"Smart and witty."

—*Woman's Day*

"A genre-bending tale perfect for readers who love romance, mystery, and mysticism." —Shelf Awareness

"This book is a wild ride." —The Stripe

"Wickedly smart." —PopSugar

"Fun, fresh, and entirely worthwhile." —*BookPage*

"A funny story of mean girls, society groups, and possible witches." —*News and Sentinel* (Parkersburg, WV)

"The best kind of satire, taking real-life absurd ideas to their most logical—and sometimes scariest—extreme." —Bitch Media

"Fans of clever, witty women's fiction with some family matters and a touch of romance will appreciate this unique story." —*Library Journal*

"If you've harbored curiosity or skepticism about secret societies or clubs, *A Special Place for Women* by Laura Hankin will be right up your alley." —The Associated Press

OTHER TITLES BY LAURA HANKIN

The Summertime Girls
Happy & You Know It

BERKLEY
NEW YORK

A

SPECIAL

PLACE FOR

WOMEN

LAURA HANKIN

BERKLEY
An imprint of Penguin Random House LLC
penguinrandomhouse.com

Copyright © 2021 by Laura Hankin
Readers Guide copyright © 2022 by Laura Hankin
Penguin Random House supports copyright. Copyright fuels creativity,
encourages diverse voices, promotes free speech, and creates a vibrant culture.
Thank you for buying an authorized edition of this book and for complying
with copyright laws by not reproducing, scanning, or distributing any part of
it in any form without permission. You are supporting writers and allowing
Penguin Random House to continue to publish books for every reader.

BERKLEY and the BERKLEY & B colophon are registered trademarks of
Penguin Random House LLC.

ISBN: 9781984806277

The Library of Congress has catalogued the Berkley hardcover
edition of this book as follows:

Names: Hankin, Laura, author.
Title: A special place for women / Laura Hankin.
Description: First edition. | New York: Berkley, 2021.
Identifiers: LCCN 2020035470 (print) | LCCN 2020035471 (ebook) |
ISBN 9781984806260 (hardcover) | ISBN 9781984806284 (ebook)
Subjects: GSAFD: Suspense fiction. | Mystery fiction. | Occult fiction.
Classification: LCC PS3608.A71483 S68 2021 (print) |
LCC PS3608.A71483 (ebook) | DDC 813/.6—dc23
LC record available at https://lccn.loc.gov/2020035470
LC ebook record available at https://lccn.loc.gov/2020035471

Berkley hardcover edition / May 2021
Berkley trade paperback edition / May 2022

Printed in the United States of America
1st Printing

Book design by Tiffany Estreicher

This is a work of fiction. Names, characters, places, and incidents either are
the product of the author's imagination or are used fictitiously, and any
resemblance to actual persons, living or dead, business establishments, events,
or locales is entirely coincidental.

For my mother, whom I see in all sorts of places.

There is a special place in hell for women
who don't support other women.

—MADELEINE ALBRIGHT

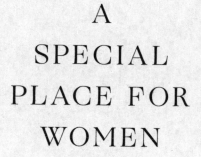

A
SPECIAL
PLACE FOR
WOMEN

PROLOGUE

Over the past few years, rumors had started swirling about a secret, women-only social club called Nevertheless, where the elite tastemakers of NYC met to scratch one another's backs. People in the know whispered all sorts of claims: Membership dues cost $1,000 a month. Last time Rihanna had been in town, she'd stopped by and gotten her aura read. Nevertheless took its no-men-allowed policy so seriously that when some belligerent guy tried to follow his girlfriend inside one night, a (female) security guard swiftly broke his collarbone.

Then, there were the more serious rumors: that the women of Nevertheless had been responsible for electing New York City's first female mayor. And the conspiracy theories: that when she'd come for their fortunes, they'd taken her down.

If you had, say, founded a judgment-free exercise studio that donated half its profits to schoolgirls in Haiti, you'd probably done

it to help the world. But you also hoped that now they would notice you. Now you'd get an invitation.

Once, a reporter had been interviewing Margot Wilding, a former socialite who'd invented a popular astrology app, and whose
presence at your gallery opening or fund-raiser immediately
boosted its chances of being covered by Page Six. "I've heard rumors that you're a member of Nevertheless," the reporter had said,
leaning in, sycophantic. "What do I have to do to get you to dish?"

For just a moment, Margot stiffened. Then she switched on a
languid smile. "Oh," she said. "We're just a coven of all-powerful
witches, of course."

"Of course," the reporter said, laughing politely. "Really,
though—"

"Next question," Margot said.

That was the closest anyone got to publicly confirming Nevertheless's existence until the night I burned its clubhouse to the
ground.

ONE

Sometimes when you're having the shittiest of days, you need to take one more tequila shot and splash some water on your face. Then, as absurd as it seems, you've got to go to a restaurant opening.

On one such shit day—the day that would end up setting everything in motion—I stood in front of a storefront lit with lanterns. In the window, my reflection wobbled, a disheveled figure in a corduroy miniskirt, dark curly hair all mussed from the windy September evening. That afternoon, I'd lost my job. The idea of hobnobbing in a crowd of loud, sparkling people made my stomach turn.

But I had to go inside. This was *Raf's* opening. He was fancy now, profiled in *Vanity Fair* as the hot new celebrity chef on the scene, but he was also still the stringy boy down the block. After my parents divorced, when my mom needed a place for me to stay with free supervision until she got home from work, I'd spent multiple afternoons a week in Raf's living room. Raf had always shared his Doritos and listened to me declaim the terrible poetry I'd written when I should've been paying attention in math class.

In and out, that was the plan. I threw my shoulders back and walked into the chatter, the sweet garlicky smells. Raf's parents had grown up in Cuba before immigrating to the States together, and the press loved talking about how this fast-rising chef was reinventing the food of his roots with distinctly American twists. The breads were baked in-house. The meat came from a farm upstate where the animals were treated like family, until they were slaughtered.

I gave my name to a young woman at the door, and she scanned the clipboard in her hand, then waved me into the throng. There were two contingents in attendance—the older investor types, and then a smattering of New York's privileged millennial crowd, who dropped by restaurant openings as casually as I dropped by my neighborhood bodega. Waiters carried trays of mojitos, or plantains speared with toothpicks. One of them offered me a miniature deconstructed Cubano, tiny and glistening with oil, like a sandwich for a doll. I popped it in my mouth, then paused to marvel at the taste of it. It was just so full of flavor, life bursting in my throat. I grabbed a mojito and took a long sip, scanning the room for Raf.

There he was, in a corner, wiry, tall, and tan, with a tattoo snaking up one arm, wearing a freaking baseball cap and T-shirt to his own opening. God, a woman could never get away with that, but if anything, it increased his appeal, judging by the gaggle of model-types jockeying for his attention. Raf was cute enough, but he wasn't the kind of guy you'd stop to look at twice on the street. Now, though, he had *status*, so he could go home with any woman he chose. We all wanted to feel that we were special, and if a special guy wanted to sleep with us, that seemed close enough. I rolled my eyes at the machinations of the women around him (although I'd been that way too in my early to mid twenties, hadn't I, jumping into bed with a visiting professor at my nonfiction graduate writing program and thinking that it made me unique). Then I walked toward him.

"Jillian!" he said, his eyes crinkling with relief to see a familiar face. He stepped away from the others and wrapped me in a bear hug. He was a little sweaty, uneasy at being the center of attention. "Oh, thank God, someone I know how to talk to."

"Hey, Raffie," I said into his chest, then held him at arm's length. "Look at you, you're such a big deal!" I leaned in and narrowed my eyes, all conspiratorial. "Tell me the truth, how much of a fuck boy are you being right now?"

His grin turned sheepish, and he tugged on his cap. "Not . . . you know . . . Maybe a little bit of one."

I laughed, or tried to anyway, and he looked at me. "Hey, you okay?"

Well, I wanted to say. *You know how I had to put my career on hold to take care of my mom while she slowly died of cancer? And how I just came back to work full-time, ready to write the zeitgeist-capturing journalism I'd spent the last couple years dreaming about? Today, the billionaire who owned my news website shut us down because he'd rather use his money to buy a second yacht. So I'm not okay at all, actually.*

Instead, I waved my hand through the air and took another long sip of my drink. "I'm golden," I said. The last time I'd seen Raf was at the funeral a couple months ago, when his family had sat with me in the pew. I'd sent my asshole father a few e-mails over the course of my mother's illness to let him know what was happening to the woman he had once loved and left. But I hadn't expected him to come back for her service, and he'd proven me right. Instead, the Morales family had stepped in as honorary relatives, providing casseroles and company. And during the years my mom was sick, Raf had regularly taken the subway all the way out to Bay Ridge, Brooklyn, to rake her leaves and shovel her snow, even after I moved home and could have done it myself. No way in hell did he deserve to spend his restaurant opening listening to my problems.

"Besides, I'm not the important one right now," I said. "Don't try to distract me from your amazing food."

"Really," he said, putting his hand on my arm, looking at me with such genuine concern it made a lump rise in my throat. "I know I've been MIA with the prep for the opening, but if you ever need anything, I'm here—" And for a moment the rest of the party fell away. It was just me and Raf on the couch in his living room, and I wanted to recite my misery to him like one of my old poems.

"So *you're* Rafael Morales," a voice said, close behind me, pitched at a husky, thrilling tone. Raf and I both turned at the same time to see her: Margot Wilding.

She was all Edie Sedgwick eyes gazing out from under dark brown bangs, her hair falling—shaggy and curly—halfway down her back, her skin glowing and smooth and like she'd just spent the summer out in the sun. If she'd been born fifty years earlier, she might have been a muse with a tragic end, a beauty who flamed out too fast, immolated by the power of her unused ambition. But now she was a maverick in a floral-print jumpsuit. Behind her, she left a break in the crowd, as if the unique force of her energy had parted the waves of partygoers. God, how were such perfectly made people allowed out in the world? Didn't they know that the rest of us had to be out here with them? It was rude.

I felt an urge to shut myself in a cabinet. It wasn't that I hated my body. I just didn't love it. I never quite knew how to move it gracefully, how to sit comfortably. Growing up, I'd longed to be one of those compact girls who got to make an adorable fuss about how they could never reach things on high shelves. But I'd just kept growing, not quite tall enough to be a model (also not pretty, thin, or interested enough), until I gave off the vibe of a grasshopper trying to masquerade as a human. My mother had once told me that when I stood still for a moment, I could be striking. But she was my mother, so she had to say that. All in all, my body and I were like coworkers. I appreciated when it performed well, I got annoyed about all the skills it lacked, and I didn't want to have to see it on nights and weekends.

"I've been wanting to meet you," Margot said to Raf, staring up at him through her long eyelashes. She didn't look at me—her world was filled with brighter things. "I haven't eaten pork since I learned that pigs are smarter than dogs, and I've bragged about it to everyone, probably quite annoyingly. So you can't tell anyone what I'm about to tell you. Do you promise?"

"I . . ." Raf blinked as she raised one of her thick, perfect eyebrows at him. "Sure, I promise."

She leaned in. "I just broke my rules for you, and it was worth it."

"Thank you . . ." Raf said, hesitating in the space where her name should have gone.

She laughed, delighted by his naïveté. How fun, that he didn't know who she was, didn't realize that her mere presence at his opening could change his life.

"Oh, I'm Margot," she said to Raf, holding out her hand to shake his. Then she clocked that his hand was occupied, still pressed on my arm in its familiar way. And suddenly I mattered, at least a little, as a curiosity or maybe as competition. She fixed me in her gaze, a pleasant, faraway smile on her lips as the thoughts passed through her head: Was Raf dating this ordinary lump? What had I done to be worthy of his attention?

I stuck my hand out. "Jillian Beckley." My voice came out very loud, like a car honk. Sexy.

"Jillian Beckley," she repeated, and the way the name rolled around in her mouth made it seem special somehow. "Lovely to meet you."

She didn't know it, but we'd crossed paths before.

It'd happened about a year ago, thanks to my editor, Miles. Ever since I'd stepped back at the news website—Quill—to take care of my mom, Miles had been assigning me fluff pieces that I could do on my own time to justify keeping me on staff. Though Miles was an intellectual powerhouse destined for bigger things and he could've gotten away with being a dick, he really looked out for his writers. Then, last September, he'd texted me:

Beckley. You said your mom loves that mayoral candidate Nicole Woo-Martin, right? Nicole had knocked on our door one day, canvassing while I was out doing errands. I hadn't even heard of her before that, but my mother had gushed about their conversation nonstop since. Miles kept typing. **I've got two press passes for a gala where she's giving the main speech. Want to come with? You can recount it all to your mom afterward and make her week.**

I accepted immediately. Miles was so kind.

I'd assumed that the gala—for an organization encouraging more women to run for office—would be a typical nonprofit fundraiser, filled with staid Upper East Side matrons, some nice hors d'oeuvres. But it was far more glamorous than that.

A beautiful woman floated past us, so close to me that her dress swished against my skin. I recognized her from Page Six, and nudged Miles. "Holy shit, Margot Wilding's here? We're in the presence of royalty. Hope she doesn't realize we're peasants."

"We might be worse than peasants," he said as we found our table. "We're journalists. Did you see that interview where the reporter asked her about Nevertheless?" He pulled my chair out for me, speaking in a low, wry tone, a crooked smile flashing across his face. "I thought for a moment there that Margot might have her shot for her impertinence."

"What's Nevertheless?" I asked.

"Ah," he said. He leaned forward and his voice got even softer. "Supposedly it's a very secretive, very exclusive club for the elite millennial women of New York." As his breath tickled my ear, I shivered.

I've neglected to mention that, in addition to being so kind, Miles was also so dreamy. I'd noticed it in an abstract way before, but as we sat next to each other in our formalwear, the abstract became *very* real.

He went on. "Word is that they're the influencers. Not the Instagram kind, who get paid to write about how much they adore certain brands. The *real* influencers: the puppeteers who pull all of our strings, whether we know it or not."

"Ah yes, my kind of people," I said, and he laughed. "Can't wait to receive an invitation."

We were interrupted by a petite, red-haired woman at the microphone. "Hello, I'm Caroline Thompson," she said in a high-pitched voice, "and I'm the founder of Women Who Lead." She basked in the ensuing applause for a moment. "Now, it is the pleasure of my life to introduce the woman who I feel confident will be our next mayor, Nicole Woo-Martin!"

Nicole jogged onto the stage. She was a forty-one-year-old public defender from Brooklyn with no polish, no political pedigree, and no chance of winning against the establishment candidate. But as she waved to us, her fierce, unexpected charisma on full display, suddenly we were no longer at a fund-raiser. We were at a rock concert. "Hello!" she shouted, and the energy in the room turned electric.

As Nicole began to speak about why female leadership was so important, Miles and I grinned at each other. I snuck a glance around the room. Everyone leaned forward, as if Nicole were a magnet pulling us all in. Some of the women watching had tears in their eyes. Only one other person was looking at the audience instead of the speaker: Margot Wilding. Her lips curled into a strange, secretive smile.

As Nicole wrapped up her speech and the thunderous applause began, my phone vibrated with a text from my mother. **How is it????** she'd written, the text accompanied by roughly a million emojis. (She'd gotten very into emojis.)

I showed it to Miles. "I think someone is excited that I'm here."

He smiled wide. "I'm glad." He nodded to where Nicole was shaking hands and posing for pictures as the applause continued. "I know we're supposed to try to remain neutral, but she's incredible, isn't she?"

"She is. Thank you so much for bringing me."

"Of course. We miss you around the office," he replied. "I can't wait for you to come back to writing full-time and blow everyone away." Suddenly I had a hard time meeting his eyes. Dammit, I was developing a *very* inconvenient crush. I turned back to watch Nicole, and Miles turned too. As he brought his hands up to clap for her, his ring flashed in the light.

Yes, in addition to being so kind and so dreamy, Miles was also so married.

Now, at Raf's opening, Margot took in my worn black tights, then my frizzy hair, then the delicate silver chain I wore around my neck. Something shifted in her face at the sight of it. "Oh, your necklace. It's so beautiful. May I?" She didn't wait for an answer, simply leaned forward and lifted it up to look at it. The audacity of her, to touch a stranger's neck! She was probably the kind of person who thought it was no big deal to use her roommate's toothbrush, except that Margot Wilding had never needed to live with a roommate in her life.

"I've been looking for a piece like this. Something antique-chic," Margot said. She examined the necklace's pendant—a small art deco flower in silver and green—as another well-wisher pressed up against Raf, monologuing about plantains. "Where did you get it? Is it Prada?"

"No," I said, suppressing a snort at the thought that I could afford something like that. "It was my mom's. Or, actually, my grandma's, and then she gave it to my mom, and now it's mine."

"Sweet of your mother to give it to you."

"Well, she was dying, so she didn't have much use for it," I said, the words coming out like a joke, spiky and flippant.

"Oh, I'm so sorry," Margot said, letting go of the necklace. She kept her hand where it was, though, and in a soft, quick movement brushed one of her warm fingers against my cheek. "I also lost a mother too young. It's a shit club to be in, isn't it?"

"It really is." For a moment, we truly looked at each other. She seemed on the verge of saying something more, but then one of her hangers-on approached, whispering into her ear. As Margot turned her head to listen, I caught a glimpse of a tattoo behind her other ear, a dark bird in flight. A raven, maybe? Margot nodded, then put her hand on Raf's shoulder. The other person who'd been talking to him ceded the floor immediately.

"I have to go to another event," Margot said, "but I'm glad I got to see what all the hype was about."

"All the hype?" Raf said, and flushed, tugging on his cap again. "Oh man. I hope we lived up to it."

"Adorable," Margot said. "You're totally a Virgo, aren't you?"

"Um, I think so?"

"Well, you *more* than lived up to it. I'll be eating here all the time, if I can get a reservation." She smiled, then widened her eyes as if the most wonderful idea had just occurred to her. "I'm having a party Thursday night. Just an intimate gathering. You must come. I'm sure my friends would love to hear about the restaurant and support you in any way they can. Let me give you the address." She dug in her bag for a pen. "I don't have any paper . . ." She looked around, then grasped Raf's forearm and scribbled an address in Soho onto his bare skin, marking him, writing the street name in looping cursive. No apartment number. Was she having it at a restaurant, or did she simply live in the entire building?

Maybe the address that Margot was scrawling on Raf's arm was that of the Nevertheless clubhouse. No, they wouldn't have a party with men allowed in there. Their clubhouse was reserved for more secretive things. Worshipping one another's menstrual blood or sitting around feeling smug about their successes while professing to feel concerned about the world.

"Come by any time after nine," Margot said. Power move to have a party on a weeknight, declaring that the benefit of being around you was worth the hangover at work the next day. "It was nice to meet you, Rafael."

"Oh, you can just call me Raf, everyone does," he said.

She smiled. "I'll see you at the party, Raf." As she turned to go, she glanced my way. "You should come too, Julia."

She waved, then swept out the way she'd come, people's heads turning to follow her. Raf looked after her, somewhat flummoxed. "Okay, so she's famous?" he asked, and I nodded. He looked down at the address on his arm. "I'm going to sweat this off in about five minutes."

"You *must* go," I said, rolling my eyes, as I pulled out my phone and took a picture of the number for him. "God, I bet all the Nevertheless crew will be there. Maybe if you get really lucky, they'll make you their male sacrifice."

"What are you talking about?" Raf asked. "What is Nevertheless?"

"Oh, Raf, you pure and beautiful boy," I said. "It's a secret club of elitists who've crawled so far up one another's assholes that they've bought themselves pieds-à-terre up there." Raf knitted his eyebrows together in confusion, so I went on. "A bunch of rich women who like to feel influential. Though I guess some of them really are. Like Margot, who, if she tweets about your restaurant, will create a line down the block. So you *should* go to her party."

"Well, then," he said, shooting me a sly look. "You should come with me, *Julia*."

"Right." I snorted and took one more gulp of my drink, the mint at the bottom flooding into my mouth. I picked it out, less than gracefully. "And go hang out with all of Margot's friends and feel terrible about myself? No thanks. Besides, it'll leave you free to get yourself some very important ass. I think she thought you and

I were dating, and I think she was disappointed." A crowd started gathering, shooting me little looks to wrap it up so that they could have their turn with the man of the hour. "Okay, I've taken up enough of your time. Talk to your other adoring fans."

He grimaced. "Do I have to? I thought part of the deal with being a chef was that you got to hide in the kitchen."

"Tough luck." I gave him a kiss on his scratchy cheek. "Congratulations again."

TWO

I stumbled out of the restaurant, drunker than I'd planned on getting. The cool night air knocked reality back into me: I no longer had a job. It came in that sudden electric shock of remembrance. You know the one? You manage to forget for a little while that your life has changed irrevocably and then: *zap*. Your heart sinks, your stomach drops, insert-other-shitty-but-true-clichés-here. Like all those mornings over the past couple months where I'd woken up thinking that I still had a mother, and then had to reorient myself all over again.

God, my finances had already been a mess. All of our savings had gone to medical bills. And all the proceeds from my mother's house, where I was still living (squatting?) while wrapping up the sale, would go to those bills too. But the money stuff wasn't the scariest part of Quill shutting down. I could probably get my old bartending job back, from the place where I worked during grad school.

The scariest part was that I had already fallen so far behind on my writing during the years I'd spent caretaking and grieving. Now it was going to be even harder, if not impossible, to catch up. And there weren't exactly a million stable journalism jobs floating around.

I headed to the subway, feeling lonely, lonely, lonely. Happy for Raf—he deserved all the success in the world—and also resentful, because how dare anyone I knew have success when I didn't? No, I wasn't going to become one of those people who just offers themselves up to jealousy like an all-you-can-eat buffet. I was going to figure something out.

My coworkers all had good clips, some contacts at other media outlets. I had exactly one contact: Miles, who'd left Quill for a job at a respected print magazine—the *New York Standard*—just a couple weeks ago.

Miles probably didn't want to hear from me. Still, with tequila and rum buzzing in my system, I pulled out my phone and typed up a text to him: **Hey there, assume you heard the exciting news about Quill—coffee next week so I can pitch you some stories for the Standard?**

I stared at the screen. "Just send the text, bitch," I muttered to myself, and did.

The train came, its cars sparsely populated at this time of night. I checked the nearest open seat for suspicious liquids and, coast clear, collapsed onto it. Then I took out a leather journal and began to scribble down story ideas, word vomit. Might as well use the hour-long subway commute for something productive. As the train lurched, the thrum of actual vomit started up in my stomach. I took a slow breath to hold it off. No puking on the train. This wasn't my twenty-first birthday.

As we crossed over into Brooklyn, the door between cars slid open, and a man came through, dragging a bag on wheels behind him. He was middle-aged, with unfocused eyes, wearing a weathered Windbreaker. He sang to himself as he dragged his bag from one end of the car to the other, singing slow and serious, like a hymn. The sweetness of his baritone voice distracted me, so it took me a moment to place the song: "Big Girls Don't Cry" by The Four Seasons.

My mother and I used to sing that song all the time. We did it to make each other laugh when we were going stir-crazy in hospital rooms, or when we felt hopeless and sharp. And I sang it to her the day we watched Nicole Woo-Martin's inauguration on TV.

Because even though the establishment candidate had every advantage, somehow Nicole had won. "Mark my words, that woman is going to be president someday," my mother had said as Nicole raised her right hand and became New York City's first female mayor, her supportive, schlubby husband at her side. Tears rolled down my mother's cheeks. She'd spent hours making phone calls to voters on Nicole's behalf. She'd ordered herself a T-shirt with Nicole's face on it. "I'm grateful I'm still alive for this."

"Hey, it's okay," I said. When her tears kept coming, I put on my most terrible impression of a Frankie Valli falsetto and began to warble our song.

"This is different, Jillian," my mother said. "This is history."

But as I sang the chorus like a cat in heat, her tears turned to laughter. We stood up and shimmied in front of the TV while Nicole smiled in her scarlet peacoat, and the room was incandescent with hope.

Now, as the subway slowed down at the Jay Street–MetroTech stop, the singing man paused by the door. Then he turned his head and stared at me, his green eyes locked on mine, as he continued his song. His eyes looked like *hers*, so gentle, like they wanted to wrap me in love as he sang our song to me. When the doors opened and he jaunted off the train, I didn't want him to go.

Because he wasn't only himself. Somehow, my mother's spirit had gotten inside of him. She had floated down and attached herself to an unlikely host so that she could see me again.

My phone dinged in the window of belowground cell service, startling me back to reality. A response from Miles. **Awful about Quill. How about we meet up Monday for a coffee?**

Perfect, I typed back.

I was being drunk and ridiculous. My mother was dead, and whatever spirit she'd had was dead too. Maybe we all had souls while we lived, but they didn't carry on after our deaths, riding the New York City subway, brushing past Showtime dancers and creeps with their dicks out. There was no need for me to have a mental breakdown. Plenty of women lost their mothers much sooner, or lost much more than their mothers. The fact that the great tragedy of my life so far was losing my mom at age twenty-nine actually meant that I was luckier than most. Big girls don't cry.

And big girls don't vomit on the subway either. They unlock their front door, run to the toilet, and hold back their own hair. So that's what I did.

THREE

On Monday morning, I dressed in my professional yet attractive best and took the subway up to the midtown coffee place Miles had suggested, a soulless chain with rickety chairs and bored baristas. Had he picked it because it was convenient or because it was the least romantic spot in the neighborhood? I grabbed myself a coffee, black, and sat at a table to wait. The coffee I'd already downed before leaving home was making my limbs jitter and my heart race, but I sipped at my new drink anyway, as if the solution to Too Much Coffee was MORE. I crossed my legs and then uncrossed them, trying to remember how to sit in a chair.

Miles walked in the door, his button-down shirt a little rumpled. He spotted me and ambled over. "Beckley, hi," he said as he approached.

"Hi!" I stood up, and we did the awkward dance—should we

hug? Handshake? We settled for waving at each other from across the table.

"Let me get a drink," he said. "Want anything?"

"Double whiskey, neat," I said. He smiled weakly. "Kidding! Bad joke. I'm all set."

I studied him as he waited to order. Miles had grown up a high-achieving prep school boy, taught to worship at the altar of Thoughts and Words, assured at every step that his mind was worthwhile. Once he'd landed in New York, his guilt at his privileged beginnings transformed into a healthy antiestablishment streak. At Quill, he'd come to work in faded T-shirts, his hair mussed, determined to hold the people in power accountable for their excess, pushing all of us under his purview to dig deeper, to be better. He was our hard-ass high school English teacher, our cool boss, and our extremely talented friend.

Now, his brief time at the *New York Standard* had already turned him distinguished. He'd started trimming his beard more neatly, strands of it beginning to gray. He looked grown-up, every inch the married thirty-nine-year-old intellectual he was. Goddamn, it was sexy.

He settled into his seat. "So, how are you doing?" he asked. I could not wait for the day when people stopped asking me that with such concern in their eyes.

"Fine," I said. "I mean, it sucks about Quill."

"I always knew Peter was liable to pull a dick move with the company, but I didn't think he'd handle it quite so horribly." He shook his head. "Anyway, how can I help you?"

I dug my nails into my thigh and took a deep breath. "Obviously I know that the *Standard* has very high . . . well, standards. But I have a bunch of long-form ideas that I think could be a great fit."

He nodded, his expression serious. "Sure, tell me what you're thinking."

I pulled out my notebook. "Okay. The New York water supply. Turns out the aqueducts that carry it here are crumbling. I could get into the dysfunction of replacing any kind of big system in New York City—"

"We've already got a regular staff writer on a similar assignment. Water is in right now, strangely. What else?"

"Right," I said, swallowing. "Well . . ." I moved to the next pitch on my list. "The plant market for millennials. Like, the new Crazy Cat Lady is a Crazy Plant Lady, but why are people *so* obsessed all of a sudden? Is it because—"

"As it becomes harder to dig oneself out from under student loans, traditional markers of stability like children are getting pushed back, and plants are an easy substitute?" he asked.

"Well . . . yes."

"Already been done."

I pitched him my other ideas, each one progressively less fleshed out, and he had a kind but firm rebuttal for all of them. Finally, he folded his hands in his lap.

"Look, I think you're a great writer, and I want to help you. But we're getting a flood of pitches right now, and I have to be incredibly selective since I'm so new. Maybe you need to take some time to think about the thing that only *you* could write."

"Oh," I said. "Got it."

"Now, I have to get back to the office."

I was an idiot. He'd come into this meeting hoping to hear ideas that he could dismiss, so that he could tell himself he'd given me a fair shot. But he wasn't going to put himself into regular communication with me again for a story on the stupid water supply, not after what had happened between us.

⸪

When I came back to work after my mom died, everyone treated me like I might break at the slightest poke. Sympathy is nice and necessary when it's fresh. But if you leave it out too long, it curdles like old milk. For the first few days, I was happy enough to take the offers of free coffee, the *With deepest condolences* cards that people left on my desk. But by the end of the week, when a coworker looked at me like I was a baby seal trapped in an oil spill, and asked me *yet again*, "No, really, how are you doing?" I snapped.

I stood up at my desk and yelled, "Office announcement!" Heads turned. Miles spun around in his chair and cocked an eyebrow. "I'm planning to get extremely drunk at happy hour today, and if you want to do something to make me feel better, you can come ruin your livers with me. Otherwise, please start treating me like a normal human being again, or I'm going to rip apart the water cooler with my bare hands. Okay?"

There was a long pause. Then Miles threw his head back and laughed. "Okay," he said.

A team of us headed over to the bar after that. We gossiped and played darts, and as our first drinks disappeared and our second came to replace them, Miles and I gravitated toward each other. "It's good to have you back, Beckley," he said. "The office had gotten too . . . pleasant without you."

"Oh, shut up," I said, and smiled at him.

We jumped from topic to topic, cracking jokes, trying to one-up each other. Occasionally, other writers joined in for a few minutes, but Miles and I kept turning back to the electric energy of our own conversation. The bone-deep weariness I'd been living with lifted. My belly hurt from laughing. Everyone else trickled out, but we only noticed when the last two said their good-byes, leaving us alone. "It got late. I should probably go too," Miles said, looking at his watch.

"Come on, Emmy's out of town, right?" I put on some jokey puppy-dog eyes. "So you could go home and rewatch *The Wire* by yourself, or you could have one more drink with your grieving friend in her time of need."

"I thought you didn't want people treating you any differently," he said.

"I don't. I'm just worried about *you*. Abandoning a grieving friend makes you a terrible person, and I don't want you to go to hell."

He laughed. "When you put it that way . . ." Then he leaned over the bar and ordered us each a gin and tonic.

When we'd finally closed out, as we were putting on our coats and lurching onto the sidewalk, the night chilly around us, I said, "Thanks for this. I just . . . Thank you."

"Of course," he said.

"I'm glad to be back at work for real now," I said, the words escaping my throat in a rush. "I'm going to write so much good stuff. Make you proud."

He stopped walking. "I have to tell you—I got another job offer. I'm giving my two weeks' notice on Monday."

A roaring started up in my ears. I did *not* care for this particular change, not at all. "No, what? You can't leave. You're the best part about Quill!"

"I've got to take it," he said, and a satisfied smile momentarily lit up his solemn expression. "It's the *New York Standard*."

"Holy shit," I said. "That's amazing. Of course they poached you. *You're* amazing."

"Thanks," he said, putting his hands in his pockets. "It's what I've wanted, forever." He cleared his throat. "I will be sad to leave you, though."

My eyes filled suddenly with tears, tears for him leaving and about other things too. Endings all over the place. The unfairness of how the bottom can be pulled out, when you thought things were so solid. "Oh God. Sorry," I said as I dragged my hand across my face and blinked the tears away.

"Jillian Beckley crying? I never thought I'd see the day," he said.

"I'm not. Shut up."

He pulled me into a hug to comfort me. We'd never hugged before. He was stronger than I'd expected.

"Whoa, man, you work out?" I said.

"Oh yeah, total gym rat." One hand of his reached up and stroked my hair, and then, with my nose against his neck, I made a mistake: I breathed in. He smelled like coffee, but more than that. Like security. Yes, I know that sounds dumb.

I watched myself put my arms around him too as if from outside myself, watched somebody who looked exactly like me doing something that I would never do. This bad decision-maker that had my face pressed herself against him, not just head against chest, but hips against hips and then, as he pressed back, I was no longer watching from outside myself. I rocketed back into my buzzing body, and oh, my body wanted him bad. "I wish you would stay," I said.

"You guys will get some great new editor and forget all about me soon enough," he said, his voice low, a hitch in his breath.

I drew back and punched his chest lightly. "Right, maybe we'll get someone who actually appreciates good pop culture."

He gave me a gentle push. "Let's hope they can put up with your typos."

I pushed him back, and then as he stepped forward again, I knew what I was going to do before I did it, and I hated myself. I put my hand on his cheek and kissed him. He drew away for a moment. And then he kissed me back.

It was like neither one of us could catch our breath. He held on to me so tight it bruised my arms. I hadn't been kissed in almost two years, since my mom had gotten her diagnosis, and my boyfriend at the time had asked if I really had to miss his work party to take her to chemo, and he was promptly not my boyfriend anymore. After I moved home, my mom worried that I wasn't dating, that I was focusing too much on her, so I'd sometimes tell her that I was going out with someone I'd met online. Then, I'd sit in a café and read a book for a few hours before coming home and spinning her tales of imaginary men—how this one had been rude to the waitress and that one had smelled like fish left out in the sun.

So I'd forgotten how kissing someone felt, the beautiful messiness of it. I was throbbing, a pulsing, exposed, EXTREMELY HORNY heart. But also, I'd never been with someone who kissed me as hungrily as Miles did, who kissed me like he'd also been denied something beautiful and messy for years, and had to make up for it all right now.

Then, abruptly, he pulled away. The flush on his face was so deep it showed even in the weak light from the cars whooshing by us. "I can't."

"Right, we shouldn't," I said, and we stared at each other for a moment before he turned aside and stuck his arm out for a taxi.

"We need to forget this happened," he said. "Please." I nodded dumbly, and then a cab pulled up. "Look, you take this home and go to bed." He opened the door for me, and I scooted inside. Before he shut the door, he leaned against it for a moment. "We just stayed out too late and got too drunk, that's all."

"Yeah," I said.

He closed the door. I gave the driver my address and we pulled away. I watched out the window as we sped down the street, Miles growing small, then indistinguishable behind us.

Now, a month later, as Miles stood up to go, I looked down at my notebook in a panic. We'd made a mistake, but he was my one contact. And we could keep things professional, if only I had something worth changing his mind. I flipped some pages—hadn't I had a million ideas over the last few weeks?—and looked at my ramblings from the subway the other night, after Raf's opening. *Raf's going to get eaten alive at Margot's party*, I'd written in a near illegible scrawl.

"Nevertheless!" I blurted.

Miles paused, in the midst of buttoning his peacoat. "What?"

I squared my shoulders. "I have an in at Nevertheless."

He furrowed his brow and gave his head a little shake, as if to clear it. "How?"

"I met Margot Wilding at my friend's restaurant opening. We bonded, because she lost a parent too. She basically begged me to come to this party she's having this week, where all her Nevertheless cronies will be." The words were coming faster now, a flood of bullshit that I almost believed myself. Miles slowly sat back down. "I could . . . infiltrate. Get invited to join, and then report from the inside."

"You can't just sign up like it's a membership to Costco. They only invite the elite. No offense. So how exactly are you planning to infiltrate?"

"I can make up some influential aunt who was on the feminist frontlines, or some project I have in the works that's going to make my name, and get my fancy restaurant friend to back me up on it."

"And if they do any kind of Google search on you, they'll know you work in media, and run in the other direction. They'd never invite a journalist. They probably think we'd sell out all their secrets. Which is fair."

"I'm not in media anymore, buddy." I crossed my arms and sat back, cocking an eyebrow coolly. "After getting so unceremoniously let go, I'm disillusioned and using my talents in other fields from here on out."

He laughed, almost against his will. "I'm not sure how convincing that will be."

"Wouldn't you love to know what that clubhouse looks like on the inside? Who's a member? Wouldn't the readers eat up ten thousand words about the way that these women put on a performance of concerned feminism while walling themselves off from any real risks because of their privilege? The *hypocrisy* of them all, saying that they need a safe space just for women while excluding all the women who need sisterhood the most?"

"Sure, that sounds interesting. But it also sounds high risk for potentially low reward, a little too ambitious—"

"What if I could prove that they're the ones who brought down Nicole Woo-Martin?"

He got very still. "What do you mean?" It was difficult to talk about Nicole even now. The disappointment stung, like a cut that hadn't scabbed over yet. She was supposed to be a hero, an icon, to do a term or two as mayor and then run for president. Instead, she'd fallen off the grid, walking in the woods somewhere, thinking about all that she'd lost.

Because shortly after Nicole started making moves to enact her most ambitious policy plan—a wealth tax on the city's richest residents—a bombshell dropped: she'd been having an affair with one of her staffers, a twenty-five-year-old boy with the face of a Kennedy (John) and the common sense of a Kennedy (Ted). It was a terrible abuse of power, particularly from someone who was supposed to be so *good*.

Still, she might have been able to come back from that. Other politicians had. Maybe, just maybe, she'd exercised poor judgment, but the two of them had been truly in love.

The publication of their text messages put the nail in her coffin. The most explosive ones received endless coverage. Everyone read Nicole's dirty talk. And everyone read Nicole's threats. **You should stay away from those women,** Nicole had texted the staffer, **or you'll get yourself into trouble.** She'd sent him a few variations on that theme: **Seriously, are you going to see her again? I wouldn't if I were you.**

At first, Nicole claimed that she was making a reference to something they'd discussed in person, that she was trying to protect him from getting mixed up in some "bad crowd." But the staffer solemnly denied it. She was threatening his job, he said, if he paid attention to other women. After that, she had no choice but to resign.

"Those text messages she sent, the threatening ones," I said to Miles. "They just came out of nowhere and never felt quite right, did they?"

"Well, no," he said.

The unabridged text messages made the rounds among journalists, and I'd read them all. Miles had too. Before the threats, everything was endearments, banter, and yes, the aforementioned dirty talk. And *after* the first threat, the staffer had written **hah, okay,** and then they'd gotten right back to banter. It was totally possible that he was just protecting himself, sure, but there was another piece of it that had never sat quite right with me.

"Do you remember her tweet? The one she deleted almost immediately?" I asked Miles.

As the scandal was unfolding, Nicole had tweeted, **Forces are** trying to stop our promise of change. **Nevertheless. Despite unfounded rumors, I will keep fighting for you.** A photo accompanied the text— Nicole beaming at that Women Who Lead gala Miles and I had gone to. In the background, Margot Wilding and Caroline Thompson, the Women Who Lead founder, watched Nicole, their faces partially in shadow.

I'd screenshot it at the time and sent it to Miles, mostly because we'd been there when the photo was taken. But that meant we were two of the only people to notice when she took down the tweet, only a minute after putting it up.

"Nicole *never* made typos, never used a period when she meant to use a comma," I said to him.

"Well," he said, shrugging. "That's probably why she deleted it, then."

"Right, maybe she wanted to correct her mistake. But then why, when she put up the new tweet, did she leave out the word *Nevertheless* and change the picture?" I'd screenshot her revision too, thinking it was strange, and now I pulled up the screenshots on my phone, flipping between the two of them so that Miles could see. The later tweet simply said: **Forces are trying to stop our promise of change. Despite unfounded rumors, I will keep fighting for you.** The picture that accompanied it was one of Nicole alone, no Margot or Caroline in sight.

He rubbed his chin, momentarily stumped. Miles didn't get stumped very often. I felt a thrill that I could go toe-to-toe with him like that.

"Why would they want to hurt her, though?" he asked. "The rumors were that they handpicked her for mayor."

"The affair came out soon after she announced that the main focus of her administration was going to be closing the wealth gap, right?" I said. During the campaign, Nicole's wealth tax had been just one part of her broad policy platform, easy enough to over-look. My mother had rejoiced at Nicole's announcement, imagin-ing that maybe their conversation at our door, when she'd told an empathetic Nicole about medical bills screwing us over, had played into the decision. I went on. "Maybe they realized that she was actually going to do something about taxing the rich, and they wanted to protect themselves."

Miles leaned forward, speaking very quietly. "You really think you could find some evidence for that?"

"I have no fucking idea," I said. "But this is my chance to try."

"It's very flimsy, Beckley," he said. "Basically a conspiracy theory."

"Oh, absolutely," I said. "But every so often, conspiracy theories turn out to be true. Besides, what do you lose if I just try to get into the club and see what happens?" He hesitated. "There's *some-thing* going on there," I continued. "Something bad. I can feel it."

He chewed on his lip. He wanted to believe, just like I did, that Nicole was simply human, instead of a monster. "An undercover operation would be very difficult."

"You think that, after the last two years, difficult things faze me in the slightest? I eat difficult for breakfast. Besides," I said, and stared him right in his beautiful blue eyes, "I can be very persuasive when I want to be. People end up liking me, more than they're supposed to."

He stared back. Then he ran his hands through his hair, leaving it sticking up in tufts. "Well, yeah," he said. "If you could get us something on Nevertheless, of course I would want it." He shook his head and laughed again in spite of himself. He had that expres-sion on his face that he got whenever someone brought him some-thing that really woke him up, a jazzed, unrestrained grin.

I floated on a wave of adrenaline as he told me to send him a written proposal as soon as I could and waved good-bye. I practi-

cally danced down the street as I headed to the subway, resisting
the temptation to twirl around lampposts and throw my arms
around strangers. This was the kind of story that could help me
catch back up and make my name, that could catapult me to a life
of credibility and regular assignments, a life where I could finally
be happy.

It wasn't until after I texted Raf that we needed to talk about
Margot's party that I stopped in the middle of the sidewalk, wondering how the hell I was going to pull it off.

FOUR

I went to Raf's apartment in Bushwick the next morning, bearing donuts and coffee, shaky from three hours of sleep. Even under normal circumstances, sleep often eluded me—my mind ping-ponged around from my Greatest Hits of past social miscalculations to my anxieties about the future. And planning to break into an exclusive club wasn't exactly "normal circumstances."

"Wow," Raf said when he opened the door, rubbing the sleepies from his eyes, with gravel in his voice. "Breakfast? What have I done to deserve this?"

"It's what you're *going* to do, I hope," I said, and he raised an eyebrow, wary. "On the one hand, I need roughly twenty favors. But on the other hand, these donuts are very good."

"I guess you should come in and sit down," he said as he took a coffee and knocked back half of it in one swig.

I followed him into his combined kitchen/living room area. His apartment didn't yet hint at the celebrity he was becoming. No fancy, expensive art on the walls, just photos of his family and a few vintage posters of musicians like David Bowie. (In high school, Raf taught himself guitar. He refused to perform in front of anyone, though, so I didn't know if he was terrible or a virtuoso.) For a chef, he had a surprisingly small amount of counter space, but then Raf saved his fancy cooking for work and whipped up elaborate meals at home only if he was trying to impress a date. Otherwise, he made himself peanut butter and jelly sandwiches. The couch we flopped onto was the same one he'd bought for his first apartment after college. I put the donuts on the same coffee table we'd been putting our feet up on for years. Someday, Raf would be forced to move to some gleaming loft in Williamsburg by whatever girl he ended up falling in love with—I pictured him wandering around it sadly, lost—but for now, his home still fit him like a turtle's shell.

"So I got an assignment to write an article for the *New York Standard*," I said, right as Raf bit into a glazed donut.

His eyes crinkled with joy, and he held up a finger and chewed as quickly as possible. "Jilly, yes!" he said as soon as he'd swallowed. Generally, I was a *Jillian*. As a child, I'd hated being called "Jill" so much that I'd spent a whole year telling people that, actually, my name was Gillian with a G (not coincidentally, this was the year I became obsessed with *The X-Files* and Gillian Anderson). When teachers expressed doubt, I doubled down, spinning out explanations of how there must have been a typo on the attendance form. Eventually, my mother had to ground me so I'd stop lying about it. Somehow with Raf, though, I never minded the affectionate shorthand.

"The *New York Standard*?" he said now, beaming. "That's incredible!"

"It is!" I said, then continued with forced cheer, "It's about that extremely exclusive social club that Margot belongs to. So all I need to do is get myself invited in, which should be a piece of cake because I'm very cool and have everything going for me right now."

"Um," Raf said.

"Yeah. At this party, can you please back me up on the stories I tell about myself? It'll be bullshit, but bullshit that they probably can't disprove."

"I don't like lying," he said. "I'm terrible at it."

"Well, you've gotta get some practice, or you're never going to survive in New York City, baby," I joked. He didn't laugh. "So, okay, don't think of it as lying. Think of it as helping your friend expose a potentially fucked-up system. And also helping her have the career she's always wanted so that she's not tempted to bash her head in with a rock."

"Hold on, you're not actually tempted to do that, are you?" he asked, concerned.

"No, of course not," I said. "Well, only sometimes."

He hesitated, then chewed on his knuckle. "What kind of bullshit are you going to tell them, then?"

I smiled. Good old Raf. "They can't know that I'm still a journalist. So, here's the plan." I stood up and faced him like I'd done so many times in our childhood, offering up the contents of my brain for him to praise. "I'm going to tell them that I'd been getting disillusioned by the state of journalism anyway. Quill shutting down was just the final nail in the coffin—"

"Wait, what—"

"Oh, right, Quill totally combusted. Anyway, this whole time, I've been working on the Next Great American Novel. You know, *The Great Gatsby* meets John Steinbeck, but from a *woman's* point of view." I paced back and forth, the words tumbling out of me and taking shape in the air. "The manuscript's not done yet, but it's close. All the agents I've met with are salivating over it, convinced that six months from now, publishing houses will be bending over backwards to bid on it. And then, when the book comes out, I pledge to donate half of its profits to Planned Parenthood." He was staring at me, his face reserved instead of open with his usual support. "This is the kind of performative feminism they eat up."

"Are you okay?" Raf asked. "This is all a little intense."

I sat back down next to him. "I know it seems that way, but let me reiterate, we're talking about the *New York Standard* here."

"I'm only saying this because I care about you, so don't get mad at me, but you're coming off as a little . . . manic right now."

Manic? How dare he? His ambition ran as deep as mine did, even if he wasn't as obvious about it. I prepared to angrily list off a million ways he was wrong, then realized that might prove his point. I took a calming breath. "Look, I get why you think that. But . . ." I scooted closer to him. "When you were trying to prove that you were worthy of your own restaurant, how many nights did you stay up until dawn, working on a recipe?"

"Um," he said. "A lot."

"Some people might've called *that* a little manic. It worked, though, so now you get to be all cool and bashful about it. But if you hadn't succeeded, you would be burning up inside, wouldn't you?" He nodded almost imperceptibly. "This is my chance to have the restaurant." I took his free hand, the one that wasn't holding a donut, and squeezed it, so that he'd look at me. "*Please*, Raf. You said if I ever needed anything . . . I need this."

He shoved the rest of his donut in his mouth and chewed it slowly. Then he nodded. "Okay. Just—we've got to practice or something. Drill me on this. I'm not a good improviser."

"Thank you! I will drill you all night long if you want!" I said, then paused. "Sorry, that came out way dirtier than I'd intended." He reached for another donut, but I grabbed the box and held it out of his reach. "Speaking of, there is another part to the plan. One more thing that I think would really clinch it all."

"What?"

I bit my lip. "I need you to pretend we're dating."

Now it was his turn to jump up from the couch, as if I'd goosed him. "Very funny."

"I'm serious, unfortunately."

"No. I don't get how that's supposed to help anything."

"Because you're getting famous now, whether you like it or not, so whatever girl you deem worthy of your homemade meals will be an object of curiosity. *Especially* if she's just sort of regular-looking and not some gorgeous supermodel," I said, pointing to myself, "she must be interesting. Worth getting to know."

He fiddled with the cardboard cozy from his coffee cup, rolling it up, ripping away little shreds of it. "I'm not that big of a deal."

"Okay, Mr. *Vanity Fair.*"

"Really—"

"'Much like Picasso,'" I began to quote, "'Mr. Morales proves that he can both respect the sanctity of classic forms and then rearrange them into thrillingly uncharted territory—'"

"Maybe I'm a little bit of a big deal," he said, blushing.

"I know this sounds like something out of a Hallmark movie, and that it might cramp your style right as you've got all these women throwing themselves at you. You can tell them that we're nonmonogamous, like all the trendiest people. I promise that it won't be for long. A few weeks maybe, a month at most. And after this, I will set you up with all of my hottest friends—"

"Your hottest friends are already married and having babies," Raf said. (Fair point. I'd never had a huge group of female friends, and somehow the ones I did have had proceeded with the typical life milestones at a steady clip, as if they were *normal* or something. They'd fallen off the face of the Earth, dealing with newborns when I'd needed them most, and I had trouble forgiving them for that.)

"I'll make some new hot friends and tell them that you're the greatest guy in the world."

"I'm gonna screw this up for you somehow. I can't do it."

"Sure you can." I winked at him. "Just imagine the plate of lasagna."

He put his hands over his face and groaned. Back in middle school, the drama teacher had put on an evening of Shakespeare scenes. I was cast as Juliet, because I was loud. Raf was cast as Romeo, because he was tall. We'd spent a week rehearsing the balcony scene, where Raf stared at the floor when he was supposed to be confessing his love.

"Speak up! Use your diaphragm," our drama teacher, Mrs. Fritz, had shouted at him over and over. "Look her in the eyes, she's not Medusa!"

Finally, Mrs. Fritz tried a different tactic. "Rafael. Honey," she'd said, sighing. "What's your favorite food?"

"Um," Raf said. "Lasagna?"

"Great. I need you to look at Jillian like she's a big, steaming plate of lasagna." Nothing helps an eighth-grade girl's confidence like knowing that a boy has to imagine she's food in order to feign attraction to her. I'd squirmed and blushed as Raf looked up and finally met my eyes. "Got it? Now try it again."

Raf had ended up performing remarkably well. I should've known then that he was destined to be a chef, if he could get that passionate about food. Neither one of us went on to become theater stars. But there was something nice in the idea that if I were going to be playing a role in this whole shebang, he'd be in it with me, playing one too.

Raf grimaced. Then he flopped back down onto the couch. "Dammit, Jillian," he said. "This is going to be so weird."

"Raf!" I shouted, throwing my arms around him. "Thank you. Thank you!"

"You promise that it won't be for long," he said.

"Not a minute longer than necessary," I said. "Now, here, take that donut."

FIVE

So two nights later, at ten P.M., Raf and I met up a block away from the party. He crossed the street toward me, a little red-faced from the heat of the kitchen. But he had made an effort, combing his hair, no baseball cap in sight. "Oh," he said when he saw me. "You look different."

"Good different or bad different?"

"Good, I guess? Nice. Just not you."

"Perfect," I said, my heart thumping, trying to fight off an encroaching light-headedness.

I'd expended so much energy trying on outfits for Margot's party that I'd had to take a nap afterward. All the current trends seemed to have been designed exclusively for—surprise!—women with zero percent body fat, whose frail frames managed to look even frailer in their wide-legged pants, whose stomachs were perfectly flat underneath their crop tops. But finally, I'd found a peasant-chic dress at a thrift store. Among at least some groups of rich people, it was cool to look like you'd found your clothes on the street, thank God. (Or thank Mary-Kate and Ashley Olsen.) Most important, the dress was cheap. My old bosses at the bar had agreed to take me back, but still, I needed to scrimp as much as possible. I didn't know how I was going to pay the Nevertheless dues if they were as high as they'd been rumored to be. One thing at a time.

I'd practiced my spiel over and over, staring into the mirror and contorting my face into different expressions. Friendly! I was so friendly! But not desperate! I'd made all my social media private and deleted my LinkedIn. I'd lain awake in my childhood bedroom for hours each night, thinking of all the ways things could go wrong.

I hugged my jacket closer and flashed Raf my best Julia Roberts, the biggest megawatt grin I could muster. "How's my smile? Effortlessly confident and appealing?"

"A little much. Like a shark?"

"Noted. I'll tone it down."

We reviewed our cover stories one more time as we scanned the street numbers and my anxiety gathered steam. Finally, halfway down the block, we found the door, painted black, with only one label on the buzzer: IN THE STARS. It wasn't a restaurant or Margot's apartment. It was the office for her astrology app.

"We grew up together," I said. "And were always good friends."

"Yeah, and then one day we stopped and looked at each other." Raf stopped and looked at me. "And we just . . . knew."

"Exactly. Here, hold my hand," I said as I pressed the buzzer. "So we look like a Couple in Love."

"Ugh," he said as he took it. "Your palm is really sweaty."

"Can't imagine why."

A low chiming noise emanated from a speaker. I turned the door handle.

"Couple in Love," I said. Together, we walked into the party.

SIX

The walls of the In the Stars office were salmon pink, but the ceiling was black and studded with gold like the night sky. I stared at it for a second before realizing: it *was* the night sky, a video of it stretched across the entire ceiling, the stars winking and planets burning bright above our heads. A few desks and long tables were scattered around the open room, along with some couches. What must have been Margot's office, at the far end of the space, was separated from everything else only by a wall of glass.

Twelve paintings hung along one wall, each one depicting a different zodiac sign. At least, I assumed that's what they were—I'd never gotten much into astrology myself, beyond some sleepovers when my friends and I would giggle over whether or not Tyson from math class was a "love match" with our signs. I knew I was a Cancer, but the assigned personality traits didn't describe me at all. I was supposed to be "watery," ruled by my emotions? Right.

The recent, meteoric rise of this pseudoscience among intelligent women confused me. Margot had built a fortune on giving people detailed astrological reports every day, right at the tips of their fingers. Maybe she believed it all herself. Or maybe she was just an excellent businesswoman.

There were about thirty party guests, drinking from champagne flutes and tumblers with dimpled bases. A bartender poured out various concoctions at a counter in the corner, and a couple of handsome young men handed them around to the guests.

"Intimate gathering, huh?" Raf said to me under his breath, and I snorted.

The guests were about half men and half women, in their twenties and thirties. I scanned the crowd to see if I recognized any of the women, trying to figure out who besides Margot might be a member of Nevertheless, so I could target them with my well-practiced charm offensive.

There, a few feet away from us, speaking so intensely to a group of listeners that it looked like she was delivering a TED Talk, was Caroline Thompson. Bingo. I'd had a hunch she might be here, and had looked her up just in case, reading a *Vogue* article about her recent wedding extravaganza overlooking a cliff in Positano, where the bride wore Oscar de la Renta and kept her own name. Her husband, whom she'd met the day after she turned thirty, had registered as blandly handsome, running a charitable organization that his wealthy family had started. Caroline put the real power in power couple, thirty-two years old, barely five feet tall, running fast on some internal generator. Her mother's family had been New York royalty for generations. Her father came from a long line of real estate tycoons. Caroline could have coasted on their money, but she was not the kind of woman to coast. She was the kind of woman to fund-raise her ass off for a worthy political cause, to go to Yale undergrad and Harvard Law School. After the 2016 election, she'd founded Women Who Lead. The article had hinted that she'd probably run for office herself someday. She looked ready at this very moment, in her high-waisted skirt and matching blazer, with her long red hair impeccably sleek.

Women Who Lead had been the first organization to back Nicole Woo-Martin during her mayoral run. They had encouraged her, *groomed* her, even. Caroline would've had a lot of access to Nicole. I squinted. Yes, Caroline had been at the inauguration in the section reserved for VIPs, beaming in the winter chill.

Caroline's uptightness made a peculiar match with Margot's free-spirited energy. What did a type A wonk have in common with someone who lived her life by the dictates of the stars? They weren't the kinds of women who seemed likely to be friends. But, linked by a common ambition and a common status, they *were* the kinds of women to unite behind closed doors to rule the world.

As I stared at Caroline, Margot appeared in front of us. "Raf, you made it!" she said, more luminous than ever, copper and gold strands glinting in her dark wild mane, her feet bare. Margot had the kind of feet that men on the Internet probably developed fetishes over. She kissed Raf on the cheek, then turned to me. "And, oh . . ."

"Jillian," I said.

"Of course." She leaned in and kissed me too, her lips barely brushing my skin. I caught a whiff of her jasmine scent. "Please, make yourselves at home."

"Thanks," Raf said.

"We're glad to be here," I said. "This office is beautiful."

"That's so sweet. I put a lot of thought into it." As Margot turned away from us to appraise her kingdom, I nestled into Raf. His body was stiff against mine. God, he was so awkward. I poked him in the ribs, and he glared at me, then put his arm around my shoulders right as Margot turned back. She registered our body language but didn't stop talking for a moment in her steady, hypnotic way. "I really wanted it to have the right kind of energy, you know? Welcoming, but also inspiring and productive."

"Mission accomplished. Too bad I didn't bring my laptop. I feel ready to post up on one of these couches and edit my novel," I said. I looked at Raf, trying to communicate that now would be an excellent time for him to rave about my impending success, but he was nervous himself. Shit. He wasn't exactly a smooth talker. Maybe I had asked too much of him. A bubble of silence hung in the air, expanding and expanding.

Margot smiled at me serenely and popped the bubble. "What sign are you, Jillian?"

"A Cancer."

"Oh, good. I thought for a moment that you might be a Gemini, and our energies do *not* mesh." She studied me. "Cancer? Interesting. I wouldn't have guessed. What's your rising sign?"

"I . . . do not know what that means."

She widened her eyes as if concerned for me, ready to help lift me out of my ignorance. "For some people, it's the rising sign that really matters. You should sign up for the app! We can do a whole star chart for you. People find it really helpful."

"Yeah, that could be great." I grasped for a segue, any segue. "It would be nice to have less uncertainty in my life, particularly as a *novelist*—"

"Oh," Margot said, catching sight of someone across the room. "Raf, I have to introduce you to this food critic friend of mine." She grabbed his arm to lead him off. "Excuse us for a moment, Jillian. And please, get yourself a drink!"

As Margot pulled Raf into the crowd, he caught my eye and

mouthed, *Sorry*. I clenched and unclenched my hands. Okay, I'd find Caroline and introduce myself. I caught sight of her in the corner by the bar, handling some work emergency on her phone. "You have to tell her that we need her statement by the morning," she said, then turned to the bartender: "No, with an orange peel, not a lemon slice."

Not an excellent moment to introduce myself, then. I took a champagne flute from one of the handsome men and stood around like I'd been sent back to a middle school formal, scanning the room for other girls who also hadn't been asked to slow-dance. (I shuddered at the memory of my own middle school formals, which weren't exactly fun events for a teenager mercilessly mocked by the popular girls for being too gawky, for being unwanted by her father, with a mother too concerned about saving money to pay for new clothes.)

Another woman stood a few feet away, holding still and observing the room. She was tall and intensely pale, almost translucent, with white-blond hair cropped short. It was a pixie cut, technically, but she had nothing of a pixie's mischief about her. She looked more like she prowled snowy Norwegian woods until she came upon a reindeer and ripped out its heart, her face never changing from its unreadable expression. I knew her somehow, and then I placed her to all the articles I'd read about her this time last year.

Vy Larsson was an experimental mixed-media artist, a millennial Marina Abramovic. Her most attention-getting project to date was an art installation that had premiered about a year ago, inspired by menstrual huts. Vy had become fascinated by an article about how, in some cultures, women and girls continued to be sent away from the rest of the tribe when they were on their periods, made to stay in huts so that they didn't "contaminate" everyone else. A few years back, a girl in Nepal had died in her menstrual hut because it was so cold, and she'd been sent out there without the proper provisions. She'd been only twelve years old.

After reading about that girl, Vy had decided to "reclaim" menstrual huts, to change them from a place where women were shamed to a place that *celebrated* women on their periods. The installation consisted of two parts. The outer room, which anyone who had paid the entrance fee could access, featured a series of black-and-white photographs that Vy had taken of menstruating women. Some whirled in the midst of activity, balancing babies and binders of important documents. Others reclined with hot pads on their stomachs. But all of them looked into Vy's camera with frank, challenging eyes. She'd even gotten a few well-known women to pose for her: a pro tennis player who bloodied her tennis whites, a sex symbol actress smearing blood all over her lusted-after legs.

That part was attention-grabbing, sure, but it wasn't the part of the installation that dominated the news, and then turned into a scandal. That was the second room. A door led to an inner sanctum, a "hut" containing . . . something. The press releases wouldn't say what it was. And the only people allowed to enter this inner sanctum were women, nonbinary, or trans people on their periods. (Or at least people with uteri who *said* they were on their periods. No one was going to ask women to pull out their used tampons to prove anything.) Two young women guarded the door and asked anyone who wanted to go in if they were currently menstruating. Even Vy followed the rules. For a few hours a week, exceptions were made for older women who had already gone through menopause, for women who were pregnant or on forms of birth control that suppressed their cycles, and for transgender women, because Vy didn't want to discriminate against those who had, as she put it, "felt the weight of oppression."

For a few weeks, it had been the most intriguing secret in town, with lines down the block. The women who were allowed inside reemerged blissed out, relaxed, a little giggly with their shared knowledge. And then a man had screwed it all up. Some asshole who had worked himself into an outrage over the way Vy's exhibit discriminated against straight white men showed up at the door claiming to be transgender, insisting that he'd been born a woman but now presented as male. He told the women guarding the door that he was on his period, and that if they didn't believe him, they were bigots. Once they let him into the inner sanctum, he took a recording on his phone and put it all on Reddit so that anyone could see.

It wasn't that special, really. Just a room covered in woven rugs and pillows, dark and smoky with incense, with a video installation projected onto all the walls. In the video, women of all shapes and sizes, dressed as various goddesses, danced on the screen, the colors turning vibrant, then fading, then becoming vibrant again. Meanwhile, a series of atonal, beautiful chants played, while "hut guides," women who Vy had hired to keep an eye on things inside, passed out chocolate and cups of green tea. (People in New York went wild for any kind of free food and drink with their culture.) It was hypnotic, the kind of place where one could get a little trancey.

The guy mocked it mercilessly, encouraging other men to try the same trick. Vy had to shut down the inner sanctum sooner than planned because dudes kept showing up at the door, demanding to be let in.

But there was a story in the *New York Post*, a month or so later, about how the guy had woken up one morning to find his house in New Jersey covered as if it had been TP'd, but not with toilet paper. With tampons and menstrual pads, all heavily used. The police hadn't been able to prove who had left them there.

Now I made my way over to Vy. "Seeing anything interesting?" I asked her. She looked down at me—I was tall, but she seemed somehow much taller—and didn't say anything. "You know, from watching the party?"

"No," she said. "But I am smelling things."

Okay, I thought. "Mm, yeah," I said. "*Love* smelling stuff. Flowers . . . tuna fish. Underrated sense, I always say."

She looked at me, her face inscrutable, then closed her eyes and took a deep breath in through her nose. "You're a very nervous person, aren't you?"

"What? No, I—"

She opened her eyes again and locked them on mine. "Yes, like a seagull gliding along the surface of the waves, afraid to plunge into the depths."

"Well," I said. "If a seagull flew into the depths of the ocean, it would drown."

"Hmm," she said, still staring at me. One pale eyebrow inched up her forehead, then back down. Abruptly she turned and walked away. I certainly hoped *she* wasn't a member of the club.

I downed my glass of champagne and got started on a second. The idea of inserting myself into one of the groups of people I didn't know felt more and more impossible with each passing minute. I spotted Raf sitting on a couch next to Margot, talking animatedly to her as she twirled her hair around her finger. Dammit, he was totally going to fall in love with her. There was one part of the plan ruined.

Who was I kidding, though? How the hell were a fake relationship and a fake novel supposed to get any of these women interested in someone like me? I didn't belong in a club with them, and they could smell it. (In Vy's case, apparently, literally.) I drained my second glass of champagne. I needed to get out of the pulsing swirl of laughter and meaningless talk before it suffocated me. I ducked into a hallway, then leaned against the wall and closed my eyes. I could just go home. I could get into my bed, and eat a pint of ice cream, and hate myself in the comfort of my childhood bedroom.

A woman's voice, high and reedy, intruded on my thoughts, coming down the hallway toward me. "Well, you think about it," the voice said, efficient. "Because you would be incredible."

I opened my eyes to see Caroline Thompson pacing back and forth, talking into her phone. She shot me an apologetic look for intruding on my privacy. I waved it off. "Okay, get some sleep. I promise you it will all seem clearer in the morning." She hung up and let out a sigh. "The work never ends, does it?"

"I know what you mean," I said, my heart starting to boom at this potential stroke of luck. "Sometimes you've just got to sneak off into a hallway and get it done. Truly any space can become your office if you have the right mind-set."

She let out a polite laugh. "Totally. I'm Caroline." Up close, her face—her reddish coloring, her small nose against her full cheeks—made me think of a chipmunk.

"Jillian," I said, and shook her tiny, outstretched hand. Her nails were painted a sensible pale pink. Surprising that she could lift her arm at all, given the size of her engagement ring.

"What do *you* sneak into hallways for?" she asked me.

"I'm a novelist," I said. "So really, at the most random moments I'll have a flash of inspiration—or what *feels* like a flash of inspiration— and have to go think it over."

"Wow, novels," she said. "I admire people who can do that so much. I need a schedule, coworkers. And calendars! Don't get me started on how much I love calendars." She spoke like someone who had been the star of her high school debate team, quick and clear.

"Oh yeah," I said. "I have to force myself to a coffee shop every morning to work, and pretend the baristas are holding me accountable."

"What's your coffee shop of choice?" She focused on me as if she were making her way down a line of voters, determined to spend one to two quality minutes with each one. And yet somehow she gave me the feeling that she was asking these questions only because she was supposed to, and as soon as she had checked off Interact Pleasantly with This Person from her to-do list, she would move on without a second thought. Maybe it was the almost imperceptible drumming of her fingers against her thigh, the studied brightness of her smile.

"Well, if you're ever in Park Slope, it's called BitterSweet, and it's the best. I milk that free Wi-Fi all day." Back when I lived in Park Slope, like a normal twentysomething with roommates, it had been my favorite place to stop each morning on my way to work. And ever since Quill shut down, I'd been spending a lot of time there. It got me out of the house, gave me a commute so that I could trick myself into feeling like I still had my job.

"BitterSweet," she repeated. "I'll have to check it out." Her eyes flitted back in the direction of the party. I couldn't lose her, not yet.

"What's your current work emergency?" I blurted.

"Mine?" she asked, a bit surprised by my interest. "I'm trying to convince this woman to run for office, and she keeps waffling. She's a perfect candidate—great credentials, fantastic ideas, incredible backstory—but she's afraid of . . ." She paused. "She's afraid to just go for what she wants."

"That's infuriating," I said. Caroline nodded, slipping the back part of her foot out of her heels, as if she were trying to prevent a blister. I glanced down. There, on the back of her heel: a small, delicate tattoo of a dark bird in flight. Holy shit. It was the same one Margot had.

"I know," Caroline was saying. "And honestly, I hate to say it, but it's a problem I run into with women all the time."

I yanked my eyes away from her foot. *Maybe they're afraid because they saw what happened to the last woman you picked*, I thought, while saying, "It makes sense. We've been taught not to ask for things, so we don't seem too greedy or ambitious. All that subtle social conditioning will keep you down."

"Exactly. No wonder true equality still is nowhere in sight. It's just like, ugh!" She shook her fist at the sky. "Ask for what you want, ladies!"

"It's tough, though, because it's a legit fear," I said. "Everyone else has been socially conditioned too, right? So sometimes when a woman *does* stand up for herself, everyone around her is like, *Wow, what a bitch*."

Caroline nodded very seriously at me. "You're so right. I have to check my own biases all the time. I never want to be the kind of person who penalizes a woman for speaking up."

Maybe it was the champagne kicking in, making me brazen. But suddenly I knew exactly what to do. "I want to get better at asking for what I want," I said.

"Yes!" she said with such enthusiasm that I half expected her to shout, *You go girl!* and then tell me that *I* should run for office.

I squared my shoulders. "Like, hypothetically speaking, if I knew I could be an excellent addition to an exclusive club, and then I met a member, the bold, feminist thing to do would simply be to ask them if I could join. Right?"

Caroline's encouraging smile froze, and she grew very still.

Something shifted in her eyes. "Hypothetically speaking," she said, her tone still light, "I guess so."

"And like you just said," I continued breezily, "if that member were truly an advocate for women, she wouldn't penalize me for it. She would recognize that it was admirable, the right thing for a liberated woman to do."

"Mm, that would all be very progressive," she said, then glanced down at her phone in her hand as if it had just buzzed, although the screen hadn't lit up. "Oh, excuse me. I have to—" She waved the phone in the air. "It was very interesting talking to you." Then she turned and walked back into the party, her heels clicking on the hardwood floors.

I exhaled, trembling, wholly uncertain whether I had just gained entry or ruined my chances forever.

"There you are," Raf said, poking his head into the hallway. "I've been looking for you."

"You seemed occupied," I said. "What were you and Margot talking about for so long?"

He stared at me like I was an idiot. "You, obviously," he said. "I've got to pee, and then I need to get out of here. I'm exhausted. Want to head out together? Do what you needed to do?"

"I have no idea," I said. "So sure, I'll meet you by the door."

I went back into the party, toward the couch where I'd left my jacket. As I grabbed it, I felt a touch on my arm. Margot.

"Leaving so soon?" she asked.

"Yeah, long day for Raf," I said.

"He's been talking about you all night," she said, studying me. "You've really bewitched him, haven't you?"

"Oh, I don't know about that—"

"No, I mean it. He loves you. I can tell." Together, we watched as Raf emerged from the hallway and headed toward us, smiling at me uncertainly.

"He's a good guy," I said.

"Well, I'll let you lovebirds go. Sorry you and I didn't get to talk more. Congratulations on the novel. I can't wait to read it." She flitted off, disappearing back into the crowd, melting into the revelry where she belonged as Raf reached my side.

But as we left, I looked back at the party one more time. Caroline was saying something to Margot and Vy. Then, all three of them turned and watched as Raf and I walked out the door.

SEVEN

Two days went by where I didn't hear anything. I became convinced that my conversation with Caroline had been a huge blunder, that my name now existed on a blacklist and no woman from reputable society would ever associate with me again. I was Hester Prynne. Typhoid Mary. The old slutty cat from *Cats*, but without the vocal chops to belt out "Memory" and make everyone accept me.

On Sunday morning, I went for a long swim at the YMCA and then dragged myself to BitterSweet for a coffee. I ordered from a barista I had never seen before. When she gave me the mug, she also handed me a plate with a ginger molasses cookie on a napkin. "They gave us extras in the shipment," she said. "So here, on the house."

"Awesome, thanks," I said, and she shrugged, then turned back to the espresso machine.

I took the coffee and the cookie back to my seat and nibbled slowly. Miles had texted me that morning at eight thirty: **Beckley! Progress report?** On a Sunday, when he wasn't even at work. Despite himself, he was getting excited about the article, just in time for me to disappoint him.

I racked my brain for alternate plans, maybe involving Raf reaching out to Margot and setting up a time for us all to have dinner at the restaurant together. But I knew that wouldn't work. If my move at the party had backfired, a meal with Margot wasn't going to change anything. Maybe it was safer to go back to the drawing board and think of other pitches, so that at least I could offer Miles something to lessen the blow.

Screw nibbling. It was time to hard-core eat my feelings. I shoved the entire rest of the cookie in my mouth, then went to wipe my hand on the napkin it had come on. I paused, my hand in midair. Someone had written a message on the napkin in small, delicate cursive: *Tuesday, 8 pm, meet on the corner of Perry and Greenwich. The password is Persist.*

I looked up quickly, searching for the barista who had given me the plate. She wasn't behind the counter anymore.

Jangling with excitement and nerves, I stared down at the napkin again. Then I pulled up Miles's text, typed out a response, and pressed send.

I'm in.

EIGHT

On Tuesday night, as the dusk turned to darkness, I stood on the corner of Perry and Greenwich and waited. The whole way over, I'd listened to pump-up girl rock, Le Tigre and Joan Jett pounding in my ears as I power walked the streets of the West Village, passing the crowds at the ice cream shops and bars on West 4th, heading toward the river, the pedestrians thinning the farther west I went. At the corner, I attempted to act casual, pulling out a copy of a Gertrude Stein book, reading the same paragraph over and over again without registering any of it. Every person who passed made my hands tremble in anticipation. They all walked right by me and carried on with their nights, paying me no mind.

I could pull this off. I was the hero of an action movie, the guy you knew was going to be okay no matter how many helicopters he jumped out of and burning buildings he dashed into. *You're Tom*

Cruise, bitch, I said to myself. *In terms of* Mission: Impossible, *not the Scientology.*

A woman turned onto the block, heading my way. Something about her registered as familiar—the tilt of her head, the way she absentmindedly fiddled with her watch, the length of her hair. I knew the *shape* of her. The uncanny sense grew as she closed in, her face shadowy in the streetlight's glow: she was my mother. My breath quickened. She was half a block away now, and I wanted to run to her but I was frozen in place, like one of those dreams where you can't move your stupid feet, and I wanted to call out but my voice lodged in my throat. Vanilla, my mother's scent, hung in the air. (I'd given her some cheap bottle of vanilla perfume for Christmas one year when I was little. She was a grown woman and probably hadn't wanted to walk around smelling like cookies, but she'd worn it ever since.) She came closer, closer still, and the light of a passing car illuminated her face, and she wasn't my mother at all, just a fiftysomething brunette with a completely different nose and mouth. As she passed by me on her way to who-knew-where, her distracted eyes landed on me for a fraction of a second. Then they flickered onto something else, because we were total strangers.

"Do you have something to say to me?" a voice asked, close to my ear.

"Shit!" I yelped, jumping back. A woman, a few years younger than me, wearing a leather jacket and a sundress, had appeared behind me. She tapped at her phone with a look of disinterest on her face.

"Um," I said, swallowing, and she glanced up. "Persist?"

She stared at me for a moment more. "I'm going to need your phone."

"Why?"

She gave me a look of disdain. "Why do you think?" Either this was the most complicated stickup in history, or they didn't trust me not to take pictures, which was smart of them, because that was absolutely what I'd been planning to do. The woman rolled her eyes. "I know we're all addicted, but don't freak out, you'll get it back at the end of the night." I turned my phone off and handed it over to her. "Do you have any other cameras or recording devices for any reason?" I shook my head. She pulled something out of her pocket: a blindfold, silky and black. "Okay, now do I have your consent to put this on you?"

"Kinky," I said, waggling my eyebrows. She didn't laugh. I cleared my throat. "Sure. Yeah, go for it."

She slipped the cloth over my eyes, knotting it tightly behind my head, her movements perfunctory as if she did this every couple of weeks, like laundry. Maybe this was a duty that the younger, less impressive members performed to work their way up. Or maybe, I thought, as the world disappeared from my view, maybe the members of Nevertheless knew exactly what I was up to, and they'd sent this emissary to lead me to some abandoned warehouse along the highway. She'd tell me to wait and leave me there until I realized, hours later, that no one was coming for me. Maybe I wasn't Tom Cruise at all, but Extra #3, whose adventure ended before it began, without any fanfare at all.

The woman gripped my shoulders, then spun me around a few times like we were about to play a very intense game of pin the tail on the donkey. She placed a hand on my back and began guiding me down the street. With my sense of sight gone, I would simply heighten my other senses to figure out where we were going, like a bat! Taking a deep breath in from my nose, I got a real strong whiff of old street piss. Okay, I would simply trust my guide to lead me without pushing me into traffic or a storm drain.

A rumble of drunken laughter grew closer. "What's with the

blindfold?" a man asked, his words a little slurry. From the sound of it, he was traveling in a pack of bros.

"Oh my God," my chaperone answered, her voice turned girlish, bubblegum. "We're doing a scavenger hunt for her bachelorette party!"

The guys whistled and whooped. One of them shouted, "If one of the things you're hunting for is your last one-night stand, Chad is up for it!"

"Thanks, but not in a million years," I said.

My chaperone giggled. "You guys are so bad!" And then, as the pack drifted off, leaving a cloud of Axe body spray in their wake, she said in a low tone stripped of any sweetness at all, "Assholes. And not even attractive ones."

"I didn't miss my chance to have Chad rock my world?" I said as I tried to keep track of when and which way we were turning.

"No. Seemed like the kind of man who pumps away for a minute and then falls asleep."

"Nice," I said. "That's what I'm looking for in a guy: someone who has never gone down on a woman in his life." She laughed, in spite of herself. Maybe she wouldn't leave me in an abandoned warehouse after all.

After a few more minutes, we paused, and I sensed her looking up and down the street. I couldn't tell if we'd gone four or five blocks, or just around in circles. Then, a buzzing noise sounded. She swung open a heavy door and pushed me inside. The noises of the outside world stopped as soon as the door swung closed again— no car horns, no conversation. Just a low hum, a faint buzzing in my ears, like when you're congested, and then elevator gears creaking, a soft *ding*, and doors sliding open.

We rode up without saying anything. The doors opened again. And suddenly, the silent world exploded into chatter and warmth.

"Ooh, a trial," someone said as my guide undid the blindfold, and I saw the inside of the Nevertheless clubhouse for the first time.

Imagine if a West Elm showroom and Anthropologie made a baby at the Women's March. That was the room before me: a little kitschy, very color-coordinated, in shades of pale blues and peach, with girl-power slogans everywhere. A bunch of lights spelling out NASTY WOMEN adorned one wall. I'M OVAR(Y) THE PATRIARCHY, read another large sign, in cursive wire letters. God, if they *had* brought down Nicole Woo-Martin, I hated them all with a fiery passion. These beautiful, dangerous hypocrites, putting up signs with one hand while desperately clutching their money with the other. Maybe they'd all plotted Nicole's downfall in this very clubhouse, talking about how she'd gotten a little too progressive in the glow from the NASTY WOMEN novelty lights.

I swallowed my anger and kept scanning the room. Anywhere there wasn't a slogan, there was a plant—succulents, ferns, vases of fresh flowers scattered all around—and yet despite this profusion of greenery and girl power, the whole space maintained a clean, clutter-free feeling. A door off to the right was marked with a sign reading POWDER ROOM. There were two other unmarked doors off to the left.

The room could hold maybe one hundred women comfortably. On this particular night, about forty of them, mostly white, floated around, sipping champagne or fizzy water in a trendy pink can that I'd never seen before. Some of them were dressed in their business casual from a day in the office—their feet in high heels, their pencil skirts perfectly tailored. Others wore artsier, cooler fare: oversize shirts and high-waisted shorts, flowing flower-print dresses. Some paid me no mind, engrossed as they were in their networking or gossiping. But others turned and smiled at me warmly. I stared at this wonderland of women. And then Margot pushed her way through the crowd.

"Thank you, Yael," she said to the woman who had brought me in. Then she threw an arm around my shoulder and turned to the crowd. "This is Jillian, everyone! She's a budding literary star." She hugged me and said, thrillingly close to my ear, "Glad you could make it."

"I'm excited to be here." I gave a thumbs-up, then regretted it.

"You're just in time," she said. "We're doing a special workshop."

All the women began assembling on couches or poufs, facing an open space by the windows where two wingback chairs had been set up. "Hey, witches!" one woman in a blazer said, waving to her friends. "Over here."

A couple of other women passed me and Margot. "No, the best psychic *I've* gone to is out in Astoria. I'm telling you, she actually makes it worthwhile to go to Queens. I'll get you her card," one of them was saying.

"That would be amazing," said her companion. "It's like I can literally feel my aura getting cloudier and cloudier. I swear my boyfriend's ex put a curse on me."

"Wow," I said to Margot, "people are really into your coven of witches joke, huh?" It had gotten popular for women to call themselves witches, to harness the danger and excitement of the term in order to assert some power. I didn't quite get it, but apparently it had struck a chord and gone commercial: I'd seen the books at Barnes & Noble, called things like *A Witch's Guide to Smashing the Patriarchy* or *Spells for the Badass Witch*. But in this gleaming clubhouse, the attempt to conjure some kind of magic seemed hopelessly awkward.

Margot pursed her lips. "I make one joke, one time," she said. "And suddenly we're overrun with cosplayers." Her annoyance surprised me. Proclaiming oneself a witch didn't seem all that different from getting into astrology. Both were ways for women to distract themselves with some illusion of control. I would've expected Margot to smile benevolently upon talk of hexes and spells, but it seemed that was a bridge too far, even for her.

She caught me looking at her and shook her head. "I don't mind it that much, but it bothers Caroline. It's 'unserious.' And I'd rather not bother Caroline right now."

Interesting. Some tension between them, perhaps? "Well, then," I said. "Good thing I left my cauldron at home."

She smiled. "Anyway, think of yourself as our guest for the night and grab a seat. Yael will escort you out again at the end of it all."

I picked my way over to a long leather couch and sat myself next to two women who were discussing an upcoming IPO for a popular tech start-up. I had nothing to add to that conversation, so I folded my hands on my lap. Since I couldn't exactly pull out my notebook and scribble everything down, I recited the details in my mind, committing them to memory while trying to appear relaxed. Like I belonged.

The problem was that I wasn't calm at all. There was something strange and thrilling about being in a room—a full, bustling room—of only women. I knew how Margot and her ilk might describe it in a promotional brochure, not that they would ever make such a thing: a paradise where you could spend time with interesting, successful women without having to worry about some asshole mansplaining or hitting on you.

But that particular kind of paradise brought its own set of complications. I throbbed with adrenaline, wanting in spite of myself to impress and ingratiate even more than I might have if men were around. The air seemed full of possibility. Certain worries evaporated (was I attractive enough to be wanted, but not attractive enough to be harassed?). New ones rushed in to take their place (was I interesting enough, warm enough, strong enough, *full enough?*).

I tried to figure out how old everyone else in this room was. I'd recently become obsessed with age. Every few minutes, men think about sex. Every few minutes, *I* thought about how old various women I admired were when they'd made their mark on the world. Whenever I enjoyed a piece of writing by a woman, I immediately Googled the year she was born. Each time I found out that some girl had published her first *New York Times* article at age twenty-six, I wanted to stab myself in the heart with the nearest sharp object and bleed out like the useless old crone I was. How dare these children simply charge forward straight out of college with a clarity of purpose and zero learning curve? I mean, I was happy for them, but how dare they? I'd started living in fear of the annual *Forbes* 30 Under 30 list. Unlike sex, age was not a fun obsession to have, since I couldn't do anything about it. (Not that I could do anything about sex either lately. My vagina had hung out a CLOSED FOR BUSINESS sign and wanted to take it down only for the most inconvenient man.)

The accomplished, accepted women around me ranged from around twenty-five to thirty-five, although they all glowed with the same good health that came from expensive skincare regimens.

"Hey, newbie, you don't have a drink!" a woman said, parking herself in front of me. "Could I interest you in some artisanal bubbly water from a female-founded company? Free samples tonight, but normally, for each case of it sold here in the U.S., one case gets sent over to dehydrated girls in Africa!" She beamed at me and wiggled one of the trendy, unfamiliar cans I'd seen earlier. She was curvy, with a hint of Southern twang in her voice, and she had one of those smiles that managed to be both entirely transformative and a little bit nervous at the same time. It took over her whole face, creasing and dimpling her cheeks, but her eyes held a hint of terror. As if she'd been one of the unpopular girls in high school, and she didn't want anyone in her new life to find out. It was endearing, in a way. I wanted to tell her not to worry. Of the two of us, I had the far more damaging secret.

"Oh, uh, sure," I said, and reached out for the can. *Fizzi*, it read on the front in a curving script, with a pretty swirling design. I turned the can to see a map of Africa, and a long block of text explaining the mission, written in a minuscule font but still dominating the entire length of the can. "Thanks so much."

"Of course!" she said, and wedged herself in next to me on the couch, staring at me expectantly. "Go ahead, give it a try. I love watching people take their first sips of it." Off my look, she smacked herself jokingly on the forehead. "Oh, d'oy! I'm not just, like, an obsessive water fan. I started the company!"

I cracked the can open and took a sip. "Mm," I said. It tasted like seltzer. "Refreshing."

"Thank you! I really think so too." She sat back and sighed with satisfaction. "It was so nice of them to let me bring in samples tonight. This is what I hoped it would be like, you know? Women helping other women! I just got invited for the first time a month ago, so I guess I'm a newbie too, although it's such a warm and amazing community that it feels like I've belonged here my whole life!" She smacked her forehead again. She was going to give herself a concussion if she kept that up. "Oh, I haven't even introduced myself. I'm Libby."

"Jillian," I said. "Are you still a trial member?"

Libby beamed. "Oh no, I'm official!"

"Hey, congrats," I said. "So how many times do they blindfold you to bring you in? Not that I don't like being blindfolded, but, you know."

Libby puffed up, excited to have the inside scoop. "Only the first few times, until you've passed the tests and they've decided that they can really trust you. *That's* when you sign the contract and the nondisparagement agreement—" Shit, was I going to have to sign something that prohibited me from fully writing about them? Would they *sue* me if I did? They were so good at keeping things secret, I should've realized that they'd have legal protection in place. Nondisparagement I could maybe deal with, as long as it wasn't a nondisclosure. I needed to talk to Miles about all of this, ASAP. Libby kept chattering. "—And start paying dues. Which, honestly, five hundred bucks a month is such a steal for this! Then they give you the address and you're allowed to come whenever you want! Well, not *whenever*—the clubhouse closes at eleven P.M., unless they've got some special event going on."

"Got it," I said. "And wait, when you said you have to pass their tests, you meant metaphorically, right? There aren't actual tests—"

"Ooh," Libby gasped, grabbing my arm. "Speaking of special events, this one is going to be *so* good!"

The women in the room all snapped to attention as Caroline emerged from one of the unmarked doors. Aha, that one must have led to a greenroom or an office of some kind. I wondered what the other one led to. Maybe a maintenance closet.

Caroline wore a plaid miniskirt, into which she'd tucked a ribbed white turtleneck. How did she get her shirt to stay tucked so neatly? Maybe good posture had something to do with it. Caroline stood up ramrod straight. She smiled at the crowd before her, ready to present, like the type of friend you'd want to give the big toast at your wedding because she would keep strictly to the time limit. Still, though, I couldn't shake the feeling that there was some kind of charisma void. She'd keep to the time limit, but she wouldn't make your wedding guests laugh. That *Vogue* article had implied that Caroline wanted to run for office someday, but she'd be so much better as someone's chief of staff. "Hello, ladies. I don't think I have to tell you how excited I am for tonight's guest."

"Tell us anyway!" someone in the crowd shouted.

"Okay, I'm *so* excited!" Caroline said. She held up a hand and began ticking things off on her fingers. "Just a few of the incredible facts about her: she's been called 'the Sheryl Sandberg of Enterprise Information Systems Technology,' she's made the *Time* 100 Most Influential People list six years running, and oh yeah . . ." She affected a blasé face for a moment, then continued, "She just officially became a billionaire!" Some of the women in the crowd whooped. I did not understand the hard-on that people had for billionaires. Being that rich was just a form of hoarding, but instead of collecting old newspapers and dead cats, you were piling up money you could never use. I wouldn't even know how to spend more than $15 million. Well, okay, no, I lived in New York City. I could probably spend $20 million if I *had* to. But not a penny more. "Here to talk to us about closing the wage gap, and how to ask for what you're worth, please welcome Louise Boltstein!"

The women applauded, with a few even standing up to cheer, as a businesswoman in her fifties walked out from the door. Louise Boltstein was sleek, with a blond bob and an incredibly subtle plastic surgeon. I'd seen her in the news occasionally. She'd testified at some hearing on Capitol Hill, where she'd shut down the ultraconservative senator who was asking her questions. Also, she was friendly with Oprah. She walked over to Caroline, money and power swirling around her in the air like dust motes, and they exchanged kisses on the cheek. Then they took their seats and leaned forward to have an Important Conversation.

"Thank you for having me," Louise said. "My daughter is jealous that I get to be here right now."

"Oh please, it is such an honor," Caroline said.

"This is amazing," my new friend Libby whispered to me. "Louise is like the ultimate girlboss!"

"I have to tell you," Caroline said, "that when I was in college, I had a picture of you hanging on my wall of inspiration, right in between Katie Couric and Madeleine Albright." Louise laughed like she heard those kinds of stories all the time. "So maybe it's a little embarrassing, but I'm not ashamed to say that I fangirled when you agreed to talk to us." Caroline *would* be the type of woman to reclaim embarrassment, to turn an accidental fart in the middle of a work presentation into an opportunity for an earnest speech about how *yes*, women had gas! And they should celebrate that, because until men saw women as equals in all ways, including bodily functions, we'd never reach true parity!

"Now," Caroline said to Louise. "You're here to give us all some guidance on what we can do about the ever-stubborn wage gap."

"That's right," Louise said, and looked out at the crowd. "There aren't that many female billionaires, and I need some of you to join me so I don't get lonely!" The crowd gave an appreciative chuckle. "But seriously, for years, I failed to reach my earnings potential because I never asked my male colleagues what *they* were making. And then one day I learned that I had been settling for thousands less even though I was just as, if not more, qualified."

"And it continues to be such an issue," Caroline said, indicating a woman in the front row of the audience, one of the business-casual set. "Just earlier this evening, Maya and I were talking about this, right?"

Maya nodded. "I'm only making three hundred thousand a year," she said. "And I *know* some of the men at my level are making more than that." I stifled an incredulous snort-laugh. In what world was three hundred thousand a year something to sniff at? In this world, I guessed.

"So clearly there are a lot of factors," Caroline said. "But, Louise, what do you think is the primary issue holding women back here?" She turned to us. "Besides long-standing structural inequality, obviously."

Louise steepled her fingers and nodded. "Great question, Caroline. Women don't negotiate as forcefully as men do. That's what I want us to work on tonight."

"One hundred percent!" Caroline gushed, then paused, her face suddenly serious. "Of course," she said, "we have to remember that the wage gap is even larger for women of color, particularly those who come from low-income households."

"Yes, of course," Louise said, and everyone nodded solemnly for a moment before she continued. "So let's get started! Everybody, find a partner."

Libby squeezed my arm. "Shall we?" I scanned the room as the other women in attendance paired off. I caught Margot's eyes on me. Did she want to be my partner? No, she'd already linked up with a willowy brunette. She was just . . . watching me. Maybe this itself was part of the test: how enthusiastically I participated, or simply whether or not anyone chose me. I felt a sudden rush of gratitude for Libby.

"We shall!" I said.

"First things first," Louise said, as everyone turned to face her in their pairs. "Women can be hesitant to take ownership of their own achievements in the workplace." She held a hand to her chest and widened her eyes, as if scandalized. "Bragging is so unladylike. Better to share the credit, so no one thinks that you're *bossy*." She shook her head, dropping the charade, her voice turning wry. "I guarantee you that men aren't thinking that when they do something amazing." The women in the audience tittered knowingly. "So pretend you're with one of your closest girlfriends after a great day at the office, and tell your partner honestly what a badass you are."

With Louise's blessing, the pairs of women around us began to chatter with gusto. Libby and I looked at each other, her with an unexpectedly shy expression.

"Ooh," she said. "You can go first, if you want!"

"No, no, you go for it," I said. "What's your story?"

"Okay," she said, and took a deep breath. "Oh my gosh, okay. Why I'm a badass . . ." She hesitated, thinking, and then pulled a face. "I don't know why this is so hard!" Now Caroline was looking over, as if to check on our progress.

"Yeah, it feels weird to be like *Hey, nice to meet you, here's why I'm amazing.* But we can't disappoint Louise," I said. Then I winked. "After all, she's friends with Oprah."

Libby smiled. "Good point."

"From my brief observation of you since we've become the closest of girlfriends, you seem very motivated," I said, indicating the fizzy water she'd been handing out.

"I *am*," she said, her spine straightening. "Thank you. I lugged all that water here tonight!"

"It was probably heavy to carry," I said. "So you are literally a strong woman."

Delight rose in her face as she laughed. And then, floodgates open, she began to catalog her achievements for me. "I was brave enough to take a leap of faith and start over in a place where I didn't really know anyone." She blinked a couple of times, cleared her throat, and went on. "I came up with the idea for Fizzi all by myself, but then built a team where everyone is treated with respect and kindness. I hadn't been sure whether the cans should feature Africa, or images of powerful women like Frida Kahlo, but I made the call for Africa, and it seems to be the right decision because we're getting more orders all the time!"

Maybe, in accepting her offer to be my partner, I'd been doing her just as big a favor as she'd been doing for me. She didn't seem to fit entirely into this room of women. She was too guileless. She came across as *younger* than everyone else even though she didn't look it, like a career gal in her twenties had body-swapped with someone's kid sister, *Freaky Friday*–style. I wondered how she'd gotten her Nevertheless invitation. Her water company must have been making a big difference.

We switched, and I tried to be as enthusiastic as a camp counselor as I listed my own attributes.

"I'm a very hard worker!" I said.

"That's so impressive!" Libby said, her own camp counselor energy much more natural than mine. Out of the corner of my eye, I caught a couple of other women I didn't know, but who also seemed to hold some kind of sway here, watching us.

Next, Louise had us reflect what we'd heard back to each other, because we couldn't tell how "truly amazing" we were until we saw ourselves as our friends did, apparently. (A woman next to us told her partner, "You are *such* a powerful witch goddess." Hmm, I could understand why Caroline was apparently so bothered—the witch stuff was already getting to be a little much.) Then we had to do power poses like Wonder Woman. With our hands on our hips and our feet firmly planted, we bellowed, "I AM WORTH IT."

All of this validation was like a self-help conference, a far cry from the rumors of shadowy doings. It was self-interested feminism in the extreme, and the women around me were *loving* it. Our collective voices were so loud, it seemed inconceivable that this clubhouse could remain a secret—surely the neighbors were wondering from whence this battle cry was coming. But it *had* to remain a secret or else the power of it was gone. Take away the secrecy from tonight, and what you had was a celebrity sighting and some mutual masturbation.

"And finally, it's time for some role play," Louise said. "Not to worry, it's the safe-for-work kind. I'll play the boss. Who wants to negotiate with me for the equal pay she deserves?"

Dozens of hands shot up, a natural result in a room full of Hermione Grangers. Next to me, Libby's arm flew into the air, and I got a whiff of her shower-fresh deodorant. But Louise picked a woman nearer to the front, the same woman who had spoken up earlier about her paltry $300,000 salary. Business Casual Maya.

"Thank you for coming in today," Louise said, giving her a firm handshake and indicating that she should sit in the other wingback chair at the front of the room. The two of them began to act out a salary negotiation. Though Maya was clearly awed by her chance to talk with *the* Louise Boltstein, that didn't stop her from going on about her work in exhaustive detail. I began to zone out.

"And how much of a raise are you asking for?" Louise asked a few minutes later.

"Fifty thousand dollars, annually," Maya replied.

Louise pursed her lips, in imitation of a hard-line boss. "Isn't fifty thousand a little much?"

Maya hesitated, then put her hands on her hips as if reminding herself of the Wonder Woman power pose. She thrust her chin up. "If anything, it's low."

Louise nodded. "I see. Well, then." She reached into a pocket in her blazer. What was she going for? A stick of gum? The women in the room leaned forward in confusion, as she withdrew a slim black checkbook and a heavy ballpoint pen. "You've convinced me." No one breathed as Louise opened the checkbook and began to write

on it, then signed her name with a flourish. She wasn't actually . . .
No, she couldn't be. Maya's body froze in anticipation. With all the
self-possession in the world, Louise ripped the check from the
booklet and handed it to Maya.

"Since fifty thousand dollars is a little low, here's sixty," she said,
and from the look on Maya's face as she stared at the check, everyone in the room realized it was true. A $60,000 gift, given as casu-
ally as a scented candle. A collective gasp rang out as Maya began
to shake and weep, and then threw her arms around Louise. The
other women in the room began cheering, a few quickly sliding
happy masks over their jealous expressions, mad that they hadn't
raised their hands just a little bit quicker. A sense of possibility
rippled through the room, the rapturous realization that at any
time in this clubhouse, life as you had previously known it could
change. (Although to most of these women, what was $60,000? A
single fancy vacation?) Yup, this group of women valued their
money, all right. Worshipped it, even. Would clearly do a lot to
protect it.

Tears streamed down Libby's cheeks, mucus beginning to drip
from her nose.

"Are you okay?" I asked, putting my hand on her shoulder.

"I'm amazing," she said. "I'm just so happy to be here."

"All right, and that's our time," Louise called out. "But before I
go, I want to remind you all that you have one more powerful tool
in your toolbox. You have each other. Women need to support
women." When Nicole Woo-Martin had announced her resignation (and thus the death of her wealth tax), had Louise Boltstein
popped some champagne, thrilled that her piles of cash would remain undisturbed? "Look your partner in the eyes." I stared at
Libby's watery green irises.

Louise spoke slowly, her words gathering force. "Next time you go in to negotiate for a raise, I want you to call your partner beforehand. She has seen you own your power tonight." Louise spoke now like a preacher, her voice rising and rippling through the room. "She will reassure you that you! Deserve! The! World!" At that, Libby stepped forward and embraced me, squashing me against her chest, as the other women in the room burst into a thunderous round of applause.

"Let's totally be buddies," Libby said to me. "I've got your back."

"Thanks," I said. "I've got yours."

The members hung around for a while after the talk was over, jostling one another in the politest possible way to get their chance to meet Louise, to experience her firm handshake and show off their own firm handshakes in return. I stood back and watched, recognizing a few faces in the crowd. Here was a young designer who had taken New York Fashion Week by storm this past year. There was Iris Ngoza, a body positivity model I'd read about in *Cosmopolitan* just the other day, unsurprisingly radiant. Vy Larsson, the experimental artist who hated me, wasn't around tonight. I couldn't imagine her bellowing "I AM WORTH IT" in the midst of a crowd. Or maybe she wasn't a member after all.

As Louise left, bound for a private car waiting outside to take her home, the other women headed for the exit too. Yael, my guide from earlier, materialized at my side, with the blindfold back in her hand, my cell phone still held hostage in her pocket.

"Time to go," she said.

"Do I need to thank anyone?" I asked her. "Or make it clear that I want to come back?"

Her mouth curled. "No, it's always clear."

"Let me just run to the bathroom," I said. In case I never gained access again, I wanted to get as full a picture of the place as I could.

"Fine, make it quick, please," Yael said.

The "powder room" was like the most luxurious gym bathroom I'd ever seen. It was inconceivable that a toilet in here had ever gotten clogged. Underneath a long mirror, the white marble countertop was laid with bottles of lotion, dry shampoo, mouthwash, and perfumes. A large glass bowl was filled with organic tampons. (I didn't fully understand what organic tampons were, but I supported them?) Above the mirror, someone had painted the words *Hello, goddess!* I stared at my flushed cheeks, my shiny forehead, and snorted. Not exactly goddess material. But good enough, maybe, to fool people tonight.

When I reemerged back into the nearly empty clubhouse, Margot was standing with her hand on the second unmarked door, the one that no one had gone near all night. Vy Larsson was with her, both of them seemingly intent on something.

"Oh, Jillian," Margot said, startling when she saw me. Her hand jumped away from the knob, like a reflex. "I didn't realize you were still here." She quickly covered her surprise, her languid smile sliding back onto her face, but not quickly enough. Vy scowled. What the hell was behind that door?

"I just wanted to say that I had such an amazing time tonight," I said.

"I'm so glad." Margot came to my side and slung an arm around my shoulder, casually walking me away from the door and to the elevator, where Yael waited with my blindfold. "We'll be in touch."

NINE

The next time I got invited to Nevertheless, the shadowy cabal in charge went through Raf. He called me one evening not long after the equal pay talk. In the intervening days, I'd been on high alert, looking for that unfamiliar barista each time I went to BitterSweet, slowing down whenever a beautiful woman passed me on the sidewalk in case she had a message for me. I'd even started checking all my receipts for hidden codes, like a Very Normal Person.

At one point, I caught the eye of a stylish woman on the train. I gave her a tentative smile. She stared at me, opened her mouth as if on the verge of saying something, then shut it again. As the train slowed down in the station, I made my way to her side through the hordes of commuters. "Do you have something to say to me?" I asked her in a low voice, not looking directly at her.

"You have lettuce in your teeth," she said.

When Raf called, I was home, vegging out on my bed and scrolling through pictures online of cats up for adoption, trying to decide if now was the right time to get one. Probably not. I had to vacate the house soon, giving it up to the yuppie couple who had bought it, and I had no idea where I was going to go next.

When Raf's name popped up on my phone, a knot formed in my stomach. It was prime restaurant hours. Why would he be calling me now? Oh God, had something bad happened to him, or a member of his family? Raf had recently sent his parents on a multi-week cruise, and all sorts of terrible things could happen on cruises. This is one of the extra fun byproducts of your mother slowly dying—you get a kind of PTSD about phone calls at weird times. Nobody's calling you just to say hi or tell you they love you. They're calling with bad news.

"Are you okay?" I asked when I picked up the phone.

"Yeah, just busy," he said, and I exhaled. "I can only talk for a minute, but I had to tell you. this woman just came back to the kitchen—she'd asked to compliment the chef, and she was at a table that spent a shit-ton of money, so we had to let her."

"Of course."

"Anyway, she said nice things about the ropa vieja, which was good, because we had a mix-up with our meat supplier and I had to do things differently, so I was kinda worried it would be an off night."

"Um, congratulations?" I said. "I'm happy for you."

"Thanks," he said. "Uh, but then she said, 'Maybe you could come over and make it for me privately sometime,' so I told her that I had a girlfriend—"

"Girlfriend, huh?" I teased. "I didn't realize that we'd defined the relationship."

"Well, yeah," he said, stammering a bit. "If we're doing this fake-dating thing, we've got to be convincing. We grew up as close family friends, so I don't think we would just start hooking up. If we were going to take the chance of screwing up our friendship, we would have to really feel . . . serious about each other, right?"

"True," I said. "Dammit, that's such a good-boyfriend thing to say. Now I'm extra sorry I cock-blocked you with this rich ropa vieja woman. Was she gorgeous?"

"Yeah. But that's not the point. After I told her I had a girl-friend, she said, all quiet, 'Tell Jillian same time, same place, Mon-day night.' And then before I could say anything else, she just walked away. I assume she meant you. I don't know any other Jil-lians that are doing weird secretive stuff right now."

"Yes!" I said, and did a victory dance in my bedroom, acciden-tally knocking over a lamp.

"Okay, so that makes sense to you?" he asked.

"Perfect sense. Thanks, Raf," I said. I heard a crash in the kitchen behind him, and a muted swear word.

"Damn, I gotta go."

"You're a gem," I said. "Call me tomorrow? Or come by the bar anytime I'm working a shift. I owe you free drinks in perpetuity."

"Yeah yeah," he said, and hung up.

I sat down on my bed, shaking my head at the brazenness of it all. There was something incredibly powerful in the way this ran-dom woman had turned an important man into a mere messenger. Half of me wanted Nevertheless's unpredictable invite system to go on forever just to see what they would come up with next. And half of me had been ready for the gimmicks to end yesterday. Be-cause honestly, it was rude. What if I had other plans? I was just supposed to drop everything in my life for them? Sure, I personally had no pressing social activities and no important commitments. (Luckily the owners of the place where I'd picked up my bartending shifts were used to employing actors and musicians who had to swap hours because of last-minute opportunities all the time.) But for all Nevertheless knew, I could be very busy and popular! Did Nevertheless do this for their businesswomen and models too, expecting them to just reschedule a photoshoot or an important phone call with Tokyo for the privilege of being led blindly down the street like a pig to slaughter? Maybe they did, and everyone wanted to be a part of it so much that they moved shit around.

I pictured my new friend Libby, beaming in the clubhouse. For Nevertheless, she'd reschedule anything, from a meeting of the board for her water company to an appointment with New York's most exclusive gynecologist. Shaking my head at the foolishness of people, I marked my calendar.

TEN

So at 7:59 P.M. on Monday I was back on the corner of Perry and Greenwich, waiting to be blindfolded. A different young woman came to meet me but the same procedure unfolded—the confiscation of my cell phone, the dizziness and disorientation, the silent elevator ride—until my blindfold was yanked off and the clubhouse appeared before me again.

The vibe was different than it had been the last time, with many fewer women around. No sign of Libby or Caroline, only a few of the business-casual crowd networking and talking at the tables. A Beyoncé song played softly from a speaker system. Someone was burning incense that smelled like eucalyptus. The lights were lower, like at a restaurant when it switches from the family diners to the date-night crowd. No billionaires would be giving a talk on this particular evening. This was a typical night at the club.

Margot sat on a velvet couch next to Vy, a pack of cards spread out between them. Candles flickered on a nearby coffee table. At first I thought they were playing a game, and laughed to myself: The true secret of Nevertheless was that its members sat around and played go fish! They went through all that hoopla and secrecy just so they could play card games without being interrupted by any men! (Or any poor people.) But Vy's and Margot's bodies were too charged with energy, too engaged with each other, to be playing a casual game. Margot was barefoot again and wearing a camel-colored shirtdress, hugging one leg close to her chest, the other one dangling off the couch. Vy curled toward her, her upper body a parenthesis, her short hair mussed and spiked as if she'd kept running a hand absentmindedly through it. High-stakes gambling? No. I looked closer. They weren't using a regular deck of cards.

I cleared my throat and Margot registered me, then smiled as if she hadn't known I was coming tonight. (Bullshit. Through my limited time at Nevertheless, I had gotten the sense that she was consulted on everything. She held a place of prominence in the group, was probably one of the founding members.) "Jillian! We're reading tarot. Come join us?"

Ah, tarot cards. Not a surprise that Margot was into them. Like astrology, they seemed a method by which one could read far too much into random information, could pick out a droplet of truth from a bucket and then profess that the whole thing was pure. I'd never had mine read before. The closest I'd gotten was going to a storefront psychic with a friend during college spring break. The woman had stared at my friend's palm and pronounced that she was going to live until age ninety-three and have a healthy marriage and successful career, that she had the kind of truly amazing energy that didn't come around very often. Then the psychic had taken my hand and told me that I was dangerously blocked, and that I needed to buy a special candle to cleanse my aura. She'd waved the candle in my face. It smelled like blue cheese, looked like a lumpy penis, and cost $250.

I didn't buy the candle. I'd known she was making it all up. But still, I'd been unsettled. She'd seen something in me that made her think I was vulnerable, an easy mark for her racket. Some energy that I was giving off—some expression on my face, some tightening in my shoulders—had made her think, *This one. This one is weak.* I'd had no desire to ever do anything like it again.

But for tonight, I could pretend to get a kick out of it. "Oh, fun," I said to Margot, determined to participate in this bonding ritual like we were all girls huddling around a Ouija board.

Vy harrumphed in my direction, then stared down at the cards, turning over a final one to reveal an image of a woman draped in cloth, wearing a sort of floppy crown, her gaze intense.

"The High Priestess," she said in a low voice. She and Margot met each other's eyes, something coded passing between the two of them.

Then Margot shook it off, whatever it was. "Jillian, you want me to read yours?" she asked, and although I worried that maybe they'd *also* try to sell me a $250 candle, I saw that if I said *No thank you*, I'd be closing a very important door. Libby had mentioned passing their tests, and this was one of them. How I reacted to the cards I drew, what I revealed about myself, even just in my body language: this was part of how they'd decide if I was worthy. Turning down this reading would be like refusing to do the math section of the SATs and expecting Harvard admission anyway.

I plastered on a smile. "Sure."

Vy grabbed a mug of tea off the coffee table and moved to the side, making room for me between her and Margot. "I think a simple past, present, future," Margot murmured to Vy, and Vy nodded.

Margot turned her gaze to me. Some people can make you be-lieve that, in a crowded room, you're the only person who matters. Margot had that gift. Her attention gave you the feeling that, at any moment, she might lean forward and kiss you.

Now, getting hit with the full force of Margot's powers sent a buzz through me. "All right, Jillian," she said, stretching out her arms, rolling her wrists in circles like an athlete warming up, even as she kept her dark brown eyes locked on mine. "First, we need to pick your archetype. The card that will represent you in this read-ing." She shuffled a stack quickly. The backs of the cards were navy blue, with thin gold lines weaving across them. Margot paused, then drew out a picture of a man in a dark cloak thrusting one hand up to the sky, the golden background behind him faded. THE MAGICIAN, a label at the bottom of the card read.

"Hmm," Margot said as she placed the card down in the center of the couch. "Resourceful. Skilled."

"Cunning," said Vy, and even as I kept my expression neutral, my stomach churned. Vy's vengeance on the man who had ruined her menstrual hut installation flew into my mind. I pictured her leading a silent fleet of women onto his lawn with bags of bloodied tampons, leaving them there as a warning. Vy, looking up at his window while the women did their work behind her, wishing she could climb inside and draw a different kind of blood. What would she want to do to me if everything worked out the way I hoped it would with this exposé?

"Now," Margot said, handing the deck to me, "think of a ques-tion you have, something that's been aching to be answered." The cards had a weathered feel to their ridged edges. This was not a deck that Margot had just purchased. This was a deck that had seen some action over the years, that had absorbed the sweat of all sorts of hands. "Hold that question in your mind, concentrate on it, while you keep the deck between your palms."

Vy took a noisy sip of her tea, sucking it through her teeth like a malfunctioning pool filter. Margot smiled at me gently. "Closing your eyes helps concentrate the energy too."

I tried to make my face serene. "Okay," I said, shutting my eyes. I didn't have an Important Question, in part because the whole thing was silly, and in part because all that was running through my mind was a series of panicky thoughts: *What am I doing here? What the fuck will happen to me if they find me out? I'm sitting very close to Margot—can she tell how much I'm sweating? Should I buy a prescription deodorant?* Seconds ticked by. A new Beyoncé song began piping over the sound system. At a nearby table, a woman was talking about the promotion she'd just gotten while her companion shrieked, "Oh my God, *yass*, queen!" My panic momentarily faded, and I rolled my eyes behind my eyelids.

"Open your eyes now," Margot said. "Shuffle the deck eight times, and then cut it into three stacks." I did as directed, laying the stacks out facedown on the couch where she pointed, below the watchful gaze of The Magician.

"So what was your question?" Vy asked, brusque, her lips downturned. I'd thought my own Resting Bitch Face was bad, but I had nothing on her. She blinked very slowly, and very rarely. It was unnerving.

"Oh, I didn't know we were supposed to say them out loud," I said.

"Well, you don't *have* to," Margot replied. "Sometimes we can dig deepest when we seek answers in the privacy of our own hearts. But I can help you interpret everything so much more accurately if you do tell us."

Right, she just wanted to *help* me. Not have me reveal the inner workings of my heart and mind in the guise of a fun little reading. "My question was . . ." I began, then blurted out the first thing that came to mind. "Am I on the right path? You know, just generally, in life."

"Mm," Margot said, sympathetically. "It's so hard to see that clearly sometimes. Let's get you some clarity." She tapped the stack of cards on the left. "This first stack represents your past." In a graceful, fluid motion, Margot turned the top card over to reveal a fleshy crimson heart, violently pierced by three swords. Cool, promising start. "The Three of Swords," she said, biting her lip. "This card generally means heartbreak. Sorrow. You've come through something difficult." She looked up at me. "Oh, that makes sense. Your mother, right?"

"Yeah," I said, and then to Vy, "She died."

Vy sucked her teeth. "Sorry about that."

"That must have been so hard," Margot said, giving me her trademarked *You Are the Only Person In This Room Who Matters*™ look again. "Was it very recent?"

Dammit, she wanted me to talk about it, to cut myself open and show her my own pierced heart just like the one on the card. This was what cult leaders did: made you vulnerable as a way of binding you to them. I'd come here to make these women vulnerable to *me*, not the other way around. Besides, it felt cheap to use my mother as a tool for my own advancement any more than I already had.

"Yeah, it happened a few months ago, and it was awful," I said, then redirected my attention to the stacks on the couch. "Here's hoping my present card is more promising." Vy blinked at me, probably picturing a seagull, refusing to swoop beneath the waves, beating its wings in great bursts of effort to stay above the spray.

As Margot went to turn over the next card, my stomach churned in anticipation. It wasn't that I believed the card was going to change the course of my life. If anything, the power of these cards was that you read into them what you wanted to see, which helped you get more in touch with what you were feeling. Margot and Vy handled the cards almost as if they held a mystical strength, but they weren't going to pull one over on me. I knew their game: the more they acted as if the cards could reveal something deep about my soul or destiny, the more authentic my reactions to them would be. The more they could gauge me, judge me. I sent up a silent prayer for a card that I could spin in some impressive way, featuring a warrior lady with a cool pet leopard, or maybe a gorgeous princess surrounded by abundance. Anything besides more bloody swords.

Margot laid the card out. Just a bunch of sticks, flying through the air in some harmonious motion toward their destination. "Huh, Eight of Wands," Vy said. "Which usually means forward momentum."

Hey, who didn't like forward momentum? Margot bit her lip again. "But the card is reversed," she said. "That can mean that you're rushing into action without fully considering steps you need to take, leaving you likely to make mistakes or even bad decisions. Does that mean anything to you?"

"Um," I said, struggling to keep my body language neutral. "I don't know."

"It could also mean a more general frustration," Margot said. "Feeling blocked or stuck."

I gave a vigorous nod. "Yeah, frustrated! It's probably because I'm trying to edit my novel and can't tell if what I'm doing is helping or hurting," I said, and then, desperate to lighten the mood, joked, "Or maybe I'm frustrated because I haven't gotten laid in a long time." As soon as the words left my mouth, I realized my mistake.

Margot and Vy exchanged a look. "Oh, but I thought—you and Raf aren't . . . ?" Margot asked.

"Well," I said, grasping at straws. "We're together and things are going really well, but we're taking it slow, physically."

"Of course," Margot said. "I didn't mean to pry."

"We totally do stuff! Hand stuff." I scratched the back of my head. "Um, mouth stuff. He's got a great mouth!" It was true, actually. Raf's mouth was one of his best features. Vy snorted—it wasn't a laugh, I'd never seen Vy laugh or even smile—and stared down into her tea. "But I feel like I've rushed into sex too much in the past and because I really like him, I wanted to . . . take our time, you know?"

I was fumbling, but Margot's eyes grew sympathetic and she reached out to clasp my hand in hers. "I do know," she said. "Please, don't feel like you have to make any excuses to me." She hesitated. "I was . . . Keep this private, please, but I was in a relationship for years where I often had sex just to please my partner even though it could be painful for me. Occasionally I would have to go to the bathroom afterward and cry."

"Holy shit," I said.

She nodded. "I think I had undiagnosed vaginismus, not that my gynecologist at the time was taking any of my concerns seriously, which is why I'm never going to a male gyno again." I hadn't seen Vy touch anyone before this, hadn't even necessarily thought her capable of tenderness, but now she rubbed Margot's back protectively as Margot went on, her voice a little shaky. "But if I didn't have sex regularly and pretend that I liked it, my partner would get . . . well, he wouldn't be happy. Not that he ever forced me, but the whole night would be off. I felt that I had to keep him content, even though that meant making myself miserable." She blinked a few times. "So I admire you for setting those boundaries. I wish I could have."

"I'm so sorry," I said, simultaneously grimy from hearing a secret I hadn't earned and grateful for the new Margot unfurling in front of me. I'd imagined her whirling from fling to fling, letting whatever man caught her fancy fly her out to Paris to woo her. She radiated so much self-possession that I'd assumed she was one of those women who could just cum seven times in a row, who were so sexually in tune with themselves that they had orgasms doing yoga, silently quaking with ecstasy in pigeon pose. "Is it better for you now? Oh God, sorry, you do not have to answer if that's too personal!"

"It's fine," Margot said. "Things are better. I know who I am, and I try to only have sex on my own terms. Maybe it's not that often, but men just have to deal with it." I rearranged the picture in my mind: a man flying Margot all the way out to Paris, taking her on a whirlwind tour of the city, buying her the fanciest champagne, and then her pecking him on the cheek and shutting the door in his face. "Most of the time, they deal with it gracefully. And if they don't, well . . ." Something flickered in her eyes. "I have ways of making them sorry."

We all sat in silence for a moment. Vy gave Margot's back one more solid pat. "I'm so glad I'm a lesbian," she said, then took another pool filter sip of her tea. "Now finish the reading. I have to go home and feed Anais." (Was Anais a dog or a kid?)

"Of course!" Margot said, tossing her head as the elevator dinged in the background. "This is supposed to be about you, not me. Let's see your future card." She leaned over and began to turn it over when Caroline motored off the elevator and toward the unmarked door that I'd assumed led to a greenroom/office area, walking furiously, stress radiating from her in an almost visceral way. Vy tapped Margot on the shoulder and they watched as a hapless club member attempted to engage Caroline in conversation.

"Caroline!" the club member said, catching up to Caroline right as she passed in front of the *other* door, the one that Margot had acted so strangely about during my first visit to the club. Caroline turned and plastered on a smile.

"Hi," she said. "What's up?"

"I wanted to propose an activity," the member went on, leaning casually against the door. Caroline stiffened, her eyes darting to the door as if to make sure it wouldn't swing open. Weird—so it wasn't just trials like me who weren't supposed to go inside. This door was off-limits to members too. My mind whirred through possibilities of what could be behind it—Secret files? Male prisoners?—as the member kept talking. "My friend would love to come in and teach this awesome workshop she does, How to Spell Your Success."

"How to spell what?" Caroline asked, her voice tight.

"Your Success—"

"It's only two words. It doesn't seem like it would require a whole workshop."

"Oh, no," the member said, laughing. "Not *spell* like letters. My friend's a witch! So, like, how to pick the best crystals for getting the promotion you want, or lighting a certain kind of candle and sending your energy out—"

"Great initiative, but I don't think that's the right fit for our members." Caroline's smile was frozen and tight on her face.

"Oh, I'm sorry—" the member began, coming out of her casual lean, a little flustered.

"No worries! Now, excuse me, I have some work for my gala I need to do." Caroline waved the member away from the door and back to her seat, and then Caroline marched off too. As she passed us, she shot a pointed look at Margot. The message seemed clear: *Look at what you've done, what you've accidentally encouraged.* Then Caroline continued her march away, a very sensible queen, watching her subjects be taken in by a charlatan, not at all happy that they were making fools of themselves. This odd-couple partnership between the two of them clearly had its problems. Why in the world had these two very different women decided to team up?

Vy raised an eyebrow at Margot. Margot nodded, then turned to me.

"Sorry, Jillian, give us one second? We'll be right back. Don't move!" She and Vy whooshed off toward the door, whispering furtively to each other, and I sat, twiddling my thumbs. There wasn't any casual way for me to sneak over to the door and listen to whatever was unfurling with Caroline. I briefly considered making a break for the secret door and trying to get inside, but there were too many people around, so instead I looked down at my future pile. It didn't matter what this last card turned out to be. It didn't.

Still, it would be nice to be prepared for it, just in case. My mistake about not getting laid had ended up much better than I could have imagined, but I didn't want to get sloppy again. I snuck a glance to my left and right. No one was paying any attention to me. I scooted closer to the stack and nudged the card over. Then my stomach dropped.

A man's body lay prone on the ground with ten swords slicing through him. Cool, so this dude had been violently killed. This card portended *great* things. I picked it up and stared at it, all the same stupid feelings I'd had with that storefront psychic rushing back again. The card trembled in my hand, even though I knew that it meant nothing at all. But how would Margot and Vy react to it? And how the hell was I supposed to react in front of them? Nevertheless was a club for women with bright futures, not women who ended up stabbed to death on the ground.

Margot's voice floated across the room, and I looked up to see her and Vy rounding the corner back toward me, still focused on each other. Before I even realized what I was doing, I stuck the offending card in my pocket, then rearranged myself on the couch as if I hadn't moved the whole time.

"Whew, sorry about that," Margot said as they sat back down.

"That's fine," I said. "Everything okay?"

"Oh, just the stress of planning the annual gala for her organization. She's fixated on getting this one woman to announce her run for representative as the centerpiece of the event. But Tiana keeps going back and forth and is nervous because of . . ." Vy put a hand on Margot's shoulder, and Margot cut herself off.

I leaned forward and said, in a quiet voice, "Because of what happened with Nicole Woo-Martin?"

A coldness slid across both of their faces. I'd misjudged. They weren't going to talk about her with a trial member. "I'm not sure what you mean," Margot said.

"Oh, just how what happened to her showed how hard it is to be a woman in politics."

"Mm, it really did," Margot said. "All right, where were we?"

"Future card," Vy said.

"Ah yes." Margot shook her wrists out again, then leaned forward, took a deep breath, and turned over the new card on top of the pile. She paused for a moment, bent over it, her shaggy hair falling around her. Then she sat up, revealing a card with three women joined in a circle, their faces beatific, their hands entwined.

"The Three of Cups," she said, and I was struck by the strangeness of this situation, by how these two intelligent and ambitious women beside me were staring at this card like believers at a church service, like it was the body of Christ and they were ready to taste of it. Maybe they *did* believe, at least a little bit, in this new kind of religion where, instead of worshipping some male deity, they worshipped themselves. Instead of reading and rereading a Bible to parse the mysteries of Jesus's words, they read their horoscopes and tarot cards to parse the mysteries within their own hearts and minds. Because what was more important than that?

I shivered. "Is the Three of Cups a good one?" I asked.

"Oh yes, very. It means sisterhood. Celebration." Margot smiled at me, a genuine smile that showed off her gleaming, even teeth. "Does that mean anything to you?"

"I think it does," I said, smiling tentatively back. "I know what I hope it means."

"Well, then," she said. "It looks like you're on the right path after all."

That night when I got home, I pulled the Ten of Swords out of my pocket. There had been no way for me to sneak it back into the deck. The dead man's hand was outstretched, curled in rigor mortis. I looked up the meaning online, clicking on the first woo-woo website in my search results, scrolling through a long description of why tarot was so meaningful, how it could help you manifest your *destiny*. (The women of Nevertheless were absolutely the type who would've believed in Manifest Destiny back in the eighteen hundreds, secure in the knowledge that they deserved whatever they could take.) God, the amount of copy on this website was practically Dickensian, but finally I found what I was looking for.

The Ten of Swords: Betrayal. Crisis, the description read. *Painful ending.*

I closed out of the window quickly. Good thing I didn't believe in that shit. Still, I preferred not to look at that card lying around all the time, so I buried it at the bottom of a desk drawer, far out of my sight.

ELEVEN

As I waited to hear if I would receive another invitation, I looked for meaning in my everyday routines. I swam so long each morning at the YMCA that my skin pruned, and my ears clogged so badly that I had to buy special drops to dry them out.

I finalized the sale of my mother's house. Twenty-five years ago, when my mom and dad bought the place—a small brick row house on a street of small row houses—the neighborhood was so far out from Manhattan that a working-class family could afford to own a home there (with the help of a mortgage, and then maybe a second mortgage). The house, though unassuming, was supposed to be an investment for the future. Thanks to my dad taking off along with his salary and to my mother's piles of medical bills, it hadn't worked out that way, even though property values had gone way up. The couple who'd bought the house were yuppies—my age, more than comfortable. They'd picked up on my current status and had told me (kindly but condescendingly) that I didn't need to move out right away. After all, they needed to take measurements and figure out all the necessary renovations to make the house "their perfect nest" and "inhabitable." They came over at night sometimes after work and walked through the rooms, frowning at the cracks in the ceiling, pointing to the blue, flowered wallpaper my mother had loved and saying, "Well obviously *this* has to go."

I picked up more and more bartending shifts. The place was a dive that catered mostly to old Irishmen. Hardly any women patronized it—occasionally a passerby would duck her head in, see the clientele, and turn right around. But the regular patrons were harmless and at times even endearing, and they usually got just drunk enough to leave me generous tips and not so drunk that they forgot to pay up entirely. All in all, it was a kind of benevolent morass of testosterone through which I could weave and serve and make a living.

Raf took me up on my offer for free drinks, and he came by the bar on nights after work when he needed to unwind. The people that he worked with at the restaurant were into hard partying—staying up until four A.M. doing coke, dragging themselves in the next morning to open for brunch. But Raf had tried the hard partying. He'd told me harrowing stories of cooking hungover, sending out bland, watered-down dishes because the regular spices he used threatened to turn his stomach. Now he preferred to have his wits about him. So while the others went elsewhere, he'd come nurse one or two whiskey sodas on a barstool across from my station and let the old regulars regale him with tales of their youth, and we'd talk whenever orders were slow. "Get any more mysterious kitchen visits?" I'd ask him each night, and he would tell me stories about how yes, actually, random women kept showing up.

It wasn't because of me, though, but because one of the restaurant's busboys was a magnet for romantic drama.

"Another one came today," he said one night as I poured a stream of soda into his glass. With any other master restauranteur, I'd be on edge about serving them, worried they'd order some fancy drink and then scoff at my poor excuse for bartending skills, but Raf never ordered anything with more than two ingredients, and he didn't care if I got the proportions wrong. "She started crying right next to the oven. I tried to give her love advice but that made things worse. So I gave her free plantains and that made things better. It's rough out there for a single person."

"Thank God we're off the market," I teased, and he laughed. I leaned over the bar toward him and said, in a lower voice, "Don't worry, I think we're close to being able to quit the charade."

"It's okay," he said. "It's not like I have time to date now, anyway."

"You are very kind," I said, then poured myself a whiskey soda to drink along with him. "It's interesting, part of me wants this assignment to go on forever, because it's so much more exciting than anything else I've done recently. But also, it's fucking stressful. I get through the day all right, but I'm grinding my teeth at night so hard that my jaw hurts in the morning."

"Hey, me too!" he said. "That happened to me with the restaurant opening."

"Really? Here's to repressing your anxiety so that it has no choice but to screw you up when you're asleep!" I said, and we clinked our glasses across the bar. "Please tell me it eventually went away on its own?"

"No," he said. "I had to start wearing a mouthguard to bed."

I burst into laughter. "Like in middle school?"

"Yup," he said. "Maybe that's another reason it's better if I don't date right now."

I kept laughing and he smiled, pleased, until I collected myself. The party of men sitting to Raf's right took the last swigs of their beers and threw down twenty-dollar bills, slinging their arms around one another as they stumbled to the door. I waved good-bye and began clearing off their section. It was just after midnight, and only a few customers remained, talking rowdily all the way down at the other end of the bar. No way to tell if they'd stay for another two minutes or another two hours.

Raf cleared his throat. "No, actually," he said. "It's been okay to take a break from . . . you know."

I raised an eyebrow. "The masses of women throwing them-selves at you?"

He blushed. "It's not *masses*, but yeah. I think it was starting to screw with my head."

"Why?"

"Just . . ." He spoke haltingly, stirring the straw around in his drink. "It's weird knowing that a lot of these women wouldn't have paid attention to me a year ago. But now that I have some kind of power, or whatever it is, there's always someone who's interested. Because are they interested in me, or would they be interested in anyone who had gotten profiled like that in *Vanity Fair*?" He tugged on his baseball cap, then took it off and began fiddling with it, bending and unbending its brim. "But also, I got that profile because I've been working hard, it's not like it just landed in my lap, so maybe I do deserve it all." He stopped and looked up from his cap, into my eyes, suddenly worried. "Not that I'm saying I deserve sex, and you know, I'm not upset about getting to hook up with pretty women. I don't know how to explain it—"

"No, I think I know what you mean," I said, and leaned over, resting my elbows on the bar, cupping my chin in my hands. "Like, I think you are one hundred percent worthy of all the interest and always have been, and if a lot of these women had gotten to know you before your success, they still would've been lining up outside your door—"

He laughed. "You're blowing smoke up my ass."

"Only a little," I said. Sure, Raf had never been rolling in the ladies, but he'd done okay. He had always been catnip for a certain type of girl—overbearing ones who loved the idea of a shy, sensitive soul who would worship them. Over the years, a few of those girls had fallen hard for Raf, had felt that they had "discovered" him. They decided that he *would* be their boyfriend and pursued him relentlessly, only to be disappointed when they realized he wouldn't drop everything to be at their beck and call, because sometimes he needed to disappear for a couple of days to work on a recipe, or because he was really close to his parents and listened to them (maybe a little too much) if they hated a new girlfriend of his.

My mom and I had spent many hours discussing this. "The Problem of Raf," we called it: that the type of girl who loved the first impression he gave off was also the type not to appreciate the fullness of who he was. When the *Vanity Fair* profile had come out, I'd brought home a hard copy of the magazine to show to her. She'd been weak and lethargic—we'd ended up taking her to hospice care ten days later, and she'd died only a few days after that—but the article recharged her temporarily. "Maybe this will solve the Problem of Raf," she'd said to me as she cut out the pages to put them up on our refrigerator, making slow and deliberate strokes with the scissors, needing to use both hands to force the scissors closed. "So if you want your chance with him, you should get in there soon." (I laughed it off. This was the same woman who had said to me, years before, *Oh no, you and Raf should never date. You'd break his heart, and then his family would hate me and I would have to move.* But in her final months, she became very concerned that all my eggs were dying, and started trying to set me up with everyone from her doctor to the barista at her coffee shop, who had literally just graduated from high school.)

"Anyways," I said to Raf, "now that you've got all this interest, I could imagine that it's hard to separate the women who are genuinely into you from the ones who want you as a sort of . . . trophy."

"Yeah, exactly," he said. "It's like they're using me and I'm using them, and that's okay for a while but then it gets kind of empty, you know?" I nodded, and he shrugged, his cheeks a little red. "Anyway, it's good to have an excuse to figure it all out."

"Well, then," I said, and patted his hand with my own, my face a perfect mask of sincerity. "You're welcome."

I slid him another drink, and he took a slightly-too-enthusiastic sip of it. "Ah!" he said, startling as some liquid sloshed onto his chin. He wiped at it with the back of his hand, a sheepish grin on his face.

The party down at the other end of the bar closed out, then pushed back their chairs with loud scrapes and headed out to their next destination, leaving a disaster zone in their wake: crumpled napkins, overturned beer bottles. We always put out little bowls of pretzels on the bar, and these men had decimated them, spewing crumbs all over the place as they talked, knocking one of the bowls off the bar entirely without noticing on their way out.

I sighed and went to go clean up. "Here, I'll help you," Raf said, and grabbed a bar rag. I studied him as he wiped crumbs into his hand with the practiced motion of a man who'd seen all sides of the service industry.

We hadn't hung out with this frequency since we were little. The hours of someone working his way up in a kitchen were basically the opposite of what mine had been at Quill. Neither one of us had ever wanted the kind of jobs where we'd just go punch a clock. We'd wanted to pursue passions, and the worlds of those passions had swallowed us up. Since he'd finished culinary school, we'd gone to each other's places only a few times a year, and that had lessened even more when I'd moved back into my mom's house. Sure, we saw each other there sometimes, but when he came home, we'd fallen into our old roles, him digging his dusty skateboard out of the basement and riding it down the block while I read a book on my front stoop, occasionally looking up to give him affectionate eye rolls.

Over the past few years, he'd grown into himself while I'd been distracted.

Now that my closest female friends had married, moved to the suburbs, and started producing little versions of themselves who demanded all their attention, and now that my mother's absence highlighted how tenuous all of my other family relationships had always been, I became hyperaware of how lucky I was that I still had someone I trusted. Thank God for this Nevertheless adventure, for reminding me of how important our friendship was. He was maybe the only person left in the world who would be willing to do this crazy thing for me. I didn't want to try his patience. I didn't want to screw anything up.

"What?" he asked, catching me staring.

"Just . . . thank you, again, for being here for me."

"Of course, Jilly," he said.

TWELVE

So yeah, I leaned into my routines when I could. But every other free moment I had, I was reading all that I could find about the women of Nevertheless, starting with Margot.

For someone who'd made a name for herself on the parties and events she attended, she was surprisingly tight-lipped about her personal life. She gave *plenty* of interviews about her business, though. I scrolled through article after article, reading up on her philosophy behind In the Stars so I could know how to talk to her about astrology, then pulled up the app to download it for myself, for research purposes. *In the Stars*, the icon said, against a blush-pink background speckled with golden stars. The app asked me to input my birthday, and then it needed to know exactly when and where I was born. Text unfurled on the screen. **This information will help us determine your moon and rising signs.** (More likely *this information will get sold to third parties and make us richer.*) I did not know what "moon and rising signs" meant, but I dutifully selected Bay Ridge, then paused at the question asking me to type in the precise moment I had emerged into the world. **Please be as accurate as possible, so that we can see exactly where the stars were positioned over your birth.**

I didn't know. I'd have to call my mom to ask. I got as far as starting to put in her cell phone number before I remembered that I couldn't call my mom because she was gone. She wouldn't pick up the phone because she didn't have fucking hands, because she was only ashes that we'd scattered into the Atlantic Ocean, bits and pieces of her floating halfway across the world by now. She couldn't remember what time I'd been born because her memories didn't exist anymore, except in the little snippets she'd passed on to me when I'd been smart enough to listen. She'd died, and a whole vast bank of experiences had died with her.

Anyway, if I *had* been able to call her, and had said, *Hey, Mom, what time did I burst out of your vagina? I need to determine my rising sign,* she probably would have said, *Honey, what in the world is a rising sign?* And when I explained it, she would have teased me about my newfound interest in astrology—she was a practical woman to the end—and so I would have told her about this whole undercover assignment and the mess I was making.

God, what would she think of me doing this? Would she be proud? Or would she advise me to run in the other direction and not look back? She'd always told me not to be stupid. But then again, she'd longed for the truth about Nicole to come out.

When the scandal first broke, we'd been going through old family photos the way that you do when someone is dying. You try to figure out what is worth saving, try to get all the stories you can from that someone before they're gone.

I'd brought the boxes to her bedroom and climbed into the bed next to her. Her limbs were so thin that she looked like an alien, head too big for her body. We laughed over awkward old school pictures, snapshots of me as a red-faced baby in her lap.

I pulled out a few pictures of her and my father, grinning next to each other in happy times, my mother still oblivious about his affairs. I put them in the trash pile.

"Maybe you should try to have a relationship with him when I'm gone," she said. "He'll be the only family you've got left."

I rolled my eyes. "Right. He's a cheating asshole and a compulsive liar." I left out the part I'd never told her—that once, when I was fifteen and annoyed with my mom, I'd e-mailed to ask if I could spend the summer with him in Chicago. He'd never responded. "I don't think I need that kind of family."

"Well, then, I guess you'll have to make your own. Soon, though, because of your eggs. My doctor said his son just broke up with his girlfriend—"

"*Mom*," I said, then paused as my phone dinged with a text from Miles. He had sent me a *New York Post* headline about Nicole. My face dropped as I read it, so my mom peered over my shoulder, and we digested the news in silence for a moment.

"No," she said, finally. In addition to the T-shirt with Nicole's face on it, my mother had acquired a Nicole Woo-Martin coffee mug, poster, and votive candle. "Rumors. They're making it up because they're afraid of what she's going to achieve."

"Yeah, probably," I said, and put my phone away. But we looked through the rest of the photos in silence, moving backward in time, past my mother as a little girl, sitting red-faced on the lap of her own mom. The photos turned weathered, black-and-white. My mother's grandmother appeared in the frame, a tall woman in her forties or fifties with a jaded look on her face.

"She used to be rich, did you know that?" my mother said, breaking the silence. "My grandmother. She was worth millions, but she was married to an abusive man, and the only way she could get away from him was to completely disappear." She traced her grandmother's face with a bony finger. "She moved all the way to Wyoming, got married again out there, only moved back East after her first husband died. He got all the money, all the property. Besides some cash, practically the only thing of value she was able to take with her was this necklace." She pointed to the necklace she always wore, with the art deco flower, which her mother had passed down to her, and which she'd later give to me so that I could wear it too.

"I had no idea," I said.

"If she'd stayed with him, we wouldn't have to sell this house to pay off all the medical bills. You could keep it, raise your own family here. Or at least I could leave you something, so that you'd be comfortable. The reason we're not rich is because my grandmother did what she needed to do, and the system was stacked against her. Wealth isn't some marker of superiority. It's a matter of luck and circumstance, and those with power using it to keep everyone else down."

My mother looked me in the eyes then. "Nicole understands that. She wants to fix it, and the people with money are desperate not to let her, and that's why there's got to be something else going on. Don't let them take her down."

"I'm not really sure what I can do to stop that," I said.

"I don't know, do journalism!" she said, throwing her hands in the air.

"Okay," I said, laughing. "I'll do journalism."

"I'm serious. You're a writer, so write. And after I'm gone, after she puts all this behind her, I want you knocking on doors for her presidential campaign. When you watch her get sworn in as the first female president, you'll know that wherever I am, I'm happy."

It was a small blessing that she'd died only a couple of weeks later, before Nicole's resignation, still believing that things might turn around.

I needed to believe that she'd be proud of me now. And oh God, all I wanted to do was talk to her, to tell her things and hear her thoughts and make her laugh her throaty laugh, but I would never be able to do that again, and instead I was staring down at my screen like an idiot, with tears pricking at my eyes.

I shook my head. I was not going to have a breakdown over an astrology app. I deleted it and went back to Googling Margot.

I found an almost overwhelming number of write-ups chronicling her see-and-be-seen event-going, all the way back to when she'd been in high school. How did a teenager have enough confidence to hang out with older celebrities? I guess it helped that Margot had looked like an angel temporarily deigning to grace Earth with her presence. I squinted at one old picture in the *New York Post*, in which a teenage Margot dangled a cigarette in one hand and slung her arm around a tiny, red-haired girl in a miniskirt whom the *Post* editors hadn't deemed important enough to identify. The girl's spaghetti straps were slipping off her slim shoulders, and she clasped her hands in front of her stomach as if she didn't know what else to do with them. Her face was partially in shadow but when I looked closer, I saw that it was Caroline. Huh. They'd known each other longer than I'd assumed. Maybe that explained why they'd decided, against all odds, to join forces. In the picture, Caroline's eyes were locked on Margot like if she studied her hard enough, she could mimic Margot's ease.

A lot of the write-ups about Margot mentioned her mother, Ann Wilding, who had been a fixture on the New York social scene in her own day. I thought Margot was free-spirited, but compared to Ann, she was practically Victorian. I clicked through pictures of Ann in the late '80s, gallivanting around the globe. She flashed the cameras a huge smile while on an African safari. She made inappropriate jokes to the queen of England. In Paris, she smoked a cigarette with a clique of thin, chic women. One of them had red hair, Caroline's eyes. I squinted at the names in the caption. Caroline's mother.

The tabloids had detailed Ann's doomed love affair with a sheikh, which ended after three months because she wasn't about to give up her life to move to Saudi Arabia (and also because he was married). When she found out that she was pregnant by him, she bucked all expectations and kept the baby, raising Margot by herself. Well, herself, plus the army of nannies and family help and the husbands from her two short-lived marriages after that.

According to her obituary, Ann had died in a boating accident when Margot was twenty. God, what a tragedy. I stared at the obituary a moment longer, my view of Margot shifting again, until I clicked over to a new article and figured out which man Margot had been talking about during our tarot reading.

Gus Wright. He was a writer and director of a certain brand of indie movies that received glowing write-ups in the *New Yorker*. I'd watched twenty minutes of one of his films once and found it to be unbearably pretentious.

Now, Gus was in his midforties, which meant that when he and Margot had started dating, she'd been in her early twenties, and he'd been in his late thirties. I found a photo that paparazzi had taken of them together, leaving a club in the early hours of the morning. He had overgrown curling hair, like Bob Dylan at the height of his fame, and even though he was lean, she looked . . . small beside him. Frail, her body hidden behind his, her gaze cast down, her legs twiggy in her leather pants.

He had talked about *her* in interviews. "Margot is a chaotic and gorgeous creature. And besides that, she's a great help," he'd told *New York* magazine once. "I'll show her cuts I'm working on, watch to see where she laughs and where she's confused so I can see how a general audience might respond." And he'd made a movie toward the end of their relationship in which a complicated, interesting man had an obsessive love affair with a young rich girl who was clearly modeled on Margot (though she was played by someone else, a former child star seeking a legitimate acting career, whose hair was styled exactly like Margot's at the time). Apparently that character spent a lot of time lounging around half-naked. There was a scene in which her underwear rode up, exposing a hint of pubic hair, that had gotten a lot of play online. I'd heard about this before, but hadn't realized it was based on an actual woman, a woman whom I now knew. What a strange and violating thing that must be, to have a doppelgänger of you turned into a sex object.

When a reporter asked Gus three years ago about rumors that he and Margot had broken up, he'd answered, "I'd rather not talk about it except to say that she broke my fucking heart." He'd made a couple movies since then, although they had both done poorly at the box office and had received mixed reviews.

Now, even though Gus Wright was on the verge of becoming a has-been, he'd still found another wealthy, wispy woman to date. Maybe "woman" was the wrong term for her. She was twenty-two. Perfectly legal, and perfectly icky. She also looked small beside him in photos.

I studied the pictures on my computer screen as I ate a turkey burger at a Park Slope café. I'd been doing my research at Bitter-Sweet all morning—making sure that my computer screen faced the wall, just in case anyone was watching me—but I'd relocated for lunch. As I took my final bite, my phone buzzed with a message from Miles. **How's it going, Beckley? Should we get a drink and discuss progress?**

A smile automatically spread over my face. **Lots of updates,** I wrote back. **When and where is good for you?**

He didn't respond immediately, so after staring unblinking at the screen for a full minute like a moron, I went to the bathroom. The women's room had three stalls, and a mirror in a shabby-chic frame over the sink. When I came out to wash my hands, a woman was reapplying her lipstick in the mirror. We smiled at each other. She seemed familiar.

Then, she leaned forward and breathed onto the glass until it fogged up. Slowly she reached out a finger and began to write in the condensation, like I'd done on car windows when I was young. *Friday*, she wrote, in a looping script. She breathed on the mirror again. *Same time.* A normal woman might have passed out from the effort to fog up so much glass, but *this* woman had the lung capacity of a deep-sea whale. I watched, fascinated by her breath support, as she traced more letters: *If you're ready to join.* Then she walked out without even glancing at me, the words already fading into the mirror behind her.

I waited there a moment, trembling. This seemed almost too easy. Also, had this woman been watching me all morning, from BitterSweet to this restaurant, waiting for her chance to catch me alone? Shit, I should have closed my screen when I went to the bathroom. I power walked back into the main part of the café. She was gone.

When I picked up my phone again, Miles had responded. **Tonight?**

he'd written, and then named one of the bars where we used to drink after work at Quill.

I hesitated, then wrote, **I actually don't think we should talk about this in public.**

Gotcha. You want to come by my office at the Standard sometime this week?

Um, YEAH OKAY!! I started to type. What I wouldn't give to be escorted around those offices, to stare at journalists I'd admired for years as they cracked their knuckles and wrote their stories. But then I paused, thinking of the woman watching me all morning, standing up to slip into the bathroom after me. I started the message over. **This sounds crazy,** I wrote, **but I think they've been sending someone to follow me around. So I probably shouldn't go into that building right now.**

The three little dots that meant he was typing appeared, then disappeared. I got ready to suggest that we rent one of those by-the-hour meeting rooms. Then, his three dots reappeared again and blossomed into a message: **Okay, how about I come to your place?**

THIRTEEN

Miles came over after work. "Damn, Beckley, this is inconvenient," he said when I opened the door. "I thought you said you lived in Brooklyn."

"You snob. Bay Ridge *is* Brooklyn."

"Is it?"

"Ha, ha," I said. "I'm sorry we can't all afford to live on the Lower East Side."

"Offer me a beer or something and I'll forgive you." He grinned, but there was something shaky in his bonhomie. Nerves in his eyes at being in my living room, even for professional reasons. Maybe especially for professional reasons. He joked with me like he was acting the part of a friendly coworker who had nothing at stake, but he wasn't going to be nominated for an Oscar anytime soon.

I ducked into the kitchen and grabbed us each an IPA. That would help. When I came back and handed one to him, he took a long sip, then looked around the room, at the flowered curtains and the well-worn armchair. "This is where you grew up, huh? It's nice. Comfortable, in that lived-in, loving-family way."

"Thanks," I said. My mom's design skills were never going to win any kind of award, but she'd done the best with what she had, making the two of us a home.

"My only complaint is that there don't seem to be any embarrassing baby photos?"

"There are. I just buried them *deep* in the basement." I took a calming sip of my beer. Then we sat on opposing ends of the couch, as far apart as possible.

He took another long swig from his can. "So fill me in."

I launched into the summary of what I'd experienced so far. I didn't embellish (I had no need for bullshit this time), and he watched me with his eyes growing increasingly wider, occasionally shaking his head in disbelief, or scorn at their elitism, or admiration at their inventiveness.

"What about Nicole Woo-Martin?" he asked at one point.

"I haven't gotten anything solid on that yet, just a few veiled comments. They're not going to talk about it with a nonmember, but that in itself says something."

"And I tried getting in touch with her staffer," Miles said. "But that seems to be a dead end—he's not responding."

I didn't tell Miles everything. I glossed over the specifics of the tarot reading, leaving out the talk about Margot's sex life and her strange comment of how she made men sorry. When I described the woman following me into the bathroom this morning, he blinked.

"Wait, this is insane. They're actually following you?"

"Um, yeah," I said. "I didn't just make that up for attention. I would've loved to come to the office."

"Ah, I thought . . ." He shook his head.

"What did you think?" I asked, and we looked at each other, not saying anything for a moment. He swallowed.

Then, a key turned in the door and the yuppie couple who'd bought the place—Sara and Rob—barged in, all sunshine and rainbows and privilege.

"Jillian, hi!" Sara trilled. "Hope we're not bothering!"

"We sent a text, but you didn't respond," Rob said.

They introduced themselves to Miles, before Sara continued, holding up a measuring tape, "We just wanted to come take another look at the downstairs."

"*You* did, you mean," Rob said to Sara, putting his arm around her. He rolled his eyes at us affectionately. "She's so excited to get started on this renovation. It's all she talks about."

"Stop, you're the exact same way!" She gazed into his eyes, swoony, practically ready to mount him right then and there so they could christen their new home.

"Sure, yeah," I said as pleasantly as I could manage, hoping they weren't getting *too* antsy. I did not have the bandwidth to think about moving right now. "We can get out of your way." I turned to Miles. "So I guess we should go to my, um, upstairs."

"Yeah," he said, and then to Sara and Rob, "Have fun."

As I led him up the stairs, he whispered, "Well, *they* are annoyingly chipper."

I forced a laugh. Up here, we had two choices. My mother's room or mine. I wasn't about to take him into my mother's—that space still somehow belonged to her, even though I'd emptied out everything but the closet—so I opened my own door. I hadn't bothered to tidy up, maybe because I didn't think he'd be coming upstairs, or maybe because I hadn't wanted to be tempted to invite him in. A self-discipline measure, like wearing dirty underwear to meet up with an ex you know you shouldn't fall back into bed with. Stacks of notebooks and magazines tilted precariously on various surfaces. I tended to shed like a dog, and strands of my hair wound along the floor. The room was close quarters, the perfect size for a kid, not so much for a grown-up woman. Still, when I'd moved back home, I'd exchanged my old twin for a full-size bed (currently unmade), and had managed to shove in a small, wobbly desk and rolling chair too.

I fantasized about someday having a Desk with a capital *D*, some mahogany behemoth that would transmit creativity to me as soon as I placed my hands on its polished surface. Sitting at that desk, words would race out of my brain and onto the page like track and field stars. I didn't believe any of the woo-woo, witchy stuff that some of the Nevertheless women seemed so into, but I reserved the right to make one exception: a certain kind of magic when it came to writing. There had been moments in my life when it didn't feel like *I* was doing the work at all. My fingers were enchanted, moving of their own accord, and I was channeling something larger than myself, grabbing that larger thing from some hazy ether and pulling it to the Earth, where other people could touch it, and be touched by it.

I hadn't had that feeling since my mom had gotten sick, and I couldn't help imagining that the right kind of desk would help me regain it. I knew rationally that desks didn't matter, and that *real* writers just sat down and forced themselves to be creative anywhere, those fuckers. But I liked my fantasies.

My desk chair was piled with clothes that weren't dirty enough for my laundry hamper, but not clean enough to put back in my drawer. Shorts I'd gone on a strenuous walk in. A sleep shirt I'd worn a few times. A black bra. Miles glanced at it and then glanced away.

"Here, you should take my laundry chair and I'll sit on the bed," I said, gathering up all the clothes in my arms and dumping them on the floor of my closet. My palms had grown damp. "Sorry, not the most professional meeting place."

He turned in a circle, taking everything in. "Hey, it's always an interesting exercise to find out more about a person by seeing their room, especially when they don't like to talk much about their personal life."

"Right," I said. "You're doing research. Preparing yourself for when I become famous, and you have to write a profile of *me*."

"'To understand the genius of Jillian Beckley,'" he said, "'you don't need to walk a mile in her shoes. You just need to walk the length of her messy childhood bedroom. If you can, without breaking your ankle.'" He turned back to his examination, pausing at a picture I'd hung up on my wall, the black-and-white portrait of my mother from her college yearbook. She was wearing a collared shirt, her dark hair blown out in the Farrah Fawcett style that people went nuts over at the time, her chest tilted away from the camera but her face looking at the photographer with a proud, almost defiant stare. I always imagined that he'd just called her something like "little lady" or "sweetheart": *Now turn your head this way, sweetheart!* And she'd turn her head, but she was not going to do it sweetly, because she had worked her ass off and now she was graduating cum laude, dammit.

I'd actually hung it up there when we were still hopeful that a treatment would work. She'd give cancer the same kind of defiant stare she was giving in the photograph. Cancer would take a step back, say *Sorry, ma'am, wrong person*, and slink off to find some other target. This picture was supposed to be a triumphant talisman. It had turned into a memorial.

"Your mother?" Miles asked, and I nodded. "Huh. She was beautiful. I also think that she could have kicked my ass."

"Probably," I said, and sat down on the bed. He sat on my desk chair, which let out a little squeak as it absorbed the solidness of him. "Okay, so what do you think about the story?"

"It's very promising so far," Miles said. "And *I* trust you. But obviously, there's the matter of journalistic integrity. Fact-checking, and all of that. Can you get me some proof?"

"Yeah, of course. They keep taking my phone away from me. But if what that woman wrote in the mirror means what I think it does, I'm getting an official offer of membership the next time I go. Then I imagine that they'll stop with the whole confiscation routine, so I can sneak you some pictures or a video. Not to mention the address of the clubhouse."

"Perfect," he said.

I bit my lip, steeling myself. "Two bits of potentially bad news. This other new member I met said that the membership dues are five hundred dollars a month and I don't . . . I don't just have that lying around. I mean, I can get it eventually—I can pick up extra shifts, but if they need it this week . . . Does the *Standard* ever give advances?"

"They don't," he said. "At least not to unproven writers."

"Ah," I said. "Okay, I'll figure something out. Maybe I can put it on my credit card—"

"Beckley," he said. "I'll cover you."

My heart thumped. "Really?"

"Yeah, I can swing it for the first month."

"That's . . . Are you sure?" Was this acceptable journalistic practice? And even if it was, was it a good idea?

"I am," he said. "I know I was hard on you at first, when you were pitching me. But then, as I've been getting excited about this piece . . ." His lips turned up in that crooked smile I liked so much. "I started thinking about that union piece you wrote, back when you were new at Quill." I nodded. I'd spent months delving into the unionization efforts at a local fast-food chain. Miles had given me incredible feedback every step of the way, pushing me further. I was proud of that piece, elated at what it might do. Then, with it all set to publish, Quill's billionaire owner had gotten wind of it and killed it. Turned out that the chain's owner was a good friend of his. He owed him a favor.

"That was a damn good piece—I *still* remember some of those lines—and I didn't fight hard enough for it," Miles said. "So now, I'm not going to let you get screwed over because of five hundred bucks. I've got you."

"Thanks," I said, trying not to blush from the fact that, years later, he hadn't forgotten something I'd written. "The other issue, though . . . That same member said something about a nondisparagement clause in the contract."

"Ah," Miles said, and frowned. "That complicates things." He rubbed his chin, leaning back in my desk chair, putting one leg up across the other. His trousers rode up, exposing his ankle, the light brown leg hair escaping from the top of his red sock. He thought for a moment, then sat forward again. "Okay. Look, you've got a good story already. Obviously I want to know about Nicole Woo-Martin, but plenty of other people will be satisfied with what you've learned so far. You've been inside the belly of the beast. It seems like you've got a thesis, that it's an unholy, elitist union of corporate interest and pseudoscience. We can get you a small camera to sneak in with you this next time you go so you can grab a picture or two even if they take your phone again. Maybe ask for a moment alone with the contract and get a clear shot of that. And then tell them that you're uncomfortable with the terms and get out of there. With your writing talent, you can still get an interesting article out of what you have right now."

"Fuck no, are you kidding me?" I sprang to my feet and began pacing the narrow room. "You think I'm going to get this far and then give up? Who knows how things change once you're a member? There must be so much that they keep from you when you're there on a trial basis!" Miles started to say something but I cut him off, so he folded his arms and watched me, an expression that looked like amusement creeping across his face. "I'm only just starting to scratch the surface with these women. There's this mysterious door that I've never seen anyone go into or out of, but that I catch Margot and some of the others staring at all the time, and I think that might have something to do with what they did to Nicole. I've got to see if I can find out what's behind that or else I'm abdicating my journalistic responsibility, and—"

"Okay, okay," he said, grinning, holding his hands up, standing and blocking my path so that I had to stop pacing. "I was hoping you'd say that."

"You were?" I asked, breathing hard.

"Yeah. Well, maybe not the 'fuck no' part—as a general professional rule, you don't want to say that to your editor's suggestions." I rolled my eyes at him, and he laughed and sat down on my bed. "But the general thrust of it all, yes. So let me take this to our counsel's office and see what they advise. Nevertheless might not want to sue you for disparagement. Getting embroiled in a lawsuit will make them look even worse. Besides, if you write something where you let the facts speak for themselves without being overtly snarky or judgmental, you can claim that you're not disparaging them at all, just recording the truth."

"Writing something without snark or judgment?" I asked. "I'm sorry, I'm unfamiliar with the concept." He grinned. "Okay, can do. And this girl didn't mention anything about a non*disclosure*, so I think maybe they just keep the secrets because it's fun for them. But if they do turn out to have one of those, same rules apply?"

"A nondisclosure is trickier," he said. "Although people get out of those all the time. Just don't sign one before we can take a look at the language and make sure it's worth the risk."

I sat down beside him. "That sounds great. I can do that. And I'm . . . I'm really glad to be doing this. I mean, it's wild, and maybe very stupid. But I'm excited."

"Me too," Miles said, and then he laughed again, scratching his beard in disbelief. "God, you actually did it, huh? You pulled it off. I thought you were bullshitting me at that pitch meeting."

"I kind of was!" I said, laughing too. "Margot didn't even remember my name after that first party—I had to get my friend Raf, who's this fancy up-and-coming chef, to pretend to be my boyfriend and talk me up to her so that she'd even take a second look at me."

"A pretend boyfriend? Uh-oh, straight out of a romantic comedy."

"Right," I said. "I'm a real Meg Ryan."

Miles shook his head in amusement, but his voice caught a little bit as he said, "Don't go falling in love with him now, Beckley."

"I'm not planning on it," I said quietly.

"Good." He looked down into his lap. "You impress me, very much."

My face grew hot. "Thanks," I said. We were sitting closer together now on my unmade bed, both not looking at each other until all of a sudden we were, his eyes locked on mine, nervous smiles rising on both of our faces. In the months since we had kissed, I had told myself it would never happen again. Thanks to my father, I'd seen how affairs could destroy a family. I was not a homewrecker. I'd even met Miles's wife, Emmy, at a work Christmas party, and she'd struck me as a pleasant person who deserved a happy, stable relationship, dammit. But sitting so close to him, our knees grazing, I knew that if he reached out for me, I'd let him touch me however he wanted. If he told me to take off my clothes, I'd shed them immediately. I'd do anything he asked, cross a divide that had always seemed unbreachable, and I wouldn't worry about hating myself until after he had gone.

In our momentary quiet, Sara's scream floated up from the staircase.

"It's a *huge* spider!" she was saying. "There!"

"Shit," Rob said, then sounds of scuffling and a stomp. "Man, that's nasty."

"Well, obviously," Sara said, "we're going to have to hire someone to do a thorough cleaning."

That broke the spell. Miles cleared his throat and stood up.

"Emmy will be wondering where I am," he said, then looked at me frankly. "We've been going through a rough patch, but she's very important to me, and we're trying to work through it."

"That's good." I winced. "Her being important to you, I mean, not the 'rough patch' part."

"Yeah," he said, and cleared his throat again. "Let's figure out a conference room or something else for our next meeting—this is a little far for me to come after work. But great job. I'll get you a camera before Friday so you can grab us some pictures. In the meantime, write up what you told me tonight, and I'm going to mail you a check."

"Got it," I said.

"Good luck, Beckley," he said before ducking out my door.

FOURTEEN

On Friday night, I stood in front of the Nevertheless meeting point, an unobtrusive camera (disguised as a cigarette lighter!) that Miles had sent to me tucked in my bag. I'd cashed the check from him earlier that afternoon.

The guide who came to get me was a familiar and eager face: Libby. "Hi hi hi, girlfriend!" she said, and hugged me.

"Since when are you one of the intimidating trial guides?" I asked.

"Since I volunteered," she said, fluffing her hair and giving her shoulders a little shimmy. "It just seemed like so much fun, and I wanted to get more involved, and—" She caught herself. "Oh, we've got to go! Follow me."

"What about the blindfold?"

She let out an excited squeak. "No more blindfold!"

"Hey, moving on up in this world!" I said as she began to walk. "So what's up? How's the fizzy water business going?"

She turned her head, an exaggerated grimace on her face. "I'm not really supposed to talk to you right now, I'm sorry!" She marched determinedly forward, and I could taste the success ahead of me, sweet as an ice cream cone. She hadn't even taken my phone! It was still safe in my bag. As she wordlessly led me west, my breath caught every time we passed a building that looked particularly fortified or fancy, every time Libby slowed her pace.

But we *kept* going west, all the way to the highway. I paused as we neared the stoplight. "Come on!" she said, and crossed the street over to the water. My old fear about being left to wait forever in some abandoned warehouse landed on my shoulder and hissed into my ear, even though this was *Libby* leading me—Libby, who had my back! (*Supposedly*, the fear whispered.) I shivered in my oversize sweater, the night air chilly for late September as it cut through the loops of fabric. I *knew* this had been too easy. We approached the river. I half expected Libby to turn and—a friendly smile still on her face but with her eyes changed into little, hard coals—tell me to climb up over the railing and jump in so they could see if I floated, or so I could be transformed by the toxic waste in the Hudson into some radioactive superwoman who actually had something to offer this club.

"Jillian," someone said behind me. Caroline sat on a bench, looking down into a leather portfolio, her hair in a bun, her feet in black heels. To anyone passing by at this evening hour, going for a run or walking their dog, she'd look just like some chic, go-get-'em businesswoman doing work by the water. She gave a small nod to Libby, who nodded back with the devoted intensity of someone who was longing to be asked to clip Caroline's toenails.

Caroline raised an eyebrow, and Libby startled. "Oh, right!" she said, then grabbed my bag and walked off with it, strolling down the riverside path without a backward glance, though clearly the effort it took her not to turn around was more than Orpheus had expended with Eurydice. Well, there went my phone. And—shit— the camera.

"Hi!" Caroline said with a perky yet professional smile as she patted the bench next to her. "Come sit, and let's chat." She looked down at a page of paper in her leather portfolio, and I followed her eyes to see a one-sheet with my name on it, like a résumé. Caroline moved it out of my eyesight before I could read it, then clasped her hands. "I'm curious to know, where do you see yourself in five years?"

Oh God, this was a de facto job interview. While I was happy enough to interview other people (I was a journalist after all), I'd always hated being the subject myself. But a Nevertheless woman would be confident. I would not stumble over my words! As Caroline looked at me with bland encouragement, I switched on a smile.

"*Great* question. Ideally working on my third novel and starting a family with a supportive husband." Impulsively, I added, "How about you?"

Her mouth opened in a little O of surprise. "Me?"

"Yeah, I mean, you're an interesting and cool person. So I was just curious." It couldn't hurt to brownnose a bit. Caroline presented herself as giving and well-adjusted, but I was willing to bet that, underneath the exterior, her ego panted, longing to be petted.

"Jillian," she said, and distractedly touched the strand of pearls at her throat. "That's sweet. No one's ever asked about me during this part of things before." She sat back. "My five-year plan," she said with no hesitation, "is to build Women Who Lead into a power-house network providing vital support to female candidates across

the country, to see our first female president take the oath of office—"
She paused for just a moment, swallowing hard, then moved on.
"I'll have my first child with my husband in three years, and in five
years' time, will be pregnant with child number two."

"Cool—"

"Also, I'll have adopted a dog—preferably a goldendoodle rescued from a puppy mill."

"That's—"

"Additionally, Derek and I will have invested in a mountain cabin
outside the city for when we need an escape, so that our children
will get to experience the great outdoors as well as the structure of
city living."

I waited a second to make sure that she was finished. "Wow.
That's a little more thorough than mine."

"Oh, if you'd like to have a clearer vision for yourself, I recom-
mend spending time each year on January first drawing up a detailed
list of your life goals. I've done it ever since I turned thirteen. But
back to you!"

She put me through a few more paces, asking me about what I
would bring to them, how they could help me personally and professionally, questions that I answered with varying degrees of comfort. Each time, Caroline moved on efficiently, not allowing any
awkward pauses to hang in the air, until she saw something on my
one-sheet that made her stop short. "It says here that you bartend?"

Dammit, I'd hoped that wouldn't enter into the equation, not
because I was ashamed of it, but because Nevertheless didn't seem
like they were actively recruiting members of the service industry.
God, had someone followed me all the way to the bar too? I
would've noticed if a glorious Amazon had ordered a drink, and
the usual crowd of old men would have noticed too, but maybe
someone had watched me through the windows.

"Yeah, a few nights a week," I said, searching for an explanation that would still make me appear to be one of the elite. Maybe I could pretend that it was research for the novel—one of the main characters was an alcoholic, so I needed to study his natural habitat! But before I could offer any caveats, Caroline spoke again.

"I see," she said. Then her face broke into an expression of approval. "That's so very Alexandria Ocasio-Cortez!"

". . . Thank you, yes," I said. "That's what I'm going for."

She sat forward again and reopened the leather portfolio, pulling out a stapled document and a pen. "Anyways, Margot has spoken very highly of you"—She had? Embarrassingly, I thrilled to this news—"and I've found talking to you to be an interesting albeit unpredictable experience. Plus we don't have a novelist yet. So we're thrilled to offer you membership to Nevertheless." Caroline handed the document to me. "Why don't you take a moment to read this over, sign at the bottom of the second page, and then we can head back to the clubhouse to celebrate?" As I took the paper from her hands, she pulled out her phone and began replying to work e-mails, her tongue poking out the side of her mouth, an impressive feat of focus. If any woman would truly be able to have it all—to mediate a fight between her children one minute while leading an important conference call the next—it would be Caroline. I stared down at the paper in front of me. *Membership Contract*, the text read, as the sheet trembled in my hands.

I'd done it. Holy shit, beautiful sweet baby Jesus, I had done it. All I had to do was sign and then she'd lead me back to the clubhouse and I'd be on my way to providing all the info I needed to the fact-checkers. The women would open up to me now, letting me in on the secrets, their history. *Fuck yes*, I thought as I skimmed the legalese about membership responsibilities like when dues were to be paid (within a week of joining, and then monthly on that date, so thank God for Miles stepping in to help). Yup, there was the nondisparagement agreement that Libby had mentioned, saying that members agreed not to speak ill of the organization publicly. (Ridiculous! Was that some kind of free-speech violation?) I turned the page to read the last bit of it.

Clause 16: Nondisclosure, the text read. Shit. So these women didn't just keep their secrets for fun, or because of some unofficial omertà. There were real legal consequences for blabbing. I read the section once, then again, trying to make sense of it. *Member agrees that all identifying information of the organization, including membership, location, and member activities, shall remain confidential.* It went on for a full paragraph in confusing legal terms, but I got the gist. By signing this contract, I wouldn't be allowed to share information about Nevertheless with anyone outside of it. Okay. I could handle this. Miles had said that sometimes, it was possible to get out of nondisclosure agreements. I just needed to check with him before I signed. That was the deal.

"Do you have a question about something?" Caroline asked.

"Oh," I said, my voice cracking like a preteen boy's. I cleared my throat. "I'm just trying to understand this nondisclosure agreement. I hadn't realized that would be a part of it."

"Yes," she said. "We had to add that somewhat recently to protect ourselves. A member told her boyfriend all about us, and when they got in a fight, he showed up at the building trying to cause trouble. Luckily we have an excellent security guard. You'll meet her later."

"Smart," I said. "So now if someone blabs, you can sue the pants off of them?"

"Basically," she said pleasantly. "Is there a problem? Otherwise, it's time to sign."

"Oh, I was just wondering, would it be okay to look this over with a lawyer before signing it?" I asked, then said breezily, as if it were a joke, "One can never be too careful with contracts. I learned that from *The Little Mermaid*."

"Love *The Little Mermaid*! And isn't it so great that the remake has more diversity?" she said. And then her smile dropped entirely, revealing the steel underneath. So Caroline could turn off her politeness with one firm twist, like a faucet, when different methods were called for. "But no," she said, and I shivered. "It's actually now or never."

Plan B, then. I'd do what Miles had said originally: call it right here and now, write the article about what I had already learned, and live with the fact that I'd written something good instead of something discourse-defining, scandal-uncovering. I'd been riding a grand roller coaster, but it was time to ask it to let me off, disoriented and unfulfilled, right before the loop-de-loops began. No chance to see the clubhouse again, to solve the mystery of Nicole, to get behind the door. I'd never untangle the complications behind Margot's blithe facade or get a smile out of Vy. It's not like they'd deign to talk to me in the real world if I turned down membership, if our paths ever crossed again.

But I'd get over that. I just needed some kind of evidence before I left. And both my phone and my camera were inside my bag, with Libby. As my brain ran through possibilities of how to make this work, Libby reappeared from her walk down the pier. She waved, beaming as she saw the contract in my lap, then leaned against the railing, watching and waiting for things to be official. Two sets of eyes burned a hole into me. My throat constricted. My brain turned sluggish, lazy. Now or never. If I didn't sign, Nevertheless would be done with me. They couldn't be done with me just yet.

"Jillian?" Caroline asked, a note of impatience creeping into her voice.

"Sorry," I said. "Just excited!" I had no choice. Miles would understand. The pen slipped against my sweaty fingers. I grasped it tightly, pressed it to the paper, and signed my name.

As soon as I'd finished, Libby squealed and clapped her hands. Caroline whisked the paper away, tucking it back into her portfolio. "Congratulations, Jillian," she said. "Let's head back to the clubhouse."

As Libby skipped ahead of us and Caroline and I rose from the bench, I asked, "So, what happened to that member? The one who told her boyfriend about everything?"

Caroline tilted her head to one side. "What member?" she asked sweetly. Then she turned and began to power walk east. "Come on," she said over her shoulder as my stomach dropped. "Time for your initiation."

FIFTEEN

I never would have picked out the nondescript, eight-story building they led me to as the site of mysterious doings. And yet that was where Caroline stopped, keying in some numbers on a push-pad at eye level on the right side of the door. "Every woman receives her own personal code to get into the building during active hours," she said briskly, but with a hint of pride in her thrown-back shoulders. "We'll get you yours later tonight."

"Are there businesses on the other floors?" I asked as Libby swung open the door to the entryway.

"No," Caroline said. "We own the whole building." Holy shit, they paid for an entire building in the freaking West Village, and just left floors and floors of it empty? The amount they'd make by renting the rest of it out for just one month could have paid off all my mother's medical bills and saved our house, but it didn't even matter to them. Every time I thought I'd adjusted to the elitism at play here, a new piece of information slapped me in the face.

A middle-aged woman with broad shoulders sat behind a desk in the dimly lit entryway, the glow of the iPad in her hand lighting up her face. She pressed pause on it as we entered, and sat up straight in her chair, her security guard's uniform neatly pressed.

"Hi, Keisha!" Libby said.

"Hi, Libby. Beautiful evening, isn't it?" Keisha replied.

"Sure is!"

"Jillian, this is Keisha, our head security guard," Caroline said. "She is *incredible*. Just *so* strong. Like, look at those Serena Williams arms! Show her, Keisha!"

"Woo! Go, Keisha!" Libby said as Keisha shook her head slightly, then flexed her biceps.

"She used to compete in bodybuilding competitions professionally," Caroline said to me, and then asked Keisha, "How many pounds can you bench-press?"

"Oh, I don't know," Keisha said, a tight smile fixed on her face.

"Come on, you totally do!"

"Two hundred and fifty," Keisha said.

"Oh my God, that's so cool," Libby said. "I can hardly even get through a Zumba class."

"That man I mentioned, the one who came here looking to start trouble? Keisha took him down like *that*," Caroline said, snapping her fingers. "Anyways, Keisha, this is our newest member, Jillian Beckley, so she's free to come and go during opening hours as she pleases."

"Hi, nice to meet you," I said, reaching forward to shake Keisha's hand.

"We need to get a picture of you for the computer system, for when the other guards are on shift," Caroline said to me, gesturing toward the large computer monitor on Keisha's desk. "So they can verify who you are if you ever want to come during the daytime to do work or to freshen up in between meetings."

Keisha fiddled with a camera attached to the top of the monitor, aiming it in my direction. I gave a stilted smile as she clicked the computer mouse. *Stupid, stupid, stupid,* a voice in my head recited. *You signed the contract and made a very stupid mistake.*

"Ooh, gorgeous," Keisha said. "Now, have a nice night, you all!" She waved good-bye heartily as we stepped onto the elevator. But I caught a glimpse, as the doors closed, of her face dropping, her performance of good cheer over.

"She's so great," Caroline said, leaning forward to press the button for the fourth floor.

"*So* great!" Libby echoed.

"Great," I said.

Stupid, the voice in my head repeated, visions of Caroline sweetly asking *What member?* playing over and over in my mind. What had I expected, that these women who had quite possibly taken down a beloved mayor would just roll over in defeat if someone spilled their secrets? What would they do to me? Oh God, what would they do to *Raf* if they found out that he'd been helping me? I wanted to vomit.

As the elevator doors rolled open onto the clubhouse, they revealed Margot waiting, a bottle of champagne in her hand. When she saw me, she loosened the cork and let it fly.

"It's initiation time," Caroline called out, and the various women scattered around the room left their private conversations and gathered in a circle around me while Margot poured the champagne into flutes for whoever wanted some. My heart strained against my chest at all the attention as they eyed me, some of them familiar, like the woman with lungs of steel who had fogged up the bathroom mirror.

Vy was there too, waving away champagne to focus on what looked like homemade kombucha in a mason jar. A white, rubbery mass floated in the liquid, the yeast and bacteria that fermented regular tea into . . . whatever kombucha was. The shiny blob bumped against Vy's lips as she sipped. She seemed unperturbed by it.

Margot pressed a glass of champagne into my hand, letting her fingers linger on my wrist, her eyes glowing as she smiled at me. Margot had the kind of eyes that could light up the dark.

Once everyone had assembled, Caroline cleared her throat, and the room grew quiet. "Jillian Beckley, raise your right hand." She demonstrated, so I switched my glass over to my left hand and raised my right to mirror hers, like I was taking a pledge, being sworn into office on a glass of expensive champagne instead of a Bible. Earnestly, with a great sense of self-seriousness, she said, "Do you swear to kick ass and smash the patriarchy?"

"I . . . I do," I said.

"And do you swear to support and take care of your fellow members, to lift them up in the workplace, on social media, and in life?" Caroline swept her arm out to indicate the crowd, and I glanced at them. Margot had a bemused expression, a slight smile tugging at her lips, as she watched Caroline lead the ritual. Vy's face drooped so much with apathy that it looked like she'd been shot full of Novocain. She lifted the blob of yeast out of her kombucha jar and began to gnaw on it. (Was that thing even safe for human consumption?) But most of the women in the circle nodded along, entirely involved, some with fond, moved looks on their faces as if they were remembering their own initiations.

"I do," I said.

Caroline raised her eyebrows. "And just as importantly, do you swear to take care of *yourself*, to be kind to the shining, special goddess you are—"

"A boss witch!" a woman in the crowd whooped.

Caroline pursed her lips in annoyance. "Please don't interrupt," she said to the circle, before turning back to me. "To be kind to yourself because you are a woman who deserves the world?"

"I do," I said.

She gazed at me benevolently like Lady Liberty, then lifted her chin, delivering the climax of a campaign speech that she had delivered dozens of times before, but that she was still working hard to imbue with passion and excitement. "Will you be a nasty woman, a badass who smashes glass ceilings and then reaches out her hand to help another woman climb through that shattered ceiling with her?"

"I will," I said.

"Amazing," Caroline said. She reached out to put her arm around my shoulder, then realized she was too short for that, and put it around my waist instead. "And now for all of the rest of us," she continued, turning to the crowd. "Do we swear to welcome Jillian with open hearts and minds, to lift her and support her as we were once lifted and supported?"

"We do," the group said as one. "To Jillian!" Then they all lifted their glasses, and we toasted. This was it, the grand initiation? Bit of a letdown. Vy tore a hunk off the yeast blob with her teeth and choked it down her gullet.

Dozens of women, a band, a pride, beamed at me. I smiled back, as all the decorative girl-power signs hummed in the background. But the part of me that smiled at the women was only a facade, while my brain stepped out of the circle and observed, taking notes and trying to remember for later. My brain took a moment to mark that this shell of my body held its arms so awkwardly. How had these women not discovered the ruse of me yet? I didn't belong with them. Some part of me would always be standing outside of the circle, of *any* circle, uncomfortable in a group, my mind buzzing with what I told myself in my more confident moments was healthy cynicism, and what I knew in my lower moments was self-hatred.

For a few seconds, before I flung it off, a pure desire shot through me, a wish that I could force my brain back in my body and look into all the faces around me with no facade at all. That I could accept their acceptance of me, and belong.

SIXTEEN

The next morning I woke to the buzz of my phone, my head fuzzy from the glasses of champagne that Nevertheless members had pressed into my hands. Miles was calling.

When I told him what I'd done, Miles was going to sigh. He had a particular way of doing it—heavy, as if the bad job that you had done caused him physical pain. His sigh was a perfect embodiment of that terrible *not mad, just disappointed* feeling. I'd never provoked it, but I had seen coworkers crying quietly at their desks in its aftermath.

As the phone rang, the door opened downstairs. Rob and Sara, back already, stomping around their new home like perky dinosaurs. Right before Miles's call went to voice mail, I finally picked it up, dread churning in my stomach.

"Beckley," Miles said. "I've been waiting with bated breath here. How did it go?"

"Great. I'm officially in, it's officially weird." I mustered up all the levity I could and continued, "Only problem is they made me sign a pretty intense nondisclosure and it seems like if you break it, they throw you into the ocean."

Silence on the other end of the line. I braced myself for The Sigh. But instead his voice got low, tight, and somehow that was worse. "How intense was it, exactly?"

"Um. They basically implied that they disappeared the last woman who broke it."

"I told you not to sign anything without consulting us first."

"I know, I know," I said, still trying to keep things light. Maybe if I refused to acknowledge how serious it was, it wouldn't be serious at all, and we could just move on. "But, God, you wouldn't believe how secretive they were about it all, like I was signing on to be a member of the fucking French Resistance." I laughed. He did not. I began to pace, desperation creeping in as he stayed silent. "I didn't have a choice. They wouldn't let me take a moment with the contract and they weren't going to bring me back to the clubhouse if I didn't sign. There was no way—"

"There's always a way!" I flinched. "Dammit, Beckley, I've been vouching for you with the higher-ups. I'd been *excited* about this."

"You can still be excited! Trust me, if I hadn't signed, I wouldn't have been able to get proof, and the story would be dead. But now—"

"It's dead anyway," he said, still in that devastating, low tone. "If it's that intense of an NDA, the bosses aren't going to fight against it for some story about how a bunch of rich women like influence and astrology, or for some catalog of the insipid girl-power posters they've got up on the walls."

"It's not going to be some insipid catalog," I snapped back. "There's more going on here, I know it. There are clearly some very real secrets that they don't want getting out. And we haven't even gotten into Nicole—"

"You keep bringing up Nicole," he said. "But it sounds like you've been having too much fun being a part of the club to get a shred of evidence about her."

"Hey," I said. "That's not fair."

"Unless you find a bombshell, and it's fucking ironclad, this whole thing isn't going to be worth it."

"Please, you have to trust me. I will get you a story." Still no sigh, just a long stretch of silence. "Are you still there?"

"Look," he said quietly. "If you want to keep going, you keep going. I hope you can turn it around, I really do. But I can't give you any guarantees that we'll publish it, and I can't give you more money in the meantime." Another part remained unspoken: that if I'd wasted the magazine's time only to screw it all up, it didn't just mean that I'd never get *this* article published. It meant that I'd never get *anything* published. Not in the *New York Standard*, or maybe, depending on how much editors talked among themselves, not in any reputable publication.

"I get it," I said, trying not to cry. "That makes sense." Three heavy raps sounded at my door. "I'm busy!" I shouted.

"We just need to get into your room for a sec!" Sara said from the hallway.

"Shit, I have to go," I said into the phone. "But I'm not going to let you down."

He made a noncommittal noise and hung up.

I tried to swallow, but my mouth was dry. I flung open the door to see Sara and Rob, plus a large man holding a clipboard. Their contractor. "George just needs to get a sense of the layout before he can start work on the renovation," Sara said, a big smile on her face. George barged into my room and began looking around. Oh God, how I hated them all.

"Look," I said to Sara and Rob, as calmly as I could. "I'm going to need you to give me a little bit more of a heads-up about these things in the future."

"Mm," Sara said. She and Rob exchanged a look.

"In that case, we wanted to give you a heads-up that George is going to be starting work soon," Rob said. "Like, next week." No. What? No, no, no.

"And we know that you're going through a tough time, and we totally don't want to kick you out onto the street," Sara said, still smiling brightly as my stomach dropped into the floor. "But we've been patient for a while, and now we think it would be best if you found another place ASAP."

SEVENTEEN

You'd think that losing your mother would put everything else into perspective. What does it matter if you have nowhere to live and your editor/object-of-lust thinks you're a disappointing speck of dirt? At least nobody's dying. But, as I dragged myself to Nevertheless that night, perspective proved elusive.

Now that all the smoke and mirrors of getting into the club were a thing of the past, logistics turned out to be practical. I'd received an e-mail newsletter that afternoon with a schedule of special events for the week—it came from a bland e-mail address and said nothing about Nevertheless itself, so if you were to forward it to anybody, it wouldn't prove anything. But still. An e-mail, just like the 92nd Street Y might send.

On the schedule for tonight was something called a "Concerns Circle." What the hell was that? A time when women could bring up their feelings of hopelessness over the rollback of women's rights across the country? Or simply a time to complain that the cleaning staff weren't doing their job as well as they were supposed to? I needed to find out. Besides, the house didn't feel like home anymore, now that George the Contractor had left a bunch of equipment all over the place, with a promise to return soon with more. I'd spent much of the afternoon searching through rental listings online. Surprise, surprise, everything was either far too expensive or a hellhole. Or both at once, as in the case of one listing for an $1,800-a-month bedroom in a sixth-floor walk-up, which claimed that it was actually a *good* thing that the room had no windows: one less way for intruders to get inside to murder you! There was no way that I'd be able to pay New York City rent *and* Nevertheless dues, if I wasn't able to get everything done in this first month.

I'd texted Raf earlier that afternoon to see if I could crash on his couch for a little bit. I got his response in the elevator: **For sure. I just went out of town for a couple days to speak at this thing** ("this thing" turned out to be a fancy-schmancy culinary conference, I saw later when I Googled that modest fucker) **and didn't leave a key, but when I get back?**

I was reading it as I walked into the clubhouse, my mask of control slipping right as Libby hurtled toward me. "Hey, lady!" she said, giving me a hug. She drew back, taking in my face. "What's wrong?"

I hadn't been planning to share the news with anyone, but in the intensity of her focus, I melted, giving her the headlines as we pulled up chairs into a makeshift circle. Her expression grew *too* sympathetic. "It's not a big deal," I said. "I'll figure something out."

"Well, sure, you can find a new place, but it's not just that. It's also losing yet another part of your mom," she said. I blinked a few times, quickly, as around us, other women laughed, helping one another push couches into formation, complimenting one another on their upper-body strength ("Thanks, I've been taking an amazing boxing class at an all-female gym!") or making self-deprecating remarks about how they'd been focusing so much on spin classes lately that they'd been neglecting their biceps.

A circle of chairs shouldn't have a head, but this one did. Caroline and Margot sat next to each other, and the attention flowed to them. "Let's open up the space for sharing," Margot said, clad in wide-legged denim, hugging one knee to her chest.

"Yes, if anyone has any concerns, whether personal or more global, with which the group can help, don't be afraid to speak up," Caroline said, sitting up straight, a notebook in her lap, poised to write down any pertinent details from the conversation. As women began to raise their hands and share their thoughts, Margot and Caroline passed control back and forth between the two of them like friends tossing a ball in the backyard—mostly easy, but with the occasional misalignment, a couple of moments where one couldn't quite catch what the other had been throwing over.

Margot rested her head on the knee that she was hugging, staring with rapt attention at whoever was speaking, and so the members tended to speak their concerns as if in a private conversation with her, at least until the other members jumped in with their responses, or Caroline interrupted to clarify something. One member shared her sadness that the family-run Puerto Rican restaurant on her block was going to have to shut down due to a rent increase, and the women discussed fund-raisers. Another member was seeking recommendations and emotional support because her personal trainer was moving to L.A.

Though the concerns may have varied, what stayed the same was the response: utter acceptance. An unspoken rule dictated that no one was allowed to say that somebody else's concern wasn't valid, even if they may have thought it. And oh, there were times when I thought it. This wasn't exactly the shadowy Let's Rule the World circle I'd been imagining. Maybe Miles was right—that this was nothing more than a bunch of insipid women.

Libby nudged me. "You should mention your housing situation! I bet someone here could help."

"Oh God," I whispered back, "I *just* joined. I can't immediately be like *Help me find somewhere livable for eight hundred dollars a month!*"

Libby's eyes widened in surprise, and a little bit of pity. Shit, I'd been too transparent about my financial situation. People in Nevertheless spent $800 a month on moisturizer.

Another woman began to speak—Iris Ngoza, the former model turned Instagram star who'd made a name for herself by decrying the industry's unrealistic beauty standards while bravely weighing 120 pounds. "A friend of mine was telling me about this man, Craig Melton," Iris said. "He's a district judge in Queens who will be hearing a case that could have huge implications for reproductive rights. And he's almost certain to rule against choice, even though I'd be willing to bet that he's paid for an abortion or six in his time." Unsurprised murmurs sounded from around the circle. "It seems that he is not a good man, not a very *clean* one, and yet he's wielding an enormous amount of power over women. So I wonder if anyone might be able to find out any information. Perhaps there is something we can do."

The response to this one was different from the others. There was a pause while Caroline and Margot exchanged a meaningful look.

"Maybe," Caroline said, her eyes flitting ever so quickly toward the mysterious door, then back again. "We'll have to be careful about it—"

Margot leaned forward. "But it sounds like he's a bad man," she said, "and bad men have been getting away with their bullshit for far too long." The crowd turned to her. Caroline watched the women watching Margot, and I realized that it killed her that, while she may have been the brain of this whole thing, Margot was the heart.

"We'll have a think on it," Caroline said. "Meanwhile, *I* have something to say. The annual gala for Women Who Lead is coming up, and . . ." She put her hand on her heart and a resigned but brave expression on her face. "Unfortunately, the woman who I'd been hoping would announce her run for the House of Representatives has decided that she is not ready to throw her hat in the ring." A few murmurs of disappointment and sympathy came from the women around the circle. "Thank you, I know. The good news is that the tables I'd been saving for her and her team are now available. So if any of you would like to attend, please come talk to me. I'd love to have anyone who wants to support. Although of course it would be good for the cause if we could get some star power." She looked at Iris Ngoza, and then at me.

Oh, right. Because of Raf. Duh. I really needed to get better at remembering that I was dating him. I gave Caroline a thumbs-up.

"Wonderful," she said, then addressed the whole group. "The last-minute change has thrown a wrench in things, so I want to apologize in advance if I'm busier than normal until the gala is over. So many things to do, so if anyone wants to help—"

"I volunteer as tribute!" Libby said next to me, her hand shooting into the air. She cleared her throat and placed her hand back in her lap. "I mean, I would love to help however you need."

"Libby," Caroline said, "you're a gem."

EIGHTEEN

When the circle ended and the women in attendance slowly began to straggle out the door, to their gleaming homes and their melatonin and their partners or their pets, Libby and I both hung back, chatting. As Libby talked about the latest updates with her fizzy water company, I watched the small group of women who showed no signs of leaving as eleven P.M. approached: Caroline, Margot, Iris, a couple of others. A few times, I caught Libby watching them too. The elevator doors dinged and Vy clomped into the clubhouse, wearing a jacket spattered with dried clay, her eyes locked on the door I'd never seen anyone go inside. She began to head that way, then noticed me and Libby. She stopped, staring at us for a minute before slouching over to the fridge and pretending to examine its contents. The message was clear: we were overstaying our welcome.

"Well, it's getting late. Should we walk out together?" I asked Libby, and so we waved good-bye and took the elevator down.

When we emerged onto the street, I walked slowly toward the subway, dreading going home. Libby matched my pace, both of us hugging our jackets to ourselves in the early-October evening, silent. Strange. Libby had never met an empty moment that she could not fill with her chatter. But now, she furrowed her brow, then opened her mouth as if to say something. She closed it. Then she opened it again. "So you've noticed the mysterious door too?"

All right, Libby. I wasn't the only person whose powers of observation were on full blast. "Yeah," I said, carefully. "It's a little weird, right?"

"Very!"

"What is it, do you think?" I asked, then rolled my eyes. "A prison where they're holding all the men who have ever wronged them?" I'd started developing a theory, strengthened by the events of that night's circle, the way that Caroline's eyes had flitted to the door when Iris mentioned the terrible judge. Behind the door, they addressed the more complicated concerns. The controversial or even dangerous ones. That was where they kept their information, their files and records, maybe where they hung up pictures of men like the judge, of women like Nicole, and figured out how they were going to destroy their lives. Maybe what went on in the back room was what had united Caroline and Margot in the first place.

Libby stopped walking and grabbed my hand, looking me straight in the eye. I squirmed at the naked intensity of her gaze. "I like you, Jillian. You really *listen*, which isn't necessarily true for everyone I've met here." Guilt came over her face. "I don't mean to be a jerk!"

"No, I know what you mean," I said, thinking of the self-satisfied air that clung to many of the women in the club. "And thanks, I like you too."

"We've got each other's backs, right?"

"Yeah. Of course."

"Okay. I'm going to tell you something that I haven't told any-one else. Swear you won't repeat it?" I half expected her to make me lock my pinky in hers, like we were children trading confes-sions at sleepaway camp. A couple of girls playing games, making meaning out of nothing, just like Miles had implied on the phone. Fuck Miles.

"I'm great at secrets," I said.

She glanced around the street, to make sure that no one would overhear, then turned back to me once she'd deemed it safe. "I think that getting through that door is the way that you know you've *really* made it," she said, her voice hushed and reverent. "That you haven't just bought your way in, but that they genuinely love and admire you. That you're truly, truly accepted." This was always the way, wasn't it? Another door, another hurdle you had to jump in order to prove yourself, in hopes of pushing off the gnaw-ing unease that you were not enough. Libby swallowed. "And the reason I think that," she began, then startled as a woman I recog-nized from the clubhouse came walking by, giving us a nod as she passed. As soon as the woman crossed the street, Libby grabbed my hand and pulled me into the alley behind us, a dark, narrow walk-way full of trash and recycling bins. Her palm was sweaty. She let go of my hand and tucked her hair behind her ear, then let out a breath.

"Okay, whew," she said, then smiled at me shakily. "I don't know why I'm so jumpy!"

"It's fine," I said. "Why do you think that, about the door?"

"Right. Because, once, I saw them go inside."

"Hold up," I said, my own palms getting sweaty in anticipation. "What? How?"

"I had to go to the bathroom before I left the clubhouse one night. And, well . . . it's embarrassing, but I was in there for longer than I expected."

"Like how long?" I asked.

"I take slow poops, okay?" she said, flushing. (Sorry.) "But they didn't realize anyone was still around, because when I came back out, the group was heading to the door. They were all, like, really excited. Giddy, even? Like it was time to do what they'd been waiting all night for. Somehow I knew that I wasn't supposed to see what I was seeing. So I hid behind a plant."

"As one does," I said, my heart pounding. "And what happened? What's behind it?"

"Well, I couldn't see behind it—I was too far away for that. And I wasn't going to try to follow them in. I'm not totally cuckoo! But I did hear them talking. Margot was saying something about how the new members were promising, and it was time to invite someone else in. Caroline was like, *Maybe*, and Margot was like, *Come on, Caroline, it's been long enough since* . . . Oh, it was some name, I don't remember what."

I'd bet anything it was Nicole. Libby just kept talking. "Caroline said she couldn't even think about it until after the gala prep was done, and Margot was like, *But we'd want to take them with us at the end of October.* Caroline sort of threw up her hands and was like, *Fine, but I get final say!* And when she disappeared into the door, Margot turned to Vy and was like, quietly, *Let's make sure they're helpful.* Then . . ." She shrugged. "Then the door closed, and they were gone."

"That's wild," I said, shoving my shaking hands in my pockets. God bless Libby. They had an opening, one that they were looking to fill soon. I had to get in there. Behind the door, that's where I'd find the bombshell that would make this entire operation worth it.

"Right?" Libby was saying. "Someone *helpful*, they said, so I've been trying to be as useful as possible with volunteering to lead the newbies, stuff like that. Caroline and I have been bonding, I think! The other day she actually asked me where I'd gotten my shoes, because she was looking for a pair like them! But . . ." She fidgeted, suddenly shy. "Could I ask you a favor? If you're talking to any of them and I come up, maybe you could say nice things about me? And then if I get invited in, I can obviously say all kinds of nice things about you! And then we can be in there together, and it'll be so fun." She hadn't even bothered to ask if I wanted to get inside the inner circle, working under the assumption that all Nevertheless members wanted to be as elite as possible. Still, I wondered why it mattered so much to her. It seemed like she more than just *wanted* it. She needed it as much as I did.

"I can do that," I said. "Totally."

She leaned forward and hugged me with a tight, quick squeeze. "You're the best!" When she released me, she cleared her throat. "You know, until your sexy chef man gets back in town, if being at home is too unpleasant, you can stay with me."

"Like a slumber party?" I said, joking.

"Yeah, exactly!" Libby answered.

"I . . ." I hesitated. It wasn't a good idea to sleep with my sources, literally. But as I looked at her cherubic face, her hopeful smile, a little bud of gratitude and something else—tenderness—took root inside of me. It would be for only a night or two, till Raf got back. "That would be really nice, thanks."

NINETEEN

So I followed Libby back to her apartment, only a ten-minute walk from the clubhouse. We passed a group of women drunkenly posing for selfies in front of a brownstone. "That's Carrie's house, from *Sex and the City*!" she said with pride, before we turned the corner and entered the doorman building where she lived.

"I was really torn between this place and a brownstone," she went on, pausing to wave enthusiastically to her doorman, who smiled at her with what seemed like real affection (although maybe he was just good at faking it for his job). "But I think a brownstone will be for when I want to buy."

When she unlocked her door, I followed her in and then stopped short, staring at her high ceilings. "Libby! This place is huge," I said, because it was, at least for a single woman in her midtwenties living by herself in New York City. God, her water bottle company must've been taking the hydration world by storm.

"Thanks! I never thought of it as being particularly giant," she said. "But I'm from Texas, so I'm used to everything being bigger."

A tiny rat dog came bounding into the living room, yapping so hard that I worried it might give itself a heart attack. "Bella!" Libby squealed. The dog rocketed into her outstretched arms and promptly began giving her face a tongue bath. "Jillian, meet my angel baby!"

"Hey, Bella," I said, holding out my hand to her wet little nose. She gave my fingers a disinterested sniff, let out a fart, and jumped out of Libby's arms, sprinting back out of the room to do God-knows-what, God-knows-where.

"Bella, come back!" Libby yelled. "Bella?" She waited a second, then shrugged her shoulders. "She's very independent." She indicated a gray couch with fuzzy white throw pillows. "That folds out," she said. "Or I do have a queen size bed, if you want to share. But no pressure!" We arrived in her bedroom, decorated in pinks and peaches. The bed in question was a canopy, fit for a princess. An open door led to a walk-in closet, stuffed with bags and shoes, an ode to Consumer Culture.

The whole place was a strange mishmash, as if decorated by a girly girl who'd been fed a steady diet of TV shows about women taking New York by storm until she'd decided that she was going to live that glamorous life, goddammit! She had a lot of *stuff*, but I didn't see any photos of family or friends. The walls remained conspicuously blank. Perhaps she was an alien in a human suit, trying to pass herself off as a modern woman. Or, more likely, she'd just moved in and hadn't had a chance to frame anything yet.

"How long have you lived here?" I asked.

"Oh gosh," she said, wrinkling her forehead. "A little over a year? Let's find you some pajamas." She pointed to a dresser drawer right as Bella tore back into the room, an old banana peel in her mouth. "Bella! Where did you . . . ?" Bella wiggled, gnawing on the peel, and then ran out of the room again. "Hey, come back here! Sorry, Jillian, just a minute."

She disappeared after Bella. I opened the drawer that Libby'd pointed out while I waited for her. In contrast to my pajama repertoire (old T-shirts, boxer shorts), Libby had a plethora of nightgowns, matching shirt-bottom sets in silks and flannels, cute little slips. Not an old T-shirt in sight. I stuck my hand into the mass of fabric. Maybe the old T-shirts were hidden on the bottom. Or maybe it was nightgowns all the way down. I brushed against something harder, colder. A picture frame. I pushed a lacy pink slip aside to find a picture of Libby—a young teenager, her nose slightly bigger than it was now, but undeniably Libby—sitting on a couch next to an older man with a healthy tan who had his arm around her. Her father? Her grandfather? Whoever he was, he looked into the camera stiffly, as if he weren't quite sure he should be there. Libby's hopeful smile broke my heart. This was how my father and I posed for pictures, back when we still saw each other. I squinted at the man, who looked familiar.

Right as Libby reentered the room, I placed him: Roy Pruitt. Miles used to rant about him in the newsroom. A Texas billionaire who believed women belonged in the kitchen, who used his vast oil fortune to elect ultraconservative politicians to do his bidding. All the wealth and maliciousness of the two Koch brothers smushed into one man with very nice teeth. Miles had always been asking his more serious reporters to dig into the latest influence of Pruitt Dark Money. "This monster!" he'd say, pointing to his picture on his computer screen. "He's one of the top five architects of our current political moment!" If I remembered correctly from some research I'd done after Miles had gone off on a particularly long rant, Roy Pruitt had a few children, boys of the Large Adult Son variety, all jostling to take over his empire one day. So what the hell was Libby doing with him? Beyond a general reverence for wealth, someone who believed the things that Roy Pruitt believed would have nothing in common with the women of Nevertheless.

"Jillian?" Libby asked as I stood frozen over the picture. She registered what I was looking at, then the expression on my face. "Oh, drat."

"Sorry," I said. "I was just looking for pajamas. I didn't mean to pry."

"You know who he is." I nodded. She chewed on her lip, then said, "I'm going to open us up some wine."

"When I was in first grade, I thought my mother was a horse," Libby said, sitting cross-legged on that extravagant gray couch, holding a glass of cabernet with one hand and picking at a fluffy pillow on her lap with the other, Rat Dog Bella snoring next to her. "That's what I heard the kids whispering. I thought maybe she was like Princess Fiona from *Shrek*, you know? One thing by day, another thing by night? It seemed kind of nice, the idea that she could go galloping through a field. I snuck into her room at all hours of the night to check if her feet had turned into hooves. I really liked horses back then." She took a long sip. "But I'd heard them wrong. They were calling her a whore."

She looked up at me then, her neck flushing pink. "She wasn't a prostitute! Although not that there would've been anything wrong

with . . . I think we need to support sex workers, I just mean—"
She shook her head, gathering herself. "She was his mistress. One
of those long-term, open-secret ones. Like, he bought her a house,
and he came around to visit a couple of times a month and gave
us an allowance. And his wife totally knew but nobody really said
anything."

"Goddamn, men are pigs," I said, and she nodded. "Did you all
acknowledge that he was your dad? Or was it just like, *This is
mommy's friend Mr. Pruitt?*"

"We did the charade for a while," she said. "Eventually I got old
enough that we dropped it, especially when my mom started lob-
bying him to set me up a trust fund. But he was never my dad in
public. Like, he didn't come to my band concerts." I couldn't stop
a half laugh from escaping, even though it wasn't funny, just fucked
up and sad to imagine little Libby at a band concert, scanning the
crowd for the evil billionaire who'd secretly fathered her. Surprised, she looked at me, and then half laughed too. "I played the
tuba! I was good at it!"

"I'm sure you were! I'm sorry," I said.

"No, no, it's okay. It's weird, that *that's* the grievance I still hold
on to! Obviously I have other grievances too, like the fact that he's
a bad man! I realized that when I went to college and met people
with different views for the first time. After that, I decided that I
wanted to use the money I got from him to help the people he was
hurting."

"Hence Fizzi?" I asked.

"Yeah, exactly! And I donate to a lot of other causes. That's how
I met Caroline—I went to her gala last year and gave a bunch of
money to Women Who Lead."

No wonder that she worried she'd only bought her way into the club. A thought struck me. "Does Caroline know? About your dad, I mean."

Libby nodded. "I didn't tell her, but she found out somehow. She asked about it at my interview. Sometimes I think that she and Margot are, like, magicians. Like they can know all your secrets just by looking at you."

"God, I hope not," I said, and she snapped out of some self-reflection, looking at me more closely.

"Do *you* have secrets?"

"Everyone who's interesting does," I said lightly. "But I think Margot and Caroline probably just run thorough background checks."

"Well, Caroline knew about my family, and she also knew that we don't speak anymore."

"You don't?"

"No, not since I decided to move to New York. I told them I thought they were closed-minded, doing terrible things to the world, and I needed to get away. They told me not to bother coming back." She picked at the pillow in her lap harder, pulling off little white fuzzies and brushing them onto the floor. "We spent a lot of my interview on that, actually, about how I couldn't be part of their lives anymore, and didn't want to be anyway. It's funny, at first I thought that I was getting the Nevertheless invite in spite of where I came from. But now I think it's because of it. That it's impressive for Nevertheless to have 'rescued' me from the dark side." She paused. "Maybe *rescued* is the wrong word. They've taken me in when my own father isn't willing to have me over for Christmas, which probably makes them feel very . . ."

"Magnanimous?"

"Yes, magnanimous!" Alarm crossed her face. "Sorry, I don't

want to sound ungrateful! I'm *so* grateful. I admire everyone in the club so much! It's just, all my life, I've never been able to tell if people like me or hate me for *me*. I thought starting over in New York would change that, but . . ." She finished her glass of wine, then wiped her mouth and hiccupped. "Well, at least most of the members don't know about it. You won't tell, will you?"

"Of course not," I said, and she gave my hand a squeeze, then let it linger in mine. Now I understood why getting past that secret door mattered so much to her. They wouldn't let people in there just to be magnanimous. And we all needed to belong somewhere. "I really am sorry."

"Thank you."

"So you and your mom don't talk anymore either?"

"Nope. She believes what he believes. Besides, I don't really know how to respect her. The major activity of her adult life has been ruining someone else's marriage."

"Maybe she really, truly loves him. You can't always help it. I mean, *I've* fallen a little bit in love with a married man, despite my better judgment."

Libby gasped. "Raf is married?"

Dammit. Again, I needed to get better at remembering that he was supposed to be my boyfriend. "Oh no, sorry, I mean it happened a while ago. Should've spoken more clearly," I lied. "What I'm trying to say is that I think everyone makes mistakes. And sometimes you go down careless, selfish paths because you want to fill up that stupid gaping hole inside of you—"

"Mm," Libby said seriously. "Your vagina."

"I was thinking a more metaphorical hole, but sure, that too." I shrugged. "I don't know. I don't mean to presume anything about your relationship with her. I guess I just feel like . . ." I hadn't said this out loud to anyone before. My voice caught. I swallowed.

"Like now that I've lost my mother, I'd give anything for a chance to talk to her again."

"Oh, Jillian," Libby said, and stroked my hair. "It's so hard to lose your family."

I didn't sleep on the foldout couch that night. I slept in the bed beside her. Like lovers, or like friends.

TWENTY

A couple of mornings later, I sat in my mother's bedroom, boxing up the remaining things of hers to give to charity as the contractor banged around downstairs. Already, sawdust hung heavy in the air of the house. I wanted to take all her clothes with me but that wasn't practical, particularly since I didn't even really know where I was going. I held a sweater of hers to my face, searching for a hint of her smell in it. Nothing.

My phone rang, an unfamiliar number with a New York City area code. "Hello?"

"Libby mentioned that you're looking for an apartment," the voice said. Of course Margot wouldn't announce herself on the phone. She didn't need to. That serene, rich voice couldn't belong to anyone else. I had a perverse impulse to ask *Sorry, who is this?* just to see how she'd react, but I swallowed it.

"Libby's apparently very concerned about me," I said. "But I'll be fine. It's the New York real estate market. That's only, what, the seventh circle of hell?"

"Caroline has a great broker," Margot said. "When she was buying an apartment, she talked about this man so much that I half expected her to leave her husband and run off with him instead." She paused. "Not actually, of course. Caroline would sooner run into traffic than get divorced. And Caroline would never run into traffic. Too messy. Want me to connect you?"

"That's really kind," I said. "Maybe."

"I can text her right now—"

"I . . ." I hesitated. "I think my budget might be somewhat lower than what Caroline's broker is used to."

"Ah, I see," Margot said. She exhaled like she was blowing out smoke. But Margot didn't smoke, did she? I could picture her with an occasional cigarette, if she were really drunk. Now, though, a joint seemed more likely. Margot, on the other end of the phone, reclining on her bed in a silky robe, holding a joint delicately between her fingertips, blowing tendrils of smoke up at the ceiling. Meanwhile, I paced around, wearing a ratty T-shirt I'd gotten for free from participating in a college dodgeball tournament ten years ago. "In that case," Margot went on, "I may have something else for you. Just give me a couple of days."

"You really don't have to—"

"I know I don't *have* to," she said, with an easy laugh. "But you're in the club now. We take care of each other. Besides, it's Libra Season." I had no idea what she meant by that, but I made a knowing noise anyway. She exhaled again. "By the way, I was reading some of your old articles from Quill. They're cutting, aren't they? You know how to destroy your target."

I tensed, even as a small part of me thrilled to her compliment, to the fact that I'd caught her attention. Maybe something I'd written had made her laugh, or maybe she'd stopped and lingered over a particular turn of phrase. But a much larger part of me heard the alarm bells starting to ring. "Thanks, I guess so. I don't do that anymore though. Gotta save all that cutting criticism for my fictional creations, you know?"

"Interesting," she said. "Are you sure?"

Shit. The alarm bells blared louder now. A fire drill, or time to start running? "I . . ."

"Because that district judge that Iris brought up at the Concerns Circle, the one who will be hearing the reproductive rights case soon, we've heard some stories about him over the past couple days." My breathing slowed as she kept talking. "Lining his pockets in exchange for favorable rulings, things like that. Some journalists might be starting to look into it, but that kind of reporting takes time, and the case is coming up fast. We couldn't help imagining how much an anonymous takedown—a well-written, incisive Twitter thread, for example—could fan the flames. Make some trouble for this piece of shit."

Was this how things had started with Nicole Woo-Martin, a casual phone call, the hitch of Margot's breath on the other end of the line? "Are you asking me to write a hit piece?" I asked.

Again, that easy laugh. "No, of course not. I was just thinking that if you were itching to stretch a muscle that you haven't used in a little while, you might be interested in hearing some of the stories too. You might have some opinions on them. And stretching is healthy. But maybe I was mistaken—"

"No," I said. I didn't love the idea of ruining someone's life for Nevertheless's agenda. But from what Libby had overheard, I had until shortly after Caroline's gala to prove I was worthy of the back room, where they'd probably devised this plan in the first place. "I'm very opinionated."

"Excellent. Come meet me and Vy tonight at eight, and we'll fill you in." She listed an intersection in Brooklyn Heights as the meeting place. "And maybe don't wear anything too flashy."

I looked down at myself. "I don't think that'll be a problem," I said, then paused. "Wait, why?"

"You'll see," she said, and hung up.

TWENTY-ONE

When I arrived at the corner, on a residential street full of lovely brownstones, I stood there for a moment, at a loss. Had I been stood up? Then, Vy and Margot materialized out of the darkness. Vy wore a men's knit hat pulled down over her pale hair, gloves on her hands, even though it wasn't that cold.

"Jillian, hi," Margot said. Vy gave a curt nod.

"Hey," I said. "Pretty street."

"Mm, isn't it?" Margot replied. "Let's take a little walk." Weird way to do an information exchange, but hey, there were worse places to wander than this manicured neighborhood.

She turned and began to stroll down the block of impressive houses as if she hadn't a care in the world. Vy and I flanked her. "So we found one of the judge's mistresses," Margot said, staring straight ahead. "A recent one. And as we suspected, she told us that he pressured her into an abortion."

"What a scumbag," I said.

"Ah, but he paid for it, like a true gentleman," Margot said in a dry tone as she turned down a narrow alley, lined by tall wooden fences shielding backyards from view. (Backyards, in New York City! We were in the lap of luxury now.) The glow from the street-lights didn't reach in here. Vy walked slightly ahead of us, examining the fence slats, as Margot kept talking. "We'll just need to find the check receipt from that procedure, though the mistress suspected that he might have a few other shady payments hidden away in his file cabinet, so let's keep an eye out for those while we're at it."

"I'm sorry, while we're at what?"

Vy stopped and tapped lightly on the fence in front of her. "This is the one."

"Oh," Margot said, looking me in the eye. "His mistress told us he keeps his records in his home office." She indicated the brown-stone, looming up from behind the fence. "He brought her here once. Wanted to fuck her on his desk. She walked us through the layout. We thought if you were going to write the article, you might like to help with the research."

"So, breaking and entering?" I asked, my mouth dry. "Are you joking?"

"If you'd rather not help out, feel free to go," Margot said. Vy grabbed the top of the fence, which came to her eye level. She shook it, checking its sturdiness.

"It's stable," Vy said. "Ready?" They both fixed their eyes on me, cocked their heads, and said nothing, waiting for my response.

This was a crime. It was also a test. To gauge my devotion, see whether or not they could trust me. Either that or they were setting me up for a fall. I swallowed. "I want to help."

"Excellent," Margot said, smiling, then pulled two pairs of gloves out of her pocket. She handed one to me. "Here, put these on."

Vy lifted a long leg up onto a horizontal slat, then pulled herself over the top of the fence in a single movement, like a great stallion leaping a hurdle. Margot climbed after her, delicately. I followed, hoping that I wouldn't impale myself on a fencepost.

Somewhere during the time that I was hoisting myself over in my ungainly way, the reality of what we were doing sank in. "What the hell," I said when my feet touched the ground in the judge's small, tidy backyard. "Do you even know if he's home? Or if he has cameras?"

"Don't freak," Vy said.

"He and his wife are out to dinner," Margot said. We walked up the steps to the judge's back door. Vy began picking the lock with a credit card as Margot went on. "Caroline and Libby are eating at the same restaurant to keep an eye on him." Libby was in on this too? I hadn't thought of her as serious competition until now. "And if he's bringing his mistresses around to his home office, I doubt he has cameras."

Vy turned the knob, and it swung open. "How do you know how to do that?" I asked.

Vy just shrugged. "Most locks aren't that strong. More for appearance than anything. If someone wants to get in, they'll get in." She loped inside. Taking a deep breath, I crossed the threshold into the judge's home.

I was too nervous to stop and drool over the place. Besides, there wasn't much to drool over, anyway. It had good bones, but the decorator had clearly just gone to a Crate & Barrel and shouted, *Bring me your finest selection of beige!* I followed Vy and Margot down a hallway and into a home office, done up to look like a library. There was a filing cabinet in the corner. Vy picked the lock on that too, this time using a paper clip she'd grabbed from a bowl on the desk. Next to the bowl, a bust of some old lawyer or philosopher— very ancient Greek—scowled at me. Margot, meanwhile, sprawled in the desk chair, looking at the pictures and knickknacks on display in a casual, curious manner, as if she'd been invited over to tour a friend's place.

They were so calm about it, so practiced. Not how they would be if it were their first time bringing about a person's destruction. More than ever, as Vy flipped through the file cabinet and Margot read some letters from the judge's drawer, I became convinced that they'd been involved with Nicole.

I, meanwhile, wasn't calm at all. My ears were alert to every creak, every sound. At any moment, the judge could come home. When he did, Margot and Vy would disappear in some puff of smoke, leaving me alone and guilty in his office.

"Do you need me to do anything?" I asked.

"Just get a sense of him, his life," Margot said. "In case it helps your writing." I looked at the diplomas the judge had displayed prominently on his walls, the framed portraits of himself draped in robes. He wasn't attractive or unattractive, just bland, the kind of man you'd pass on the street without a second thought. But sometimes the blandest-looking ones were the worst of all.

"Bank statements," Vy said, stepping back from the drawer and holding up a sheaf of paper. "There's a charge at a women's health clinic for the right amount, around the date that the woman told us it happened."

"Perfect," Margot said. "Jillian, unlock your phone?"

I did, hesitant, and Vy grabbed it from me, using it to take a picture of the evidence. Margot, meanwhile, held up the letters she'd been reading. "Notes too. From some prominent antichoice advocates, thanking him for coming to dinner and complimenting him on his golf game, making veiled allusions to what they hope he'll do for them." She too took pictures with my phone, until her own phone buzzed. "Oh, they're leaving the restaurant." She sighed. "I suppose we should go."

Quickly, they put everything back in its place, as if we'd never been there at all. Then, right before we were about to leave the office, they exchanged a look. Margot stepped forward and picked up the bust of that scowling lawyer, moving him from the desk to the top of the file cabinet, a tiny act of mischief. "All right, then," she said, and turned to the door.

"So go ahead and start writing," Margot said to me, a hitch in her breath as we half ran back down the hallway, out the back door, and reentered the night air. She stopped moving for a brief moment and smiled at me. "And obviously we won't tell anyone about this if you don't."

TWENTY-TWO

Okay, which do you think is more evocative?" I asked Raf as we stood in his kitchen chopping onions in the morning light, both of us sniffling from the juice. "'He has no soul, like a cardboard cutout of a man,' or 'He's pure appetite, like a sentient Hungry Hungry Hippo'?"

"Hmm," he said, and paused in his chopping to consider, rolling the words around in his mind. "Hippo."

Libby had told me I could stay as long as I wanted ("Seriously, I love company!" she'd insisted). And even tiny rat dog Bella had been growing on me. But it wasn't a good idea to get too attached. So when Raf had gotten back into town the day before, I'd moved to his couch.

He had tried to give me the bed, saying that he'd be rattling around in the kitchen early anyway. He was working on a new recipe for his fricasé de pollo. (Of course he was. The glowing *New*

Yorker review of his restaurant had gushed over everything else and then called his fricasé "simple and homey, if not particularly complex." That had probably been driving Raf nuts.) I'd refused his offer. I wasn't going to inconvenience him even more than I already was. Besides, it wasn't like Raf's old couch was going to ruin a blissful night of slumber—I hadn't been able to sleep well for weeks now, and my entrance into the world of crime a couple nights ago hadn't helped. At random flashes, I was back there, standing in the judge's office, waiting for my consequences.

Raf had refused my refusal. After a ten-minute standoff during which we'd repeated each other's names in increasingly firm tones while he carried my bag to the bedroom and I wrestled it back to the living room, he'd finally relented.

"Ha, I win!" I'd said, parking myself on the couch.

"Or I do," he'd replied, his eyes crinkling, and let out his signature Raf cackle, a belly laugh that seemed all the heartier coming from his beanpole frame.

That morning, I'd woken up early, going through the document photos we'd taken the other night, the notes from the stories that Margot had told me. The more I learned about the judge, the more incensed I became. This wasn't a Nicole Woo-Martin situation. This man deserved what was coming to him.

Raf had come out of the bedroom in a T-shirt and old running shorts, rubbing his eyes. "Trade help for help?" I'd asked.

"Oh. Uh, yeah, sure," Raf had said. Then he'd made us both some strong cups of coffee and, with him unshaven and my hair unbrushed, we'd gotten to work.

"I can't get the flavors quite right," he'd said, throwing an onion at me. I caught it with one hand. "Hey, look at those reflexes!"

"That's it, I'm giving up writing for sports. Don't try to change my mind."

He laughed and we started chopping, our shoulders almost touching thanks to his limited counter space. He cut his entire onion in the time it took me to slice a quarter of mine. We moved on to other ingredients. He handed me some firm, plump tomatoes to dice, then poured oil into a saucepan on the stove. It was all a little thrilling, cooking like this, since my typical mealtime routine had recently consisted of shoving fistfuls of cereal in my mouth, or when I wanted to get *really* fancy, heating up some frozen Indian food from Trader Joe's. Now, as I explained what Margot had told me about the judge (though I left out the part about breaking and entering), Raf sautéed the onions, their pungent smell making my stomach rumble, and simmered the chicken in a sauce.

He didn't need my help—if anything, I was slowing him down—but still, he made me feel as if he appreciated it. And I appreciated *his* help as he listened seriously to the takedowns I'd come up with, letting me know if they were withering or entirely toothless.

At one point, in the close quarters, we bumped into each other and nearly knocked the saucepan off the stove. Raf caught it just in time. "You know you have a huge, beautiful restaurant kitchen," I said. "You don't want to do the recipe testing there?"

"Nah, I never do. Too much pressure that way. Makes me get in my head, having all those other people around." He took a spoonful of the sauce out of the pan and handed it to me. "More or less cayenne?"

I rolled the flavor around in my mouth. "I'm hesitant to mess with near perfection. But . . . a little more."

He shook in some spice and added a handful of fresh herbs. We each took a taste at the same time, closing our eyes, savoring it. Then we turned to each other, almost laughing with how good it was. "Holy shit, Raf. I think my taste buds had a full-on orgasm."

"Welcome to Flavortown!" he said.

I squinted at him. "Are you doing Guy Fieri?"

"I'm doing Guy Fieri."

"Cool."

"Yeah, I'm not going to do that again."

We laughed and dished ourselves up heaping platefuls of chicken stew, then leaned against his counter, feasting on five-star dining in our pajamas at nine in the morning.

"Thanks for your help with the article," I said once I'd regained my ability to make words, instead of just noises of contentment. "I'm feeling jazzed about it."

"I'm jazzed to read it. Thanks for your help with the cooking."

"Oh, psh, I barely did anything."

"No, really."

"You probably try out new recipes with all your fake girl-friends," I teased.

"I've never tried out new recipes with any girlfriend." He stared at his fork, twiddling it in his fingers. "Or with anyone, really."

I suddenly became aware that I was not wearing a bra. Shoving the final bite of my food into my mouth, I chewed quickly and put my plate in the dishwasher. "Well, I'm honored. Now I guess I should actually write this thing instead of just talking about it, huh?"

It probably wasn't a good idea to stay with Raf too long either. I'd finish the article that day, I told myself, and then I'd rededicate myself to the apartment hunt with a vengeance.

TWENTY-THREE

I went to a coffee shop and wrote like a fiend. A poisonous side of me poured out, but it was *righteous* poison. How freeing it felt to be vicious in the name of justice. This man had wormed his way into power by virtue of nothing but his membership in the old boys' club and now he was using that ill-deserved power to ruin the lives of people who'd worked harder than he ever had. He needed to be destroyed. I barely lifted my fingers from the keyboard the entire time, my coffee growing cold beside me as I crafted something that could work as either an article or a very in-depth Twitter thread. I wrote my concluding sentence. Only then did I feel how desperately I needed to pee. When I stood up to do so, my hip hurt from hours of sitting in the same position.

Stephen King says that, after finishing a draft of a novel, you should put it in a drawer for six weeks before coming back to reread so that you can see it clearly. I left what I had written on my computer for the time it took me to go to the bathroom (roughly three minutes), then read it over and decided I was fucking in love with it.

I texted Margot. **Hey, I finished writing that thing.** I added an exclamation point, then a biceps curl emoji, then deleted them both. "Just send the stupid text," I muttered under my breath, and did so.

Ten seconds later, my phone rang. "You're quick," Margot said. "Can you bring your computer and meet me in an hour?"

"Sure. Yeah, absolutely. At the clubhouse?"

"No, just us," she said, and gave me an apartment address on the Upper West Side instead. Funny that she lived there. That neighborhood seemed much more Caroline than Margot. It was too normal, too full of Juice Generations and The Gap. Unless . . .

"We're not breaking and entering again, are we?" I asked.

"No," she said, and laughed.

A few subway transfers and one elevator ride later, I knocked on a door. Margot answered with a glass of red wine in her hand, her feet bare, wearing no makeup except for a slash of bright scarlet lipstick. I hadn't imagined Margot to be messy, per se, but I *had* thought her place would be cluttered, full of love letters and half-finished bottles of perfume. Like a Parisian garret, except huge and expensive. Instead, this living room was tastefully furnished, with everything put away in its place and what looked like Real Art framed on the walls. Through a large window, the trees of Central Park swayed, their leaves starting to turn orange and gold.

"Please, go ahead, sit," she said, pointing to a brown leather armchair, so I did. I expected her to sit on one of the multiple other chair or couch options, but instead, she sprawled on the rug, lying on her stomach and cupping her head in her hands, her dress fanning out on the ground around her. I was starting to think that Margot was allergic to sitting up straight like everyone else. "All right. Read it to me," she said, staring up into my eyes.

I blinked, not sure if I'd heard her right. "Now? Out loud?"

"In your head, but think it strongly in my direction," she said, then smiled. "Or we could do out loud, if you prefer."

I cleared my throat. "Um, okay," I said, my hands shaking a bit with nerves. I needed Margot to like this for what it could do to my standing in the club. But also, this was the first whole thing I'd written since my mother had died, and maybe I needed to prove that grief hadn't permanently altered my abilities. Maybe too I wanted to show myself that Margot could respect me for something real, not just my made-up relationship and my bullshit novel. I took a deep breath and began.

"'Attention, women: Despicable men hide in plain sight. You pass them every day without a second thought. But if you've ever felt an unexplained shiver of revulsion, an involuntary clenching in your uterus, maybe you've just entered the orbit of the Honorable Craig Melton.'" I paused and looked at Margot. She was listening thoughtfully, toying with a strand of her hair. "Are you sure . . . Do you want me to keep going?"

"Please," she said, and so I did, reminding myself to breathe as I began to catalog the list of the judge's faults. When I got to the Hungry Hungry Hippo line, Margot tittered. My shoulders loosened infinitesimally. I stood up and began to pace back and forth, balancing my laptop in my hands as I read more and more. When I described how this sack of shit who viewed the world as his own personal abortion buffet was more than happy to be taken on expensive golfing trips by pro-life lobbyists, Margot sat up from her sprawl, her eyes dancing with amusement and with something else. Maybe I was flattering myself, but I could have sworn it was excitement.

"'But,'" I continued, "'how could the honorable judge possibly keep a promise to remain fair and impartial when he can't even keep a promise to pull out?'" At that, Margot full-on cackled.

I went on for a few more adrenaline-filled minutes, reading more details, more ways in which I'd ripped Judge Melton to shreds, until I finally came to the end and caught my breath, flushing. "So, uh, that's what I've got," I said. She bit her lip and I waited for her to say something. Pockets of sweat had collected in my armpits.

"You are vicious," she said.

"Well, when it's warranted."

Silence stretched between us for a moment. I cleared my throat again and sat back down in the chair. Then she broke into a smile. "It's perfect."

I exhaled. "Yeah? Good!"

She unfolded herself, rising to her feet, and pulled a flash drive out of the pocket of her dress. "May I?" she asked as she perched on the arm of my chair and then, without waiting for an answer, reached across me and inserted it into my computer. I breathed a quick sigh of relief that I'd renamed all the files where I kept my Nevertheless notes, as she moved the draft of my article over to her drive, humming something to herself. The way she was leaning over me, her head practically touched mine, her dark hair in my face, strands of it glinting gold. I didn't actively try and smell it—I didn't want to be some weirdo, smelling her hair!—but it was right in my face.

Anyway, her hair smelled like jasmine.

She righted herself and pocketed the drive again. Then she stood up and moved her arm through the air to indicate the living room, the magnificent view of dusk falling outside the window. "I forgot to ask you, what do you think?"

"I mean, it's gorgeous," I said. "It's funny, though, it's not what I imagined your place would look like."

"Probably because it's not my place," she said. "It's yours."

"You're very funny. And very cruel," I said. She just raised an

eyebrow, a smile curling on her lips, and I blinked, my heart starting to pound. "No. What? Shut up. I can't . . . I can't afford this."

"There's nothing to afford. It's my aunt's pied-à-terre. But she's
in a mood where she only wants to be in the Italian countryside.
City life clouds her chakras. She doesn't want to sell, though, just
in case something interesting comes to Broadway, or her Italian
lover dumps her. So it's just sitting here empty most of the time."

"Stop it," I said.

"I spoke to her about it, and she actually thought it would be nice
to have someone around, to get a little life in the place. It would be
like you were doing her a favor, keeping an eye on everything.
Think of it as indefinite house-sitting."

"If you're playing with me right now—"

She laughed and held her arms up. "Not playing! It's all yours.
Just don't start any fires or punch any holes through the wall."

I couldn't accept a gift this big. I had to turn it down. "All right,
fine, no punching," I said.

"I told you." She stepped right up to me, cupping my cheek in
her hand. "We take care of each other."

"I . . . Thank you so much," I said.

"Oh, it was nothing." Forget their secrets and their rumors. To
bypass the New York real estate market? *This* was true power.
Margot smiled, then stretched her arms out, rolling her head from
side to side, reaching down and touching her toes as if psyching
herself up for something. "Okay!" she said when she straightened
back up again. "I have to go to an opening. But the key's on the
kitchen table for you. I'll be curious to hear how you like it. You
have my number, so call me tomorrow. I love talking on the phone,
don't you?"

"No!" I said. "It makes me anxious and I'm bad at it."

"Well." She winked. "Practice makes perfect."

As soon as Margot left, I started whirling through the open hallways, sliding down the hardwood floors in my socks. I opened and closed all the drawers in the bedroom, pressed my cheek against the marble countertops in the kitchen, rolled around on the king-size mattress in my new bedroom, alternately laughing and on the verge of tears. Margot had described it as house-sitting, but more than that, it felt like I had a patron.

I found a new place. Will move the rest of my things out tomorrow, I texted Sara and Rob.

Good for you, Sara wrote back. She and Rob were probably pitying me right now, imagining that I'd landed in some dump with six roommates and no fridge. I fought the urge to send them a picture of my new bedroom like a petty little bitch. Luckily, a text from Raf popped up, distracting me from my worst impulses.

Hey, our supplier accidentally gave us a ton of extra bread. Want me to bring some home for breakfast?

Normally: yes of course why are you even asking, I texted back. **But I won't be there for breakfast cause I got an apartment! You're once again free to do whatever weird stuff you want on your couch.**

The three dots that meant he was typing appeared, then disappeared, then appeared again, until finally he sent back a thumbs-up emoji.

I bit my lip. **But if you're desperate to get rid of the bread and want to check the place out, you should come by,** I texted. **Prepare yourself: it's a shithole.**

TWENTY-FOUR

Raf showed up a few hours later, a couple of crusty loaves in tow, and I ushered him inside. "You're pranking me," he said, turning around in circles and staring with his mouth ajar, so I explained the situation.

"Damn, maybe you should forget the article and stay in the club," he joked. A sudden paranoia seized me.

"You've gotta come see the bathroom," I said, turning on my heel and power walking through the hall. The moment we entered the bathroom, I shut the door behind us and turned on the shower. (Of course it was a rainfall showerhead, spraying steady, soothing jets.)

"Uh, what are you doing?" Raf asked, shifting his weight. He tugged off his baseball cap and held it in front of his chest, fiddling with it.

"The *Gone Girl* thing," I said. He looked at me uncomprehendingly. Right, Raf didn't really watch movies. (In his free time, he devoured fantasy books, the kind with cheap-looking covers and complicated titles like *The Mists of the Krampledern*.) "I know this sounds nuts," I whispered, leaning in close, "but remember how they had people following me around? What if this apartment is bugged?"

He let out a breath. "They wouldn't do that, would they?"

"They sent a woman to hit on you and make sure we were dating, so I'm gonna go with . . . yes?" We were very close now as we whispered, steam rising up around us from the shower. It swirled in the air.

"Okay," Raf said. A bead of sweat glided, slow and smooth, down the side of his cheek, along his neck, down underneath the lip of his T-shirt. I realized I'd been watching its progress only when Raf cleared his throat. "Should we check? It couldn't hurt."

I stepped away from him. "Yeah, let's."

After a quick how-to session on Google, we searched the apartment for hidden cameras, recording devices on the walls. "Just look at these gorgeous paintings!" I said, surreptitiously running my fingers along the sides of the frames.

"You could write a whole new novel at this desk," Raf said, ducking underneath it and checking the wood.

We opened the cabinets and shook out the curtains, doing our Couple in Love playacting the whole time, just in case. "Not to get ahead of ourselves," I said, looking closely at the walls in the kitchen, "but if we ever move in together, I'd want our apartment to have this color scheme."

"You don't think it washes me out?" he asked, striking a pose, and I laughed.

As the prospect of finding a bug began to diminish, our pretending got goofier and goofier. "This flat-screen is nice," Raf said, inspecting the gigantic TV, deepening his voice, contorting his face into a parody of a 1950s sitcom dad. "But *our* children will have limited screen time. It's important for kids to play outside and eat dirt!"

"Yes, darling," I said. "Dirt will be the main dish at every family dinner."

Finally, after we finished our search with a thorough sweep of the bedroom, we collapsed on the bed, turned onto our sides facing each other. "I think we're safe," I whispered, and we high-fived.

"Shit, this bed is comfy," he said, and pretended to fall asleep on it, closing his eyes and letting out big fake snores until I poked him repeatedly in the stomach. He held up his hands to protect himself. "Okay, okay! I guess I should head out."

Words rose up in my throat, words that scared the crap out of me, so I swallowed them. Raf furrowed his brow at the look on my face. "What?"

I sat up. "Oh, just realizing how late it got. It's been a long day."

I walked him out and closed the door after him, then leaned against it, the words I'd swallowed pinging around in my head: *Or you could stay.* In the moment when he'd said he was going to leave, all I'd wanted was to tuck my head into the crook of his neck, to press my body into his and let him wrap his arms around me until we fell asleep together.

It wasn't too late for me to fling the door open and run after him, to stop him before he got into the elevator. And then what? I'd ask him to stay and he'd turn me down, and things between us would get all awkward. Or worse, he'd say yes, and yes again, yes and yes and yes until one day a few months from now, one of us decided to say no. And then things between us would be more than awkward. They would be ruined.

Get a grip, Beckley, I chastised myself. *You're just lonely and horny.*

I was not going to screw up the best friendship I had, the only relationship I could truly rely on, just because of a strange, voracious urge to feel Raf's lips on my collarbone.

What I needed was to get laid. I was entering my sexual peak, baby! I shouldn't be depriving the world of my bedroom skills, which were adequate. New York City was full of attractive strangers. I'd download Tinder.

No, I couldn't exactly go on a public dating app, where someone connected to Nevertheless might find me. Besides, I'd never been great at casual sex. The liberated women of today were supposed to be able to fuck their way through anything—boredom, grief, existential despair—but I never enjoyed sex that much the first time with someone new. I was always anxious about what they thought of me. Were my hands too sweaty? Was my cellulite too glaring? What if they, God forbid, wanted me to call them "Daddy," so I tried but it came out sounding dumb? And then there was the running commentary in my head about *their* body. What was that mole on their shoulder? Was it malignant? Would I fall for them only to lose them to this CANCEROUS MOLE?

No getting laid tonight for me, then. Instead, I masturbated, trying to keep the faceless figures in my head (going at it in the backseat of a parked car) from morphing into me and Raf, me and Miles, Raf and Margot, me and Margot.

When I finished and caught my breath, I decided that we should end the dating charade after Caroline's gala. It had served its purpose, so it was time to "part ways" amicably. Then, the weirdness it had caused to spring up between us would simply disappear.

Later, swaddled in sheets with a thousand thread count, drifting off to sleep more easily than I had in weeks, a thought occurred to me, hazy and half-formed, prompted by Raf's joke that I should just forget the article and stay in the club: There was a version of my life where I didn't sell them all out. Where I was their kept woman, their pen-is-mightier-than-the-sword warrior. I lived in the apartments they found for me (with no rent to pay, and with me picking up more bartending shifts, I'd have enough money for dues!) and eviscerated their enemies, and I never had to disappoint them, never had to watch the regard they had for me drain from their faces. In my half-asleep state, that kind of life didn't sound so bad.

TWENTY-FIVE

The piece I had written went up the next morning as a Twitter thread from an anonymous account and spread like wildfire. Iris Ngoza was the first woman to retweet to her hundreds of thousands of followers. She posted the thread with an outraged, surprised comment, as if she'd just stumbled upon it and had never heard of the man before. (Probably a better strategy than going with the more honest *Please read! I set his destruction in motion a week ago!*) Soon enough, prominent women who *weren't* in Nevertheless began tweeting about it, and some prominent male allies too. A petition went up online, calling for the judge to recuse himself from the case, and garnered thousands of signatures.

It had been strange, thrilling, to watch the fuss and furor over my words all day long while in real life, no one gave me a second look. I moved the first round of my things to my new fancy apartment, lugging boxes and suitcases on the subway, and every time someone glared at me for taking up space, I just nodded at them serenely. I was Elena Ferrante. No, Banksy! I began to understand how power could be addictive. How, maybe, the women in Nevertheless developed a taste for it, and started wanting more.

I held on to that feeling when I went back to the house for my second and final round of belongings, letting my victory keep me warm as I said good-bye to my empty childhood bedroom, as I breathed in the air of my mother's room and pressed my hand against her old blue wallpaper for the last time. As I lost her in one more way.

Later, as I was hanging up clothes in my new closet, Margot sent me a wave emoji. *Just call her,* I told myself. *You won't be annoying her. She* asked *you to.* I shook out my whole body, and then pressed her number.

"Hi, you," she said when she picked up. "How did you sleep?"

"Like a fucking baby," I said.

"I've always thought that was a strange expression. Aren't babies notorious for waking up multiple times a night?"

I laughed. "Excellent point. Like a teenage boy?"

"Much better. Do you think the place will start to feel like home soon?"

We talked all about the apartment, and then I prepared myself for the good-bye, but she didn't want to stop. Instead, she whirled from topic to topic as I—dizzy and excited—ran to catch up. She was rereading *Sense and Sensibility* and asked if I'd ever cried while reading Jane Austen, because she wept at every single one.

She wanted to talk about the gallery opening she'd gone to the night before. "I thought I was just going as a favor to Vy—she's looking for inspiration for her next project, so she's trying to see what's out there right now—but I found myself unexpectedly moved by it. There were all these gigantic sculptures, evocative of

Stonehenge, asking all sorts of questions about faith and belief. It really made you think about the role of the mystical in everyday life, how so many things just happen but we don't think about why."

"Whoa," I said. I imagined Margot trying to have this conversation with Caroline, Caroline halfheartedly feigning interest and then changing the subject.

"Do you believe in anything?" Margot asked me.

"Climate change."

"Well, obviously. But beyond science, I mean."

"Nah, I've always been pretty certain that life is random and that eventually we all become nothing but worm food."

"Hmm," she said, and I sensed that it wasn't the answer she'd been looking for.

"But," I added hastily, "I've also always thought that I could be convinced to change my mind."

She got quiet for a moment on her end of the line. She was probably gathering her thoughts, getting ready to say something, but I wasn't sure. Dammit, this was why I hated talking on the phone. Right as I opened my mouth to break the silence, she spoke. "For me, after my mother died, the idea of us all turning into nothing but worm food became unbearable."

"Oh," I said. "Of course. I understand that."

"And yet you still believe the worm food?"

"Yes, but also . . ." I hesitated, then plunged on, feeling that, of anyone I knew, Margot might understand. "Even though I know that my mother is gone entirely, I keep thinking I see her everywhere. Like I'm catching little glimpses of her soul, attaching itself to other people so that she can come check in on me or tell me something—" I cut myself off. "It sounds silly, I know."

"It doesn't," Margot said. "I've felt that way sometimes too. I even went to a medium once, not long after mine died."

"Did . . . did it help you?"

"No, that medium was so clearly faking it all."

"When did your mom die?" I asked her, even though I already knew.

"When I was twenty. It was so sudden. One day everything was fine, the next she was gone. I think the grief made me lose myself a little bit. Do you know what I mean?"

"Yeah, I do."

"It led me to that controlling relationship I told you about, and it's why I stayed in it for so long. I just wanted someone else to tell me what to do. I didn't even notice when he stopped helping and started hurting me instead. And then I looked up and realized I had spent years and years with someone who didn't respect me. Someone who didn't trust me or think that I was smart, who only wanted me to be a little plaything he could take out and use, and then shut away."

I wished I could pass through the phone to Margot's side and wrap my arms around her. "Oh, Margot, I'm sorry," I said. "But you got out."

"I did. And I won't let people control me again," Margot said, then let out a noise of surprise. "Oh, it's been forty-five minutes! I suppose I should go work or something." She paused, and then, her voice full of mischief, all traces of our serious conversation gone, said, "By the way, I wanted to ask: Have you heard about this Twitter thread that's been making the rounds today? I think it's really going to have an impact."

"Hmm, interesting," I said. "Who wrote it?"

"It was some anonymous account," she said. "They didn't even have any kind of profile image. But whoever they were, I'm very impressed by them." I smiled. "I wonder," she went on, "if you might be interested in saying yes to other things within the club as well."

"More articles? Sure."

"That, maybe. But also, opportunities to get closer to some of the women. A more . . ." She paused. "Curated experience. More intense too. It would require a certain commitment. Certain sacrifices."

My heart began to pound. "Yes," I said. "Yeah. I could be very into that."

"Good to know. I'll be pulling for you."

TWENTY-SIX

That night, I worked a shift at the bar, a secret smile on my face. Of course none of the patrons, who were glued to the football game, had any idea that I'd become an Internet vigilante. I doubted that any one of them even had a Twitter account. I closed out a group of customers and turned to a new guest who had just slid onto a stool.

"What can I do for—"

"It was you, wasn't it?" Miles asked.

"Um, hello," I said, and blinked a couple times, confirming that my eyes weren't lying to me. Yup, Miles, wearing a gray sweater with the sleeves pushed up. He looked like he hadn't been sleeping particularly well, and yet somehow he pulled it off, dammit, as if he weren't sleeping because his mind was too busy with fascinating thoughts, thoughts that you'd be lucky to know. "What was me? And what are you doing here?" I'd mentioned the bar to him before, but he'd never come. And considering how things had gone the last time we talked, I hadn't exactly been expecting that to change.

He shrugged. "I was walking by, so I thought I'd get a nightcap, see if you were on shift." The bar wasn't near the *Standard*, and it wasn't particularly close to Miles's neighborhood either. I smelled bullshit. I also smelled tequila—this wasn't his first drink of the evening.

"Well, here I am."

"Could I get a gin and tonic?" I poured him one, and when I handed it to him, he said, "It was you who wrote the thread about Melton."

"I don't know what you're talking about," I said.

"Right," he said, and gave me a small, wry smile. "Once you spend some time editing the Jillian Beckley voice, it becomes unmistakable." Screw Cinderella's prince, searching far and wide for the maiden whose foot would fit the glass slipper. Miles could see words I'd written and know immediately that they belonged to me. I hated that he recognized me like that, and I loved it too.

He took a sip of his drink. "Unclear if any of it was properly sourced or just total hearsay, but it was good. Really good."

I threw the bar towel over my shoulder and put my hand on my hip, affecting a much cooler posture than I actually felt. "So you're being nice to me again? To what do I owe the honor?"

He looked up from his glass and leaned forward against the bar, hangdog eyes looking into mine. "I was too harsh on you. I'm sorry. A whole combination of things was going on with me, and I shouldn't have spoken to you like that."

"Well. Thank you," I said, then added, "What combination?"

He leaned back again. "Oh, you know. Another piece I'd been working on got bumped from the issue, Emmy and I were in the midst of a huge fight, things like that." He was silent a moment. "It's been a bigger adjustment to working at the *Standard* than I thought it would be."

"Poor Miles," I said. "It's hard for you not to be the undisputed top dog?"

"Yes!" he said. I rolled my eyes as he continued, "I know, I know, I'm a dick."

"A little bit."

"But I'm smart! I'm good at what I do. And so far in my professional career, whenever I've worked hard enough at something, I've mastered it. Since I've started at the *Standard*, though, I . . ." His voice got lower, so low that I had to step forward to hear it. "I keep screwing it up. I'm worried that I won't be able to stop."

I grew careful—no sudden movements—afraid that I'd startle him off before he could finish talking. He'd never shown this kind of weakness to me before. Not that he'd pretended he was perfect in every aspect of his life—he'd shown me that he wasn't when he sucked my face. But I'd never heard him express vulnerability about his professional competence. He always seemed so naturally good, so certain that he was right. Historically, I'd been turned on by talent. Nothing made me want to tear my clothes off like a big, throbbing brain, and Miles's was one of the biggest, most throbbing ones I'd encountered. But now, as Miles let me glimpse his doubt, puncturing the illusion, I didn't lose a single ounce of respect for him. I only loved him more.

"I've finally gotten my chance at bat, and I've forgotten how to swing. That's the biggest reason I was a jerk. When you told me about the NDA, I realized I'd made one more misstep."

"Hey, it was *my* misstep, not yours."

"No. It belonged to both of us. I probably shouldn't tell you this, but—" He sighed. "Oh, screw it. After I knew you were getting invited into the club, I passed up a different story that my bosses wanted me to take on so that I could focus on yours. They didn't understand why, so I talked you up more than I should have, created a situation where there was no wiggle room. I made an error in professional judgment and staked too much on this story, because I know you're wonderful and wanted the bosses to see it too."

I had no idea if anyone else was trying to get my attention to order a drink, and I didn't care. In the dim lighting, Miles and I were the only two people in the whole place. "Are you in trouble with your higher-ups now?"

"Don't worry about it."

"Don't dodge the question," I said as he ran his fingers through his hair, then rested his hand on the bar. "Tell me the truth." I put my hand on top of his, and he looked up again, right into my eyes.

"I don't know. But they want to schedule a performance review."

"I mean, that's got to be normal, right? In a new job?"

"I asked around, and I don't think it is. Not this soon."

"Shit. I am so sorry," I said. "I didn't mean to—"

"Hey. It's not your fault. Or, I guess it is in a way. Your fault for being so talented and making me want you to succeed."

"We're still going to succeed," I said. "Maybe you've never experienced this before, but when the rest of us mortals start a new job, there's always an adjustment period. You're not getting sent back to the bench, though. You're too fucking good for that. I'll get you something unassailable that you can bring into that performance review."

"You don't need to . . ." He cut himself off, chewed on his lip. "You don't need to make promises that you can't keep."

"I'm not," I said, and smiled at him. "This mess, right now? It's just a hiccup. You're still going to ascend to that Media Throne.

King of the Editors. David Remnick had better watch his back."
He let out a soft laugh.

"Jesus, Beckley," he said, shaking his head. My hand was still
resting on top of his, and he turned his over so that our palms were
touching. "You make my life very difficult."

"I know," I said. He curled his fingers over mine, brushing my
skin with his thumb, back and forth. We stayed like that, not speaking, just touching, breathing, until a man down at the bar started
waving his arm frantically for my service.

"All right, I'll let you do your job," Miles said, putting some
money on the bar. "But I'll see you soon?" He paused. "I want to
see you soon."

"The Women Who Lead gala is at the end of the week. I'll be
there, along with a lot of the women from the club. Maybe you
should get yourself a press pass, like last year," I said.

He raised an eyebrow. "Maybe I will."

TWENTY-SEVEN

Things happened quickly with the judge. My post had struck a nerve—the right words at the right time—and caused some legit reporters who had been quietly digging to kick their work into high gear. Only a few days later, on the night of Caroline's gala, the *New York Times* published a more substantiated account of his conflicts of interest, citing my anonymous post in the body of the article. It seemed Craig Melton might not be long for the bench.

Margot texted me the link as I was getting ready for the gala, and I read it while brushing my hair. "Holy shit," I said, my heart thumping.

Raf ducked his head out of my bathroom. "What?" Since the gala was only a ten-minute walk from my place, he'd come straight to my apartment from the restaurant to get ready with me, toting a garment bag with his tuxedo inside of it. He'd bought this tux—

his first one—a couple of months ago, when he'd started getting invited to fancy events, but still felt self-conscious and constrained in it. Now he wore only the tuxedo pants and an undershirt, waiting until the last possible moment to put the rest of it on.

"Look at this article," I said, holding out my phone to him, and he began to read. His undershirt showed off the muscles in his arms. They weren't large—he wasn't chugging protein powder and doing dead lifts in the gym—but still, they were sinewy. Solid. Sexy? No!

"This article is happening because of what you wrote?" he asked. Our eyes met as I nodded. "Jilly, that's amazing," he said, his face breaking open into a smile, and I felt a weird zing inside of me. *Stop that*, I told my vagina.

"Hopefully it'll be enough for the inner circle," I said, breaking our eye contact, moving away from him. "Okay, I'm gonna put on my dress."

I emerged from my bedroom a couple of minutes later, struggling with the zipper of an off-the-shoulder floor-length gown. It was black, velvet, and '80s inspired. Or rather, not '80s *inspired*, but actually '80s, since that was when my mom had bought it. This was the one thing I took with me from her closet. The one thing that still smelled like her. (Even though that must have been just my imagination. She hadn't worn it in decades.)

"You look . . ." Raf began, then cleared his throat. "You look nice." He had changed fully into the tux by now. It made him into a man. He came behind me to zip my dress up the rest of the way, and his fingers brushed against my back.

"Thanks. All dress credit goes to my mom."

"Damn," he said, stepping back and taking in the dress again. It was fitted around the waist and hips, with a slit to show off some leg. "This was Kathleen's?"

"Yeah. She wore it to one fancy event in her twenties, and then she saved it forever because it was the nicest outfit she ever owned. Well, besides her wedding dress, but she threw that off a bridge after the divorce."

"No," Raf said. "She threw it off a bridge?"

"Yeah," I said. "At least that's what she told me. When the divorce was finalized, she drank a bottle of champagne and threw her wedding dress into the river."

"Kathleen," Raf said, laughing. He shook his head. "She was the best. And that was her necklace too, right?" I touched the chain around my neck and nodded. His face grew contemplative. "We used to hang out my senior year, when you'd gone off to college. Did you know that? I'd go over to your house on Sunday mornings when my parents were at church, and we'd have breakfast together. She made the strongest coffee I'd ever tasted." He paused. "It was not good. It was tar."

"Oh, it was fully disgusting," I said.

"Yeah, and she didn't like milk or cream, so she never kept any around the house!"

"When I realized you could add things to coffee to make it taste good, it was a revelation."

Raf smiled. "Anyway, I thought I was doing her a favor, going over on Sundays. You were gone. She was lonely. It was a way to get my parents to stop bugging me about church. But then when she went out of town for a couple weeks on vacation and we had to skip the breakfasts, I was kinda sad. She was fun. Funny. Just . . . nice to be around."

I swallowed. "She loved you. She was really proud of you. One of the last things she ever did was hang up your *Vanity Fair* article on our fridge."

"Really?" he asked. "That's nice to know. I miss her. Not as much as you do, I'm sure. But sometimes when I'm lonely, I think about how nice it would be to call up Kathleen."

I wasn't going to mess up my makeup for the gala by getting all teary-eyed and sentimental, so I shook my head and said, "Strange, I think about that sometimes too." I squared my shoulders. "Okay, let's go. Couple in Love?"

"Couple in Love," he said.

TWENTY-EIGHT

The gala was on the top floor of a hotel overlooking Central Park. Floor-to-ceiling windows revealed an expanse of dark trees on one side and the lights of Columbus Circle on the other. The red taillights of cars glittered down below. When you were so far above everyone else, even traffic looked pretty.

Caroline had gone for an autumnal theme, with staff tastefully placing bowls of freshly picked apples from Hudson Valley farms on various surfaces. Knobby decorative gourds adorned the tabletops where we would be sitting down to dinner. Everywhere, the well-dressed elite milled around, including a few minor and not-so-minor political figures. Some of the Nevertheless women were there, Iris Ngoza and a couple others whose names I didn't know. They murmured something to each other and sent approving looks my way. Because of Raf, who had cleaned up so nicely, standing by my side.

Sure enough, Iris turned and made her way over to us. "Rafael Morales? I'm a huge fan of your restaurant," she said, and then focused on me. "And, Jillian, you're a writer, yes? I've enjoyed some of your work. I'm finishing a book too, nonfiction, a manifesto on body positivity that a publishing company asked me to write. If you ever want to talk shop or have me put in a good word for you at my imprint, please let me know." She smiled at me and walked away, as if getting a book deal were just that easy, like all one had to do was snap one's (unequivocally accepted and loved) fingers. So the hum in the air wasn't all about Raf. People knew about the *New York Times*.

"I'm going to go check our coats," Raf said.

"I'll grab us some drinks." I held out my hand as if we were in a sports huddle, and he put his on top of mine.

"Break!" we said. I turned back to the crowd.

An official photographer loped from group to group, snapping pictures, while some members of the press chatted with the luminaries. I looked for Miles but didn't see him. Probably better if he didn't show up. Whenever Miles and I had been in the same room together at Quill, we were connected by an invisible string. I was always aware of his presence, tugging quietly at me, even as I did whatever else I needed to do. If he came to the gala, I would have to acknowledge that I knew him—after all, we had a proven track record of working together at Quill—but not let on anything about our continued acquaintance. Tonight, I needed to assure my invitation to the inner circle, not get all distracted by whether or not Miles was looking at me. Still, I longed for him to see me in this dress.

I wandered into the fray as a jazz trio played standards in the corner and waiters walked around offering bacon-wrapped dates.

There, waiting for cocktails at the bar, were Caroline and Libby, smiling at each other.

"It's only my second East Coast autumn," Libby was saying to Caroline as I made my way toward them, "and it's truly blowing my mind. Like, I just want to leaf-peep all day long?"

"That's adorable," Caroline said, putting her hand on her heart, looking at Libby like she was a loyal puppy. "And correct. Autumn is the best season."

"Yeah, summer can go fuck itself with a butternut squash," I said.

Caroline blinked. "Jillian. Hi."

Libby squealed and threw her arms around me. "You look gorgeous! So retro." She looked pretty herself, pink-cheeked, in a gold-sequined dress that showed off her curves. Caroline, meanwhile, wore an ivory dress with a feathered bottom (like a bride, marrying her nonprofit), and a diamond necklace that managed to convey that, while she was *very* rich, she wasn't the kind of woman to spend all of her money on luxuries when she could use some of it to save the world. Her eyes darted around the gala as if she were running through the world's longest to-do list in her head, checking things off in record time.

"You've done a beautiful job," I said to Caroline. "I mean, I know the night has barely started, but already I'm impressed."

"I had a lot of help from Libby in pulling everything together this week," Caroline said.

"Oh, it was my pleasure," Libby said. "Seriously so fun. I felt like I was in *The Devil Wears Prada*, but with a *nice* boss!"

"Exciting day all around," I said. "A gala, some interesting stories in the *New York Times*—"

Caroline's eyes landed on a server with a tray of hors d'oeuvres.

"Excuse me." She marched off toward him. "Are those mushroom tarts? No, the senator is allergic!"

As Caroline continued to lecture the waiter while greeting whichever important new arrivals came her way, Libby glanced around, then said, almost shyly, "I wanted to tell you . . . Keep this between us for now, please. But I've been thinking a lot about what you said at our sleepover, about your mother and how much you wished you could still talk to her. And so . . ." She blew out a breath and then said, in a rush, "I called my mom last night."

"Holy shit," I said. "How did it go?"

"Oh," she said, her eyes growing a little red, "we talked for two hours straight and then I agreed to go home for Thanksgiving. She even said she was going to work on my dad to convince him to stop by at some point. Which I have more mixed feelings about, and he probably won't even come, but it's sweet anyway."

"I'm really happy for you," I said, and I was, even if I did feel a tingling in my throat—treacherous, jealous tears—as she glowed, lit up from within like a jack-o'-lantern, very on theme for this gala's autumnal decor.

"We'll just have to watch a lot of movies and not discuss anything political. But it'll be nice, I think." She cut herself off, looking at me. "Oh, I am being so insensitive. Do you have a place to go for Thanksgiving?"

"I . . ." I hesitated.

"I'm sure Raf will want you to go home with him, but if for whatever reason that doesn't work out, you should come with me."

"You don't have to say that."

"I mean it! I know how hard it is not to have a place to go. And besides, it'll be fun. We're going to stuff you full of so much good food, and my mom will have to be extra nice to me because we have a guest. So, win-win." She beamed. "I've got your back, you've got mine!"

"Thanks, I'll think about it," I said, the tingling in my throat intensifying. How dare she be so thoughtful, to offer a solution to something I didn't even realize I'd been worrying about? I grabbed two glasses of champagne, taking a large swig out of one. "I should go find Raf."

I found him, all right, in the middle of a conversation with Miles—the two of them in their tuxedos angled toward each other, bean-pole Raf nearly half a head taller than distinguished Miles. Neither one of them was entirely relaxed in this upscale scene. Or maybe something else was causing the tension in their bodies.

Raf turned toward me as I approached, and I watched Miles watch Raf watch me. And then Miles turned and saw me for him-self. His eyes traveled over my body, and it got very warm in the event hall.

"Um, hi, guys," I said.

"Ah, Jillian," Miles said, and casually shook my hand, although he squeezed my fingers before letting go of them. He held a half-empty scotch in his other hand. "I was just introducing myself to your celebrity chef, hoping to get a quote or two from him on why he's attending this gala. What do you say, Mr. Morales?" He pulled a voice recorder out of his pocket and held it up to Raf's mouth. "Any thoughts on the patriarchal underpinnings that prevent women from reaching true representational parity?"

Raf flushed, uncomfortable. "Oh, um, I don't need to—"

"You know why he's here, Miles," I said, and put my arm around Raf's waist, handing him my extra glass of champagne. "Because he is a wonderful, supportive boyfriend."

"Right, right, of course." Miles took another sip of his drink. "You two make a beautiful couple." He lowered his voice and continued, in a sardonic tone, "Very convincing. I would never have guessed that you're not actually into each other."

"You're not into each other?" a voice said from behind us, and I turned to see Vy, standing very close, her face unreadable, wearing a canvas jumpsuit and work boots just like she'd wear to anything else, holding a napkin full of shrimp. Miles, Raf, and I startled.

"No!" I said. "No, it's a stupid joke."

"I was teasing," Miles said. "Because they're so clearly smitten."

Vy picked a piece of shrimp out of her teeth, staring at us.

"You know, when you really like someone," I said, "and so you're like, *Oh, I can't stand him?*"

"No," Vy said.

"Like," Raf said, "Um, *I hate her so much that I think about her all day.*"

"Right," I said, looking at Raf, putting my hand on his cheek, "Like, *Ugh, your stupid mouth is so disgusting that I just want to kiss it all the time.*"

"You can kiss," Vy said, dead-faced. "I won't be offended."

"Oh," I said, "No, I didn't mean, like, *now.* In public—"

"All right, well, I should—" Miles began.

"No one cares," Vy said, not looking away from our faces as she began to chew one of the shrimp from her napkin. "So why not?"

I let out an awkward laugh as Raf shifted uncomfortably beside me. "Oh, I don't know," I said after a beat of silence, when I realized she was actually expecting an answer. The wheels in her head were probably turning now—first my comment during the tarot reading about how I hadn't gotten laid in so long, now this.

"Then go ahead and do it if you want to," she said, almost a dare.

"Um. Okay," I said, panicking. I turned to Raf and tried to telegraph a *Be cool, man* message with my eyes as I put my hand back on his warm cheek. I leaned forward and brushed my lips against his. At first he was rigid, and then he put his hand on my neck and kissed me back, tangling his fingers in my hair. I forgot about our strange circumstances, the people watching us, for a moment. The only immediate thing was the unexpected, lovely feel of Raf's mouth on mine.

We broke apart slowly, and I came back to myself. Raf's ears were pink. Miles had a strange expression on his face.

"Okay," Vy said.

Miles cleared his throat. "Well, thank you for the interesting quotes. Enjoy the rest of the gala." He gave a small salute and sauntered off, right as Margot appeared, resplendent in a diaphanous, dark green gown, looking like an ancient Greek goddess.

She noticed us and made her way to our side. Margot moved through the room, through *all* rooms, as if she were floating on a rowboat, trailing her fingers through the water while someone else did all the paddling.

"What an incredible event," she said as she hugged each of us in turn. Then she pulled me aside as Vy began to talk to Raf. "So the *New York Times*, huh? I'm glad you said yes to our little writing assignment."

"I'm glad I did too," I said. "It's wild."

She faced out, surveying the crowd, and we both concentrated on drinking our champagne, not looking directly at each other. "I've been talking to Caroline about what we discussed," she said. "I made the case for you."

"Oh yeah?"

"There's limited space, though." Her eyes flickered over to Caroline, who had somehow ended up talking to Libby again. "And she has someone else in mind." Libby leaned in to Caroline like a flower bending toward the sun. The two of them laughed so heartily it was like they'd gone into slow motion, heads thrown back, eyes closing. I'd never seen Caroline so at ease. Maybe Libby's constant adulation filled some need inside of her, proved that someone could be drawn more to her than to Margot.

Margot bit her lip. "She gets final say on this one. I owe her, and she won't let me forget that." A stormy expression passed over her face, a note of agitation in her voice. "I want it to be you and I'm still trying, but if there's anything you can do to convince her yourself, do it tonight." She put her now-empty champagne flute on the tray of a passing waiter. "Good to see you." She kissed my cheek, then turned and tapped Vy on the shoulder. "Shall we?" Together, the two of them waded into the crowd while Raf and I stared after them, silent for a moment.

"This night is very weird," Raf said.

"Sorry about the kiss and all of that. That was so stupid of Miles—"

"Yeah, what was that dude's deal?"

"I don't even . . . He's going through some stuff." I shook my head. "How was your conversation with Vy?"

"Well, she said she couldn't stay long because she had to feed Anais, and I asked if that was her dog, but no. It's her emotional support snake," Raf said. "And then she showed me five pictures of the snake."

"What? What kind of snake is it?"

"I don't know. Big. And then she looked at me for a long time and told me I smelled like I had an honest heart. And then . . ."

"And then?"

Raf gave a funny little cough. "That was pretty much all she said."

"Really—" I began. But I didn't have time to prod him on that because Caroline excused herself from Libby and headed toward the bathroom, and I knew it was my shot to catch her alone.

"Be back in just a minute," I said to Raf.

TWENTY-NINE

I was standing in the bathroom, redoing my lipstick in the mirror, when Caroline emerged from behind the floor-to-ceiling door of her stall.

"Oh, hey, girl!" I said, too enthusiastically. I reined myself in. "Great gala so far."

"Thank you," she said, pulling an oil-removing wipe out of her purse and dabbing at her face with small, sharp movements. "Yes, it's a fun night, but it's really all about the funds we can raise to help female candidates."

"Of course," I said. The *New York Times* was the best chance I had of impressing her. "God, you must have been so busy today. Did you even have a chance to look at the news?"

"Hardly," she said, and threw the wipe away. She gave her cheeks a little slap, for energy or for color, maybe, and then looked toward the door. "Well, once more unto the breach!"

"The *Times* picked up my thread on Judge Melton!" I blurted as she began to leave. Caroline froze, then turned around and stared at me as I continued, in a lower voice, "So it's a good day for women in general—" In another stall, the toilet flushed. I froze too.

Caroline grabbed my arm, her tiny fingers digging in, her manicured nails sharp against my skin. "Come here," she hissed, and dragged me out of the bathroom to a small alcove down the hall leading to the kitchen. A few members of the waitstaff passed by us, but Caroline didn't care about them as she rounded on me.

"Why the hell would you bring that up like that?"

"I am so sorry, I didn't realize anyone else was in there—"

"That was careless, Jillian," she said, pointing her finger at me. "Don't do it again." She tossed her head, finished with the conversation, and I knew it was my final chance.

"I won't," I said. "I did something stupid, because I was trying to impress you." Caroline was a negotiator, so I threw my shoulders back, praying I was making the right move. "I should have just asked you straight out for what I want, like we've said that women should do." I lowered my voice and looked her straight in the eye. "I know that you're picking someone new for the inner circle." Caroline stiffened, pursing her lips, as I went on. "I could be helpful to you in it. I'm asking you to choose me."

Caroline let my words hang in the air for a moment. Then she sighed. "I appreciate your candor, Jillian." She shook her head. "But the inner circle is serious. I've made my decision. I need someone I can trust. Someone steady who puts the group ahead of themselves, like I do, or like Libby."

"Like Libby," I repeated, a roaring noise beginning in my ears. They were going to pick Libby, who would weep with gratitude for it.

"Yes. She's so dedicated to us. For her, we're her *family*."

The words bubbled up and overflowed before I could stop them. "Are you sure of that?"

Caroline furrowed her brow. "What do you mean?"

An image appeared in my mind: Libby, with her bright and trusting eyes, in her lonely apartment modeled after TV shows, cradling her sweet rat dog in her arms. She was so close to getting what she'd wanted, to knowing there was a place where she belonged. And she deserved that. She was a good person, who'd been nothing but generous since the moment we met, who'd snuck her way into my heart and invited me, with no hesitation, to fucking Thanksgiving. Libby would fight for me if they ever had another opening, but when would another opening arise? Sometime long after the women of Nevertheless had inflicted more damage on their enemies, long after Miles's performance review, after I'd ruined my chance to write for the *Standard* or anywhere else of repute. I could keep up with the lies only so much longer. Soon, I'd have to leave the club and the apartment it had given me. Libby would put in a good word for me after the ax had fallen on my neck, and that good word would be useless.

Libby was only one person. The information I would find in the back room could help so many more. I didn't have a choice, but I would make it up to her. I'd make sure that she got in too, eventually. I just needed it first. "Just that . . ." As if in a dream, I watched myself say, "Well, she's going home for Thanksgiving."

Caroline's nose twitched. "No. Sadly, she's had to reject her family. Their actions and beliefs—particularly about women—are toxic. We've talked all about it."

I hung my head and said, quietly, "She reached back out to them the other day. She just told me. She even invited me to come along."

"Well, that's . . ." Caroline said, and then trailed off, leaning against the wall.

"I love Libby. I do. And yes, she is so passionate about everything you represent," I continued, as the roaring in my ears got louder. "She's also going through a rebellious phase. And sometimes those phases last. But sometimes they don't, and if she goes back to them . . . I don't want to betray her trust. But I also don't want you all to open yourselves up to something that could hurt you if, after you let her see all the inner workings, she decides that her true place is with the people fighting against you."

"This is all a very interesting story, Jillian, but why should I believe you?" Caroline asked, straightening back up and blinking rapidly. Were her eyes turning just the slightest bit red?

"Here," I said. My stomach starting to churn, I pulled out my phone and typed up a text to Libby. **Thanks for inviting me to Thanksgiving. In case it wasn't clear, I'm really excited for you, and I hope you and your dad get to make some peace.**

I sent the text and we waited, silent, our heads bowed over my screen as the three dots that meant Libby was typing appeared. Part of me hoped that she wouldn't be stupid enough to trust me.

But then the words came through: **Thanks lady, fingers crossed!**

Caroline clenched her entire body—her jaw, her fists. Then she gave a little sniff out of her nose, turned on her sensible heels, and walked back into the main gala space. I followed her out, watching as she glad-handed and checked in with her invited guests, all the while making her way toward Libby, who was standing at the bar, trying to figure out how to insert herself into the conversations that various groups were having around her. As Caroline approached, Libby lit up, waving. I grabbed another glass of champagne from a nearby tray and tucked myself into a corner close enough to hear their conversation.

"Whew," Caroline said. "What a night."

"Everyone is having the best time!" Libby said.

"Honestly, I'll be relieved when it's over. I've been so consumed with planning that I've barely thought about anything else, and now Thanksgiving is just around the corner."

"I know!"

"Will you be spending the holiday in New York?" Caroline asked innocently, tilting her head to the side.

Libby paused, for just a second, and then said, "Hmm, I think so? I've been dying to see the parade in person, ever since I was little. I always thought it would be so fun to perform with one of the marching bands! I actually used to play the tuba, and I'd—"

"Interesting," Caroline said, her tone grown cold. "Excuse me, I need to announce dinner." She walked away and Libby stared after her, befuddled by the abrupt shift in energy. Caroline passed by me on her way to the dining room and shot me a glance. *You win*, it seemed to say, but it gave me no pleasure. I felt only a chill, as if all the blood pulsing inside my body had been sucked out and replaced with ice, as Caroline approached a microphone and announced that dinner was served.

The rest of the gala, I sat through the food and the speeches, through the auction where the attendees pledged hundreds of thousands of dollars for the cause. (And yet people pledged much less than they had the year before, now that there was no Nicole to pin their hopes on.)

That invisible string unspooled and connected me to Miles. Whenever I turned to look over at the press table where he was sitting, he was looking back. At one point, my phone buzzed in my purse and I pulled it out to see a text from him: **Dammit, Beckley. I'm an ass. Forgive me?**

But other strings tugged on me too, from so many directions—

Margot and Caroline, conferring in a corner. Raf, next to me, his leg brushing against mine under the table, sending aftershocks of our kiss rippling through me. And always, Libby, who chatted with the elderly couple seated next to her with only a fraction of her usual animation, sensing that something, somehow, had gone amiss.

As Raf and I were waiting in line to get our coats at the end of the evening, Margot passed by, touching my shoulder lightly.

"Whatever you did worked," she said to me, and a brief, unguarded smile—full of joy or maybe triumph—flashed across her face. "Will you be sleeping at your apartment the next few nights?" I nodded mutely.

"Good," she said. "Make sure you're alone."

THIRTY

The night after the gala, worn out by stress and shame, I fell asleep earlier than I had in weeks, at the entirely reasonable hour of eleven P.M. Who was I, a retiree?

I dreamed of Margot, underwater, her toes just barely kissing the sand beneath her, her cloud of hair rising up above her head as she beckoned me. I was underwater too, trying to get to her, a humming, groaning noise all around us, everything greenish, brackish, and somehow, despite the water, I could smell her. I blinked, and she flickered, and then she wasn't Margot anymore but my mother. She reached out an arm toward me, and her arm was *healthy*, not stick thin like it had gotten over the years of chemo. I tried to swim to her but I couldn't breathe, and I woke to find that I couldn't breathe because a hand was covering my nose and mouth.

There were people in my apartment.

Before I could consciously make sense of anything, a yell from some primal, terrified place tore through my throat. But the calloused hand over my mouth muffled it, and I knew that nobody would come to help me, that I was finally in that moment so many women experience, the moment when our luck runs out.

Then, the familiar jasmine scent of Margot's hair, and her voice in my ear. "We've come for you." In the faint light from the traffic outside my window, the dark figures around me came into focus, their faces hidden by hoods. Maybe six or seven of them? I saw them only for a second before one of the figures tied a cloth over my eyes, and then I couldn't see anything at all.

Someone slid a pair of shoes onto my feet. Then, mute, efficient, the figures led me out of my apartment and into the back of a vehicle. The seat was rough under the thin leggings I'd worn to bed. One of the women closed the door after me, sliding it instead of slamming it. So we were in a van, one that smelled faintly of paint and sweat. Maybe the sweat smell was coming from me.

The engine roared to life, and we began to move. From outside came the nighttime noises of New York: the honks of warring taxis, people coming home from the bars, others rowdily heading to a second location. But inside the van, all was silent except for some faint rustling, shifting of the bodies around me. "I've gotta say, I give this Uber points for good driving, but the 'fun conversation' is a little lacking," I joked. Nobody answered. Nobody laughed. (Which, given the quality of the joke, was fair.)

It's only Margot and the rest of them, I told myself. Once we'd gotten to the inner sanctum, they'd tear off my blindfold and hand me some champagne and show me their diagrams of all the people they wanted to take down and how they were going to do it.

Maybe it would be like a dimly lit club with cigars and snifters of brandy, or maybe it would be more like a classroom, or maybe it would look exactly like a meeting room in the White House where politicians gathered to decide on matters of life and death. All of these options flashed through my mind as the women pulled me out of the van and into an elevator, as I put myself into their hands and let them move me where they wanted. I heard a door open— this was it, we were going behind the door!—and we stopped. I braced myself for them to remove the blindfold. But then we entered *another* elevator, not smooth and quiet like the clubhouse one, but old and creaking. A freight elevator. When the doors opened with a grinding sound, the women pushed me out into someplace colder, ripe with the rich, loamy scent of earth, plus something smoky. A hand pulled the blindfold from my eyes, and what lay before me was something I hadn't prepared myself for at all.

I was standing in a forest. No, I saw, as I got my bearings. Not an actual forest. But we were surrounded by trees in planters, tall ones arcing up from their pots, spreading their branches, amid trellises covered in ivy. And the floor was actual dirt, dirt that they must have trucked in from somewhere. In the center of the trees stood a circle of small stones with wood arranged inside, ready to be lit. That had to be a fire code violation, right? Did this room come equipped with sprinklers? I looked up to the ceiling to check, and saw sky. We weren't in a room at all, but on the rooftop under the stars, or at least as much of the stars as could be seen in the smog of New York, arranged around the glowing orb of a nearly full moon. The ivy-covered trellises closed us in, so that a casual observer looking over from the window of a nearby building wouldn't be able to see anything but a beautiful rooftop garden. Besides, there weren't many nearby buildings this tall anyway—most were at least a floor or two shorter. I looked back down again and saw, at the edge of the stone circle, a dark wooden chest with drawers, standing at about waist height. I narrowed my eyes to bring it into focus in the sage-smoke rising around me. On the chest sat candles, bundles of herbs, and a large, sheathed knife. Almost like an altar? But that couldn't be right.

Two of the figures appeared in front of me and pulled the hoods back from their heads, revealing one head of straight auburn hair and one with wild, dark curls. Caroline and Margot. "Welcome," Margot said, "to our coven."

THIRTY-ONE

Okay. What? Hadn't Caroline and Margot hated the casual references to witchiness that some of the members made, pressing their lips together whenever other women went on and on about crystals? Margot had said that she'd made a mistake, joking that Nevertheless was a coven in that interview. Type A, corporate Caroline had practically bitten off the head of that member who proposed a Spell Your Success workshop. But now, they were wearing full-on floor-length black robes made of velvet, taking it way further than those other women ever had.

I searched their faces for a hint of embarrassment, an acknowledgment that they knew they were playacting. But they were contained, sincere, as the other women removed their hoods. Vy was there, and Iris, along with four others whom I recognized from the clubhouse but whose names I didn't know, all of them luminous, their bodies alert with anticipation. Vy bent down to the wood in the center of the stone circle, pulled out a lighter from her pocket, and lit a fire. As the flames began to crackle, they sent dancing shadows over the faces of the women before me.

"Coven?" I asked.

"Mm-hm," Margot said, a smile curling on her lips.

"Like everyone talks about in the clubhouse?" I asked haltingly. "Like, rah-rah, love my witches, we're totally a coven?"

"Not quite," Margot said.

"For those members who want to talk about spells and such, it's just a fun fad," Caroline said. "Some casual appropriation. Up here, it's different."

"How?" I asked.

"Simple," Margot said, and smiled at the women flanking her before turning back to me. "Because *we* actually do magic."

"Um," I said. I waited for someone to flip on the lights and for them to shriek with laughter, for them to point at my face and crow about how I was so fucking gullible. But they just kept looking at me, even and appraising.

"What kind of magic?" I asked, trying to maintain a mask of impressed sincerity. Most of me was trying not to shriek with laughter myself, although another, smaller part half expected Margot to whip out a wand and transform Vy into a cat, for Caroline to peel off her skin to reveal a crone's face beneath. "The magic of sisterhood?" Maybe saying that they "actually did magic" was like when I said that I could "literally eat a horse"—I felt like it in the moment, sure, but I knew it wasn't really possible.

"No, real magic," Caroline said.

"Right, okay," I said. "Like Harry Potter? Enchanting mirrors and hanging out with dragons?"

"Of course not," Caroline continued. "I told you, *real* magic. The kind where we make things happen."

"With every spell we do, we're influencing things, carving grooves in the world so that the water flows where we want it to," Iris said.

"Like, for example, I wanted to focus on my career for as long as possible before settling down," Caroline said, "but I also didn't want to wait *too* long to start a family, so the day I turned thirty, we did a summoning circle to find my husband. I met him the next day. A man who checked all of my boxes."

"And she had a lot of boxes," Margot said.

"I had an *average* amount of boxes," Caroline said.

"When that troll ruined Vy's art installation," Iris said, "we did a blocking spell so that the police wouldn't look too hard into who had vandalized his home. And they never even brought anyone in for questioning."

Or, the voice inside me snarked, *Caroline glommed on to the next attractive man she met, and the police left you alone because you had money and power.*

The other women, the ones I didn't know, began to speak too, introducing themselves—Tara, Ophelia, Gabby, and Nina. They each told their own story, the ways in which this coven had protected and promoted and shaped their lives, and the whole time I just kept waiting to wake up.

"And, well, we've done bigger things too, in service of some larger goals," Margot said. My ears perked up, but Caroline cleared her throat, so Margot didn't elaborate. She just leaned over the altar and began to light the candles on it.

So this was the big secret. That they were absolutely nuts.

"Wow," I said. "Were you really into Wicca in high school, or—"

"This isn't Wicca," Vy said.

"Although it might look that way at first, from the outside," Margot said.

"It's not some hobby," Caroline said. "And we're not going to move to Salem and open up a witch store to sell candles. It's sacred, and it's secret."

"Our great-grandmothers started it," Margot said. "Mine and Caroline's. Almost a hundred years ago, they began to meet in this building. It was just an old abandoned button factory at the time, with three women sneaking in to start a fire."

Three? I wondered as Caroline took over the story. "Back then, hardly anybody came out this far west. That changed over the years, of course, thanks to us practicing here. We basically made this neighborhood."

"I'm sorry, are you saying that you *made* the West Village—" I began, but Caroline was still talking.

"They passed it down to their daughters. My grandmother bought the building and invited in more members. Then our grandmothers passed it down to their daughters too. The Coven seemed like it might die with our generation. When Margot's mother . . . well. I thought maybe it was antiquated and unnecessary anyway. But after 2016, I saw that it wasn't, that we could use our magic in the service of a new goal—" Caroline cut herself off, then shook her head. "Anyways, we found our way back to each other."

What goal? I wanted to ask, but Margot had jumped in.

"At first it was just me and Caroline," Margot said. "Then we tracked down some of the daughters of women who had belonged over the years." Margot looked at Vy, who gave her a nod. "And then we started the club."

"Wait, so Nevertheless itself is just a beard?" I asked.

"No!" Caroline said. "Sure, we're doing the real work up here. But I knew there could be a way to help other women in the process, to give them community and connection while we drew inspiration from them on the other side of a door. That's why I said that we should start it." She tossed her head, making sure she got the credit, still a *little* passive-aggressive even in what, for her, seemed a holy space.

"And besides," Margot said, "now we keep an eye out for members who have an extra power inside of them. A . . . potential. Those are the ones we bring in here. Most of them haven't ever realized the extent of what they could do, haven't ever thought of themselves as witches, at least not in a serious way. But when we all worship together, our magic can be unlocked."

What the ever-loving fuck. Magic was not real. This madness was not what I had signed up for. I just wanted to write an article and move the hell on.

"I know it's a lot to take in," Margot said, touching my hand gently. "This part is always strange for the initiates."

"I almost ran away when they first told me," said one of the women—Tara, she'd said her name was.

"But soon," Caroline said, "everyone believes. Do you have more questions?"

A million fought and jabbered inside my brain. "*Why?*" I asked.

"Why what?" Caroline asked.

"Why do we do this?" Margot asked, and I nodded. She straightened her shoulders. "Because of power and sisterhood. Because to be a woman in this world is to know that you're never truly equal, even when you put in ten times the work. Because it scares the men who want to keep us quiet, those who want to control us." I thought of the pictures of Margot with her ex-boyfriend, who made her look small. Now, in the darkness, in this pocket of forest in the middle of the West Village, as tree branches rustled around us and firelight danced on her wild mane of hair, she seemed ten feet tall. "Witches used to be respected, used to heal and help until men decided to take their power away, to burn them, to call them hags. But in here, in the dark, we clasp hands and make things happen, and we will be equal despite them, or we'll be better."

The other women watched Margot, rapt, as she spoke. But something flickered on Caroline's face along with the firelight, a kind of envy at the speech. She swallowed again. Maybe it wasn't envy, but discomfort.

"So, no offense to your picking methods and obviously I'm honored and everything, but . . . why me?"

"You've known hardship and come out the other side. Your words have the power to take down a powerful man." Margot paused, then smiled, radiant. "And, beyond that, your tarot reading predicted you'd be here."

"What?" I asked.

"The Three of Cups, the sisterhood card. You only would have drawn that if you'd truly belonged."

With a quick jolt of fear, I remembered the card I'd turned over before the Three of Cups, the card I'd hidden in my pocket and then buried in my drawer. The Ten of Swords. Betrayal. Clearly their "magic" didn't extend to knowing that I'd lied about that. All during the reading, I'd assumed they were playing a mind game with me. But it had been so much more.

"No one had drawn it for so long, not as their future card," Margot said.

"We'd been waiting years, and then, within a month, two of you did it," Caroline said.

"Caroline thought it would be poetic justice to have Roy Pruitt's daughter involved," Margot said, and a flash of annoyance or regret passed over Caroline's expression. "But you proved that *you* were the one who would be loyal, who was willing to do what needed to be done for the good of the Coven."

"So we invite you in. Join us, Jillian," Caroline said.

"*Join us, Jillian,*" the other women echoed, these women who took taxis and went to yuppie juice shops and who, now, were chanting my name, shrouded in mystery and darkness. And here I was, standing among them in my pajamas, not knowing where to put my arms.

"Are you ready?" Margot asked, holding out her hand.

Fuck no. I did not want to entangle myself in this. I'd come to find out what they'd done to Nicole Woo-Martin, not to get my-self trapped in some mass delusion. Clearly things would only get more dangerous and unstable from here on out.

But . . . this was a story too. The elite of New York City, drawn into a cult of the occult, so drunk on their own power that they'd lost touch with reality. And they'd made other things happen, Margot had said with that mysterious smile. Did they believe they'd magicked Nicole out of office? If it was all connected, my God, the waves this reporting would make. I couldn't get this far only to run away in fear.

"Are you ready?" Margot asked again, and it wasn't a question.

I placed my hand in Margot's. "I am," I said.

The women let out a breath as one, a soft sighing noise.

"Then let's start the ritual," Margot said.

By now, the flames were crackling higher in the stone pit, hiss-ing and spitting. Maybe I was still dreaming. Maybe they were still screwing with me. Caroline turned and walked to the altar, pick-ing up a bundle of herbs and the silver-handled knife that lay there. She passed the herbs to Margot, who placed the bundle in her right palm.

Margot closed her palm into a fist and held it out over the fire. "Once we do this, you won't be able to share the details of what you'll go on to learn here with anyone outside the Coven," she said. "Not a partner, not a best friend. We've all had to make that sacrifice. If you break the circle, there will be consequences." Cool, so this was like a *magical* NDA, where instead of sending fancy lawyers after me, they'd send Satan? Thank God I didn't believe in this. (I was more afraid of rich people's lawyers than some demon from hell.)

Murmuring something soft, words that weren't in any language I knew, Margot crumbled the leaves into the flames. I kept one eye on her but I trained my other eye, obviously, on the freaking knife. It was smaller than a butcher's knife but larger than your average silverware, and I was getting the discomfiting sense that it would play a starring role in this ritual.

Caroline unsheathed the knife and held it delicately, revealing its smooth, sharp edge. "Your blood is mine, and mine is yours," she said, and in one swift movement, dragged the blade down her left palm. Okay, they weren't screwing with me. *Shit.*

The incision she made was about a couple of inches long, shallow. I winced as a line of red sprung up on her skin. Caroline turned her hand over the fire, letting the droplets of blood seep into the flames, which sizzled and smoked in response. "So mote it be," she said, then straightened up, her smile more blissful than I'd ever seen it, her shoulders loosening as if she'd just taken a Valium. From her robe she pulled a jar of some kind of ointment and rubbed it over the cut. Margot took a strip of cloth from her pocket and tied it around Caroline's palm. Then Caroline passed the knife to Margot, who dug it into her own palm and repeated the same words.

Again, the sizzle as the flames absorbed her blood, and then she passed the knife on down the circle to Iris, who took her turn and sent it down, getting ever closer to me, as the women who'd opened themselves bound up one another's wounds.

Nope. Nuh-uh. I didn't even like going to the pharmacy for a flu shot, so I wasn't about to plunge an actual knife into my skin. Also, had these women been tested for STIs recently? I thought we all acknowledged nowadays that mixing blood with strangers wasn't generally a great idea. I'd never shared a hairbrush at sleepovers back in the day because of lice, so clearly I was too neurotic to be a witch, and I should just gracefully bow out and let them carry on with their spell-casting and bloodletting without me—

Vy placed the knife in my palm, interrupting my thoughts. Its handle was heavier than I'd expected, with a raised pattern of vines and fruit on it. I stared at the vines, hesitating. "What are you waiting for?" Vy asked.

The flames, the smell of the herbs, the tang of the blood—all of it mixed in the air, a cloying, suffocating scent that made me lightheaded. Nausea roiled in my stomach. My face was reflected in Vy's eyes, and I could've sworn that for a moment, amid the smoke, the image twisted and turned into that of a gull, batting its wings to stay above the waves.

I pressed the blade into my skin, at the base of my thumb, chewing on my lip to stifle any whimpering. The sharp pain of the knife as it bit into me was what finally convinced me that I wasn't dreaming, and then my skin split, my dark red insides revealed to the air. "Your blood is mine," Margot prompted.

"Your blood is mine," I said, "and mine is yours." I held my hand out. My fingers trembled as the blood began to trickle down my wrist, staining the sleeve of my cotton shirt. I turned my hand over and watched the blood run into the fire, the rest of my body starting to tremble too. "So mote it be."

"*So mote it be,*" the women repeated, and repeated again, over and over, a kind of monotonous chanting. Caroline took the knife back from me and placed it on the altar. Margot dabbed the ointment onto my hand—it was cool, smelling of some herbs I couldn't identify. She bound up the cut. Then the women all reached out and clasped hands in the circle, Margot taking my right. Vy's calloused hand gripped my left palm, and I recognized it—she'd been the one who'd held her hand over my mouth when I'd woken in the dark that night, lifetimes ago.

We circled around the fire, and the women all began to take deep, slow breaths. "Breathe it in," Margot said to me, so I followed their lead, my stomach expanding and contracting, the dizzying scent of the fire flooding into my nose and down my throat, a tingling within me spreading and spreading as, distantly, a church bell began to chime, twelve times. The final chime lingered and faded, and when it was gone entirely, Margot released my hand.

"We are bound together, our secrets safe within this circle," she said, her voice ceremonial, her eyes closed, lashes fluttering. Then she opened her eyes and smiled. "Now for the fun part."

THIRTY-TWO

The fun part?" I repeated dumbly.

"Each new initiate gets a spell," Caroline said. "To welcome them to the circle."

"Something we can do for you, something you want," Margot said.

"What should it be? Oh, I know." Caroline clapped her hands, the most efficient witch I'd ever seen. She turned to the altar and opened the drawers, which contained jars and herbs and also, incongruously, a few cans of LaCroix. "Success for your novel."

"Oh, maybe," I said.

"Protection," Iris said. "As the Judge Melton consequences continue to play out."

"Or," Margot said, "we could summon your mother."

I turned my head toward her so fast I nearly got whiplash. "What?"

"Bring her spirit here. Let you talk with her," Margot continued, her tone almost dreamy, and anger at her flooded into me, anger that she would dangle this in my face when my mother was gone and nobody would ever be able to bring her back.

"Margot, no," Caroline snapped, the anger in her own voice startling me. "We're not doing that kind of magic here." The two of them locked eyes. They'd had this argument before. Already, the power dynamics in this coven were coming into focus. Maybe Margot gave the speeches, but Caroline was the boss.

"I know," Vy said. "Raf." We all turned to her.

"What?" I asked.

"At the gala," Vy continued. "After you sucked face, I asked him if he loved you. He got all red." So *that's* what he hadn't told me about their conversation. "He does, but he's scared to say it."

"Sweet Raf," Margot said.

"He's the only good man in the world," Vy said. "But he's shy."

"Aw," one of the other women in the circle—Ophelia—said. "That's adorable. Also, his restaurant is incredible." The women on either side of her murmured their approval of Raf's cooking.

"And you two were so sweet together at the gala," Iris said.

"Sometimes he has trouble expressing things. So let's loosen his tongue," Vy said.

"The supplies, though," Margot said.

"I brought a cow tongue." Vy reached into her robe and pulled a Ziploc bag out of her pocket. The bag was filled with ice and something else: a hunk of meat. Great, she'd just been carrying raw meat around with her all night. I looked at the other women, expecting to see their faces pinched in distaste, but only smiles beamed back.

"Perfect!" Caroline said. "It's settled, then. Ready, Jillian?"

"Uh," I said. Eight pairs of eyes turned toward me, bright with anticipation. I couldn't think of a way to protest now without seeming suspicious. Besides, it's not like it mattered. It wasn't real, so I should let them have their fun. Maybe someday I'd tell Raf, and we'd laugh over it, after things had gone back to normal, long after I'd forgotten the feel of his mouth against mine. (The memory of our kiss had slammed into me a few times since the gala, very inconveniently.) "Ready."

Vy plopped the slimy, cold cow tongue into my unbloodied hand, which didn't exactly help my nausea. Caroline went back to the altar, where she picked up a vial filled with some kind of oil, plus the knife again. Oh God, I'd hoped we were done with that particular prop. She opened the vial and spilled some of the liquid into her hand, scattering drops of the oil on the cow tongue. She rubbed the rest of the liquid on my forehead. It smelled of ginger and cloves. Then she handed me the knife. Did they want me to stick it into the cow tongue now? How many germs were on this blade? As soon as I got out of here, I was going to have to make an appointment for a tetanus shot. (Yes, I was turning into my mother.) *Get ahold of yourself, Beckley*, I told myself. *Pay attention to it all, so you can write it down.*

"Carve your initials in the tongue," Margot said, her breath hot in my ear. She watched over me, her hand on my shoulder, as I inscribed them unsteadily into the meat: *JAB*. Jillian Abigail Beckley.

When I was done, Margot lifted the meat from my hand, and held it above the flames. Caroline came up next to her on one side, with Vy on the other. The other women flanked them, linking themselves by putting hands on one another's shoulders.

"May tongue uncurl and speak its truth," Margot recited.

"May tongue uncurl and speak its truth," the other women repeated, and then said it again, the words echoing and growing

more urgent. Again and again, they said it, their voices lifting
louder and higher until the words became almost a shriek, and the
women's eyes blazed. When it seemed that the words could not
possibly gather any more force, the women all took in a breath as
one, and then Margot threw the tongue into the fire. Sweating, the
women arced their heads back, releasing a guttural yell up toward
the sky.

I was sweating too, the heat of the fire flushing my face, as the
meat began to char and the panting, shrieking sounds continued.
The meat threw off a rich smell—shit, now I was hungry—and the
smoke hung heavy around us. I was back in the dream I'd been
having when they'd startled me awake, where everything was
underwater, the world around me a slow-motion haze. And then
Iris took off her robe. She wasn't wearing anything underneath it.

What. The. Fuck. Was. Happening. I tried not to stare, but . . .
well, I could see why she was so body positive. One by one, the
other women followed, shedding their robes, until they were entirely bare. Nipples everywhere: tiny ones the size of dimes, large,
puckered ones as big as sand dollars. So many nipples, and a lot of
full bush. They tossed their robes to the side and began to dance,
leaping and twirling, uncoordinated movements around the fire.
They swung their hips and clasped their hair in all their naked,
uninhibited glory, while I clenched my body tighter, not knowing
what to do, on the outside again.

Margot appeared at my side and put her hands on my face. *Eyes
on her eyes, not on her boobs*, I told myself. *Don't be a perv.*

"Sometimes we worship sky-clad," she said to me, as the women
whirled around behind us. Even Caroline was naked, totally hair-
less and well maintained, her breasts like pert round apples. She
danced like someone who'd been obsessed with ballerinas as a little
girl and would have wanted to be one herself if not for a total lack

of talent. Still, she was unabashed in her ungraceful movements, throwing in the odd pirouette or arabesque, and it was weirdly hypnotic to watch.

"Sky-clad?"

"Naked. When the body is released from all the things that constrict it, it has a power unlike anything else. Try it with us."

"I'm not quite comfortable with my body," I said quietly.

"Why not?"

"I just don't . . . love it."

"Oh, Jillian," Margot said, with such sympathy in her voice. "That's exactly why you should do it." She stepped even closer to me, and the sounds and people around us blurred, growing smudged and fuzzy like the two of us were a photograph at the center of an Impressionist painting. She reached out and grasped the bottom of my pajama shirt. "May I?"

I nodded, my throat dry, trembling. Slowly, she drew the shirt up, lifting it over my head in an unhurried movement, so that the fabric scraped against my far-too-sensitive skin. I started to cross my arms over my chest, but she cocked an eyebrow, and I put them back down at my sides. She made no attempt to avert her eyes like I had. Instead she ran them over me, a lazy, contented smile playing around her mouth, then looked back up into my face.

"You're beautiful, Jillian," she said. Next, she combed her fingers along my hips. My skin prickled and sent off sparks as she drew her fingers underneath the waistband of my leggings and hooked them on the cotton band of my underwear. We rested like that for a moment as the other women continued their worship. Then, gentle and deliberate, Margot pulled the fabric down until it rested at my feet. She held her hand out to me, and I took it, our hot, sweating hands pulsing against each other's. I stepped out of my clothes and into the circle, which opened up to welcome me in.

Enthusiastically, Margot jumped into the dancing. I moved stiffly, trying to copy her ease, so that no one would realize their mistake in letting me in here. *Dance like no one's watching, you dumbass*, I told myself. And nobody *was* watching. No one was rating my movements on a one-to-ten scale. The other bodies passed in front of me. Up close, they were a feast of imperfections. Cellulite dimpled some of their thighs. I saw a birthmark here, a stretch mark there, and yet the dancing women didn't care, didn't try to hide it in the shadows, because they were too busy moving in an ecstatic communion.

I rolled my shoulders back. I dug my toes into the dirt below me. I went into the smell and the fire and the humming, and my body was no longer some ungainly shield I used to keep the world out but a flowing thing all of its own. I forgot to pay attention, I forgot everything except the rush of my arms and feet, moving in ways they never had before. I was in my own private world and I was terrified and alight all at once.

We danced for I don't know how long, until they handed me back my pajamas to put on, then led me down a warren of stairways and out onto the street. They kissed me on my cheek, put me in a cab, and disappeared into the dark.

THIRTY-THREE

Margot had given the cab driver my address, and for a minute as he headed toward the West Side Highway, I sat in the backseat, drenched in perspiration and frozen still. I'd been turned inside out and then right side in again, but some of my veins had been left on the outside of my body in the process, and now they throbbed. The driver asked me if I was all right, and I just sort of whimpered and shook in the backseat. Then I leaned forward and gave him a different address and sat in a daze as he took me to the only place I could possibly go.

"What the hell, Jilly, it's after three A.M.," Raf said, rubbing his eyes, when he finally opened his door after a minute or two of my pounding on it. "You almost gave me a heart attack." Then he took me in—my wild eyes and hair, the sweat-drenched clothing, the bloodstains on my sleeve—and he immediately threw off any remaining sleepiness. "Are you okay? Are you hurt? Who did this to you?"

"No, not hurt. But maybe not okay. I don't know. Can I come in?"

"Of course," he said, and swung the door open wide for me.

"What happened?" he asked as I paced around his living room. Just being in his presence—my familiar, solid beanpole, someone who was going to stick a knife in my hand only so I could help him chop onions—allowed me to anchor myself back to the Earth, although my blood still pinged around inside of me, bouncing off my skin, making everything buzz and tingle. Imagine the feeling you get when the hair on the back of your neck stands up. Now imagine it doing that for an hour straight.

"So it turns out that they actually think they're witches. That they do real magic. Not, like, card tricks, and not just sending some positive energy out in the world, but that they can truly influence events."

"They . . . what?"

"Yeah. They're out of their minds. And now I guess I'm one of them."

"What did they do to you?" he asked.

A strangled noise erupted from my throat at the thought of having to tell him any more details, having to relive the chanting and the knife and the cow tongue, so I just shook my head. Raf came over and put his arms around me as I tried not to cry. "I'm not sad! I'm just kind of overwhelmed," I said, my face against the threadbare T-shirt he'd worn to bed.

"Okay," he said. "It's okay."

"Yeah, it's fine, it's just that I got freaked out by it all and I didn't want to be alone in my apartment because they showed up there and kidnapped me earlier and"—here I caught a whiff of myself, reeking of the herbs they'd burned and the oils they'd pressed onto me—"Oh God, I smell like a feral child who's been raised by wolves, so here I am stinking up your apartment and I'm sorry but I didn't know what else to do."

He stepped back and looked at me, a little overwhelmed himself. He nodded a couple of times, quickly, and then asked, "Would a shower help?"

My whole body drooped with relief. "A shower would be amazing."

I followed him to the bathroom, watching as he knelt down and turned on the water for me. He knew that his tricky faucet confused me to no end. I stood there shivering while he adjusted the temperature.

"Okay, that should be good," he said, turning to go, and I so desperately didn't want to be alone that I just said it without thinking it through:

"Will you stay in here with me?"

He hesitated. Then he nodded, put the toilet lid down, and sat on it. I pulled the shower curtain—a solid, shiny blue—and he turned away as I took off my clothes and stepped in.

Raf's shower was not the cleanest place in the entire world. Of course he had a three-in-one body wash/shampoo/conditioner. I was grateful for all of it, for the bits of mold blooming on his tile, for the stupid boy bath products that I used to dab the cut on my palm, which had already begun to scab up. Through a crack between the wall and the edge of the shower curtain, I could see him sitting, jiggling his leg, his head turned away from the shower for propriety even though he wasn't going to see anything anyway. He swallowed, then adjusted his athletic shorts.

"I have to keep going back," I said as I soaped up my hair, as my heart continued to pound against the walls of my chest. "It's good for the story, right? That the tastemakers of New York are in this weird cult?"

"It's definitely not what I would have expected," Raf said. He adjusted his shorts again.

My skin still prickled, sensitive, as I tried to scrub the night off it. Faint streaks of red marked my hip bones where Margot had moved her fingers. "But the wildest thing is that when you're in there with them, it feels . . . almost real. They sweep you up in their delusion, even though I know that actually, they're all having this mass psychotic break."

"Well . . ."

I paused in my scrubbing. "What?"

"I don't know if they're having a breakdown. A lot of people believe in things that we can't prove."

"Yeah, but you don't know . . ." I started. "Some of what they were doing was just . . . Oh, I can't think about it anymore to-night."

"Sorry," he said. "I'm not saying what *they* . . . I just mean, my grandma practiced Santeria when she was growing up, so she was always making potions and stuff when my mom was a little girl. And you know my mom. She's a realistic person. But even now, she swears that she saw ghosts in her childhood bedroom. I don't think that makes her crazy."

"No, I didn't mean to say that—"

"And *I* don't mean to . . ." He let out a breath of frustration at himself, at his imperfect words. "This shit is scary and weird, and I get why you're freaked out. I just mean that I don't know if you can say for sure one way or another what's real and what's not."

If I'd been with Miles, we would've snarked about this like snark would save the world, and everything would have seemed less real and less terrifying. But instead Raf was saying in his sort of stumbling way that there was no certainty, that maybe I'd just fully insinuated myself with an all-powerful coven, and the tingling feeling was growing all over my body instead of going away like it was supposed to.

I turned the water off and stood still, staring at the shower mold, water dripping off me, my body covered in goose bumps. In the sudden quiet, I became very aware of Raf's breathing on the other side of the curtain. "Sorry," he said. "That's probably not helpful right now."

"It's okay," I said. "You don't have to apologize. You're being so kind to me. You've *been* so kind to me this whole time."

As if to prove my point, he handed me a large, fuzzy bear of a towel through the gap between the curtain and the wall. I wrapped the towel tightly around me and emerged, face-to-face with him.

"Well," he said, "I care about you." His dark hair was mussed from sleep, a single curl falling over his forehead. He had a slight line, an indentation from his pillow, on his cheek.

"I care about you too."

He looked at me for a moment more, then averted his eyes. "You want to sleep here?" I nodded, and he paced out of the bathroom, calling over his shoulder, "I'll get you something to sleep in."

I toweled off, then followed him to the door of his bedroom, waiting at the threshold like a vampire who couldn't come in unless invited. His sheets were rumpled from when I'd startled him awake. A few different baseball caps sat scattered on top of his dresser. On one wall, he'd hung up a corkboard on which he'd pinned notes to himself, an article announcing the restaurant opening, and some pictures—his family at Christmastime, him with a group of his guy friends hiking in the woods, and a photo of a block party in our neighborhood years ago, where I'd slung my arm around him, my mother on the other side of me, his parents on the other side of him, and we all grinned, naive, no premonitions about the sadness that was coming our way.

He rummaged around in his drawer, then pulled out an oversize T-shirt and a pair of mesh shorts. "Here," he said, handing the clothes to me. "I'll take the couch."

"No, you take the bed," I replied.

He shook his head. "You're taking the bed."

"We could both take the bed."

My breath caught in my throat for the eternity in which my words hung in the air. Then he nodded and climbed in.

I pulled the shirt and shorts on quickly, hung my towel on his doorknob while he turned off the lamp, and got in beside him, still shivering. We lay there, both looking up at the ceiling, his body heat radiating from a foot away. I scooted a little closer to him and turned onto my side, craving the warmth of him, hoping that he would turn too. After a moment, he did, and wordlessly lifted his arm to wrap it around me. I nestled into him. Behind his wall, the pipes clanked and murmured softly, the only other sound besides our shallow breathing. The ice in my bones began to melt, coursing and rippling around, an almost ticklish sensation inside my skin.

But still we hadn't crossed a line. Still, this could all be explained away in the morning, just another hazy thing that had happened on this unexpected night.

"Are you feeling any better?" he asked.

"It's all so much . . . *more* than I expected," I said.

"You could always stop," he said, his breath hot in my ear. I pressed myself closer to him, against the hardness at his hips, and his voice grew husky. "You don't have to do anything you don't want to do."

I turned my face to his. "But I do want to," I said, and kissed him.

Like at the gala, he stayed rigid for a moment. And then he kissed me back. His arms tightened around me, and I ran my hands over his scratchy cheeks, and our tentative movements turned urgent. He pulled my shorts off me, and I wanted him more than anything. When he pushed inside of me, it was inevitable and safe, but thrilling too. I wasn't overthinking it at all. Everything was only need and instinct and our ragged noises until it was done, and then sleep came and pulled me under.

THIRTY-FOUR

The next morning, though, the freaking out set in.

I woke up, locked in Raf's arms, drool crusted on my chin, and for a moment, it was right and warm. Then came the electric shock of remembrance. You can't unfuck someone. I'd ruined things between us. And to top it all off, I hadn't peed afterward, so I was probably going to get a UTI.

The night before, I'd been out of my mind, light-headed from the smoke and the oils and the sight of my own blood spilling into a fire. Infected by their way of thinking, I'd very nearly believed that the women in the Coven had summoned a certain kind of power. And then I'd carried that infection here.

With a clear head came reality: Those women could make things go their way, but it wasn't because of magic. It was because of their wealth. In so many ways, magic and wealth were just the same thing.

Raf stirred. When he opened his eyes and saw me, still there in his arms, a sleepy, hopeful smile came over his face. "Hey," he said, his voice froggy. He cleared his throat. "So."

"So," I said, and an awkward silence hung in the air for a moment. "I need coffee. You want some?"

I made a noncommittal noise, and he rolled off the bed and disappeared out the door. As the sounds of him clattering around and grinding beans rose in the kitchen, I searched for the shorts he'd given me last night. There they were, balled up under the covers at the foot of the bed. I caught a glimpse of myself in the mirror and looked away quickly, both because of the shame and because, with my purplish under-eye circles and lightning-struck hair, I looked like a troll doll.

God, everyone had seen me naked, dancing around tits-out like I'd gotten too drunk at a college party. And now I was supposed to go back to Nevertheless and act like everything was normal. How did the other women do it, slip into these ecstatic states, do and say things that daylight would render ridiculous, and then slip back into reality to go about their lives? It was like they were pulling on a costume, transforming themselves in the firelight. Or maybe it was the other way around. Maybe everything they did in the daytime, every casual conversation they had in line at Sweetgreen, every meeting they led at the office, was the costume they wore, and when they danced in the firelight, mad and wild, *that* was the reality that mattered.

I slunk into the kitchen right as the pot of coffee finished brewing. Raf poured me a cup and handed it to me with a nervous energy, then scratched at the stubble on his cheek. I took a sip.

"Um," he said. "We should talk."

"Yeah," I said. "I'm really sorry about just . . . throwing myself at you."

"You don't need to apologize for that."

"We can forget it ever happened. A weird one-off night. Probably most friends do it at one point, right?"

"I don't know if they do."

"And I'm sorry that this fake-dating thing has dragged on so long. We should end it. I've been depriving you of your ability to hook up with all these hot ladies, and it's not fair to you—"

"Jillian, stop it." His face flushed. "I don't want to hook up with all the hot ladies."

"Right," I said. "I know. Because it's overwhelming."

"No," he said, his thick dark eyebrows knitting together, a little curl of chest hair sticking out the top of his undershirt. "Because I love you."

I froze. An image flashed before my eyes, that of Margot throwing the cow tongue into the fire last night as all the women chanted for Raf to tell me his feelings.

"Did you talk to Margot?" I asked. "Did she tell you to say this?"

"What? Why would she— No. No one *told* me. But I just . . . do." He looked down at the floor, then took a deep breath and looked straight at me, and he was both the shy little boy down the block and a man who it turned out that I didn't know at all. "I love you."

Bear with me on a tangent here: researchers once conducted a study where they showed a roomful of subjects a line segment and then asked them to identify a matching line from three others of varying lengths. Visually, it should have been the easiest task in the world. Only most of the subjects weren't subjects at all. They were confederates hired by the experimenters. Their job was to point at a line of a clearly different length and say, with conviction, that *that* was the matching one.

And so, for the real subjects in the room, it screwed with their heads. They knew which line matched, but, as more and more people pointed to another line, they began to doubt themselves. Were the other subjects seeing something they weren't? Some of them braved potential ridicule and stuck to their guns. Others picked the same line as everyone else just to save face. But others, I think, truly didn't know what reality was anymore.

I was not going to be like them. I was not going to start doubting what I knew to be true. The women hadn't made this happen, with their cow tongue and their chanting. This was a coincidence. An extremely inconvenient one.

"Well, sure," I sputtered. "Like, you love me as a cousin. Who you had sex with. Which isn't illegal, so it's fine the one time but probably shouldn't happen again."

"Not as a cousin, Jilly," he said softly, and the hair on my arms lifted into the air. "I want to be with you, for real."

"Stop it," I said, and collapsed onto the couch. "You're confused. I confused everything by making us do this fake-dating thing. I thought it was symbiotic, you know? An excuse to help you figure out this new life of yours. And you went along with it, because you're so nice—"

"I'm nice, but I'm not *that* nice." He sat down next to me. "I think I've probably always loved you."

Inside, a part of me thrilled to this news, and it was like I was seeing our childhoods together in color instead of black-and-white—Raf watching me recite my terrible poetry, hanging on my every word. Raf playing the Romeo to my Juliet and not picturing me as lasagna at all. "It's not like I was pining away all of this time," he was saying. "Sometimes it was stronger than others, but it was always there on some level. But now, I don't know, I just feel like shit's getting real, and I had to tell you."

I turned to him and took his hand. My palm was sweating, and so was his. "You're one of the most important people in my life."

"Yeah, and you are for me too."

"No, but listen, it's different. You still have your family, and you have all the people at your restaurant and so many others who love you. But for me, you're like my family and my closest friend rolled into one, and that's why we can't screw things up by trying to date each other and then having it go wrong."

He looked down at our clasped hands and traced his thumb over my fingers. I didn't want him to stop touching me. "What if it doesn't go wrong, though?" he asked.

I stood up and began to pace. "On the off chance that it doesn't, it's not like we could be together after the article comes out anyway. You'd have to break up with me, pretend you were outraged at what I'd done, because if it came out that you were my accomplice they'd ruin you, ruin the restaurant, and I'm not going to let that happen."

"I think we could figure it out," he said, standing up too.

"No. No, this is . . . we're being ridiculous. Sure, maybe it's been nice at times, being together in that way. Maybe we've developed little crushes on each other. Maybe last night was extremely satisfying." A tingling shudder ran through my body at the remembrance of his hands grasping my hips, the feel of him against me. "But if we cut it off here and now, and just go back to the way things were—"

"Jillian," he said with a firmness that stopped me short. "I don't want to argue you into loving me. I don't think I'd be very good at that anyway. But I do need to say—" He walked right up to me, took my face in his hands, and began to speak with more clarity and conviction than I'd ever heard him use before. "I think it would be worth it for us to try. Because there is a world where it works with us, a world where it works so well, and we have a house with a big kitchen for me and a big writing desk for you and a couple of kids who eat dirt." Here, he smiled, and I couldn't help smiling back even as a lump grew in my throat, because I could see them too, these long-limbed, dark-haired children, laughing at family dinners, and the possibility of so much joy. "So if you're pulling away just because you're scared, I . . ." He trailed off. The long-limbed, dark-haired children winked at me, then turned and vanished, and I needed to end the conversation however I could, give whatever excuse I had to help us go back to normal.

"It's not just that," I said. "There's also . . . I still have feelings for someone else."

"Ah." He took a long, slow breath in. Then he exhaled, his shoulders dropping. "So it's a no, then?" I nodded. "Okay," he said, automatically reaching for the top of his head like he was going to fiddle with his baseball cap, before realizing that he wasn't wearing one. "Then I'm going to need some time to not be around you."

My eyes began to smart. Part of me wanted to take it all back and tell him to get into bed and hold me again, to rewind to the moment where I'd woken up in his arms. "That's . . ." I said. "Sure. Yeah, that's understandable. We can take a couple weeks and talk after that—"

"It might need to be more than a couple weeks, Jilly," he said, his voice sad and wise, and for the first time I felt like he was older than me, that I really knew nothing of the world.

"No, don't say that. Don't do this." He was swallowing hard as if he were trying not to cry, and then he looked away from me. "I can't not have you in my life, that's the whole point of—" I said, before my words got tangled up because I was so angry at him for needing this time, and at myself for crawling into his bed in the first place.

"Jillian," he said, but I turned and went into the bedroom to find my stinking, bloody clothes from the night before, throwing them on as quickly as I could. This was for the best, for the long term. We had to break it now, break into two even, slightly chipped pieces, so that we didn't shatter entirely. With time and care and the right kind of glue, you can put two chipped pieces back together again.

I came back to the kitchen and hugged him tightly. And then I walked out his door.

THIRTY-FIVE

I avoided Nevertheless for the next couple of days. I avoided everyone and everything I could, pushing off Miles's apologetic texts asking to meet up, swimming for hours each morning, working double shifts at the bar until my feet began to ache from standing so long, trying not to miss the sight of Raf arranging his long limbs on a stool so he could keep me company. I got a tetanus shot.

But on the third day, Margot sent me a text. **Tonight**, it read, simply, and then a fire emoji. So, when I got off my shift around nine P.M., I headed back to the clubhouse.

When the elevator doors opened, I had a disorienting sensation, that of returning to a familiar place but as a different person, like going back to visit your high school after your first semester in college. You know so much more than you did the last time you walked through those halls. You look at the seniors and marvel that you were ever that ignorant.

Libby caught my eye and jumped up from her seat by the window, waving. She'd been sitting alone, reading a book with a pink cover. "Hey, lady! You're here late tonight."

"Yeah, life's been nuts, but I wanted to swing by."

"Sit, sit," she said. I was going to make some excuse, but she just kept talking, indicating the coffee cup on her table, a whirlwind of friendliness. "I got this decaf pumpkin spice latte on a whim tonight, and it is *so* good. Want a sip?"

"Nah, I'm fine."

She took a gulp of it, still all in on autumn. She wore a chunky sweater and a jaunty little knit beret, her hair in two thick braids beneath it. "Do you think anyone's ever done pumpkin spice fizzy water before?"

"No, and I think there's probably a reason for that," I said, scanning the rest of the clubhouse. The ranks were thinning at this late hour, but I recognized all of the witches (or rather, women who thought they were witches), chatting in various groups, lounging on different couches, entirely casual. No indication that, soon, they'd be ripping their clothes off and chanting in tongues.

"Why have things been so crazy?" Libby asked, then looked at me still standing. She made a goofy face of concern. "What, your butt sore or something? Sit down!" So I sat and talked with her about how my week had been, like a millennial Judas. Eventually, she started showing me videos she'd taken of Bella the Rat Dog learning how to shake her hand. She scooted her chair next to mine and leaned in close as she grinned down at the screen, the scent of her coconut shampoo in my nose as the clubhouse cleared out even further and eleven P.M. approached.

"Oh, goodness!" she said at one point, temporarily interrupting her dog chatter. She grabbed my hand, peering at the scabbed, scarlet line that lingered on my palm. "What happened to you?"

"I was trying to keep up with Raf in some onion chopping. Clearly a fool's errand."

"Poor Jillian," she said, stroking my palm with utter tenderness. Oh, that sweet little dumpling. How she would hate me if she knew.

Caroline walked through from the back office to get herself a tea. Libby sat up taller in her chair, waving, trying to catch her eye to no avail. She sighed and sat back. "Maybe I'm totally in my head, but I feel like Caroline's gotten kind of cold to me all of a sudden. Have you noticed?"

"Hm, no," I said.

"I guess it hasn't been that long. Only since the gala, which is weird, since it seemed to go so *well*."

"Maybe it's just the comedown from all the excitement."

"Although," Libby said, tapping her fingers against her mouth, "I guess it started part of the way through the gala. Like we were having so much fun, chatting about all sorts of things, and then she asked me about Thanksgiving and it was almost like . . ." She was talking so quietly now, her gaze fixed on the table, that it was as if I weren't even there. I wished I weren't. "But I don't know how she would've known." The last few remaining women were filing out now, as the Coven surreptitiously arranged themselves near the door. "I just hope it doesn't affect . . . well, you know."

She shook herself out of it, noticing the time and the atmosphere. "Anyways! Should we walk out?"

"Oh, it's okay, I've got to go to the bathroom, so you go ahead."

"I don't mind waiting, really," she said. I hesitated, my eyes flitting to Margot, who was lingering by the back door. Libby followed my gaze. And then understanding settled over her.

"Oh," she said in a quiet, heartbroken voice. "You're going to stay." She bit down on her lip, her eyes reddening, as I nodded. "Got it." She swallowed, then attempted a smile. "Congrats—" She took a sharp intake of breath, and her expression hardened as she connected the dots. She had told me her secret, and now Caroline knew. "Yes, I get it."

"Libby—"

Swiftly, clumsily, she began putting on her coat and gathering her things. "I should leave you to enjoy it, since it clearly meant so much to you."

Libby wouldn't like the Coven anyway. She had about as much of the dark witch about her as a tuna fish sandwich. And she was too concerned with pleasing others to want to impose her will on the world. Sure, Libby could get into the kitschy stuff. She'd gamely hold a crystal in her palm and imagine that she felt its vibrations, but the moment a knife came out, she'd get spooked and wish she were back in her apartment watching reruns of *Real Housewives*. (At least this is what I told myself at the time. Now I think that she would have raised that blade high in the air and thrilled at how it gleamed.)

Let me explain, I wanted to say, even though there were so many reasons that I couldn't. Maybe, when the article came out, I could show up at her building. The doorman would wave me through with a genial, familiar wink, and I could knock on her door, and when she flung it open (too trusting for New York City, never looking through her peephole, assuming that each knock meant the delivery of an exciting package or an introduction from a friendly neighbor), I could stop her before her smile curdled and she turned away. Maybe I could make her understand that she'd been only collateral damage in service of the greater good.

Once, in fifth grade, I hadn't finished my math homework because I'd stayed up too late watching *The Breakfast Club* for the first time. When my teacher had called me over to her desk to ask about the missing assignment, a story had come spilling out: My older brother had gotten into a horrible accident on his bicycle. We'd had to race to the emergency room, where I'd spent the night anxiously waiting as the doctors reset the broken bone in his leg. Details had bubbled up out of nowhere, details of the screams coming from passing gurneys, the way my mother had wept with relief when the doctors had told her that he *would* be able to walk again, how my brave brother had emerged from his hospital room, limping but smiling, in the early hours of the morning and, to show us he was truly okay, had stopped and pumped his fist in the air, just like at the end of our favorite movie, *The Breakfast Club*. My teacher had agreed with me that yes, that was a good movie. Then she'd told me she was so sorry to hear about my brother and had given me an extension on the assignment.

That night, when I'd come home from Raf's, my mother called me into the kitchen. My teacher had telephoned to express her hope for my brother's speedy recovery, and my mother had had to explain that not only was my brother not injured, but I didn't have a brother at all.

"You've got a gift for stories," my mother had said, interrupting my attempt to bullshit my way out of the new mess I'd created. She sat at the kitchen table, back straight, with her gaze locked on mine. "Your father has that too. And that can be such a superpower, to have an imagination like you do, to have the right words at the tips of your fingers and to be able to say them with conviction. But it can lead you down a dangerous path. You can end up hurting people." Something had flickered in her eyes then. I'd realized only later that she'd still been talking about my father. She'd leaned forward, taking my hands in hers. "I need you to promise me now that you are only going to use that gift for good."

"I promise," I'd said.

"Also," she'd said, shaking her head, "you know you're not allowed to watch *The Breakfast Club* yet. Obviously you are grounded."

In the years since, I'd done a pretty good job keeping my word to her. But as I watched Libby's retreating form step into the elevator, her shoulders hunched, her jaunty, ridiculous beret wobbling on her head, I didn't know if my mother would be proud of what I was doing and who I had become to do it.

I would have given pretty much anything to ask her.

THIRTY-SIX

When we went upstairs—behind the mysterious door, down a hallway to a freight elevator, and then passing through a sort of antechamber with a door opening onto the roof—I was relieved to find that the excitement this time was of a different kind than the plunge-a-knife-into-your-palm variety. Instead, the women were planning a trip, talking among themselves about logistics and supplies. Margot floated over to me, Caroline walking briskly at her side.

"Clear your schedule for next weekend," Caroline said.

My fingers itched to check my calendar, but we'd all put our phones in a bucket in the antechamber. It was where the women normally changed into their robes (although not for this meeting, this was a planning meeting and needed to be briefer. Besides, my robe hadn't come in yet from the special, high-end store where such robes were apparently made, and they didn't want to make me feel left out). We dropped our phones and other distracting devices in that antechamber, so that nothing took away from the worship. Then we passed through a door that locked automatically behind us, and we were out under the stars.

Next weekend. I didn't *think* I had any plans. Who would I even have them with, now that Raf didn't want to see me? Libby certainly wasn't going to swoop in to invite me to anything either. "Halloween?" I asked. "Are we doing something wild? I should warn you, my thing with costumes tends to be that I think of a pun at the last minute—"

"Oh, beautiful Jillian," Margot said. "Who cares about Halloween? It's Samhain." She pronounced the word *saw-when*.

"What's Samhain?"

"The best weekend of the year," Caroline said.

"The time when magic is most potent," Margot continued. "When the moon is full, and the veil between the worlds is thin."

"Oh," I said. "Of course."

"We have a tradition now," Caroline said. "A trip."

"It started when I bought a cabin in the Hudson Valley, deep in the woods, a few years ago," Margot said offhandedly. "After my big breakup." *Gus*, I thought. That controlling, pretentious film director with whom she'd lost herself.

"We'd reconnected that year, and we went there, just the two of us, for Samhain."

"Caroline had told me about her idea to start Nevertheless, so we did some spells for the success of that," Margot said. She paused and put a hand on Caroline's arm. "Honestly, us reconnecting, Caroline telling me about what she thought we could do together— it was part of the reason I had the strength to leave that relationship in the first place."

Caroline put her hand on top of Margot's. "We did all the typical post-breakup things at the cabin, of course," she said. "Wine and chocolate and hexing the ex." Maybe that was why Gus's movies hadn't done well since he and Margot broke up. *No*, I reminded myself. *Coincidence, not real magic.*

Caroline smiled at Margot, and Margot smiled back at her as they reminisced in silence for a moment. It was the most tenderly I'd seen them look at each other. I'd assumed that Caroline was the type of woman to have ten bridesmaids (no, more than assumed— I knew! It had been in the *Vogue* article about her wedding) but no one to whom she was truly, deeply close. But now, watching her and Margot, Margot who had not even been one of those ten, I saw that I had been wrong. The two of them weren't just business partners. They cared for each other. They had history, *good* history, despite the tension I sensed between them.

"Our magic is so much more powerful once we can get into nature and away from the noise of the city," Caroline said. "Although obviously we could never live in the country full-time." She shuddered slightly at the thought.

"What we do here is nothing compared to what we've done out there," Margot said.

"Like what?" I asked.

"Well, last Samhain was right before the mayoral election," Margot began.

"Margot—" Caroline said, a warning note in her voice, the tenderness between them starting to turn prickly again.

"All right, all right. Let's just say that, at that point, our preferred candidate was down ten points in the polls, but things turned around for her after that."

"You all were responsible for electing Nicole Woo-Martin?" I asked.

"We don't want to say *responsible*," Caroline said. "We just gave her a nudge."

"Well, to call it a 'nudge' might be downplaying it," Margot said.

"I would love to know what you do to make something like that happen," I said, but neither of them answered. "I mean, I was so excited about her. It was a shame, how it all played out."

"Yes, you have to be careful what you wish for," Caroline said shortly. "That's why we're not doing things like that anymore." Margot bit her lip. "On that note!" She turned to the rest of the group to get everyone's attention. "Let's discuss what we want to accomplish this Samhain."

"Yes," Margot said. "There are a lot of exciting possibilities."

"I've been chatting with a bunch of you individually about your goals," Caroline said, "and I've drawn up a list of our most promising ideas for the agenda."

"The agenda?" Margot said under her breath, her dark eyebrows knitting together.

"A lot of you mentioned that you were hopeful about your career developments, so I propose that we concentrate this year on doing something that will support our individual successes."

"Or," Margot said, "we could think bigger, start getting back to the original goal—"

"I think it's plenty big to focus on things like bestseller status for Iris's book about body positivity, a promotion for Tara, more national recognition for Women Who Lead, and so forth. What do you all think about that?" The other women all chimed in enthusiastically. But not Margot and Vy. They were staring at each other, and they did not seem pleased at all. Margot opened her mouth to speak, but Caroline cut her off.

"Great!" Caroline said. "I'll nail things down further in that direction, then." She turned back to me and Margot. "And, Jillian, I'll send you a packing list and all the other necessary details."

"Cool, yeah. I can bring some booze. Ceremonial wine maybe?"

"No, we do *not* worship under the influence," Caroline said. "That's one of our most important rules. It can screw with the magic and make you take risks you shouldn't. But if you want to bring a nice Tempranillo or something for after the circle, that could be lovely."

"Got it," I said.

Caroline glanced at Margot, registering her displeased expression, and said in a low voice, "Stop it. We've talked about this. We're not getting careless again."

"That doesn't mean we have to be useless—"

Caroline ignored Margot and clapped her hands to get the group's attention. "Now, for tonight, let's do a spell for a successful and safe Samhain. Shall we prepare?"

As the other women began to build a fire, Margot turned away. I sidled up to her.

"You okay?"

"Mm. Fine." She shook her head. "Oh, I've been meaning to ask. How are things with Raf? Any . . . movement since the spell?"

My stomach dropped at the reminder. "Um," I said. "He did tell me that he loved me."

Margot's face broke into a smile. "Good! I'm so glad."

"But then we . . . we had a fight, so we're taking a bit of time."

"Oh no. A fight?"

"Things are just a little confusing." I waved my hand through the air. "Let's not talk about it now. Should we help build this fire or, I don't know, smudge some sage or something?"

"I'm going to give you a spell," Margot said. "To help you gain clarity. It's helped me in the past." She proceeded to explain it to me, intently, staring into my eyes, as the wood began to crackle and smoke, and the others arranged themselves in a circle.

"Thank you," I said, and then in a lower voice, "But seriously, are you okay?"

"Imagine you had a direct line to God," she said, putting a placid look on her face, though her tone was sardonic. "You knew that whatever prayer you sent up would be answered—true equality, say, or an incredible person being elected to lead the country— and you chose to pray that your famous friend's book would sell. It would be pretty hard to look at yourself in the mirror after that."

"Margot?" Caroline asked. "Come on. We're ready."

A look of annoyance passed over Margot's features. Then she shook it off, took my hand, and we went to join the group.

THIRTY-SEVEN

The next day, I tried the spell that Margot had given me. For research purposes. Although if I happened to gain some clarity along the way thanks to the placebo effect, I would take it.

First, I grabbed an egg from the refrigerator. I held its cold, speckled shell to my forehead. *Focus on the negative, confusing energy inside of you*, Margot had said. *Let it flow out of you and into the egg.*

Why an egg? I'd asked.

It represents a fresh start.

Feeling faintly ridiculous, I rolled the egg down my nose, over my neck, and onto my chest. I rubbed it in three clockwise circles over my heart, thinking about the causes of my inner turmoil.

Miles's face appeared in my mind. I'd finally texted him back earlier that afternoon. **Sorry, I needed time to digest some things**, I wrote. **But I have updates for you.** His response came immediately, suggesting that we meet up the next day. He could come to my place, he said, which was strange, since he'd previously made it clear that he didn't think we should have business meetings in my bedroom.

New apartment now, I'd written, **and it's owned by Margot's aunt, so it's probably not the safest.** We'd settled on a neutral location instead, one of those rent-by-the-hour meeting rooms in an office building. My heart thumped against the egg's shell in anticipation.

No contact from Raf, or from Libby. Not that I actually expected it, but still, every time I glanced at my phone and didn't see their names, a foolish burst of disappointment rose up inside of me.

I rubbed the egg back up my body in the opposite direction, and around my head a few more times for good measure. Then I took it out my door, down the elevator, and, cupping it in my hand, jaywalked across Central Park West, narrowly avoiding an overeager taxi. (What a way to go *that* would be: *Police declared it a normal hit-and-run, although they could not understand why the victim was clutching a raw egg.*)

Once I made it into Central Park, I found a secluded spot, a grove of trees slightly off the beaten path. I knelt down in the grass. Then, as dusk began to fall, in one fluid motion, I smashed the egg into the earth. The shell cracked, and golden yolk spurted onto my fingers. I rubbed it off in the grass, then covered the whole mess up with dirt. I sat back on my haunches to find a tourist couple—in matching *Phantom of the Opera* sweatshirts—staring at me.

"I'm a performance artist," I said to them. They blinked, then politely applauded.

After I'm done with the egg, Margot had said, *I take a long bath, and when I emerge, everything seems clearer.*

So I went back into my apartment, lit some candles, and soaked in the tub until the water around me cooled and my fingers pruned, thinking about everything I'd done and everything I had left to do.

When I finally got out of the bath and wrapped myself in a towel, one new bit of knowledge was crystal clear: I had just wasted a perfectly good egg.

THIRTY-EIGHT

When I arrived at the office space where Miles and I had arranged to meet, he was already there, sitting at the table, leaning back in his chair. He jumped to his feet as I walked in. "Hey, it's good to see you," he said. The room was muted, We Work–esque, with a small round table and a white-board, plus one piece of mass-produced art meant to liven things up. Within its sterility, Miles seemed extra alive.

"Good to see you too," I said. He pulled out a chair for me. He'd shaved his beard off in the week since I'd seen him last.

"Wow," I said. "New look. Is your face cold all the time now?"

"I'm constantly on the edge of contracting hypothermia," he said, and laughed. Goddammit, I loved his laugh, which he didn't give out to just anyone. Whenever he laughed with me, I felt like a chosen one, swirling and jittery and high on adrenaline.

Suddenly, Raf's face flashed into my mind, the sadness on it when he told me that he needed space from me. I needed space from Miles, who wasn't available and wasn't *going* to be. I had to finish my article and then take some time before working with him again, if I worked with him again ever. Maybe the egg had given me some clarity after all.

"So, I want to apologize again about the gala—" he began.

"It's fine. That's not important right now," I said. "These women are not well. They believe that they did things that got Nicole Woo-Martin elected."

"Sure. Like, donating to her? Holding fund-raisers?"

"No, more than that."

"What—"

"And I got into the back room."

"Holy shit," he said. "What's inside?"

I'd been thinking and thinking on my way over about the best way to tell him. Now I opened my mouth, but something held me back. I swallowed. "Have they scheduled your performance review yet?"

He blinked. "Yes, next Thursday. As in, not tomorrow. The first week of November."

"Okay," I said. "Okay, good, so there's still some time." I put my hands on the table. "If I tell you everything right now, you'll think that I'm lying."

"I won't," he said.

"No, I promise you, it's going to sound like I'm making up some batshit story that's just going to get you deeper into trouble, and I don't want that."

"So, what does that mean?"

"Give me this weekend. They're taking me away with them. Let me really find out everything I need to know and then figure out how you can see it for yourself. I think that's the only way this is going to work."

"Beckley," he said.

"Trust me."

"You've gotta give me something here—"

"I need you to trust me."

He paused. "Okay. I do." Another beat of silence stretched between us. "It's not . . . dangerous, is it? You're taking care of yourself?"

I shrugged. "Oh, you know, some things might be dubiously legal, but I'm fine." I waved my hand through the air. He squinted at it, then reached out and clasped it in a fluid motion, bringing my palm close to his face.

"Wait, what happened?" he asked, pointing at my scar. "This is new." I pulled my hand back, covering it with my other one, and he leaned forward. "Is this part of it?"

"It's okay," I said. "It's basically a glorified scratch."

"You don't need to put on a front for me," he said, wrinkling his forehead in concern. "Seriously. I want this story, but more than that, I want to make sure that you're okay. We threw you into something that turned out to be far more intense than we expected, and if it hurts you somehow . . . I'm not all right with that."

"I'm taking care of myself," I said.

He bit his lip. "Okay, then." He sat back. "And listen, I know you said it's not important, but I think it is—will you tell your friend that I'm sorry for how I was acting at the gala? He seems like a nice guy."

"I—" I began. "Um, you might need to tell him yourself. He doesn't want to see me for a little while." Miles raised an eyebrow. "We put the fake-dating thing on hold."

"He got too invested in it, huh?" Miles asked, and I looked away. "Damn, Beckley, you're stealthy about it, but you're a heartbreaker, aren't you?"

"Fuck you," I said. "I'm not."

"Well, then, just to you: I'm sorry I was being a dick. At the gala, and like five seconds ago."

"And some other times too. You've kind of been a dick a lot lately."

"I have," he said, and stared down at the table, toying with a pen he'd taken from the cupholder. "Emmy and I are getting divorced."

My mouth went dry. I'd fantasized about him saying these words to me and had hated myself for it. "I'm really sorry to hear that."

"Thanks," he said. "We gave it our all, but it just—" He put the pen down and looked at me. "It just wasn't right." His clear blue eyes held mine. "I don't want to complicate anything, with you working on this story, but I wanted to let you know."

I cleared my throat. My face felt hot. Under the table, my hands trembled, so I sat on them. "Thank you for the update."

"Let's talk again when you get back from the trip?" His voice was so soft that I had to lean forward to hear it. "About the article, and everything?"

All my egg-gained clarity disappeared. "Let's do that," I said.

THIRTY-NINE

The e-mail Caroline had sent me about the Samhain trip was extremely detailed, with bullet points, packing lists, and a weather forecast. On Saturday morning, I stood outside my apartment to play my role in Caroline's efficient carpool schedule: Iris would be taking the Coven members who lived downtown, Vy and Margot would ride together from Brooklyn, and Caroline would pop over from her home on the Upper East Side to grab me from the Upper West.

I was looking down the avenue for a sensible, expensive car keeping perfectly to the speed limit when a big white van swerved up next to me, and Vy leaned her head out of the driver's window.

"Get in," she said.

I blinked. "Oh. Hey. I think I'm supposed to ride with Caroline?"

"Change of plans. Just get in."

I slid open the door and climbed into the backseat. Music—something Icelandic and keening—pumped through the stereo as Margot turned around from the passenger's seat and gave my hand a squeeze. "Hey you," she said. She'd wrapped a scarf around her hair, like a classic movie star, driven by her lover down a winding European road. "Caroline's not coming." Vy put her foot on the gas and the van roared into action.

"She's meeting us at the cabin?"

"No," Margot said. "Unfortunately, she's ill. She's been throwing up all morning. She can't come at all."

"Holy shit," I said. "Do you think it's food poisoning or something?"

"Maybe," Margot said.

"Maybe she's pregnant," Vy said.

"Let's hope not. According to her life plan, that's not supposed to happen for another year and a half." Margot's voice was dry. "She'd be *very* upset to deviate from the schedule."

We bumped down the avenue. The van smelled of paint and something faintly like rotten meat, and I was willing to bet anything that it was the same van I'd ridden in the night that they'd taken me from my apartment. "Well," I said, "that really sucks for her. I know she was excited about the trip."

"Yes, it's terrible timing," Margot said, and she and Vy exchanged a look, one that I could've sworn contained a hint of amusement. Vy sped up suddenly and we pulled onto the highway.

Vy was an unpredictable and casually terrifying driver, not bothering to put her blinker on until she'd already started changing lanes, but Margot seemed unruffled by it. We left the city behind us and entered the suburbs. Then we left the suburbs behind too. We passed farmland and fields. An hour and a half after we'd set out, Vy turned the van onto a road made of dirt and gravel, a nar-

row, winding path. We drove past a sign that read END STATE MAIN-
TENANCE. The road dropped into a steep decline, and I grasped the
seat beneath me as Margot began to hum in the passenger's seat,
some excited, cheery tune. Then we turned again, into a driveway
with a sign reading PRIVATE PROPERTY.

"Welcome to the cabin," Margot said as it came into view before us.

Sure, it was a cabin, if you were judging only by its wooden exterior. The dark, stacked logs, in and of themselves, gave off the
requisite Abe Lincoln vibes. But if you were going by anything
else—like, say, its size—it was not a cabin at all. It was a behemoth:
three stories, with a large porch on one side, and two separate chim-
neys. Behind the cabin, the woods loomed, the trees a riot of color—
scarlet and burnt sienna and golden leaves trembling in the breeze.

We all stepped out of the car and stood in the yard. Vy pulled a
stick of beef jerky out of her pocket and began to gnaw at it. Margot stretched her arms up high, taking in a deep breath as the wind
whipped her hair around her. "God," she said. "The air here. It's
ambrosial."

I'd never been taken in by all the hoopla about fresh air. Fill my
lungs up with that sweet, sweet city smog and let me slowly suffo-
cate in a place with bodegas. Still, I followed Margot's lead and
took a deep breath too, the sharp chill filling up my lungs. I thought
of Caroline sitting miserably in her apartment. While we were on
the road she'd sent out an e-mail to the group with a checklist of
reminders for the agenda she'd drawn up, expressing her disappointment. **I'm devastated not to join. But while I rest and hydrate, I
expect the rest of you to carry on. Try to have a great time without worrying about me too much!** she'd written. Margot, in the front seat,
had scanned the e-mail and then deleted it. And then we'd lost cell
service entirely.

No cell service. No neighbors. This was the perfect place to get murdered, or to sacrifice a new member for her betrayal.

"Yes," Margot continued as Iris pulled into the driveway in a sleek red sports car, from which the other women piled out with their luggage and their chatter. "This is going to be an excellent Samhain."

FORTY

There were enough bedrooms for us to each have our own. Mine had a comfortable queen bed covered in a flannel goose-feather comforter, topped with more pillows than I'd ever seen in one place before. There was just enough of a rustic feel to the decor that you couldn't forget you were in a "cabin"— exposed beams, the paint on the walls distressed in a very intentional way, a little wood-burning stove in the corner. Had Margot gotten some fancy interior designer from the city to drive all the way out here, down these winding roads, to consult?

After we all put our luggage in our rooms, some of the women went on a nature walk. Others decided to cast some individual spells, to work on their own magic before we all came back together for our nighttime rituals.

"I don't really know any spells. Besides the egg one. Which was great. Loved that egg spell," I said to Margot as we stood in her living room, which somehow managed to feel gigantic and cozy at the same time. Its ceiling was two stories high, and all the windows were hung with gauzy curtains. In addition to a couple of large midcentury modern couches, throw pillows and poufs littered the floor, which was covered by an artfully faded woven rug. A huge fireplace lined almost the entirety of one wall.

"I can teach you." She opened up a chest of shabby-chic drawers to reveal a variety of candles, herbs, and other supplies. I'd have felt like I was in an apothecary in Shakespeare's time, if not for the clean Avenir Next labels on everything. More of an apothecary designed by Gwyneth Paltrow. Herb by herb, candle by candle, Margot went through the supplies with me, explaining the types of spells you might do with each one. She radiated authority, standing up taller and taller as she went, even though what she was saying didn't make any sense to me, as if I'd signed up for a course with a respected college professor without realizing that it would be taught in a foreign language.

"What's your favorite spell?" I asked at one point.

"Hmm," she said, giving me a strange look. "I've had good luck with a summoning one, to find someone that you've been looking for. You take one of these candles"—here she pointed to a thin white taper—"and carve some representation of the person into it. So for example, a heart, if you were trying to summon a lover. Then you scatter sea salt in a circle around the candle, light it, and say a prayer to call that person into your life. It can be very effective." She smiled a private, small smile. "But there are so many others too." And she went on to explain spells for prosperity, for protection, and more.

"That was the one Caroline and I did, the first time we came up here," she said at the end of one explanation, her tone lapsing a bit into melancholy.

"I hope you don't mind me saying this, but you and Caroline are a . . . funny match. To have started a coven together, I mean."

She smiled. "Well. Some of it was our family history. And some, I suppose, is that a big goal can make strange bedfellows. When we started out, what we wanted to do was so strong that our differences didn't matter."

Caroline and Margot had both alluded to a goal now, a goal that didn't seem to be Caroline's driving force anymore. "What you wanted to do?" I asked. "Boosting your careers and such, you mean?"

"Not that," she said, her expression stormy. "It was supposed to be more than just helping each other and ourselves, and maybe bringing down the occasional bad man. We had something bigger in mind."

"What was it?"

She hesitated. Then she looked me straight in the eye and said, almost against her better judgment, "We wanted to elect the first female president."

Well, shit. Way to set achievable objectives.

Margot went on. "We didn't know if we could do it, of course. But we wanted to try. We'd seen how a woman could be far more qualified, far more intelligent, and still be passed over, time and again. And we were done being helpless about it. We had influence and we had magic, so why couldn't we be the queen-makers?" She shrugged. "And sure, we thought it would be nice to have the ear of the person in charge, particularly since Caroline always had such great policy ideas—her thoughts on parental leave were transformative—but more than that, we wanted to do it for equality, for all the girls out there."

"Was that why you all worked so hard for Nicole Woo-Martin?" She hesitated, so I leaned forward and continued, in a low voice, "What happened there? You can tell me."

"Why do you want to know?"

"Because I'm a curious little bitch." She smiled, just slightly, so I went on. "And because I'm a member of the Coven now. Shouldn't I be up to date on the history? The good, the bad, and the ugly?"

"I've probably said too much already. I like you, Jillian, but not even the other members know the full story. The details are between me and Caroline, and she asked me not to get into it with anyone new, which I understand," she said. "I'm sorry." She turned and headed toward the door. "Now, I have some things I want to work on myself, but go ahead, use whatever supplies you need."

I watched her disappear into the yard. That had been . . . informative? Supremely frustrating? If the details needed to be kept just between her and Caroline, that certainly made it sound like something sketchy had gone on.

To pass the time more than anything else, I took one of the white candles, a matchbook, and a pinch of sea salt, and found a spot, just beyond the tree line, where I was hidden from the other women.

I didn't know what kind of symbol would represent a failed mayor. So, with a pen in my pocket, I carved Nicole Woo-Martin's initials into the candle. I made a circle with sea salt, then lit the candle. "Um," I said quietly, and called up Nicole's face into my mind, the last time I had seen it, when she had given the speech announcing her resignation. It was also on the steps of City Hall, just like at her inauguration, but hope and grandeur no longer swirled around her, and her supportive schlubby husband no longer stood by her side.

I made an error in judgment, and for that I am truly sorry. But I would never have threatened someone's job over this, she'd said, her voice strong, but her hands trembling at her sides. *I hope you can believe me. Still, I recognize that the distraction caused by this has damaged my ability to fight for our agenda, and the work can only be done if I step aside. I am heartbroken. But at the end of the day, the work must be done.*

I had been heartbroken too, for my mother and for the world. I was still heartbroken. Nicole's replacement was a business-as-usual woman who'd done nothing of note since she took over. All the exciting legislation Nicole had introduced was just sitting there, stalled. I stared at the candle. "Nicole," I said, "I call you into my life. Let me find you, so I can talk to you and figure out the truth of what they did to you, and what the fuck you were thinking." Maybe not the holiest of prayers, but it couldn't hurt.

The small flame wavered in the breeze. A rustling sound came from the trees to my left, where the woods began to thicken. I turned, and for a split second I expected to see Nicole emerge—perhaps she'd been wandering in the forests all this time, and her compass was now spinning and sending her my way. But instead Vy stomped into the clearing, and over her shoulder was a bag filled with plants she'd gathered from the woods. I snuffed out the candle quickly and stuck it in my pocket.

"We're gonna make dinner," she said. "Come on."

As darkness fell, we roasted root vegetables and sautéed halibut. Iris had brought along a loaf of dark pumpernickel bread. The kitchen was all gleaming marble countertops, an eight-burner stove. Margot had an old record player in the corner, and she put on Ella Fitzgerald to serenade us as we cooked. We slapped on some organic bug spray and ate on the porch. For a moment, as Margot turned the fairy lights on and Iris told a story about some celebrity who kept sending her flowers, it felt like we were at a fun, rustic bachelorette weekend, and maybe a firefighter stripper would come knocking at the door.

It wasn't very much food when it was all split up among us. More like the first course of a tasting menu, an appetizer. My stomach rumbled, primed for the actual meal. It didn't help that I hadn't had lunch, assuming we'd stop somewhere on the road. None of the other women seemed bothered, though. Maybe they'd brought snack bars in their bags, or maybe they were used to more restrictive diets. Or maybe they wanted to feel lighter, more alert—like tech bros, with their intermittent fasting—for what was coming next. Margot stood up. "It's time," she said. The women all disappeared into their rooms as Margot beckoned me over.

"Here," she said, and handed me a black robe of my own.

"Very chic," I said. She raised an eyebrow and looked at me. "I mean, thank you. Do I . . . do I wear anything underneath?"

"What do you think?" she asked, then laughed her throaty laugh. She stepped closer to me and reached out a finger, tracing my mother's necklace, the one we'd talked about at Raf's restaurant opening the very first time we met. "Keep this on, though."

FORTY-ONE

We made our way into the woods. Margot led the group, holding up a lantern. I carried some logs for the fire, grasping them haphazardly in a quest to avoid splinters, hoping that we weren't going to wander into poison ivy or a spider's nest. Crickets chirped and tree branches rustled. Dead leaves crackled underfoot. A few of the women whispered to one another, an isolated giggle breaking out, but for the most part, we were silent as we swished through the bramble.

Besides Margot's lantern, the only source of light was the glowing orb of the moon above, bigger and more golden than I'd ever seen it. A moon on steroids, surrounded by pinpricks of stars. I wasn't used to such darkness. I shivered, both because I was cold underneath my robe, and because I was scared.

Do you remember the kind of fear that you felt as a child, when you had the sense that anything was possible? Ghosts might be lingering in the shadows. A hand could reach out from underneath your bed and drag you down. Perhaps a vampire lurked in your attic, waiting for the moment when you were alone and defenseless to bare his fangs. As a grown woman, I had plenty to fear in the real world—a man walking too close behind me at night, a man yelling hateful things in people's faces on the subway, a man coming through my window or revealing his true colors or doing any number of things. But the fear that came over me as we walked deeper into the dark woods was like it was in childhood again. Terrifying, but tinged with a sense of possibility. Spooky, and just a little bit full of wonder. I didn't fear a man tonight. I feared these women, and the strange things I could not see in the darkness, and maybe, just maybe, myself.

We emerged into a clearing, and Margot stopped. She held the lantern up high, looking for something in the trees at the edges. Then she moved toward a large oak with a hollow in its center. The lantern light revealed the deep ridges in its bark, the greenish moss growing over it. She put her hand on the edge of the hollow, where the wood formed a kind of ledge.

"Our altar," she said. The women spread out around her and began to set up, pulling offerings from their bags. Vy assembled wood for a bonfire inside of a ring of small stones. Tara placed a gourd on the altar's ledge, along with some dried flowers. Iris handed us each a wreath she'd made, woven with berries and leaves, and we put them on our heads, our hair loose and flowing beneath them, like we were going to a Renaissance fair or a trendy wedding in a barn. We all kicked off our shoes and left them at the edge of the clearing.

"Anyone thirsty?" Vy asked. As some of the women began to murmur in the affirmative, she pulled a bottle of wine out from her bag.

"Oh. We shouldn't, should we?" Iris asked. "We should wait until we're finished, I mean. Caroline wouldn't want—"

"It's hardly anything, split between all of us," Vy said. She twisted off the screw top with one jerk of her hand, then tipped her head back and took a large swallow.

"Are you sure?" one of the other women—Gabby—asked.

"Yes, it's so little, it won't interfere," Margot said. "If anything, it will only enhance. Besides, it's a special occasion. It's Samhain." She took her own swallow, then passed it on. The women sent the bottle down the line as we continued to set up, although I noticed that Iris didn't take a sip herself. When it came to me, I held the wine in my mouth for a moment before swallowing. It was spicy and warming, but still my teeth chattered in the autumn night.

"You cold?" Vy asked. She took out a thermos and unscrewed the top. Steam rose from it. "I brewed some tea," she said, and held it out to me. "Here." I took a swallow of that too, then recoiled at its bitterness. Vy noticed the look on my face. "It's good for you," she said. "All natural."

"Mm," I said, and took another sip, then handed it back to her.

Vy lit the fire, and the kindling began to catch. As the larger logs caught too and the women finished setting up, we all gathered in our circle. Again, we linked hands, and again, we began to breathe in long, slow inhales all at the same time. It reminded me of warm-ups we did in an acting class I took freshman year of college. Pretty soon, if we kept following that theater class trajectory, we'd be reciting tongue twisters for diction, and making out with each other.

"Sisters," Margot said. Or maybe "intoned" was the right word for the way she spoke, her husky voice resonant. "Summer is over. The harvest has been gathered and it is time to plant new seeds. Let us plant them now and pledge to care for one another's." Margot walked around the circle, handing each of us an herb that Caroline had selected for us, an herb that was supposed to represent what we were hoping to have success with. Caroline had assigned me rosemary, for creativity.

One by one, we played our starring role in the ritual. Iris held up her handful of mint. "I plant the seeds for my book's success."

"*Let them grow tall and full,*" we chanted as she knelt to the ground and buried the herb in the dirt in front of her.

When it came to me, I said my piece about planting the seeds for my writing. The women gazed at me, their faces shining and supportive, and I knew that my true success would mean their downfall. For a moment, it was the strangest thing, but I almost wanted to cry. The smoke from the fire was clouding my head. My stomach rumbled again. The dirt under my feet had been cold and scratchy ever since I'd kicked my shoes off, but as I pushed the herb into the ground, the earth was soft, comforting even, against my fingers, and I was sad to take my hand out.

Margot's smile, when it came time for her, was hooded, faraway. "I plant the seeds to make real change again," she said.

"*Let them grow tall and full.*"

Together, we each took a small sprig of basil and planted it for Caroline in absentia, chanting for the success of Women Who Lead.

"Now, we seal our spell," Margot said. "And toast to the future." Vy took out another bottle—more red wine—and passed it around the circle. This time, everyone was less hesitant with their swallows, though Iris held the bottle to her lips for only a second. She disapproved of it, still.

When we'd drained the bottle, some of the women began to pull at their robes, as if ready to move on to the dancing and the celebration. But Margot stopped them. "One more ritual," she said. She knelt down and took something out of her bag: a round, red fruit that she held in the firelight. "A pomegranate," she said.

Everyone besides Margot and Vy looked confused. Caroline's agenda hadn't included anything about a pomegranate.

"In Greek mythology," Margot continued, still locked into her ceremonial focus, her shadow tall as the trees, "Persephone ate its seeds in the Underworld, the land where the spirits lived after death. Tonight, when the veil between worlds is thin, we eat its seeds to connect with the spirits of those we've lost."

"Hold on," Iris said. "We're not going to *summon* them, are we?"

Margot hesitated, then shook her head. "We'll just send them a message. Ask them for protection, if you want. Remind them of your love." She held the pomegranate up, then dug her finger into its skin. Red juice seeped out, and I flashed back to my first ceremony: the knife in the base of my thumb, the red spilling from my hand. A full-body shiver passed through me.

Margot closed her eyes and took in a deep breath, thinking—I assumed—of her mother. Then she tore the fruit open and held it to her mouth. A trickle of juice—scarlet, the color richer than it should have been in the darkness—traced its way down her throat as she tilted her head back. She straightened up, her eyes glittering, and handed the fruit on to the next person.

I was feeling strange, light-headed, almost a little drunk, and I looked around the circle to see if anyone else's eyes were too bright. Something glowed at the edge of my vision and I narrowed my eyes to bring it into focus: a patch of mushrooms at the edge of the clearing. They seemed to glow in the firelight, their white tops pulsing. A suspicion hit me.

"Vy," I whispered, leaning over to her as the women passed the pomegranate down the circle.

"What?"

"Was that normal tea, the stuff you gave me?"

"What do you mean?"

"I mean, did you put something in it?"

Vy stared at me, one pale eyebrow traveling very slowly up her forehead and back down again. Then she gave me the strangest look—I think it was supposed to be a mischievous smile but it came out like a grimace?—and turned back to the circle, accepting the pomegranate from Tara for her own bite. The other women looked on, their eyes blinking in slow motion.

I'd never done a drug besides pot because I was generally a wuss, present circumstances excluded. But I'd written an article for Quill once about people getting high and going to see bad movies, and I'd read up extensively on all sorts of drugs for research. Shrooms had a bitter taste. They were often brewed into tea, and they distorted things—textures, colors, emotions.

Had Vy laced the tea with fucking *shrooms*? That unreadable, potentially sociopathic asshole. But there was nothing I could do about it now except go with it. And if I were going on a trip, at least it wasn't a bad one. No nightmare panic. The fire, the women, my own hands in front of me—everything just looked more beautiful.

Vy handed the pomegranate to me and I tore open a new patch of skin. The seeds glistened, droplets of juice from the other women's bites quivering on the fresh, untouched sections. Almost without realizing it, I put my fingers to my necklace, staining my skin beneath with the pomegranate juice. My mother's face flashed into my mind. *God, I wish you were here*, I thought. Then I bit into the fruit, and the seeds burst in my mouth.

Vy threw another log on the fire. Margot began to hum something that I didn't recognize. Vy joined in, and their voices vibrated together, traveling through the air and into my body, where they made a strumming, a thrumming, inside of me.

This time, I was the first to lift my robe off, my arms prickling in the cold as the others followed. I'd been clenching my shoulders for months, maybe even years, and they'd finally loosened.

As the music grew around me—the gentle, throaty voices weaving with the crackle of the fire, the crickets chirping their own contributions, the rustle of the leaves our steady drumbeat—we all began to dance. And I didn't lose myself in my own private world, going into my own body as if no one else existed. This time, Margot put her palm up in the air in front of me and I touched mine to hers. We stood there like that for a moment, and then we began to move, together, as if we knew exactly where the other one was going to turn.

Then we were *all* dancing together, joining hands, breaking apart, circling. We were gliding and graceful, the fire beating hot on our naked backs. The fall wildflowers at the edge of the clearing—hearty, surviving stalks—opened and closed their petals in time with our breathing. We lay down in the dirt and made angels with our arms and my body was so full of sensation, my heart was so full of bliss.

I understood that to be a woman in the world was to spend so much time trying to act the right way. Be loud enough, but not too loud. Stand up for yourself, but pleasantly. Beauty was everything, but you shouldn't rely on your looks. Always, always I was trying to get it right, to find the balance, but here around this circle, naked but not sexualized, together we could flail and scream and open ourselves raw without worrying about anything else at all. We were powerful and free, and I felt like I had when I went skinny-dipping for the first time: I was moving through something larger than myself, but also I was a part of it, no barriers between us.

Time slowed down and then sped up again. Margot handed Iris her lantern, and a few of the women made their way back toward the cabin for bed. Then Margot took my hand. "Come with me," she said, and led me to the other side of the fire from where the remaining women danced.

"Hi," she said, and smiled at me.

"Hi," I said, and smiled back.

She let go of my hand and moved her fingers very slowly until they rested on my necklace. "Your mother wants to talk to you."

FORTY-TWO

What?" I asked as a roaring in my ears started, like ocean waves. "I don't—"

"You must have called her, and now she's here," Margot said. "I can't stop it."

And then her eyes went unfocused for a moment, as if she were in a kind of trance. When they focused on me again, they were different. Instead of Margot's appraising, languid gaze, her eyes looked out on me with pure love.

"Jillian," she said, and her voice was higher, still Margot's voice but as if it had been mixed with a different one.

"Margot," I said, stepping back. "Do not fuck with me like this."

"My little skeptic," she said, and leaned forward, her hair swinging toward my face. It didn't smell like jasmine now. It smelled of smoke, yes, but also the faint scent of vanilla, like the perfume I'd given my mother as a present so many years ago. This wasn't happening. This wasn't happening. Oh God, how I wanted it to be happening.

"Stop it," I said.

"It's okay." She reached out and touched my cheek gently. "Are you keeping your promise?"

"I . . ." I said, my breath leaving me as if I'd been punched in the stomach. *You have a gift for stories. I need you to promise me that you're only going to use it for good.* I stared into those wide, concerned eyes as they waited for my answer. "I'm trying," I said when I could speak again. "I'm really trying to use it for good, but I don't know."

All those times I thought I'd seen her in the man on the subway, the woman on the street, only to have her disappear—I'd felt so strongly in those brief seconds that there was more of her waiting for me. Always, I'd come back to my senses. She was gone, irrevocably gone, and I was never supposed to be able to talk to her again because that was just the way that the world worked, but now Margot was saying in that strange, un-Margot-like voice, "You'll figure it out. You always do."

"I'm not sure about that this time," I said.

"I wish I could help you." She shook her head. "But how's our Raf doing?"

"He's—" I began, then cleared my throat. "You'd be really proud of him."

Margot gave me a look my mother had given me a million times before, one that managed to be both wry and empathetic at the same time. "You need to figure that out too, don't you?"

"I guess I do."

"I just want you to have a family," she said, and I couldn't stop a little laugh from escaping me.

"Right, because my eggs are dying."

"Well, yes," she said, with a slight smile. Then her face turned serious, searching again. "But it doesn't have to be that kind of family."

A lump rose in my throat, and before I even knew what I was doing I had reached out and clasped both of her hands in mine. "Are you all right? Are you . . . warm? Sorry, that's a stupid question—"

"I'm warm. I just miss you."

"I miss you so much. All of the time." My lip trembled, and I bit it, trying to swallow the tears. *Big girls don't cry.*

"It's okay," she said, and traced the corner of my eye, where a tear was threatening to spill out. "You can. You should."

With that, the floodgates burst open. I wept in an all-consuming way like I hadn't in forever, maybe not since I was a child. Sounds escaped me, gasping, wretched sounds over which I had no control, and I couldn't catch my breath. I sank onto the ground, onto the cold dirt.

Margot wrapped her arms around me and began to cry too. I clutched her tightly, and our bodies shuddered and heaved against each other for a long time. Maybe minutes. Maybe hours. When my sobs ran out and we grew still, I wiped my nose and took a sniff in. I couldn't smell vanilla anymore. Whatever had just happened, it was over.

The strange expression on Margot's face drained away. She wiped her nose too, her tear-streaked cheeks, and blinked a few times as if she were waking up. My head was heavy, but the rest of my body had grown lighter. I was devastated that it was done and so grateful that it had happened at all.

"Thank you," I said.

Margot gave me a small, sad smile. "I've never been able to do that with my mother. She won't come. But maybe next Samhain, you can help me."

"I can try," I said, my voice rusty from the tears. Margot leaned forward and brushed her lips against my cheek, so lightly I barely felt it. Then she looked up at the sky, stood, and pulled me to my feet.

"Come on," she said. "We only have a little time." She grabbed our robes and we ran through the woods, barefoot, thrashing through low-hanging branches, scrambling over rocks. As we ran, a strange thought hit me: I wanted to tell Raf what had happened, how I'd been able to talk to my mother again, to tell him how she'd asked about him. I shook that thought off and kept running. The ground before us rose in an incline and we climbed it, emerged through a grove of trees onto a ridge as the sky began to lighten around us. We sat on the grass, panting softly, as the others who had stayed up came through the trees behind us. We all wrapped our robes around ourselves like blankets and watched the sunrise. Pinks and oranges streaked across the sky. The only sounds were the rustle of a breeze in the leaves and our own awed breathing.

I realized then that I hadn't tried very hard to talk to anyone about Nicole Woo-Martin because I wanted to believe that they couldn't have hurt her. They'd only ever wanted to build her up, not bring her down. Maybe too they weren't as elitist as I'd thought. Margot had figured out that I wasn't rich, that I wasn't even close. That's why she'd found me a free apartment. And still, I was here beside them, worthy of their love.

As the morning light caught in Margot's hair and brightened Vy's face, I didn't want to betray them anymore. I didn't want to write about this night, to try and make sense of it. I didn't want to lose this beautiful, precious place, where things were magic and I belonged.

FORTY-THREE

We all slept until the afternoon. When I woke up, my feet ached. I turned my heel over to reveal scratches and bruises from the night before. I had a splinter that I didn't remember getting. I pulled it out with my fingernails.

The smell of coffee and butter drew me to the kitchen, where I found Tara, frying up potatoes at the stovetop while Iris and Ophelia sat at the table drinking coffee as if their lives depended on it. Tara shoveled some of the potatoes onto a plate and handed it to me.

"Thank you," I said. "God, do shrooms make you ravenous the morning after? 'Cause I am starving."

"Shrooms?" Tara asked.

"From Vy's tea." Tara gave me a blank look. At the table, Iris's back stiffened. Oops. "Did she not pass it around to everyone?"

"Apparently not," Iris said.

"I'm not mad or anything that she did it," I said, and it was true, even though I should have been livid. "It was a really wonderful night."

"Sounds like next time she should share with us all," Tara said.

We ate in the living room, sitting on the couches and the pillows, our feet tangling together under plush quilts, recovering and relaxing. My mother and I used to veg out on our couch together all the time, in those couple of years that I'd taken care of her. We'd spent multiple afternoons a week under the blankets cupping huge mugs of tea, gossiping about everything like middle school girls. My mother had always been so busy when I was growing up, trying to earn enough to support a family as a single mother, so our leisurely afternoons together were the one unexpected upside to her illness.

Now I had a kind of warmth like that again, as we moaned about our aching calves and told each other stories. Iris sat, lost in thought, by the window, every so often exchanging looks with Nina. But the rest of us passed one another snacks and laughed until finally, regretfully, we knew it was time to go home.

In the van, Iris's sports car zipping ahead of us, our phones all dinged at once. We'd driven back into service, and we had a new e-mail from Caroline.

Feeling much better today, she'd written to the group, **and cannot wait to hear about your trip! Let's all meet at the clubhouse when you arrive back in the city so you can fill me in? Let me know your ETA. There might be people around, so use the back entrance, obviously.**

We sped toward the West Village, a new camaraderie among the three of us. Margot and I sang along to Vy's yowly Icelandic music, making up lyrics, and she pretended that it didn't bother

her. I felt a sudden, deep surge of tenderness for her and her un-apologetic weirdness.

"I thought you hated me for the longest time," I said to Vy, who gave a kind of harrumphing noise in response.

"Oh!" Margot said. "Why?"

"Basically the first thing she ever said to me was that I was a seagull who was afraid of the ocean."

Margot laughed, delighted.

"I still think you're a seagull," Vy said.

"No! Can't I graduate to a heron or a hawk, or something cool like that?"

"When seagulls do go beneath the waves, they actually have excellent lung capacity." She swerved into a different lane. "Those birds are stronger than they look."

"Thanks," I said, biting my lip. Now that the floodgates had opened, all my emotions were bubbling very close to the surface. Oh God, I was going to become the kind of person who cried at commercials.

I wished that time could extend infinitely between now and when I was supposed to talk to Miles again, so that I could keep living like this. For the first time, I pictured telling him that I'd chosen the Nevertheless women over him. I wanted the things that they had: the power, yes, but more important, the sisterhood. Vy swerved onto the streets of the West Village as dusk started to fall, and parked somewhere far away from the clubhouse's entrance. In-stead of walking into the front door, she and Margot turned down a back alley.

"So there's a secret back entrance?" I asked.

"Yes," Margot said. "Just in case we need to get to the roof without anyone else seeing."

We came to an unmarked, unprepossessing gray door with a

small keypad to one side of it. Margot typed in a code—2823—and then pressed the door handle. We entered into a small dark hallway. No security guard here. At the end of the hall was a staircase, and also a musty freight elevator, the same one I'd only ever taken from behind the door in the clubhouse a few floors up. Its gears ground and squeaked as we rose through the air. Laughing, talking, we stepped off the elevator and through the door leading to the roof, along the narrow pathway between trellises to where the trees began. Caroline and the others were already there, locked in whispered conversation. When we emerged into the circle, they turned and looked at us. Iris had a strange, resolute expression on her face. Caroline's coloring was still a little green, but her eyes were dark. Furious.

"Welcome back, Margot," she said, her voice like ice. "They just told me everything."

FORTY-FOUR

Margot straightened her shoulders and looked at Caroline with a level gaze. "What do you mean?"

Caroline began to pace, practically spitting as she talked. "Summoning the dead? Drinking during the rituals? And I hear you allowed Vy to put *shrooms* in her tea and drug Jillian?" Vy shot me a *what the fuck?* look, as if she couldn't believe that I'd sold her out like that. "It's like everything I've asked you not to do—"

"It doesn't even get close to everything," Margot said drily.

"—and the moment I couldn't be there, you just did whatever the hell you wanted! And yes, I do have suspicions about how all of a sudden I started to feel badly right before Samhain—"

"Well, now you sound crazy."

"Don't call me crazy!" Caroline snapped.

"I'm sorry. But nothing bad happened," Margot said, her voice calm, as if she were dealing with a child having a tantrum over nothing. "We're all fine. We didn't even do any magic toward the old goal, I promise. Maybe you and I should discuss this somewhere—"

But Margot's measured tone seemed only to make Caroline more upset. She steamrolled on, as the other women exchanged uncomfortable glances. "It never seems bad right away. It didn't seem bad with Nicole until months later, and then it was a disaster."

"When will you let us move on from that?" Margot said. "I don't know how much longer I can sit around and do small, selfish magic about Iris's *book*—"

"Excuse me," Iris said.

"—when we have a potential to be such a powerful force in the world!"

"I can't deal with another mess like that again!" Caroline said, throwing her hands in the air. "Do you know what the guilt has been doing to me? I haven't been able to sleep since! I've told you over and over again that we have to stick to stricter boundaries, and instead it's always *oh, what if* this, and *maybe we should do something huge* that!"

"Caroline!" Margot snapped. "I wanted to help you fix it, and you wouldn't let me! Stop trying to control everything. You're not the queen of this coven."

"I'm not the queen, but I am the one who restarted it," Caroline said, drawing herself up to her full, not-very-high height. "You're taking us down a dangerous path again, and I should kick you out."

Margot looked at her for a second. Then she laughed. "You can't. Yes, you came to me, and yes, you own the building, so you think you're the one in charge here, but you and I are both the great-granddaughters of the founding members. One of us can't just kick out the other. You don't have the authority."

"You're right," Caroline said. "So I'll have to do the next best thing." She turned to Vy. "I'm kicking out Vy instead."

Vy blinked. The other women shot one another worried looks. Margot's face went white. "*What?*"

"Yeah, what?" Vy repeated, her eyebrows slowly traveling up her forehead.

"Something needs to be done, or we'll be right back on track to repeating the mistakes we made with Nicole, and nobody else here wants that, do they?" Caroline glared at all the other members of the circle.

"Of course we don't. But you can leave Vy out of it," Margot said, putting her arm around Vy.

"Vy started the drinking, didn't she? Vy's your little confidant in all this, and encourages your behavior. Vy's not related to an original founding member. So all I need is a simple majority to kick her out. All those in favor?" Caroline shot her hand up like she was punching the air.

"Maybe we could all talk about this—" I began.

"Jillian," Caroline snapped. "No offense, but you're the newest member and you don't know what's been going on—"

"Then maybe someone should *tell* me," I said.

"This is not the moment. You don't really get to talk right now, okay? If Vy wants to advocate for herself, she can."

"Well, I'm not gonna beg," Vy said. She stuck her hands in her pockets, her face still unreadably blank.

Caroline sniffed. Way down on the street below, a car honk sounded. "Then it's time to vote. Everyone?" The other women hesitated. "Let me remind you," Caroline said, "of how we all felt the day that Nicole resigned. Do any of you want to go through that same disappointment again? That heartbreak? Knowing that we elevated a candidate into power so quickly that it went to her head, and she felt she could threaten someone's job if he wouldn't keep sleeping with her? If we don't set strong boundaries, it's only a matter of time before we go too far again. So it's time to choose what you want the future of this coven to be."

Slowly, all of the other women besides me, Margot, and Vy put their hands in the air, their expressions solemn. Just a couple of hours ago, we'd all been lounging like sisters. Caroline counted, taking note of my hand at my side, then addressed the group.

"That settles it," Caroline said, solemn. "I'm sorry, Vy, but you broke the rules. You're no longer in the sisterhood. So mote it be."

For the briefest of moments, a heartbroken expression crossed Vy's face, before it returned to its usual inscrutability.

"Caroline," Margot said, her jaw clenched.

Caroline whirled on her. "If you want to quit in protest," she said, "go ahead."

Everyone turned to look at Margot as she swallowed. After a long moment, she shook her head, avoiding Vy's eyes.

"I didn't think so," Caroline said.

Vy turned on her heel without any last words, without even a good-bye, and clomped over to the door. The elevator let out its soft, high shriek as Vy descended.

"I'm sorry, Margot," Caroline said, a flush coming over her cheeks. She'd won the war, but her voice wavered, as if maybe she were wondering if she should've fired shots in the first place. "But you didn't give me a choice. Now we need to do a casting-out ritual, and then we can begin to heal."

Silently, Margot knelt to gather little pebbles from the dirt, and soon everyone else joined her. Someone else—Tara—began to build the fire, like Vy usually did, and it wasn't nearly as good.

FORTY-FIVE

I dreamt of Raf that night. We were in his old living room, teenagers again, and I stood before him, holding a sheet of paper, ready to recite some of my terrible poetry. I began to read the words in front of me. "'There is a world where it works with us, a world where it works so well, and we have a couple of kids who eat dirt.'" I stopped, confused, because those weren't my words at all, but his. And when I looked up from the paper, he was walking toward me. We weren't teenagers anymore. We were older, middle-aged, maybe. He took my face in his hands and drew me to him, but his hair smelled like Margot's, and when I woke up, she was sitting on my bed.

"Jillian," she said.

"Jesus!" I flinched, then rubbed my eyes. "Can you knock from now on?"

"I need to talk to you. I was hoping it wouldn't have to be so soon, but . . . well." She sat very still, almost a statue in the darkness. I reached over and flipped on a light, registering the time.

"I'm generally not a great conversationalist at four A.M."

She sprawled on her stomach, her face in her hands, and gazed up at me, dark circles under her eyes. She was still wearing the same long dress she'd had on earlier in the day. She needed a shower. "It was fun when we did the bigger magic, wasn't it? Just more . . . fulfilling."

"Nope," I said, pulling the pillow over my face. "No way. I'm staying out of this."

She pulled the pillow gently off my face. "I don't think that's going to be possible."

"Look," I said, and sat up, a bad taste in my mouth both literally and figuratively. "I'm mad about Vy too. But maybe we have to let this blow over and then try to reason with Caroline to let her back in."

"It's not going to blow over."

"I think Caroline has already realized she went too far—"

"I don't want it to blow over." At the wary look on my face, she scooted closer to me. "We were on the right track to achieving our goal, to electing the first female president. But then we messed up—*I* messed up, I can admit it. And because of that, Caroline has decided that we can only do selfish little magic instead. But you look at everything going on in the world and . . . I can't just sit back anymore."

"Margot," I said. "Don't take this the wrong way, but the kind of magic you're talking about . . . that feels like a whole different scale, and maybe it's not worth it to blow everything up because—"

"Because you don't think it's possible," she said. When I didn't respond, she reached into the pocket of her dress and carefully pulled out a black-and-white picture. She placed it on the bed between us like it was a sacred object. "My great-grandmother gave me this. She was still alive when I was young," Margot said. I leaned forward to look at the photograph. "I showed it to Caroline once, and she glanced at it for a minute and then moved on to other things. But I studied every detail."

The picture showed three women, rich women, dressed in evening gowns—all satin and puffed sleeves and furs. It must have been the 1930s, but these women had clearly escaped the austerity of the Depression. The one in the middle sat in a leather armchair. The women on either side of her placed their hands on her shoulder. They all looked at the camera with frank, proud gazes.

"It's the original coven," I said, and Margot nodded.

She pointed to the woman on the right, who had catlike eyes and Margot's straight, elegant nose. "My great-grandmother. She'd tell me the history, when I went to visit her in her nursing home. How they began to meet in secret to protect their families and their fortunes and themselves. When they worked together, they were free. Powerful. So much more powerful than women were supposed to be."

Their faces showed it—power in the tilt of their chins. The one in the middle held a cigarette between her lips and smirked at the camera. "They used to do undeniable magic," Margot went on. "She told me that once, they actually flew. Just lifted off the ground and soared, landing on the spire of the Chrysler Building." She paused and looked at me. "I know, you're thinking that was probably the dementia talking."

"Or they were doing some very powerful flapper drugs."

"I don't think so. I swear it was the most lucid I'd ever seen her. It was like the Coven was the one thing she could remember in vivid detail."

We both looked down at the picture again. The woman on the

left had Caroline's thin lips and pale coloring, her hair in a platinum bob.

"What happened to the third member?" I asked.

"She left the city. Afterward, they added more people to the circle, and they had influence, sure, but they never got back to the same level of magic after she was gone."

"No more night flying?"

"Jillian," Margot said, her voice urgent. "Listen. I forgot about all this as I grew up. But one day when things were really bad with Gus, I was in the bathroom, staring at a bunch of pills, thinking that maybe I should just take the easy way out. But then I remembered there was another option. I could do what my great-grandmother did, build something where I could fly." Her eyes were shining now. "Shortly after that, Caroline and I saw each other again for the first time in a long while. She told me her plans for Nevertheless, and that night, I left Gus."

"So it sounds like your relationship with Caroline has meant a lot to you," I said, even as I wondered—was I trying to keep everything simple (or rather, as simple as it could be in this batshit situation) for the sake of an article, or because I had so recently begun to feel a kind of belonging in this circle, and I didn't want to watch it rip itself apart?

"It has," Margot said, her voice small and sad. She straightened her shoulders. "But now Caroline's trying to control everything too, like Gus did, and it's making all of us small. I think I can change her mind, but I need you to help me."

"I get it, why you feel that way. And I'm so sorry about the shit you had to go through. But I can't get mixed up in this."

"It has to be you," she said, clasping my hands, staring up at me with such a strange intensity that I had to laugh.

"As Caroline very helpfully pointed out today," I said, "I'm new, and I don't get to talk, so I really don't think I'm much use to you."

"Look," she said, and moved her finger on the photograph to the woman in the chair, the cigarette dangling from her lips. Something about her face struck me as familiar. "My great-grandmother's biggest regret was how they treated the third member. When she asked them for help escaping her abusive husband, they tried to keep her in the circle instead. So when she left, she didn't even say goodbye. She just disappeared. My great-grandmother always hoped that she was all right, that maybe one day, someone from *her* family would rejoin the circle and make it whole." Margot moved her finger down the photograph until it rested right below the necklace around the third woman's neck. My necklace.

"I summoned you," she said. "When everything was getting bad with Nicole, I did a spell to bring you into my life. And then one day, a local paper printed some feature on In the Stars, as part of a trend piece on astrology. I never read the paper anymore, but for some reason I read it cover to cover. Even the obituaries section."

She reached into her pocket again and pulled out a newspaper clipping: *Kathleen Beckley, beloved mother, dead from cancer at age fifty-seven, leaving behind a daughter, Jillian.* I'd spent hours looking through family photos, trying to find the right one to send in to the paper, finally settling on one I'd taken of her years before, where she was giving me her signature wry look. Where she was wearing the necklace.

"No," I said, my heart thumping. Coincidence. This was a co-incidence that had spiraled far out of control. "I'm sure a lot of people have necklaces like that."

"They probably do. That's why I double-checked. I looked her up, and I worked backward. Your great-grandmother had gotten married again and had her children with her second husband, but I figured it out."

It fit, as much as I couldn't believe it. My mother had told me about her rich grandmother, who had left an abusive husband in New York and gone far, far away. Her grandmother who talked sometimes of the luxury she had given up but wouldn't talk about so many other things. She was the reason Margot and I were here in this bedroom, having this conversation.

Margot looked at me, so vulnerable all of a sudden, and for the first time I realized how much power I had.

"So then, what?" I asked. "You stalked me?"

"I just made sure that our orbits overlapped," she said.

"This is so fucked up, Margot," I said. "Why this whole riga-marole, with me needing to *prove* myself, me needing to screw over Libby? Why didn't you just tell me?"

"You're guarded, Jillian. A skeptic. I've learned my lesson about telling people all of this before they're ready. If I'd told you right off the bat, you would have run screaming in the other direction." That was true. Part of me wanted to run screaming even now, while another part thrilled as Margot kept talking. "You had to want to come yourself, to think it was your idea. Besides, you needed to prove yourself to Caroline. I could talk you up to her, sure, and fudge your background check, but you still had to im-press her on your own merits. I couldn't have her knowing who you were too soon because, if things went wrong, it would just be another unforgivable mistake from me."

The room spun as I tried to process it all. I was someone who belonged. Someone who still had a family of sorts after all. When I'd felt that communion around the circle at Samhain, it wasn't just delusion. It was written in my blood.

"I think that the lost coven member returning might be the

only thing that could make Caroline come around. But if she doesn't, well, one member related to a founder can't kick out another, but *two* . . ."

Her words hung in the air between us for a moment. Outside, a car screeched down the avenue. I swallowed.

"If I'm going to do this," I said, "and I'm not saying I am, but if I *were* to, I would need to know that you really trusted me. No more sending people to follow me around or sneaking into this apartment at night without letting me know that you're coming. It freaks me out."

"Of course," Margot said.

"And I need to know the extent of things. I need to know exactly what happened with Nicole Woo-Martin."

She nodded. And then she told me what they'd done.

FORTY-SIX

Caroline had fallen in love with Nicole at first speech. She saw her give a talk at some luncheon, when Nicole had been a lowly public defender, and had beelined for her afterward. That humor! Those brains! The clear, good head on her shoulders! Had Nicole ever thought about running for a higher office?

Nicole hadn't. She liked her life as it was—working hard to do small, good things during the day, coming home to her husband at night. But if Nicole *did* decide she was interested, Caroline ran an organization that wanted to support female candidates. Plus, she had a lot of . . . influential friends. Caroline planted the seed, and eventually Nicole came around. It was a long shot, but why the hell not?

So Caroline set Nicole up with a campaign manager, held fundraisers for her, introduced her to the other women in the Coven.

They all hung out with Nicole, brought her with them to their events, and introduced her around to the people she needed to know. Nicole was cool, if a policy nerd, with a previously untapped charisma that was just dying to show itself to a wider audience.

"I think this woman is the one," Caroline said to Margot. "She could be our president."

Margot's body had tingled with anticipation. "We're doing this?"

"We're doing this," Caroline said. They'd hugged each other then and squealed like little girls. And then they'd started casting spells for her without her knowledge.

And Nicole kept doing better and better on the campaign trail. She went on *The View* and killed it. She knocked on doors with her husband (sweet but introverted, slightly dazed by the new turn his life had taken), and made people laugh in the mayoral debates, and got the common people excited to knock billionaires off their pedestals, and got women excited to make history.

Still, she was down in the polls against the establishment candidate. So that Samhain, the Coven tried some new things, did some new rituals. They sacrificed a possum they'd found in the woods. Caroline was a little nervous—the spells were so much bigger than anything they'd tried before—but then, holy Jesus, Nicole won.

It happened so fast, the nationwide interest in her. People were making votive candles with her *face* on them. Out of nowhere, she'd become an icon. And that kind of thing can fuck with your head.

Not long after Nicole took office, Caroline and Margot met with her to discuss priorities, to invite her to come speak at the Nevertheless clubhouse. Nicole gave them the tour of City Hall, introducing them to her staffers, including a particularly handsome one. His interaction with Nicole was strangely charged. She turned almost giggly in his presence.

"He's a babe," Margot said when he left.

"More like a baby," Nicole replied, but she blushed.

"Okay!" Caroline said. "So first on your agenda, better parental leave?" That was Caroline's cause, the one she was most vocal about. She'd consulted with Nicole on it during the election, spending hours researching the best policies for families, helping Nicole draw up the specifics of the plan.

"Yes," Nicole said. "That and closing the wealth gap in the city."

"Are you sure about that one? It could be bad for business, and it's going to make a lot of powerful people angry."

"I'm sure."

Caroline sighed. "Well. You need to do what you need to do."

Later, when they were all saying good-bye and Margot started chatting with the handsome staffer, exchanging numbers with him because he *loved* going to art openings and she often had an extra invite, she'd noticed Nicole looking over far too often. Huh. That was something to keep an eye on.

So she cultivated a little friendship with the staffer, taking him along to the occasional opening. He was idealistic, totally in thrall to Nicole. Not the brightest bulb, but Margot enjoyed his company enough, and it was another good way to keep track of Nicole's doings as she got busier and busier.

One night, Margot went to an event where Nicole was giving a speech. Caroline couldn't come—she'd promised to attend a work function with her husband—so when Margot saw the staffer across the room, she made her way to his side. The staffer drank his beer too fast and stared at Nicole darkly as she spoke with her usual inspiring platitudes. Margot nudged him. "You all right?" she asked.

He shook his head. "She's going to sell out," he said. "On a bunch of issues. Trading them so that she can get support for her wealth tax. Don't get me wrong, I'm fine if she wants to make the wealth tax her centerpiece issue, but there's got to be a way to fight harder for all the other things she promised too." He frowned as Nicole finished her speech, then began hobnobbing with all the people who wanted something from her. "See that man she's shaking hands with now? They're solidifying a deal tonight, and then it's good-bye parental leave and prison reform. I thought she was different, that she'd actually stick to all of her principles, but maybe she's just a typical politician."

"What?" Margot asked. Parental leave was the thing that Caroline cared about most, the cause that really lit her up. If Nicole only knew about the power she had behind her, that she could just let them work some magic on her behalf, she wouldn't have to make these compromises. Margot had one glass of champagne too many, then cornered Nicole in the hallway and told her about the Coven.

"Just listen," Margot said, because she thought that Nicole would be thrilled. Nicole froze as Margot talked about what they'd already done, the exciting possibilities of what they *could* do, how she couldn't tell her the details, of course, because the circle was sworn to secrecy, but maybe Nicole could *join* the circle! A wary look came into Nicole's eye, but Margot didn't see it until it was too late.

"You all think that you're witches," Nicole said, when Margot took a breath. "Got it." The subtext was clear: *Oh, these women are crazy.* Margot's cheeks burned with shame, her mouth dry with apprehension. She had made a terrible mistake.

Nicole made her excuses and left the event. Then she immediately iced them out. Caroline couldn't understand why her calls went unanswered, why her meetings were rescheduled. Margot wanted to tell Caroline, but she was afraid to disappoint her. Maybe if Nicole had some time to digest, Margot could make her come around without having to worry Caroline. But then the handsome staffer stopped responding to Margot's texts too. And then a few weeks later, the first report of the affair came out, an affair that had been going on for months.

Caroline and Margot read the story with sinking feelings in their stomachs. "How could she do this?" Caroline said. "It's *such* a bad misuse of her power." Caroline kept scanning the article, and gasped. "Oh my God. Listen to these texts she sent him: **'If you don't watch out for those women, you might get sacrificed . . . '** **'Seriously, are you going to see her again? I wouldn't if I were you.'** Is she threatening his job if he sees other women?" Caroline put the article down and began to cry in a way that Margot had never seen her cry before. "It's my fault," she'd said, snuffling, as Margot handed her tissues. "I brought her in, and then we pushed her too far, too fast. She didn't get a chance to learn the boundaries."

"No, it's my fault," Margot said, trying not to cry too. "Those text messages are about us, I think. Warnings, maybe, or jokes, or both."

"What do you mean?" Caroline asked, blinking her bloodshot eyes.

"I told Nicole about the Coven, and she must have told him," Margot said, hanging her head. "That's why he hasn't been responding to me lately. They think we're insane."

"You . . ." Caroline stiffened, her face growing flushed with anger. "I'm sorry, you *what*?"

"She was giving up on parental leave! I just wanted to let her know that we would support her so that she didn't have to make sacrifices!"

"And you didn't even talk to me about it first? What the hell were you thinking?" Caroline yelled. "Clearly you weren't thinking at all." A news alert on Caroline's phone interrupted them:

Nicole was denying that the texts were threats. She'd said something about trying to protect the staffer from "a bad crowd." He would be giving a press conference the next day to tell his side of the story.

Caroline grabbed her phone and dialed Nicole's number over and over again. Each time, the call was sent to voice mail. Caroline slammed the phone on her desk. "Goddammit!" She rounded on Margot. "Do you think the staffer's going to tell the truth? If he explains it all, we'll be a laughingstock."

"He doesn't have to explain. He could just deny that they were threats, say it was part of a private conversation."

"You think the media's going to let that go, when Nicole dangled something about a 'bad crowd'? No. Unless there's a more salacious explanation, people will keep digging. And if it all comes out, that's the end for the Coven and all the work we're doing, the end of Nevertheless, maybe the end of all our careers." Caroline clenched her fists, a battle raging inside of her. Then she gave a little sniff. "She's going down anyway. She can't take us down with her."

"Let me help you fix it—" Margot began, but Caroline whirled on her.

"You've done enough. I'll handle it myself."

So Caroline showed up at the staffer's apartment that night (scaring the shit out of him) and they had a little chat. Though he'd thought it was love originally, he'd grown disillusioned enough with Nicole to open up to the reporters who were sniffing around. Caroline had been right: the wealth tax *had* made Nicole a lot of powerful enemies.

But he wasn't going to lie about Nicole threatening him. That is, until Caroline offered him a bribe of $50,000. Then he was willing to say what he needed to say. He *was* out of a job, after all.

And if nobody else was going to stick to their principles, why should he?

Nicole couldn't exactly contradict a serious claim like that with some story about witches. Then *she* would seem insane. She must have realized pretty quickly that protesting, trying to implicate Nevertheless, was futile.

So Nicole had gone down and the Coven had stayed a secret. But after the dust had settled, Caroline had declared that was it. Their original goal—to use their magic to be the queen-makers— was off the table, at least for a long, long time. Things hadn't been the same between Margot and Caroline ever since.

FORTY-SEVEN

Holy shit," I said when Margot was done. "You guys did take her down."

"No, she was going down anyway."

"And then you made it that much worse with a fucking bribe," I said.

"Caroline was the only person involved in the bribe. So she's the only person who you'd have proof did something wrong." She fixed me with a stare. "If, say, the whole reason that you came to us in the first place was to write an article."

My stomach dropped. She'd been more than one step ahead of me this whole time.

"I don't know what you're talking about," I said.

"The second time we met, I spent almost the whole party talking to Raf about you. He knows you very, very well. He's shy about most things, maybe, but start him on the subject of you, and the floodgates open." *Dammit, Raf*, I thought, and as if she'd read my mind, Margot said, "Oh, he was very good. He stuck to the party line, but still, I learned things. You're not the kind of person to care so much about being in a club. Certainly not to the point of cornering Caroline in a hallway and blatantly asking her to invite you in."

I didn't say anything. "It's all right," Margot said. "You didn't know us then. But now you do." She tucked a strand of my hair behind my ear, so close to me, and said, in a quiet voice, "I wouldn't write about us if I were you. I'm not trying to threaten you. I'm telling you the reality. You could sell us out, and sure, it might make a splash for a little while. But that splash wouldn't last, because you'd have made a lot of influential enemies. Besides, you'd be selling yourself out too. You *did* break into a judge's private home." God, of course that was why she'd brought me with them, why they'd used only *my* phone to take the photos of the evidence, so I'd implicate myself. "Or you could take over the Coven with me and Caroline like you're meant to, and we could change the world. What's one article against the real change that we could do?"

At the doubt on my face, she leaned forward, almost glowing with purpose.

"By holding the Coven back, Caroline's not just punishing *me* for my mistake. She's punishing everyone that we could help. Stand with me at the next meeting, and we'll talk to her, and then we can start fresh. Find a stronger Nicole, someone who can break that last glass ceiling and lead the country with the interests of women in mind. There's so much potential, if we work together," she said, her eyes shining with hope. "Will you help me?"

I hesitated.

She gave me a searing look, one that seemed to cut all the way inside of me. "It's a way to keep your promise. To use your power for good," she said, calling me back to that moment in the woods when she'd held me in her arms and spoken to me as my mother. I shivered.

Tears began to well in her eyes as she reached for my hands. I looked down at her palm, at the scar at the base of her thumb that matched mine. Her nails were bitten, uneven. Her voice wavered. "We can make things right. Get Vy back in. I know you've only seen a little bit of the magic so far. I wanted to be able to show you more before I asked this of you. But please, will you think about it?"

"I—"

"Let us be your family," she said. I'd heard those words before, recently, hadn't I? *I just want you to have a family*, my mother had said to me in the woods. Or perhaps the only person who'd been saying it was Margot. My eyes flickered to the clipping of my mother's obituary, the photograph I'd sent the paper of her, where her face wore that classic look of wry empathy. The look that Margot had given me by the fire.

"I don't need to think," I said. "I'll do it."

FORTY-EIGHT

I closed the door after Margot and collapsed against it, one thought racing in my mind: *Fuck that manipulative bitch.*

Was everything she'd done this whole time, all the intimacy she'd cultivated with me, simply so that I'd be her faithful lieutenant in her fight for more power? It wounded my pride, sure, injured the small part of me that had believed that, through my own merits, I'd made someone like her interested in someone like me. But that wasn't why I ached with anger.

I ached with the knowledge that, during Samhain, summoning my mother must have been an act too. Margot wanted me to see magic, so she'd put on a show. What had she done and said that had convinced me so fully? Nothing all that special. *Are you keeping your promise?* People made promises to their dying mothers all the time. My mother's look. She must have studied the photograph until she got it just right. Everything else she could have found out from looking up my mom, or from Raf, when they'd spent a whole party talking about me. I'd wanted to believe she was channeling something bigger so badly that I'd made it easy for her to pull the wool over my eyes.

Sure, it was tempting to just believe Margot's big speeches, to throw myself into this new family now that she'd told me I truly belonged. But I wasn't going to be a naive little fool again. None of what had happened over the past two months was sisterhood. The reason our magical weekend together had felt so magical was because I'd been high off my ass. Them bringing me into the inner circle wasn't proof that they were rising above their elitism, like I'd been telling myself. I was a legacy, the most elitist choice of all. And all the magic I was just beginning to think about without rolling my eyes, that sense of possibility outside of my understanding? It wasn't magic at all, just a puppet show with Margot pulling the strings.

I was going to burn them all to the ground. Maybe they'd drag me down with them. But at least I'd go down in a blaze of glory.

I texted Miles. **Call me when you wake up**, I wrote. **I have a plan**. And then I sat down at my computer and began to write.

FORTY-NINE

Two nights later, I paced in my living room, waiting for a knock on my door. I thought of the time, way back at the beginning of this whole saga, when I'd gone to try on clothes for Margot's party. I'd ended up trying on a whole life, a life where a place like this was my home. But I wouldn't be here much longer. I'd left the tags on this life the whole time, and now I had to return it.

The knock came, quiet but firm. Miles. He had his hands in his pockets, and wore a black jacket over a dark blue shirt. "I don't think anyone saw me in the hallway," he said as he ducked into the living room.

"After tonight, it won't matter anyway." I'd get the proof tonight, then turn in my article. When the payment came, I could stay at a cheap motel or something until I could figure out a new housing situation. Besides, Margot had promised to stop keeping tabs on me, and she couldn't risk breaking my trust, at least not until I helped her take over the Coven.

Miles registered my surroundings, then let out a whistle. "Wow, I can see why you wanted to milk this as long as possible." I glared at him. "Sorry."

"Thanks," I said, and we went over the plan. I'd text him when we were heading up to the roof. I would make sure that I walked through the door last, so that I could slip a piece of cardboard over the automatic lock, leaving it just slightly ajar. Then Miles and one of the *New York Standard*'s fact-checkers would head into the back alley, to the unmarked entrance I'd described, the door with no security beyond a code that I remembered. The freight elevator was too noisy, so they'd have to take the stairs. I walked him through the layout of the roof, the path they could use to avoid being noticed by anyone. If they stayed on the other side of the trellises, they'd be able to see what was happening through the gaps in the plants, but we'd all be so blinded by the fire, so caught up in the smoke and the ritual, that they'd remain undetected for as long as they needed to confirm what they needed to confirm. They could take some blurry video footage and then get out of there.

Margot and I had agreed that we wouldn't make our stand until after the worship had already begun. Let everyone else get a little blissed out, let Caroline loosen up, remind her how good she felt when she gave in to the magic. Miles and the fact-checker just had to get in before that so that they could see the height of the ritual.

"So if they catch me," he said, "do you think they'll prosecute me for trespassing, or go ahead and tear us all limb from limb?"

"Hard to tell, honestly."·

"You nervous?" he asked.

"Oh, terrified," I said. "You?"

"Yeah, kind of. I feel like I'm in a movie."

We smiled shakily at each other. "I wrote the article," I said, indicating my laptop. "Turns out it all came pretty easily."

"Hell yeah, you did," he said, a smile growing wide. "Can I get a sneak peek?"

"Fine. But just the first sentence," I said. I opened my computer, cleared my throat, and read the words I'd spent two months preparing to write, words into which I'd packed all the beauty and anger I had inside of me.

He listened. The sentence hung between us, so solid that I could practically see it shimmering in the air. Then Miles shook his head. "Jesus Christ, Beckley, what a lede," he said. "In case I haven't communicated this clearly enough, you're a fucking fantastic writer."

There it was, all over his face: his approval, of the beauty and the anger alike. He was looking at me the way I'd looked at *him* for so long, with a little bit of awe, unable to stop himself from smiling when he met my eyes even though we were about to do something nerve-racking, maybe even dangerous. I flushed. "Thanks."

He took a step toward me. "Any way I can convince you to keep reading?"

"No," I said, and shut the computer, turning away to put it down on the coffee table. "Tonight, after you've seen it all for yourself, then I'll send you the whole thing." I rolled my shoulders, then turned back to him. He'd moved even closer when I'd put my computer away. There were only inches between us now. "I . . . I guess I should get going. See you on the other side?"

"Wait," he said. He put his arm around my waist and drew me in close to him. He smelled like pine, and when he leaned in to kiss me, he had coffee on his breath. He kissed me hungrily, like he had the first time, and this time he was free, we were *both* free, to keep pressing against each other.

I'd spent so much time thinking about the night when we'd

done this before, turning over the memory, living in the feeling of it. Now, though, he moved his lips on mine and trailed his fingers up and down my back, and I was distracted. Maybe I was too nervous about what was to come later in the night. Maybe it was the flash of Raf's face in my mind, how it shone as I'd turned toward him in the dark, the night I'd gotten into his bed. Maybe it was the fact that Miles was still my editor, and that was a little screwed up, wasn't it?

As my mind was still processing all of it, Miles stepped back and grinned at me. "I've been wanting to do that again for a long time," he said. "Perhaps not the best moment for it. But also no time like when you're about to do a risky recon mission, right?"

"Right," I said. "Sorry, I just—I'm all over the place right now."

"Of course," he said, and touched my cheek briefly before walking to the door. "Well, shall we?"

FIFTY

When I turned onto the block that held the Nevertheless clubhouse, I couldn't make myself go in just yet. It was still early, and I had too much jittery energy buzzing around in my body to go make chitchat with the other club members while we shot furtive looks at the time and at the door. So instead, I headed over toward the water to practice some deep-breathing techniques.

With a dull roar, airplanes flew through the dark sky overhead. A barge glided down the river, slow and unbothered. The wind picked up, so I hugged my jacket closer to me as I approached the water. Putting my hands on the railing, I stared at the Hudson River. It churned and rippled, making me so dizzy that I had to look away.

A few feet down from me, another woman stared at the water, lost in thought, wearing sweatpants and a baseball cap with the brim pulled down low. As the headlights from the cars behind us illuminated her face, I glanced over at her, then glanced away. And then I looked again.

"Excuse me," I said, my heart pounding. "I'm so sorry to bother you, but are you Nicole Woo-Martin?"

She turned, a wary look on her wide face. "Hello," Nicole said. "Yes."

I'd spent so long thinking about her that I couldn't believe she was actually standing in front of me. But there she was, not an illusion, a little worse for the wear—rumpled, no makeup, gray strands in her shoulder-length black hair—looking up at me as if I'd dreamed her into being. As if I'd summoned her. Which, back in the woods for Samhain, I had.

She waited for me to say something, bracing herself for my disappointment—disappointment with her for failing, maybe, or disappointment with the system that chewed her up and spit her out, but it would be disappointment of some kind, because that was what she got from the world now.

But instead, what came out of my mouth was, "What are you doing here?"

That caught her off guard. "In New York City? Technically I live here."

"Right, sorry, I just mean—I thought you were off the grid somewhere, walking in the woods."

"Ah," she said, sliding a politician's veneer over herself, standing up a little straighter to give me a canned answer. "Yes, I was taking some time to reflect and consider how I could be of service in the future. But recently, I felt it was time to come back."

"This is so fucking weird," I said, dazed. "The timing. The coincidence."

She furrowed her brow, trying to keep up her polite political smile, but one of her feet lifted slightly as if poised for flight, in case I turned out to be an unstable stalker, someone who'd spent all my money on votive candles of her face. "I'm sorry, who are you?"

"No, I'm . . . My name is Jillian. I know Caroline Thompson and that whole group."

At the mention of Caroline's name, her jaw tightened, and she clicked her tongue. "Huh. Well, it was nice to meet you, Jillian. Keep fighting the good fight. Now, I should—" She began to turn away.

"I'm going to get justice for you," I said in a low voice, and she turned back.

"Justice?" There were hardly any people around at this late, cold hour, and those who did pass by were paying us no mind. "I'm not sure what you mean by that."

"I'm a journalist, and I've been looking into things."

At the word "journalist," she stepped back. "Oh. No. No thank you. I'm sorry, I've already talked to a lot of journalists. I've been followed and hounded even when I asked for privacy, and I would rather not—"

"But I know you weren't threatening him," I said. "I know that other people were involved, that bad crowd, and you didn't deserve . . ." She blinked a few times and swallowed, so I continued. "Maybe we could go somewhere and talk, just for a little while."

"I don't think so. I'm trying to move on, and I don't have any interest in relitigating or reliving it all."

"But I'm angry!" I said. It just burst out and then, embarrassingly, tears began to well in my eyes. I remembered my mother telling me that when Nicole was sworn in as president, she would be happy, wherever she was. "They played God with you, and they ruined you, and I'm so angry about it all."

She considered the pathetic spectacle of me for a moment, then walked up very close so that we were side by side at the railing, the water lapping before us. She put a hand on my arm. "Jillian, yes?" I nodded. "I'm going to say what I need to say now and then we're going to be done with it, and this is all off the record, okay?"

"Sure," I said, and wiped my eyes.

She let out a heavy, exhausted sigh. "I was getting good work done in that office, and I'm angry that it got cut short too. I'm heartbroken. But I also . . . Well, you know. I made a huge error in judgment. I've been trying to figure out why I did what I did, because I always thought I was pretty good at knowing what was right."

"I know why," I said. "You had all these outside influences pushing you—"

She gave a dry laugh. "Well, so what? So I was weak enough to change who I was entirely based on some outside influence?" She shook her head. "No. Pardon my French, but that's bullshit. I made my own decisions."

"But—"

She raised an eyebrow and said drily, "Do you want to know the grand result of my self-examination or not?"

I laughed, just a little bit, then sniffled. "I do, yes."

"All right, then. I think . . . I think my foundation for running in the first place was shaky. A whole big house was built on top of it so quickly, but I hadn't made sure that its base was secure. And because everything came so easily all of a sudden, I began to believe that I deserved it. I began to think that I was special."

"You *were*—"

"Not just special. Better. That what I thought and wanted mattered more than anything else. Of course a handsome young man would fall for me. Our love was exceptional, so I was allowed to enjoy it, even though if someone else did it, I would think it was wrong. That's what power will do to you, if you're not watching out for it. I didn't want to let go of a single thing that I had. I was ruining *myself*. So maybe it's good that I have to start over. Because if I ever step back into the public eye, if I ever ask people to consider me in that way again, it's going to have to be not for the glory or the flattery, but for something deeper." She stared into my eyes, her voice growing fuller and more certain. "Sometimes, to make something strong, we have to tear out the rot in the foundation and start again."

As she continued speaking, I felt the full force of her charisma. This woman truly could have been our president someday. Maybe it wasn't too late. Maybe she still could be. "It's fine that you're angry, Jillian. I'm angry too. But we have to use that anger to rebuild."

Then she shook her head again, and the flame that had been roaring within her sputtered out, and she was just an ordinary woman in sweatpants, standing by the river. "Or not. I don't know. I'm still figuring it all out." She waggled her finger at me. "So again, do not quote me on anything."

I nodded. She gave me a sad smile, patted my arm once more, then turned and walked away into the night.

FIFTY-ONE

By the time I arrived at the clubhouse, waving shakily to Keisha at the security desk, most of the more casual members were trickling out. I looked toward Libby's favorite table in the corner. She wasn't there. I wondered if she'd been back to the clubhouse at all since the moment she had realized my betrayal. Maybe it was a good thing for her to give up on this nest of vipers. She could make better, safer friends by taking an improv class or joining an after-work softball team. Vy wasn't around either. If she couldn't be part of the Coven, she would never come back.

I made small talk with the sparkling women who had passed all the tests that Caroline and Margot had set for them and who continued to toe the line, to perform and shine and pay their dues so that they could wrap themselves up in the exclusivity that Nevertheless conferred. So that they could feel that they were special. Better. That they mattered more.

The clubhouse was lifeless without Libby and Vy there.

As the final members who didn't belong to the inner circle said their good-byes, I put my phone on silent and sent a text to Miles. **We're about to head upstairs.** Margot appeared at my side. "Ready for this?" she asked in a quiet voice. I nodded, and she gave my hand a squeeze. Before I'd really gotten to know her, when she'd seemed all surety and ease, I would have bet anything that Margot's palms had never sweat in her life. But now her hand was as clammy as mine.

Caroline unlocked the second door and we filed through, walking down the short hallway to the freight elevator. The energy was different tonight than it normally was, less excited and more nervous, some of us preoccupied with our own impending betrayals, others perhaps thinking of the discomfort that had happened the last time we'd all assembled on this roof.

When the freight elevator let us off in the antechamber, we changed into our robes quietly. As the speedy, impatient ones among us dropped their phones into the bucket and opened the door to the roof, I took my own phone out to give Miles a ten-minute warning before turning it off. But he was already typing something.

We're at the entrance to the alley, but there's a woman in it. Can't tell if she's security, or casing the joint herself. I stared at his words. What the fuck?

Another message came through: **She looks like a Viking, crossed with a ghost?**

Dammit. Vy. What was she doing there? Margot was sitting on a bench against the wall, taking her shoes off. I sat down next to her to take off my own, then leaned over and said, quietly, "Hey, have you talked to Vy recently?"

Margot's eyes darted toward the rest of the group. Then she looked down at her laces and said, out of the corner of her mouth, "She's not taking my calls. I texted that I had a plan for getting her invited back tonight, if she wanted to come to the neighborhood just in case. But she hasn't responded." She stood up and put her phone in the bucket, then headed to the door, her robe swirling as she walked.

I thought quickly and sent Vy a text. **FYI plan's not going to work tonight, so I wouldn't bother coming to the neighborhood. We're going to try next week instead.**

I looked down at the screen. No response, no little dots that meant she was even starting to type. If she was angry with Margot, she was probably livid with me too, for being so obvious about what she'd put in her tea at Samhain. Maybe she thought I'd tattled on her to Caroline. I sent another text. **Also, I didn't mean to out you with the shrooms, and I'm really sorry if that contributed to you getting kicked out.**

Still no response. Fuck. What if she didn't have her phone on her, or she was wary of trusting me? "Are you coming, Jillian?" Caroline called from the doorway, a strange edge to her voice. Everyone else had already filed out onto the roof.

"Sorry, yes!" I said, standing up quickly. We had to get evidence tonight. There was no telling what would happen, how badly things might blow up, when Margot made her stand. Maybe Caroline would retain her control, and I'd never be invited up here again. Maybe the Coven would tear itself apart. I turned toward the bucket as if to put my phone in it. But instead, moving as fast as I could, I pulled up my voice recording app, pressed record, and slipped the phone into the pocket of my robe. Just in case Miles and the fact-checker couldn't make it up to the roof, at least there would be *some* record.

"Well, come on," Caroline said, holding the door. I followed her out, stopping to slip a piece of cardboard over the automatic lock like I'd promised Miles.

Already, the fire that some of the women had built was starting to roar, and they were assembling in a circle, reaching out their hands to one another, a few of them beginning to take the deep breaths that we would all breathe together to begin the worship.

Caroline took her place next to Margot, the tension between them crackling in the air, but she didn't reach out her hands. "Stop the breathing for a moment," she said, looking around the circle, her red hair glimmering in the firelight, strands of it lifting and dancing in the wind. "Before we begin, we have something we need to discuss." Her eyes landed on me. "It's about Jillian."

FIFTY-TWO

My breath caught in my throat as everyone's faces turned to me. I glanced over at Margot, who shot me a look of confusion and barely suppressed panic. "She's not who we think she is," Caroline continued as wind rustled the ivy on the trellises. Holy shit, had Caroline found out about my family history too? Was she going to preempt what Margot had planned and try to claim me for herself, or present some sort of well-prepared legal defense as to how I'd forfeited any rights to my authority? The panic on Margot's face grew.

Caroline stood up straight, lifted her chin. "She's a journalist." Somehow, I had not been expecting that at all.

"What?" Iris asked as the other women began to mutter, looking at me with growing distrust. God. Dammit.

"Well, yes. I mean, I was," I said, my mind racing for the spin.

"I told you all that. But the website I wrote for folded, and I realized I didn't want to keep doing—"

"That was what you said, yes," Caroline said. "But I've been making some inquiries over the last few days."

"Wait. Why over the last few days?" Margot asked.

"That's not important." Caroline pressed her thin lips together.

Margot's eyes narrowed. "Because you saw that she sided with me when you kicked out Vy, and you're looking for any possible excuse to quash dissent?" She let out a hollow laugh. "I should've expected it. You're such a—"

"She's writing an article about us!" Caroline snapped. "A friend of a friend knows someone who works at the *New York Standard*, and they've heard whispers about some top-secret undercover story that they're planning."

Stunned noises echoed from some of the women like the wind had been knocked out of them, shock at my betrayal all over their faces. And anger too that I would dare to try and take away this clubhouse, this circle, from them.

"I knew something was off," Iris said.

"No," Margot said firmly. "No. Listen. She *was* going to write an article about us, sure. That's why she wanted to join at first." Margot turned to me. Things weren't going how she'd planned, but she could still turn this around. "But you're not going to anymore, right, Jillian?"

"Right," I said, my face burning, my fingers trembling. "As I've gotten to know you all, I've realized—"

Caroline rounded on Margot. "You *knew*? You knew the whole time and didn't tell me?" She gasped, as if she'd been slapped. "Because you knew that *I* would be the one who would go down, that I had the most to lose because the bribe came from me—"

Caroline cut herself off abruptly as the other women turned their shocked faces to her. "Bribe? What bribe?" Iris asked. Because of course Caroline and Margot had never told them that part. As far as the rest of the Coven knew, their only mistake had been elevating Nicole too fast, and she'd destroyed herself.

"I . . ." Caroline began.

"It was to fix a mistake I made," Margot said to the others. "Don't blame Caroline, blame me." Then she turned back to Caroline, her voice rising. "And that's not why. I kept it from you because you wouldn't have wanted to take a chance, but I knew that she would change her mind when she realized who she was." Down on the street below, a siren wailed, then faded away.

"What the hell do you mean?"

"She's the third!" Margot said, coming to my side, putting her arm around my shoulder. As the others stared at me in confusion, I felt like a prize pig being presented at a fair, unsure whether my fate was to be feted or slaughtered. "The original founder who left the Coven—Jillian is her great-granddaughter. I found her."

For the first time since I'd known her, Caroline was speechless. She opened her mouth, then closed it, then took in a shallow breath.

"That's why I wanted to do more magic at Samhain," Margot said to her. "Not to screw with you, but to show her what was possible. And now, she's not going to sell us out. She knows that she belongs here. We're whole again, and it's time to get back to the important work."

As the others whispered to one another, Caroline touched her hand to her throat, staring at me with a strange mixture of awe and joy and horror for what all of this meant.

"Margot," she breathed.

"I know," Margot said. "With the three of us, united, think of what we all could do."

Caroline ran her eyes over me, from my face to my feet, seeing me in a new light, as my heart pushed against my chest. "Maybe we could—" she began, and for a moment I almost felt bad that Margot would get Caroline back on board only for me to ruin it all, but I kept my spine straight and my face composed. Then Caroline's eyes locked at my waist, caught by something they saw there. In a low, ice-cold voice, she said, "What's in your pocket, Jillian?"

I looked down. Ever so slightly, through the dark cloth of my robe, something glowed. *Shit*, I thought. "Shit," I said. "I was all distracted texting before this and I forgot to put my phone away. That was dumb of me. I must be getting some messages—"

I fumbled to pull the phone out of my pocket to see a series of new texts lighting up my screen. "I am so sorry, I'll go put this in the bucket," I said, backing toward the door, my eyes flitting to my screen. I'd received a thumbs-up from Miles, plus a message from Vy: **Don't bother with plan. Done w/ Coven. It's gotten all fucked up.** But I didn't have time to register what any of it meant because I needed to close out of the voice recording, stat.

I swiped over to the app but before I could stop it, Caroline moved to me at lightning speed (God, she was little but quick, like a fucking hummingbird) and grabbed the phone from my hand.

"Wait—" I started, as she stared at what she saw.

She held up the phone for everyone in the circle. "She's been recording this whole time."

A series of murmurs—angry, sad, shocked—burst from the women, rippling out as my betrayal sank in. Margot stepped back from me. "Jillian," she said. "But I thought . . ."

Miles was probably entering the code on the downstairs door now, ready to start up the flights of stairs. I needed to buy some time, to keep the circle from disbanding and extinguishing the fire before he got up here. He wouldn't get to see them in full worship, but at least he'd get to see the roof, the fire, the robes. That would be enough for something at least.

"What about all the good we could do?" Margot asked, and the fact that she had the nerve to try to make *me* feel guilty is what set me off.

"This isn't *good*," I said. "This is insane." Margot stepped back, her mouth opening. "You're all a bunch of delusional, elitist assholes, playing with the rest of us as if we're not real people, as if we don't matter!"

"No," Caroline said. "We're trying to help—"

"Right," I said in a withering tone. "You've built this ivory tower and stacked it with only the shiniest women who can pass all your tests—never mind all the other women out there who just don't happen to be as rich or credentialed—and yet you want to keep all these shiny women downstairs because you *still* think you're better. How dare they call themselves witches when you're the only true ones with the power, according to your family history or some other metric that shouldn't really matter?" The others bristled, uncomfortable, as I went on. "You've appointed yourselves the gatekeepers and played God, and then you want to whine about how everyone's trying to control you?" I stared at Margot, practically spitting the words at her. "You're the controlling one now. You're exactly what you claim to hate."

"No," she said, her eyes turning red. "I'm not."

"Oh, spare me. The whole reason you had to bring down Nicole was because you wanted her to enact your agenda over anyone else's. That's why you told her about the Coven, and then you had to go scorched earth on her to cover your mistakes."

"It wasn't for *my* agenda," Margot said. "Caroline's work on parental leave, on *everything*, was so good, I just wanted it to get out in the world."

"What?" Caroline asked.

"Same difference," I said, my voice dry and steady even though my body was shaking. "And besides, what's more controlling than pretending to summon someone's dead mother to get them on your side?"

"I wasn't . . . Oh God, that's what you think? I would never pretend with something like that," she said, her voice choked. "I felt her there, I swear to you." For a split second, as she held her trembling hands up to me, she seemed to have no guile at all. She was just a defenseless, scared child telling me the truth.

"Okay, I'm getting rid of this," Caroline said, holding my phone up and moving her thumb over the delete button, making the voice memo vanish off into the ether. She threw the phone down onto the ground, where it skidded back over to me, its screen cracking. "I hope you know, Jillian, that if you publish this article, we will sue you so hard. If you want to take us down, prepare to be taken down in return. And as for *you*, Margot—"

In front of me, the phone lit up again, glowing with a new message from Vy, barely readable through the shattered glass. **Also I don't do shrooms. Brain's weird enough as is.**

"You keep hiding things from me," Caroline was yelling at Margot. "And now look what's happened! We're supposed to be a team!"

"Oh, we haven't been a team for a long time now," Margot yelled back. "You've always lorded it over me: you own the building, you'll take care of Nicole all alone, I make one mistake and you're going to punish me forever."

I picked up my phone and stared at Vy's message, trying to make sense of it. Vy hadn't put anything in the tea. But I had seen things, felt things, that I never had before, things that I wasn't supposed to be able to feel unless I was under the influence of something, because I was the kind of person who stood on the outside watching, my arms folded around myself, a snarky comment always locked and loaded.

I'd told myself that I'd been able to lose myself in the circle only because of the shrooms in my system, but I was just looking for an excuse. Deep down inside of me, I wanted that communion, didn't I? And more than communion, I wanted to believe in something, whether it was magic, or the possibility of something greater, or maybe just the idea that people could be better than they were.

I wanted to believe that *I* could be better. Because I had been playing with them all like they weren't real people too. Throwing Libby under the bus, letting them open up to me while planning to expose them all. I told myself it was for a greater purpose, and in some ways it was, but really, I wanted that impressive byline so that someday I could be a gatekeeper myself.

"I know I messed up, but you didn't trust me to learn from it—" Margot was saying.

"And I was right, because you did it again! Again, you've shared it with the wrong person, and jeopardized us all!" Caroline screamed. She lunged toward Margot as if she were going to kill her, as if she were going to push her backward to the roof's edge and throw her off. The other members were all arguing among themselves too, yelling about what to do, about if anyone else had known that there was apparently some kind of bribery involved, hurt and rage and resentments that had been simmering between them all coming out. Nobody was watching Caroline as she hurtled forward except for me and Iris. Iris's eyes widened, and she moved as if to restrain Caroline, but she was too far away to stop Caroline's wild, violent body as she collided with Margot.

But Caroline didn't push Margot backward. Instead, she wrapped her arms around her. "I'm not doing any of this to punish you. I'm scared. I *want* to trust you, but you make it so hard, and I just don't know how we're going to fix things this time. And what if we've never fixed things at all, just broken them?"

I thought of the coincidence of seeing Nicole by the water. I'd been having a whole lot of coincidences lately, more than one person should have in her entire life.

Maybe there *had* been something swirling around us in the woods that night. Unseen currents. Unseen spirits. I didn't know if it was magic, but maybe it was more than sheer randomness. Even solid Raf, whom I trusted more than anyone, believed there might be things in this world we couldn't explain. And if that were the case, maybe Margot hadn't been coldly pretending to be my mother after all.

Margot was crying now too, wrapping her own arms around Caroline in return. "I've only ever wanted us to be better, to get back to how good and hopeful it was when we started," she said. "But it's gotten so bad."

Nicole had rot in her foundation, but she was so afraid of losing anything she had that she'd tried to prop up a shakily built house anyway. There was rot in the foundation of this coven too, rot inside the cloistered walls of Nevertheless. The power had gone to everyone's heads. Still, as Caroline and Margot held each other, trembling with guilt and sadness and regret, I saw that there was a spark of something here worth saving. If I exposed them to the public, they'd be ruined. But if I didn't write the article and I let them go on like they were, getting away with it all while gripping tightly to everything they had, they'd be ruined too.

"What do we do?" Caroline asked Margot, her voice catching.

Miles was probably well on his way up the stairs now. Even if I withdrew my article, he could pick up the torch and carry it himself if he saw everything, now that he knew where the building was. Oh God, how could I have invited a man here, to watch these women the only time that they were able to be free?

Everyone was arguing or crying, a cacophony of angry voices around me. Nobody was paying attention as I walked to the edge of the fire, which snapped and danced in front of me. *Use that anger to rebuild*, Nicole had said.

A stick, a larger piece of kindling, burned at my feet. I drew it from the fire and held it in the air. Then I touched it to the ivy on the trellis nearest to me. The ivy was dry, and so was the wood it wound around. It all caught immediately. For a moment, the sound and the smell of it was covered by the bonfire we'd already built, and I watched as the flames began to spread, racing from one trellis, one tree, to another.

Then Caroline turned and saw the forest around us starting to catch fire. She gasped, and the others turned too. "Run!" Caroline shouted.

We sprinted to the door and threw it open right as Miles and the *Standard*'s fact-checker (a short, unassuming man) were entering the antechamber from the other side, out of breath. "Who the hell are you?" Caroline said, then shook her head. "No time, the roof is on fire!"

I grabbed my shoes. Iris grabbed the bucket, because you've always got to save the phones. She began to fumble around inside for her cell so that she could call the fire department, but Margot grabbed her arm and began to pull her to the stairwell.

"Get outside first," she shouted, and we all kept running down the flights of stairs in shock, our gasping breaths and our pounding feet the only sound besides the rush of wood catching, this old building that women had been hiding themselves away in since the 1920s, a building built before the fire codes had changed, threatening to collapse around us. I hadn't expected it all to go up so quickly and, as we fled, I realized that the flames might kill us, that my impulse had actually been a deadly one, and there would be no rebuilding at all. The stairs seemed endless. In the mass of moving bodies, I stumbled, falling to the ground as women in robes pushed past me. Overhead, the sound of shattering glass rippled through the air.

"Jillian?" Margot called, turning around. "Jillian! Come on!"

I picked myself up and ran toward her through the smoke. Another face appeared in my mind: Raf, smiling at me in his shy, hopeful way. He was the person I wanted to see when I was scared. But it wasn't only that. I wanted to see him when I was happy and sad and all the other things too. I ran faster. I had to get out of this building. I had to see his face again.

I sprinted down the final flight of stairs. Ahead of me, Margot held open the door to the alley, and I plunged into the fresh air. Iris was dialing 911. Miles was looking at the door, frantic, relief coming over his face when I emerged. He started toward me, but Caroline charged up to him and asked, "Sorry, *who* the hell are you?" Some of the other women were shouting, asking one another if they'd seen how the fire started.

Margot turned to me. "You did it, didn't you?" she asked, her eyes blazing. The fire hadn't killed me, but she still might, so as the flames began to shoot out the windows of the floor below the roof, I turned and kept running, flying through the darkness down the streets of Manhattan, all the way to a storefront lit with lanterns on the Lower East Side.

FIFTY-THREE

When I burst into Raf's restaurant, the hostess at the front tried to stop me. "Sorry, we're closed for the evening," she began, but I ran past her and back into the kitchen, skidding to a stop next to Raf, who was arms-deep in a sink full of soapy dishes. When he saw me, he froze, wary.

"Hi," I said, then bent over to catch my breath.

"Uh, guys," he said to the few remaining dishwashers. "You can take off for the night." Reluctantly, they did, shooting furtive, curious glances at me. (Right. Because I was still wearing a fucking *robe*, like I'd escaped from a fancy church concert.)

"So . . ." he said, removing his arms from the water and reaching for a dish towel. "What's up?" Just like the first night I'd found out about the Coven, simply being in his presence made me feel better, safer, hopeful. A cute, dark curl fell across his forehead and I wanted to brush it back. How I hoped he hadn't changed his mind and thought better of things. If he'd healed his heart and taken up with one of those lithe model-groupies in the weeks since we'd seen each other, I didn't know what I was going to do.

"I just did something that was probably very stupid," I said when I was able to speak again. "And there's a chance I'll go to prison forever, or that the women of Nevertheless will send a hit man to kill me in the night."

"Jillian—" he said with concern, dropping the towel and stepping toward me.

"No, it's okay. I had to do it. It was the right choice. Probably. Yeah, now that I know everyone made it out safely, it was the right choice. But I was thinking about what I'd regret, if they kill me or lock me up forever, and it was only you."

"Me?" he asked, a glimmer of hope beginning to shine in his eyes, and that glimmer of hope gave me what I needed to keep going.

"It was only that I wanted to tell you that I love you."

He folded his arms across his chest and raised an eyebrow. "Like as a cousin?"

"Not at all," I answered, and stepped forward to kiss him.

Our hearts pounded against each other. He wrapped me up in him and kissed me back, and it was exactly where I wanted to be. I never wanted to stop touching him. We'd been children together, and we'd be old together, or at least we'd give it our best shot as life threw its typical curveballs our way. I melted into him as he backed me up against the counter, both of us smiling and gasping and clutching each other like we'd never get enough.

"Hold up," he said, pulling away for a moment. "Are you not wearing anything under this weird robe?"

"No," I said, pulling him back in. "No, I am not."

FIFTY-FOUR

I went to Margot's aunt's apartment the morning after spending the night with Raf to find that all my stuff had been boxed up and left outside the door, and that my key no longer worked.

As I stood in the hallway, staring at the meager contents of my life, Miles called me. I'd gotten four missed calls from him over the course of the night. "Beckley, thank God," he said when I answered, his voice ragged. "I've been worrying about you. Where the hell did you go?"

"They found out I was a journalist, right before the fire started," I said. "I had to get out of there."

"Oh shit. Are they going to retaliate? Do anything to you?"

"I don't know," I said. "Probably? But so far, they just locked me out of that apartment and, honestly, that seems fair." He laughed a little, but it was a worried, halfhearted sound. "I saw Caroline cornering you. What did you say to her?"

"I said we were building inspectors, but obviously that wasn't true, and then we got out of there too." He sighed. "Jesus, what a mess. I'm so glad you're okay, though."

"Thanks, yeah, you too."

The line was silent for a moment, both us of taking a breath. "What's our next move here?" he finally asked.

"Well, the evidence is all gone," I said. "So I think there is no next move."

"No," he said. "Come on. You already wrote the article. There's got to be some way to make this work. E-mails they sent you, *something* we can fact-check."

"I'm sorry. There's no way to back up the bigger claims in the article without the clubhouse. And like you said when I signed the NDA, it's just not going to be worth it for some catalog of the insipid girl-power posters they've hung up on the walls."

"Look, you know I didn't mean . . . There were a bunch of women in robes on the roof—it's clear that you were right, and something juicier was going on."

"Mm," I said.

His voice got softer. "Can I see you? Come over to my place, and I'll go into work a little late." I swallowed. The switch from editor to lover jarred me, even though it had been happening all along in subtler ways, hadn't it? "And if you need to stay with me for a bit—"

"Did you ever think that maybe this article was doomed from the beginning?" I asked.

"What?"

"I was never going to make the best decisions about it because I had such strong feelings for you. You must have known that on some level."

"I . . . well, no, I trusted you to be professional."

"And you had feelings for me, even though you didn't want to admit it, so you made bad decisions too. You said so yourself—you talked up the story too much, created an impossible situation."

"Are you trying to say I just gave you the article to get into your pants?"

"No—"

"Because that wasn't it at all. I respect you as a writer—"

"I know that you do, but still, on some level, the whole thing was fucked up. Don't you see that?"

He let out a grunt of frustration on the other end of the line. "I think you're exaggerating a little." I chewed my lip. He wasn't admitting it, or he truly wasn't getting it. I'd wanted to feel that I was special by proving myself to a special man. But maybe I didn't need to prove anything, and Miles wasn't that special after all.

"I'm not going to come to your place, because I'm staying with Raf," I said.

He was silent for a moment. Then he said, "You're really screwing me over here, Beckley."

"I'll repay the money you gave me. It might take some time, but I will. And in the performance review, you can say what you need to say. Tell them I'm too scared of retaliation to keep going, if that helps. The fact-checker you brought can back you up that there was a fire and shit got dangerous. Now I should go—"

"Did they get to you somehow?" he asked.

"What do you mean?"

"Are they blackmailing you, or promising you things? You're not being yourself."

"Actually, I think I am," I said, and hung up.

FIFTY-FIVE

They didn't come for me that day, or the day after. I waited and waited, expecting them to show up, looking for them around every corner.

There were some news stories about a fire in a West Village building, which burned entirely to the ground. No one was hurt, and it didn't spread. The building, an old one, hadn't been up to code, a tinderbox just waiting for a spark to set it ablaze. And still no one came for me, no cops wanting to question me about arson, no mysterious beautiful women ready to plunge a knife in my back.

At random moments, I smelled the flames again. How many people knew what I had done? Had Margot told the whole coven, had word gotten around to all the members, to the staff? Oh God, in my burn-it-all-down impulse, I hadn't even thought about the fact that I might be putting people out of a job. A sinking feeling of guilt took up residence next to the fear in the pit of my stomach.

A few nights later, I was working in the bar. Raf was going to stop by at the end of my shift to pick me up since I was nervous about retaliation, about walking in the dark by myself. Together, Raf and I would go back to his place, which, at least for the moment, was my place too. I was going to start looking for a (probably shithole) apartment soon—living together immediately was not a great way to start off a relationship—but, God, it felt nice to be around him all the time, to kiss him good-night and wake up next to him. Nice, and also terrifying.

At eleven P.M., the regulars were still going strong, but the rush was over. I stretched my neck, rolling my head from side to side. The door swung open and I looked up, nearly dropping the glass I was holding when I registered the identity of the new patrons: Margot and Caroline. I briefly considered ducking out the back. But, no, I needed to hear what they had to say. So I braced myself as they looked around the bar, something strange like trepidation on their faces.

They spotted me and made their way over to the bar in front of my station. They were far from the bar's usual clientele, and the regulars stared accordingly. One older man wolf-whistled at Margot as she walked by, and she stopped right next to him, whispering something in his ear. His face dropped and, chastened, he went back to watching the game with his buddies. Caroline took a tissue out of her purse and cleaned off the barstool before sitting down on it, so as not to ruin her tailored gray skirt. The two women settled themselves and looked up at me in silence.

My heart pounded. "Are you here to hex me off the face of the Earth?" I asked.

"We considered it," Caroline said. "Especially when I found out that the insurance company was going to deny my claim because the roof wasn't up to fire code, so your actions are going to be costing me hundreds of thousands of dollars—"

Margot put her hand on top of Caroline's. "But then we thought about the men coming up the stairs. I saw the way that one of them started moving toward you, when you came out of the building, so I looked up pictures of the *New York Standard*'s staff, and we put two and two together."

"I guess Margot was right," Caroline said. "That in the end, we could trust you after all."

"I didn't do it just to destroy the evidence, you know," I said quietly. "You were fucked, doing things the way you were, and I thought that if it was all gone, you could start fresh. Start better."

"It's funny, we talked about that," Caroline said. "Once we got over the shock of losing so much, of course."

"We've been talking pretty nonstop over the last few days," Margot said. "About everything, including how to move forward with Nevertheless. Caroline made a very detailed chart of the possibilities."

"It was a normal amount of details," Caroline said, and Margot smiled at her. Caroline smiled back. In the background, the bar hubbub raged, but there was a new calmness between the two of them.

"The conclusion that we came to," Margot said, "is that Nevertheless, as it was, is over."

"No more clubhouse, no more club," Caroline continued. "Though we're committed to paying the cleaning staff and security guards until they can find new work, of course."

"Good," I said. "But the members aren't going to be too pleased about the club shutting down, are they?"

"We'll just have to deal with their displeasure," Caroline said. "And they'll just have to get over it. If they need to call me a bad leader or drag my name through the mud, well, that's probably what I deserve."

"We'll still try to hold some events, talks and workshops and such, maybe through Women Who Lead and In the Stars," Margot said. "But they'll be first come, first served. And, whenever possible, they'll be free."

"That sounds . . . nice, actually," I said.

"And are you still going to write an article about Nevertheless?" Caroline asked. "Obviously I wish you wouldn't, but if you have to, you have to, and we won't sue." She pursed her lips. "Unless, of course, you make any false claims about us. Then we will sue you for libel."

"No, I'm not going to write the article. I . . . I think I have something else in mind."

At that, Caroline let out a small breath of relief, but to her credit, she tried not to look *too* pleased.

"So," Margot said.

"So," I replied.

"That obviously leaves the other . . . matter," Caroline said. *The Coven*, she mouthed, trying to be discreet, and I held back a laugh.

"We talked about how to move forward with that too," Margot said.

"Together," Caroline said. "With a new kind of focus, somewhere in between. Not selfish, or at least not as *purely* selfish."

"Helping," Margot said, "but not controlling. Only with people's best interests in mind, instead of trying to be the queen-makers so we can have the ear of the queen."

"And we wanted to ask . . ."

The two of them looked at each other, then back at me, and Margot said, "Will you start fresh with us?"

This time, I couldn't hold back the laughter. "Right. Because I'm a legacy? I almost sold you out, I lied to you for months, I burned down your clubhouse, and you *still* want me? Wow, I feel like a boy applying to an Ivy where his grandpa donated a building."

"Not just because you're a legacy. Because of everything," Margot said.

I pushed an old beer bottle out of the way and leaned forward onto the bar. "I didn't draw the Three of Cups, you know. In the tarot reading. You all left me alone for a minute and I turned over my third card, and then I hid it in my pocket because it freaked me out. But it was supposed to be the Ten of Swords."

"Huh," Margot said, the corners of her mouth turning up ever so slightly. "Betrayal. That tracks."

"I don't think I belong with you. I'm not even sure if I believe in magic of any kind. You should've chosen Libby instead."

"Maybe," Margot said slowly. "Or maybe we should have chosen both of you. Or we shouldn't have chosen anyone at all, and just let people choose us. It's like what you said on the roof—we made people pass so many tests so that we could feel like we were superior. It's so much nicer to give the tests than to take them, but perhaps everything we were using to decide doesn't actually matter."

"What matters is that, when we started locking the door behind us, we told ourselves it was for protection," Caroline said. "But then it became about keeping other people out."

"And now that building is gone," Margot said. "But it was always better when it was just us in the woods anyways, with no locked doors at all."

The two of them leaned toward me. And maybe I couldn't say

for sure that together, we would make magic. But I thought—I hoped—that we would make *something*.

"So we try again, but different this time?" I said, slowly. "With Vy back in, and anyone who thinks they have something to offer?" Caroline nodded. "Doing it for the right reasons, without all the fancy shit?"

"We try again," Margot said.

FIFTY-SIX

When I knocked on Libby's door, Rat Dog Bella began to bark wildly inside her apartment. "Okay, okay, honey," Libby started saying in a soothing tone as she swung the door open wide. When she saw me, the expectant smile on her face dropped and she began to close the door, hard.

"Wait," I said, and stuck my foot out—an idiotic reflex. The door slammed on my foot before bouncing back open, and I let out a cry of pain. "Mother*fucker*."

"Oh my God, sorry!" Libby said.

"It's okay," I said, shaking my foot out. I was going to have a bruise tomorrow, but it didn't seem to be broken.

"I mean, no! Not sorry. I'm not apologizing to *you*, you should apologize to me!"

"I know. That's why I'm here."

That flustered her. "Well," she said. "Well, maybe I don't want an apology!" She glared at me and went to close the door again.

"Now that you've maimed me, can you at least hear me out?" I took a deep breath. "I want to bring you to the back room."

That stopped her short. "You can't," she said. "Haven't you heard? The clubhouse burned down."

"I'm taking you to the back room. I'll explain everything on the way," I said, and held out my hand.

FIFTY-SEVEN

So, there is no article. There is only this instead. It's the truth, as much of it as I could tell, though I've had to change some names and identifying details. I'm hopeful that I'm telling it for good, like I promised my mother.

If you want to come find us, wait until dark on the night of the new moon. Then come to where the sounds of the city can't be heard, down a dirt path that winds and bends, where it passes a grove of crooked, gnarled trees: we'll be meeting there at midnight.

You don't have to prove that you're worthy. You only have to want to try. The fire we build will be a large one, with plenty of room around it. We'll gather in our circle and join hands, and we'll dance with our imperfect bodies.

Maybe nothing will happen. We'll just be a bunch of women dancing in the woods, and it will be really fucking fun. Or maybe, just maybe, we will lift into the air, and we will fly.

ACKNOWLEDGMENTS

Even though much of writing is quite solitary, it takes a village to make a novel, and I've got one incredible village. I'm so grateful to the following people for their help in bringing this book to life.

My editor, Jen Monroe. The text you sent me when you first finished reading a draft of this book was so wonderful, it almost made me cry. Working with you is a dream. I'm very lucky that I get to enjoy both your expert editorial guidance and your friendship.

My agent, Stefanie Lieberman, along with Molly Steinblatt and Adam Hobbins. Thank you for pushing me to be the best writer I can be, and for not letting me spend too much time on book ideas involving complex magic systems/multiple realities that don't make any sense outside of my own head! I value your guidance so much. And thank you to everyone at Janklow & Nesbit for working on behalf of this story.

My writing group, Kate Emswiler, Becca Roth, and Celey

Schumer, who never blinked when I sent them e-mails like "I HAVE A DEADLINE COMING UP IN A WEEK, CAN YOU READ THESE 75 PAGES AND GIVE ME YOUR TYPICAL THOUGHTFUL, BRILLIANT FEEDBACK?" We jokingly called ourselves "the Coven," but the magic of drinking tea and discussing writing together was real.

My excellent friends who have cheered me on during the highs and lows of publishing. I'm writing this acknowledgments section during COVID-19, and my God, I miss hugging you all so much. Special shout-outs to Sash Bischoff, whose feedback improved this novel immensely, and Rebecca Mohr, who texted me title ideas at all hours of the night when she was up feeding her new baby (one of which, *There's a Special Place in Hell*, inspired the eventual title).

The whole team at Berkley, from the social media experts to the copy editors. Special thanks to the core four—Jin Yu, Jessica Mangicaro, Danielle Keir, and Tara O'Connor—who have headed up my marketing and publicity for two books now with good cheer, lots of patience, and excellent Instagram comments, and to Emily Osborne, Craig Burke, Diana Franco, Jeanne-Marie Hudson, Christine Ball, Claire Zion, and Ivan Held. I look forward to the day when we can once again drink wine and gossip together.

The people at Paragraph, my quiet, friendly writing oasis in New York City, and Laura, my host in Hastings-on-Hudson, whose tiny cottage was where I wrote some of my favorite scenes in the book. Like Jillian, I envy those writers who can just churn out their brilliance anywhere, because I'm certainly not one of them!

Cas, the guide of a Salem Night Tour that I took while figuring out this book, whose enthusiastic but questioning attitude about witches helped inform Jillian's arc.

The whole reading community. I'm in awe of the booksellers

and librarians who spread the word about *Happy & You Know It* with such passion and kindness, the readers who let my characters into their lives (and took beautiful pictures of my book to boot), and the other authors I've gotten to know, who support one another with such enthusiasm, write the best blurbs, and inspire me with their talent. I got to meet some of you bookish people before the world turned upside down, and I hope I get to meet more of you when we're right side up again.

My father, Mark, and my brother, Matt. I put your actual names in here this time!

And Dave, who took me to Salem, talked through tough scenes with me (for what sometimes probably felt like eight hours!), and recommended that Vy have an emotional support snake. I left you out of the acknowledgments last time, but I can't wait to include you in all the ones to come.

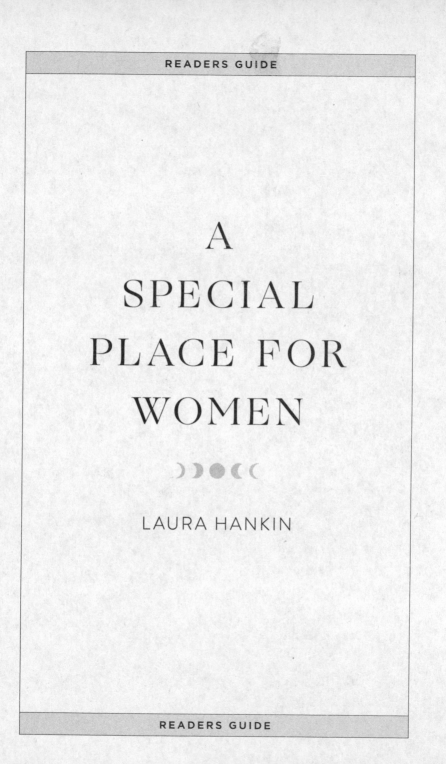

A
SPECIAL
PLACE FOR
WOMEN

LAURA HANKIN

QUESTIONS FOR DISCUSSION

1. What's your opinion on spaces meant for women only? Have you had any personal experience with them?

2. What do you think of Jillian's ultimate decision about her article? Would you have made the same choice?

3. The novel's title references the famous Madeleine Albright quote, "There's a special place in hell for women who don't support other women." How do the characters embody or go against her words?

4. What do you think of Jillian's view of things we cannot

prove—like astrology and the occult—and how that view changes over the course of the book?

5. How did you hope the love triangle would resolve? What do you think drew Jillian to each of these two very different men?

6. One of the book's major themes is about the appeal of truly *belonging*. Would you want to belong to a club like Nevertheless? If so, how would you get yourself in?

7. Did you find your perceptions of any of the characters changing over the course of the book? Who surprised you the most? And if you could hear the events of the book from another character's point of view, who would you choose?

8. What did you think of how the book played with different genres, from satire to romance to the occult?

9. Share your thoughts on the scandal involving Nicole Woo-Martin, and how that relates to the book's view of power and ambition. How do you think that such a scandal would have unfolded with a male politician at its center?

10. What do you think is next for the women of Nevertheless?

BEHIND THE BOOK

A few years ago, an acquaintance invited me to have coffee with her at an exclusive women's coworking space in New York. I'd heard of this place before and had been intrigued by the utopia it promised: a sisterhood where you didn't need to worry about men bothering you—as long as you could afford the dues. As I sipped my expensive cold brew on a fancy, peach-colored couch, I remember being fascinated by the peaceful clubhouse. I was also wildly intimidated by the women roaming around, exuding effortless cool. I didn't belong among them. They were all so sparkly, so accomplished! On the elevator ride back down to the real world, I overheard a woman telling her friend about the big struggle in her life: that it was really hard dating a celebrity chef, because he was never free for brunch.

The experience stayed in my mind as I watched these types of spaces grow in popularity and then face a backlash. Critics slammed them as a luxury good that, in trying to rectify one kind of inequality (gender), ended up reinforcing others (economic and racial). The COVID-19 pandemic didn't exactly help with membership. CEOs resigned, doors shut, waitlists disappeared. At the time that I write this essay, the majority stakeholder in that "utopia for women" that I once visited is now a man.

And yet, the idea of these spaces still appeals. After all, what's more seductive than belonging? We all want to find a place that feels like it was made for us, where we can be safe and celebrated and loved by like-minded people. But does making a place special always have to mean keeping others out?

With *A Special Place for Women*, I wanted to explore this kind of environment, heightening it even further by making my fictional women's club secret and more than a little bit witchy. That coworking space I'd visited sometimes called itself, semi-jokingly, a coven. A lot of the women I knew had begun dipping their toes into the occult—from getting more into astrology and crystals to casting spells in their apartments. They did it partially for fun, but it was more than that. It was also a way to feel some sense of power as the world spun more and more out of control, as the promise that "leaning in" would fix everything began to feel more and more false.

Ultimately, I set out to leave readers with a sense of hope. Trying to make things better doesn't always work perfectly the first time around, but that doesn't mean you give up. You come together and try again. So . . . meet you in the woods at midnight?

READING LIST

Enjoyed *A Special Place for Women*? The following books are all related in one way or another, and very much worth a read.

1. *The Secret History* by Donna Tartt
The GOAT of secret society novels, about a clique of brilliant college students and the outsider who gets drawn into their unstable world. Spooky and atmospheric and extremely compelling, this is the kind of five-hundred-page novel that simultaneously flies by and sucks you in deep.

2. *Trick Mirror* by Jia Tolentino
Jillian would probably kill to be the next Jia Tolentino and

write something like this book of brilliant, incisive essays about the way we live now.

3. *Witches of America* by Alex Mar
Interested in what it's actually like to be a witch in America today? Mar is a journalist who spent years exploring modern-day paganism with fascinating results.

4. *The Ex Talk* by Rachel Lynn Solomon
If you're looking for more of the "fake relationship" trope, Solomon does it brilliantly in this sparkling, swoony, actually-laugh-out-loud rom-com about coworkers who have to pretend to be exes for a new public radio show they're cohosting.

5. *The Secret Place* by Tana French
I am devoted to Tana. I will read any book she writes, probably over the course of one weekend during which I do not do anything else and the dishes pile up in my sink. This murder mystery set at an all-girls boarding school is full of brilliant interrogation scenes and hints of magical realism. The dreamy but dangerous girls at the center of this novel could very well grow up into the women of Nevertheless.

6. *The Immortalists* by Chloe Benjamin
Four young siblings visit a fortune teller who predicts the day they're each going to die. I admire Benjamin's balance between the real world and the mystical here—is the fortune

teller really predicting the future, or simply creating self-fulfilling prophecies?—and tried to strike a similar one in my own writing.

7. *True Heart Intuitive Tarot* by Rachel True
Want to learn more about tarot so that you can also manipulate and/or see deeply into the souls of the people around you? Rachel True's book, which comes with a deck too, is one of the best!

Author photo by Ricardo Quinones

Laura Hankin is the author of *Happy & You Know It*. She has written for publications like McSweeney's and HuffPost, while her musical comedy has been featured in *The New York Times*, *The Washington Post*, and more. She splits her time between NYC, where she has performed off-Broadway, and Washington, D.C., where she once fell off a treadmill twice in one day.

CONNECT ONLINE

LauraHankin

LauraHankin

LauraHankin

YouTube Feminarchy

Ready to find
your next great read?

Let us help.

Visit prh.com/nextread